WE DID WHAT WE COULD

Nancy Wynen

Nancy H. Wynen © 2020

Print ISBN 978-1-09834-174-9
eBook ISBN 978-1-09834-175-6

PROLOGUE
Early May, 1936 – Leaving Day, St. Martin's

Miss Archer kept a vigilant eye on her three protégés. They would not leave without playing one more trick, she was sure of it.

The girls at St. Martin's School were groomed to be ladies of social position: wives able to carry on intelligent conversations as good hostesses for their husbands, ready to lead privileged lives as they oversee households with servants. For Miss Archer, that was all secondary, if not irrelevant. The girls needed a real education, one leading to independent careers, however brief those might be. A few students each year became her protégés – girls who had the potential for future greatness.

As both Assistant Headmistress and Director of Athletics, Miss Archer was demanding, intimidating, and a strict coach. Students avoided her. She didn't mind that reputation; it allowed her to keep an eye on the girls without interfering in their lives. She rather enjoyed her life.

Sadly, she had to work for Headmistress Lady Lattery, a most mean-spirited and unpleasant woman. Her latest disastrous decree centered on an 'incident' one month before the end of the school term. It involved a bridge, a student, and a car.

The bridge, ancient, beautiful, and unique, crossed a small stream on the edge of the school grounds. The sides of the bridge were solid stone arches. It was a landmark in the region, a symbol of the school, and it linked the school to the local village.

The student from one of the lower forms had been playing on the bridge. She slipped and fell into the shallow stream below, breaking her foot. A typical accident on school grounds. She was carried to the infirmary on a stretcher. The stretcher scratched the car.

The car in the story was Lady Lattery's pride and joy. It was a brand new blue 1936 MG-TA Midget, two-seated convertible. It was garaged in the stables near the bridge, and was parked that day directly in the path taken to get the student to the infirmary. Lady Lattery proclaimed the bridge off limits to everyone. The one-mile walk to the village became three, impossible to do in under two hours, especially in winter when the sun sank at 4pm.

It was now the two-day Leaving Holiday at Saint Martin's. The first day was mostly social. Parents, benefactors, trustees, and dignitaries gathered at meals that were far superior to what was normally served at the dining hall. Displays of the girls' creations filled the gymnasium, and there was an evening program of theater, music, and dance. On the second day, the Leaving Class received their certificates and awards, followed by lunch and a special Dressage exhibition.

Just before the Dressage, Miss Archer was wondering where her protégés were. She reviewed each girl's personality to guess what they might do.

Ellie De Wever, tall, graceful, and fair, and with a sweet personality, dreamt up most of the pranks and adventures for the three. Quite the creative writer, and consummate actress. She wanted to join her father in foreign service for The Netherlands.

Agnes Fletcher was Ellie's opposite – short, with curly dark hair, and constantly in motion. She worked in spurts of high concentration, learned quickly, and designed how their pranks would work. Her immediate future was to enter nurse training in London.

Maggie Shelford was in the middle of the three in height, coloring and temperament. She was unaware that she was a natural leader, the responsible one, the doer, capable of anything asked of her, clever in finding solutions and patterns that others missed. Miss Archer found her a job at the *London Times,* a type of extended general education.

A formidable trio at the age of sixteen. As adults, who knows what they will accomplish?

On their last day at school, they were not sitting together. They stayed with their parents, a highly visible choice, that was highly suspect to Miss Archer.

The bell sounded to begin the Dressage. As the crowd settled into the arena, the three girls got up from their seats and casually strolled away in separate directions. Ah, observed Miss Archer, there they go.

The girls, unaware of being watched, circled around the school buildings to the stable area on the opposite side of the school grounds. Agnes and Maggie entered the stables just after the last horses, riders, and stable hands left for the arena. Ellie climbed a ladder to the hayloft for a better view of the area.

"Did you forget something, Miss?" asked a stable hand, looking up into the hayloft and startling Ellie. He couldn't see the other two girls, but the needed to know he was there. She called out loudly enough for the other two girls to hear, "Not really. One of the riders teased me and threw my cap up here. I can't be caught without full school uniform, even on our last day. Oh, I think I found it. Go on, I'll be fine."

"Very good Miss," was the reply as he left the stable. The three girls exhaled in unison before getting back to the job at hand.

"The keys are still in the motorcar," whispered Agnes.

"Headmistress is with the parents, and all of the stable hands have left. I can't see anyone else from here," Ellie reported.

Maggie went over to the car. It's now or never. Agnes walked the short distance to the arched bridge. She crossed over it and waited for Maggie.

Maggie carefully opened the car door and dropped into the seat. The crowd cheered in the distance as the horses entered the arena. The noise covered the closing of the car door and the starting of the engine. She drove slowly out of the stables. The crunch of the gravel under the car's tires and the sound of the motor were also drowned out by the crowd. Maggie urged the car forward.

Maggie remembered their discussion about the unfair closing of the bridge and what they should do about it. The plan evolved from that. Now was not the time for memories; she had to concentrate on her driving. Maggie hoped that Agnes had measured the distance between the bridge walls exactly. She reported that the inside width of the bridge was the same as the inside width of the car's wheel base (45"), and the thickness of the walls was greater than the tires (walls 12", tires 8").

"Easy job," said Agnes. Agnes hoped that Maggie's driving skills were as good as she claimed. Ellie, as look-out, hoped they would be gone long before they were discovered.

Agnes crouched and guided Maggie towards the bridge. For both of them, it suddenly looked too steep, too narrow (or wide), but the commitment was made.

The front wheels rolled onto the bridge. They fit. When about half the car was tilted onto the bridge wall, the back wheels began to spin. No more traction at that angle. Maggie stopped and rolled the car back onto the level ground. Then she remembered what her father's farmers had done in rainy weather to get their tractors up hills.

She got out of the car, and called to Ellie. "Find two long boards and bring them here!"

There was no time for Ellie to question the strange request, she followed Maggie's orders. She found a few boards in the back of the stable and dragged them outside.

"Got them," called Ellie. They laid them over the tire tracks and on to the bridge and ran back into position. Maggie started the car again, using a bit more pressure on the pedal hoping that her steering remained true. She drove onto the boards; the front began to climb up the wall again. The back wheels held firmly as she drove the car onto the bridge. At the top of the arch, Agnes signaled Maggie to stop. Maggie turned off the ignition, climbed over the driver's seat, over the back of the car onto the bridge itself, and walked down toward the stable. Agnes, unsure of going over or under the car, waded into the shallow stream, shoes and socks between her teeth and skirt held high, and joined Maggie.

Ellie climbed down from the hayloft. They returned the boards to where they had been.

They stared silently at what they had done. The car rested on top of the arch of the bridge, as if placed in a toy village scene. They had done it. Suddenly they heard cheers and applause coming from the arena, signaling that the Dressage was over. They ran back between the buildings before weaving into the crowd unnoticed.

Miss Archer, however, did notice them. And here they were, coming back into view from separate places at the same time, flushed from some sort of exertion. She smiled to herself and pretended not to notice them. If they had been up to something, everyone would know soon enough.

PART ONE

CHAPTER 1
Summer, 1936, Ellie

The home in The Netherlands that Ellie knew from vacations and family leave was now her permanent residence. Her father was in the Dutch Foreign Service, and her early childhood had been in Baghdad. The De Wever family had loved the six years in that luxurious home, with nannies, extra servants, and an extravagant social life.

Life was quite different now. Her father was Charge d'Affaires in the London Embassy. She and her twin brothers went to boarding schools, and their social life was, well, English: restricted and traditional.

She was taking the now-routine trip by train from London to Dover, the ferry to Hoek van Holland, and then the family motorcar to their home near Leiden.

Ellie considered the time spent traveling as transition time. The start of each journey is anchored in past. Normal life is suspended in the middle, with no responsibilities. The end of the journey is the beginning of the future. She was becoming an adult with an unknown future.

Finally in the family motorcar, she watched the scenery changed from the harbor to the built-up city of The Hague and then to open farmland. The De Wever home lay between The Hague and Leiden, nearer to Leiden.

As the car turned onto the gravel drive framed by linden trees, she took in the familiar view. The well-proportioned manor was made of stone and brick, each tall window had its own set of shutters, framed by climbing roses. Early summer flowers bloomed brightly. The great front door stood partially open, with Ellie's beloved grandmother there to greet her.

Gran and Ellie were kindred spirits; age was never a factor. They spoke a mix of English and Dutch. Gran was English by birth and had married a wealthy Dutch businessman. She had lived in The Netherlands ever since. "Gran" never took the name "Oma," even after living in The Netherlands for many years and speaking Dutch perfectly.

"Welcome home," Gran smiled. They hugged, followed by kisses on both cheeks. Gran studied her granddaughter. "I wish I had seen your last days at our old school. I didn't expect my cold to become pneumonia. I fought it off quickly, just not quickly enough. Even at sixty, I am still quite healthy. How are Maggie and Agnes?"

"Fine. We all missed you," Ellie hugged Gran again.

"And your brothers?"

"Theo, as usual, is doing very well – many friends, good marks in class. Ben, as usual, is Ben – not doing well in class or in making friends. Mama wants to send them to different schools. It must be horrible to be twins. Like two parts of one person that gets split in half. Anyway, what's our plan for the summer?"

"Dinners with everyone, beginning tomorrow night at the Westerveld's. Then Saturday at the Van Horn's," said Gran, "but just us tonight."

Ellie climbed the stairs to the second floor. Familiar old family portraits greeted her. The furniture and Persian carpets collected by her family over several generations gave her their own welcome. Her room was near the central staircase. A strip of sunlight shone through the door sill onto her feet. She opened the door into a flower garden. Flowered wallpaper and drapes. Pictures of flowers, and of course, fresh flowers. Loving flowers might be a Dutch trait, but this is too much. I need a simpler décor, thought Ellie.

Her traveling trunk was already in her room. The maid opened it, and began hanging and putting away her clothes. Ellie took out a few small items, her school ribbons, and a handful of books. She placed them on a corner shelf, dispatching toys and dolls to a place under the window. Her green lace dress was laid out for dinner, a formal affair, as was their family tradition.

Gran planned a dinner of Ellie's favorite dishes – clear vegetable soup, then white asparagus and ham. While waiting to be served, Gran asked, "So, what *did* you do at school? The report about you three girls sent by your parents has piqued my interest. Your imagination does carry you away – just like mine still does," Gran's eyes twinkled as she waited for the story.

"Why, Gran, we were perfect angels. Quite misunderstood. Besides, our awards show that we were the top three girls in the entire school! Hardly time to study *and* misbehave!"

Gran laughed. "Yes, and congratulations on your Ribbons of Excellence in Foreign Languages and in Theater Arts. I heard that your performance of Lady Macbeth's mad scenes was fantastic. But I really want to hear about the car."

"Fine," Ellie sighed. "After making the Guy Fawkes straw figure that looked like the Headmistress last November, we really did try to behave," Ellie tried to look contrite, failing miserably. "But she deserved something for closing down the bridge to the village."

Gran, her daughter Carolina, and now her granddaughter Ellie had all been educated at St. Martin's. Gran remembered her own mischief there. (That time when the neighborhood sheep were decorated in graduation ribbons and set loose in the village was her favorite memory.) "So, was it your idea? I suppose you and I will always be the ones to start the fun."

"Mostly. Though Guy Fawkes was Agnes' idea. Maggie put the plan into action."

"Well, just as I thought. You were quite clever as a toddler, starting mischief and letting your brothers take the blame. Your innocent look and sweetness fooled us most of the time," Gran left the comment hang in open silence.

Ellie asked between bites of ham, "So what were your school days like, Gran?" (She already knew the stories – except about the sheep – and loved hearing them again.) The evening went by quickly.

Gran finished her last story and added, "As I said, tomorrow we're at the Westerveld's. You and Tinie played together whenever you were here. It will be nice for you two to catch up."

"Honestly, Tinie and I only got along because our parents were friends. She can be very annoying, always needs to be the center of things. No room for anyone in her life except her worshippers. I hope I make it through dinner."

"Oh," Gran was startled. "I apologize. Well, she might be an introduction to other young people here, so take advantage of what you can."

"I'll give it a try," Ellie said.

Ellie spent the next day wandering around the house and property. The flowers, especially the irises and roses that her mother loved, greeted her, along with blooms she couldn't identify. Everything looked like it always did. Same gardens outside, same furnishings inside, same staff keeping it pristine. Not as many servants here as in England, though, and most went home to their own houses at night. Interesting, thought Ellie, as she dressed for dinner.

"Ellie," Tinie welcomed Ellie into the house. "You've changed so much."

"As have you, Tinie," Ellie said. "You look lovely."

"Oh thanks," Tinie said. "But call me Katrina now. We're nearly adults."

Tinie's father was a colonel in the Dutch Army and the whole family was known for being snobbish. They reminded Ellie of some of the stuffy English families she had met.

Tinie's father smiled, "I hope you and Tinie will come to the *Kazerne* next week. The newest Army officers are being commissioned – dinner and dancing will be the 'Order of the Day.' Just don't distract my men too much from their duties after that."

Tinie shook her head, smiling, "We wouldn't dream of it, Father. Besides, it is also your promotion to general and you want a big audience."

Ellie smiled and said, "I'd love to come. I feel like such a stranger. Any chance of meeting new people sounds wonderful to me."

Tinie turned to her and said, "I'll introduce you around. But stay away from Pieter Van Horn. You remember him? He is one of the new officers — and he's mine. Though he doesn't know that yet." Her smile was more warning than friendly.

Ellie nodded. Same old Tinie, center of the universe. No problem staying away. Pieter was at least five years older than they were. They had all grown up as next-door 'cousins.' She asked Tinie what to wear at the Commissioning, and the evening continued.

Gran turned to Ellie on the ride home. "Sorry about that — I see what you mean about Tinie. Well, just use her as your open door. Then you can venture out on your own. And Saturday night, the Van Horns. But stay away from Pieter."

They laughed and relaxed like two old friends.

CHAPTER 2
Summer, 1936, Agnes

Agnes sat at the window feeling empty, sad, and extremely lonely. Ellie was in The Netherlands, and Maggie was in Oxfordshire, while she sat in London.

She stood up when she heard the bell for tea. She checked her dress for wrinkles (such a scandal, wrinkles) before going downstairs for afternoon tea with her parents.

She entered the sitting room and looked at them. They were like wax figures, lacking any movement. She could never sit still for more than a few minutes. Her mother sat in her overstuffed ancient armchair, erect and solemn; her father sat at his desk, looking at the afternoon's post. The housekeeper, Mrs. Millie, came in with tea and sandwiches.

"Well," said Father, waving a piece of paper. "As much as we were proud of your Ribbon of Excellence in Mathematics and Science, we are quite distressed by Lady Lattery's letter about your behavior." He continued waving the letter. "I can hardly wait to hear how you defend yourself this time. What will people be saying about you?" He sat back, waiting. Her mother said nothing.

Agnes was tired of her father being obsessed with status and personal reputation. When she was a child, he had been fun to play with; now all he wanted to do was impress his colleagues. She was tired of her mother's imperial attitude towards everyone simply because she was the head of the family's business. She was tired of being "the poor excuse of a daughter," not being the perfect little angel.

Agnes replied, "Headmistress was horrid. She deserved what we did. No harm done."

"No harm done? How shall we ever make a proper lady out of you, Agnes," her mother asked. "Next year you will be presented to King Edward. There will be outrageous gossip, you know. Lady Lattery will make sure of it."

"It seems you are more concerned with the gossip than with me. Well, you will be rid of me this week," Agnes announced. Taking a sandwich offered by Mrs. Millie, she continued, "I can't go along with all this 'what would people think' society fluff any longer. You want me to behave like a dog – like Juno. Behave when commanded, sit in a cage until someone choses to marry me so I can breed little society pups. For all of your perfect public behavior, your private lives seem to me like total misery. That is not the way I want to live. It is not what I want to do."

"What then?" her parents asked in a chorus of surprise and shock. Their daughter had never spoken to them like that.

"Nursing," Agnes replied. For the first time in her life she wasn't as confident as she sounded. But on she went, "maybe even a doctor."

"Dreadful. We forbid it," said her father. "We already have our work, our responsibilities, and your duty is to take over the family business in due time."

"Sorry, but I have already been accepted into St. Bartholomew's nursing program beginning in September. I'll stay in the nursing quarters, and Maggie's aunt, Lady Charlotte Donne, has agreed to my staying with her at Shellings in London until then. I can pack and leave at any time." Agnes stood, preparing to leave the room.

"Why didn't Miss Archer tell us this?"

"Because I asked her not to. Because I knew what you would say," Agnes replied. With that, she went to her room, looked around, and began rearranging things in her trunk. She half expected her mother to come into the room, but no one came, not even a maid with dinner. She went to bed and woke up without feeling any emotion at all. She knew a line had been crossed, but she couldn't stop now.

Breakfast was served to her in her room as if nothing had happened. Her mother's lady's maid helped her get dressed, saying very little. As she left to go downstairs, the maid murmured, "Good luck."

When she entered the sitting room, she saw Lady Charlotte sitting with her mother.

"I phoned Lady Charlotte to confirm what you had said," her mother said. "This is what will happen. You are barely seventeen years old, and cannot be officially on your own. You must be eighteen before you can inherit anything, as it is written in your trust accounts. Training expenses will come from that trust, along with your allowance. You may live with Lady Charlotte until you are of age, which we will remind you is next June.

"You will be presented next year, with us sponsoring you." Agnes wanted to protest, but her mother held up her hand. "You will be presented, not because you want to be, but you shall receive every and all advantages you are entitled to. Even if you do not value it now, every privilege you have will be worth something in the future. That is all we shall say about this. I am leaving the house for the rest of the day, and I expect you will be gone before my return."

Agnes watched her mother rise slowly, pick up her handbag that doubled as a business case, and go to the front door. Without pausing or looking back, she left.

"Well," said Charlotte, "Shall we go?"

Speechless, Agnes nodded.

Agnes and Charlotte became good companions for each other. They both felt a bit of reluctance when September brought the first day of the new term at St. Bartholomew's School of Medicine and Nursing.

Agnes walked slowly through the high arch in the outer walls and into the courtyard of the building complex. She felt the impulsive urge to flee. Agnes thought, of course, that's how I am usually described – impulsive. Maggie and Ellie weren't there to talk her out it. She climbed the large multi-level staircase. On each wall was an enormous museum-quality (and sized) painting. All who entered knew this was an institution with history and significance. She made her way to the Nursing School Office.

"Good morning," smiled the woman at the desk. "Are you a new student?"

Agnes nodded.

"Come this way. You can leave your valise here."

Agnes followed the woman down a brightly lit white corridor and into an equally brightly lit white room. It was a classroom, like those at St. Martins. She sat in the first empty place that she saw. The girls already in the room sat silently with their own thoughts. A few more girls came in, found seats, and the waiting continued.

With a suddenness that only happens when you wake from a dream, an older woman dressed in a white nurse's uniform entered the room. She was the woman who interviewed her for admission to the program.

"Welcome, ladies. I am Matron Drenton, the Director of the Nursing School, and your most beloved and most hated vision for the next few years. Behind my back, I know I am called Matron Dreaded or Dreadful. But, because of me, you will become the best nurses in the British Empire."

My mother all over again, Agnes feared. Matron Drenton continued, "You will be part of an experimental program here. Mornings will be in this classroom. Afternoons and scheduled night duty will be in one of the hospital wards. You and a third-year student will pair up to share ward duty and a bedroom. Two years here gives you a diploma as a general nurse, three years for the full nursing specialty certificate. School starts officially tomorrow. Settle in today and meet your student partner. Until tomorrow then."

With that, Matron left the room. Another nurse, leading a group of girls in light blue dresses with starched white aprons and caps, quietly entered the room. As the nurse called each name, a girl rose from her seat. A girl in blue walked up to meet her and the two left the room together.

When Agnes' name was called, a tall, confidant, strong-looking girl with red hair approached her, with a big smile on her face, and they left the room together.

"I'm Emmy, short for Emerald," she said, leading Agnes down the corridor. "Are you from around here?"

Agnes replied. "I'm Agnes. Not short for anything, just Agnes. And yes, I'm from London."

"Here we are. You sound posh. What's your story?"

"Not very interesting. My parents and I didn't have the same future in mind for me."

"Well, here we are. Since I am your senior, I have already chosen my bed next to the heater. You're next to the window. Your uniform is on the bed. Everyone gets small, medium, or large. Matron figures out your size during the admissions interview. This is a medium. Hope she got it right." Emmy laughed. "Sometimes she doesn't, and the girl is in a bother about whether to report it or not. Well, we sort that all out quickly."

"No, it looks like it will fit." The pale blue dress and white apron looked both welcoming and intimidating. The real sign of a new life. Her curly brown hair needed to be tightly pinned to fit into the white cap. With Emmy willing to help her get it done, Agnes was feeling less nervous. Emmy's warm greetings made her feel almost relaxed.

The girls began making friends that night over dinner. The next morning was like any class at school. The afternoon round was in the general women's ward. The new students learned how to bathe and feed patients, and make up beds. She and Emmy were assigned to night duty that very first evening; Agnes was already exhausted.

"Don't worry. Most patients are asleep. We chat with the 'awake ones' and try to take short naps. Eat as much as possible now so you have the energy to stay up." With that, Emmy walked off with the other third year students.

In the evening, Agnes found her way to the Central Nursing Station in the charity wards where student nurses worked. The administration felt that if students made mistakes, charity patients were less likely to complain. During the day, second and third-year students worked the "better wards" on the other side of the hospital. The same with the medical students.

She and Emmy each had a chair at the night station. Emmy was prepared with a pillow, a shawl, paper-wrapped sandwiches, and a deck of playing cards.

"Tell me about your family," Emmy said.

"Not much to tell. Very formal, proper, never spontaneous. I am the total opposite, usually getting in trouble," Agnes wanted to get this conversation over with. "How about you?"

"Very spontaneous and informal. Mum is a midwife, raising us three girls by herself," Emmy explained. "I'm the oldest. She saved enough money to pay most of my way here. Now she is getting the other two set up. Ruby, the middle girl, works with a seamstress, and Pearl, the youngest, is still at home watching other peoples' children. She wants to be a teacher, so Mum is saving up for her now." She paused. "What's it like to be rich?"

"I don't know. Normal. What's it like not to be rich?"

"Normal."

A bell rang in the distance. The Men's Ward.

"Let's go!" Emmy stood up. Agnes followed.

"It's Weejun, Sister," said one of the patients, holding the call bell. "Again. What a stink!"

"All right Freddie, we'll fix it," Emmy replied. She stripped the top sheet off a large man, both in height and physical size, writhing in his sleep. Bandages wrapped his unconscious head, and he was suffering from diarrhea from the smell of him. Emmy pulled the bottom sheet from the bed, rolled the linens up in a ball along with the soiled hospital shirt, and tossed them on the floor. She turned to Agnes and told her to clean up Weejun while she retrieved some new bedding.

Agnes was as still as a statue. Along with the smell and the mess, she was looking at only the second naked male body in her life. Her first experience had overwhelmed her, and she quickly put it out of her mind. She grabbed a wash cloth, and like she had done for the women in the afternoon, she began to bathe him.

From the next bed, Freddie began to laugh. "Well, Sister, even I know that cleaning his face is not what he needs. That might be where he's injured, but you might want to concentrate on the smelly parts. You needn't be gentle with that one either," he ended in a chuckle.

Swallowing hard, she somehow got through the procedure, wondering what took Emmy so long to get a few clean sheets.

"Done, then?" Emmy asked when she returned. "Well, let's make the bed. This will take both of us." They rolled him to one side, made half of the bed, then rolled him over to make the other half. The patient never woke up. They returned to the Night Station.

"Let's write it up and have a snack. Not hungry? Get used to it – welcome to nursing."

"What's wrong with Weejun? You know him?" Agnes asked, trying to sound casual. All was perfectly normal one minute, then all was turned upside down, then all normal again. Could she learn to switch moods like Emmy did so easily?

"Weejun's a regular here, usually injured from falling down or fighting during a night of hard drinking. This time his head and a beer bottle met, and both broke. He has a concussion. Sometimes he is delirious and has terrible dreams. Pain meds get him through the first part of recovery. Nice enough chap when he wakes up. His full name is Bruce MacFagin originally from Glasgow, hence Weejun. He works as a butcher at the Smithfield meat market down the street. The diarrhea, though, is something new. Hey, tomorrow night a few of us are going to the pub. You want to come? You deserve it – you've had a tough start."

"Sure. Thanks." Agnes hoped that she didn't look too young. And what about the strict school curfew rules?

The next evening, Emmy showed Agnes the ancient tunnel that connected St. Bart's to the outside world. She explained that though the nursing school was strict about curfew and student nurses staying in, the officials understood the need for an escape. The tunnel was an open secret. The school kept all in balance by remaining extremely strict about classroom attendance, exam performance, and enforcing a no tolerance policy in the wards.

Emmy led Agnes into The Sickly Doctor. What a name for a pub near a hospital! No one checked for her age. At one point she went to the loo. When she returned, Emmy was telling a story to their group. Everyone was laughing and enjoying the story.

"Then, towards morning, the Men's bell rang. Agnes and I saw that it was Weejun again. The whole filthy routine all over. Well, I came back with new sheets just to hear Agnes talking with Weejun. He was fully awake, she was washing him down, right near his privates, and Weejun was getting flirty. And then," Emmy stopped to catch her breath, "and then, Agnes said, 'put that thing away – you can't use that here.' I doubt she had ever seen an undressed man, let alone at full salute!"

Emmy turned and saw Agnes. "And here she is the star of the evening. Agnes, the first-year nurse who survived her trial by fire a lot earlier than everyone I know, and she's is still here! Free drinks for her all night from the rest of us!"

"Cheers!"

CHAPTER 3
Summer 1936, Maggie

Time in London was over. Maggie's family, the Shelfords, was heading home to Oakstone. Father sat in front of their motorcar with their driver. Mother, Herbert, and Maggie sat in the back. They shared what they had done while staying at Shellings House, their London home and the primary residence of Lady Charlotte Donne, Maggie's aunt.

Maggie's father, a Peer in the House of Lords, and her older brother, Herbert who was following his father's footsteps, talked about politics. Maggie's mother reported the gossip she had collected during her visits with friends, shopping, dress fittings, and making plans for the family's summer calendar.

Father turned to face her. Here it comes, Maggie thought.

He began, "Headmistress Lattery asked us what we knew of the incident with her car. Well, out with it."

Maggie chose her words carefully. "You and Mother encouraged all three of us to act with justice and fairness."

Father was insistent. "And?"

"Totally justified," Maggie admitted, "and we were very careful."

Silence.

"Well done!" Father, Mother, and Herbert all cheered at once. It was the first time Maggie had received such an acclamation. Everything she did was considered 'expected', with no fanfare or compliment. Even receiving the

Golden Ribbon for Highest Overall Student at school was "well done" and nothing more. She knew they were proud of her, just not likely to show it. Not knowing how to react, she simply looked out the window. The rest of the ride continued in simple conversation.

The family turned silent, as they turned into Oakstone, in reverence to the place. The trimmed trees and shrubs that lined the drive opened onto a meadow that wrapped around the three-story mansion. It was U-shaped, with an open garden area in the back of the stone structure. Behind and to the side were outlying stables, a garage, and farming sheds. Part of one wing of the mansion had its own entrance for the offices of Shells Bakery.

Herbert later explained to Maggie that Mother and Father thought that Maggie was merely following Agnes, not strong enough to think for herself. Luckily, they found the Headmistress annoying, and agreed that she deserved some form of come-uppance.

Later, when the dinner gong sounded, Maggie felt it signaled the beginning of her life after leaving school, Fitting announcement, she thought.

"I would like to go back to London as soon as possible," she said during dinner.

"What? Why not stay home with us for a while?" Mother said in a surprised response. "We do like Miss Archer's idea that you work at the newspaper before choosing a final career. But leave so soon?"

"And I hoped that you would join Herbert in learning more about running the estate," Father added. "However, we can understand that London is more exciting than Oxfordshire. What will you do, pester Aunt Charlotte?"

"I want to meet with Lady Davids right away. She is editor of the social pages at the *Times*, and my boss," Margaret said. "Miss Archer said that I would work as a clerk and proof reader. Agnes starts training in September, so we want to visit some museums and such before then. And hear how our school mates survived the Season."

Herbert joined in, "I thought you weren't keen on the Season. You want to see how your friends 'survived'? So that you can gloat at their suffering?"

Maggie said, "Maybe. Perhaps they'll convince us that it isn't as awful as it sounds."

Father said. "Tomorrow, though, you and Herbert need to be here and the village."

Mother added, "And you might want to start doing more lady-appropriate things, like taking interest in the village charities."

"Yes, Father," Maggie and Herbert said in unison. She kept quiet, but thought, do I have to start acting like an adult already? "Yes Mother," Maggie added.

The following morning, Father, Herbert, and Maggie rode around the property. Maggie was asked to drive the estate car, a Ford wood-sided truck. (Proof that she could drive anything?) The rolling hills of Oxfordshire were covered with farm land. After the recent economic hard times, many people had moved away for better-paying jobs. In order to keep up with taxes and other expenses, changes had to be made. Oakstone's fields were now mostly grain which didn't require as many workers, and Oakstone continued to thrive.

After lunch, Herbert and Maggie walked to the village. For centuries the village of Hillford depended on Oakstone, and Oakstone on the village. The biggest change of all was at Shells, the local bakery. It expanded into a regional success and was on its way to national recognition. Oakstone's grain supplied the bakery and the Shelfords helped sponsor training programs and schooling for the village which grew along with the fame of the bakery.

"I'm jealous of you," Herbert said. "You're getting to do as you like. I'm stuck following Father – estate business, government politics. Even little brother Sam has more freedom than I do. Right now, his first-year reports at Oxford are quite poor. He studies local pub culture rather than books. But, for better *and* worse, he picks up enough from class discussions to get by without working. Hopefully he will figure it all out."

"Won't Sam take over Shell's Bakery?" She thought Sam feared success would bring on greater expectations. He hid behind poor performance and a sense of humor to avoid responsibility.

Herbert nodded. "I think that's the plan. He can get people to do what he wants."

He stopped mid-step and turned to her. "By the way, another topic, the Season. I've been to some of those debutante balls. You're right, it is a nightmare for you girls, but it's not much better for us males. If that's how we are supposed to find our future mates, I almost want to remain single. So, when you do get presented next year, promise to help find me a 'suitable' girl. Please! Most of the available girls seem too silly to be seriously considered and I haven't had the time it takes to find the few who are worth the effort."

"Of course. At least I have until next year. Besides, with new King Edward, things this year are rather confusing. Be patient," Maggie laughed. "I'll do my best to hunt for you."

In late June, Maggie moved in with Aunt Charlotte and Agnes in London, and went immediately to the offices of the *Times*. Maggie knew that Miss Archer had made Agnes' acceptance at nursing school and her own newspaper job possible. They were too young and inexperienced to be accepted in any other fashion. She felt great pressure to be worthy of those family and school connections.

Lady Davids often accepted the children of her friends as new employees. They lasted a few months and were gone. Maggie was one more 'social hire'. After a proofreading test, and re-writing a few articles, Maggie was assigned a desk with the typists and copy editors near the reporters' room. The reporters wrote the articles for the society pages, the copy editors created the final copy. Maggie sat next to Letty Jenkins.

"I help the Fashion Editor, Miss Carlisle. Sometimes I go with her on visits to the various design houses and bigger shops to spot the newest looks," Letty explained. "I take her notes and make them into readable articles. Clark goes with her to get photos. What area will you be working in?"

"Don't know yet," Maggie answered.

"Lunch time," Letty announced. "Join me?"

Maggie had made her first friend. Letty, it turned out, was another 'social hire' like she was. Letty had been presented to the King at Court two years earlier, and was waiting for a proposal from "a boyfriend from way back in my childhood."

"I wanted a bit of time to see the world before settling down. What better than a newspaper job, especially doing write-ups on the latest fashions," Letty explained, waving her sandwich in an elegant gesture. "I'm just about ready to leave here. You will love it. The writing can sometimes be a bore. Just put up with it. It's better than school."

Maggie listened, charmed and curious at the same time. Letty didn't seem interested in a career, only as a way to spend time until she was married. And she had gone to Gorton, a school higher status than St. Martin's. What would Miss Archer have done with her, she wondered.

"Miss Shelford," Lady Davids asked, walking past Maggie's desk. "Can you type?"

"No Lady Davids," Maggie answered.

"Well, you must learn quickly. The others in our section will turn a polite eye on your youth and connections, but not on your lack of skills."

That evening at Shellings, Maggie received a large, heavy package. A typewriter like those in the typing pool. Maggie smiled and began that night to teach herself to type.

Each day, Maggie sat at her desk, and just typed random keys at the same speed as her co-workers. If anyone came near, she ripped her paper off the typewriter roller and walked away. Lady Davids smiled, because Maggie only handed in her typed work at the very beginning of the day – obviously done at home.

In all other ways, Maggie was as good as the 'real' members of her staff, just so very young. Against her own judgment and experience, but trusting Miss Archer, she asked Maggie to write a few pieces of her own. She enjoyed Maggie's observations and writing style. Again, contrary to her instincts on social hires, she decided to take a gamble.

"Miss Shelford," Lady Davids began, at the end of a long day. "You've only been here a month, but I am impressed. You write well. Let's see if you can be a journalist. Perhaps you could do a few more pieces like that one about your classmate. We'll print it and watch for reactions. If it is successful, we could expand it to a small series for the Tuesday papers. It is normally a slow day for social news, so anything might fill the space. Your thoughts?"

"Thank you," Maggie said. She wanted to squeal or jump, but stayed rooted to the floor. Her brain already churned with possible ideas.

One week later, "Eighteen" debuted in the Tuesday editions of the *Times*. It described the life of young debutantes making the weekend social news. Maggie's pseudonym (protecting both writer and subject when needed) was Betty Bonder. Each article vaguely referenced a girl's family as listed in Debrretts and Burkes, schools attended, and the girl's plans for the future.

Maggie expected that most girls might show little interest in national or world affairs. She promised them anonymity. That relieved some of the girls, disappointed others. At first, she invited friends to interviews over lunch or tea at the Ritz Hotel. Agnes often joined her. "As long as I don't show up in the series as 'tea heiress runs away to become nurse'. I'd rather be the editorial conspirator," Agnes said after one incredibly boring interview.

Maggie now worked for the paper, not to prove herself to anyone, but as someone who had earned her place. Each Sunday evening, Maggie wrote – and typed – what might make the girls sound interesting. There were only a few girls who were truly interesting; the rest of them were so similar, she had to stretch her imagination to come up with characteristics and descriptions to make them worthy to the readers.

She routinely arrived early each Monday morning to deliver her work before the other reporters came in. That was the only way she could make sure the typing was acceptable. It was difficult to do, as the *Times* staff worked every hour of every day. She worked hard every night to get up to speed, nearly ready to type during work hours.

"Morning, m'lady," the young man in casual clothing said in a cheery voice. He was the only one who came in as early as Maggie. He pushed around a cart filled with paper and office supplies. At each desk, he stopped to deliver paper, pencils, and other items on the order list he held as he went. Maggie knew that later in the morning he became the 'postman' distributing mail and messages to the staff and stopping to chat with Letty.

"Hello," Maggie replied politely.

"We've never officially met, though I've heard about you," he continued. "I'm Maxwell Howard. Max. Would-be reporter working my way up the ladder. Jealous that you jumped in ahead of me. Tell me, who do you know?"

"Pardon?"

"Sorry, didn't mean to put you on the spot. Let's start over."

Max twirled around again like Fred Astaire. "Good morning, Miss. Need any office supplies?"

Maggie laughed. He was rather good looking, though he dressed like a newsboy from the street. She thought, I need to stop judging people either by looks or dress. "No thank you. Getting back to your introduction, working your way up the ladder, what do you want to write about?"

"Politics, crime, danger, intrigue, adventure," Max bowed deeply. "Gotta go!" And off he went, checking his list and tossing supplies on desks as he went.

They saw each other in the early mornings. He explained that he came from the "poor side of town." He started as a newsboy on the city streets, talking to reporters coming out of the news office about what was in the headlines. He read thrown-away newspapers. He studied how reporters wrote, and studied up on those topics by going to the local library. He was preparing for interviews to move up in the world of journalism. Still a delivery boy, but, "on his way."

Maggie tried to keep her personal information to a minimum. She was still very conscious of being a social hire. She wondered what being "on her way" might mean. She asked Letty about Max over lunch one day.

"He is a love, but no one takes him too seriously. He's too cocky, too ambitious," Letty said. "But he is rather dashing. At least he thinks he is. Actually, he and I have become rather close friends. I might have a little fun with him while I am still free as a bird."

Maggie pretended not to be shocked by the suggestion.

Later that week, Max invited the two girls into the Dark Room, where the photographer Clark demonstrated how film was developed into pictures before being engraved onto the newspaper press plates. Max was Clark's unofficial apprentice and very excited by the process. Maggie was fascinated by it as well. She decided to take more photos, but also decided to leave the developing to the professionals.

Only a week later, Letty told Maggie that she and Max had used the Dark Room for "another purpose." And hinted that they might use it often. It didn't take too long before Letty came to Maggie in a panic.

"My dress got smudged from some chemical in the Dark Room. How do I get it out? People are already suspicious about us – this will ruin everything if word gets out!"

Maggie thought fast. One of the chemicals was silver. She suggested, "Try silver polish or a tarnish remover. Or one of the rinse solutions for the photos themselves – and – maybe leave before you are asked to leave."

Letty actually followed both pieces of advice. So did Max. He left three weeks later.

Maggie was lonely after they left, but not for long. She hoped to see both of them again, but didn't go out of her way to do so. "Eighteen" was taking more of her time, and she found new friends among the newspaper staff.

CHAPTER 4
July, 1936, Ellie

Twilight comes late from May through September and the sun's long shadows gave the landscape a golden glow. The flat land looked even flatter. On the way to the Van Horn's house, Ellie watched the dairy cows return to their fields after milking. Farmers walked or rode their bicycles home from tending fields of vegetables planted in long narrow rows between equally long narrow drainage canals. Windmill vanes turned slowly in the warm breeze. If the ride had been longer than five minutes, Ellie might have fallen asleep.

Gran interrupted Ellie's daydream, "Tonight's dinner will be large, maybe twenty people. I fear we shall see the Westerveld's once again. Simply sit quietly and learn all about the latest local news."

Ellie and Gran smiled. Both disliked the trivial talk at formal dinners. Here were national decision makers, heads of businesses, diplomats like her father. Yet they seemed absorbed by conversations about how much milk each cow should produce and the traffic problems of motorcars and horses on the same road. Maybe they did care about 'bigger things' and just didn't bring then home. That was at least what Ellie hoped.

"I often daydream until the topic becomes more interesting," Gran admitted. "You probably do that too."

Ellie was grateful for the advice. It confirmed what she already did.

The Van Horn's house was similar to their own. The De Wever ladies, in variations of light blue silk dresses and pearl jewelry, were greeted warmly.

This was their circle of old friends. The dinner celebrated Pieter's new job as a Chemistry professor at Leiden University. They were greeted warmly, and before Ellie knew it, she had a glass of champagne in her hand.

"Is this little Ellie, the pesky annoying child of my youth?" A tall young man stared in disbelief at her.

"Hello, Pieter," Ellie replied. "Are you the annoying tall teenager who always picked on me?"

They both laughed and began catching up. Ellie had lived in foreign lands for most of her life, including boarding school in England. Pieter had been an awkward boy who grew too tall too fast. He never fit into the sports scene with the other boys and was a scholar from an early age. They were both used to being slightly out of the normal groups of people their age. That understanding led to a desire to find out more about each other. He seemed nicer and more good-looking than she remembered.

"Hello, Pieter," sang Tinie, entering the room as dramatically as she could – and totally ignoring Ellie. "I believe we are sitting together tonight."

Ellie hadn't seen the Westervelds enter the house. Pieter mumbled something as Ellie turned to find anyone else for conversation.

"Dinner is served," Mrs. Van Horn announced. She led them into the dining room.

Ellie thought that Pieter wasn't suited to Tinie, but that was none of her business.

Ellie's dinner partner was a friend of Pieter's, polite and friendly. The evening became quite pleasant.

Tinie waved as she left, "See you at the Commissioning."

Ellie went alone to the Commissioning Ceremony. She wore the same blue dress that she wore to Van Horn's. Actually, it was her only formal dress (other than a winter gown from London), and it was comfortable in case she was asked to dance.

The late afternoon sun gave off nearly horizontal light as the guests at the Army *Kazerne* were escorted to chairs set up outside the main building. Ellie sat next to Tinie and her mother. They were barely seated when a trumpet announced the start of the ceremony. A military band played traditional march music. The highest-ranking officers marched up the central aisle to the podium with the young cadets following behind them. A round of speeches were each followed by polite clapping.

The officer candidates stood, heard a charge of duty, and swore to defend Queen and Country. Insignias of rank were pinned on their uniforms and the crowd of family and friends erupted in clapping and loud cheers. A similar, but more dignified ceremony was then given to Colonel Westerveld as he became the newest general in the Dutch Army.

After more applause, the band began to play again, leading the officers and guests in order of importance into the main building.

The *Kazerne's* hall was large. For the commissioning celebration, regimental flags and brigade honors hid military equipment pushed against the wall. Ellie was reminded of her school dining hall, greatly enlarged and decorated for a scene in a romantic play. Tables were set with linens, crystal, and china of the highest quality. The military band took its place behind the head table along the back wall. The new officers, including Pieter, were seated on one side of the room; opposite them were tables of older officers with their wives, adult children, and guests. Ellie guessed that they were Col. Westerveld's colleagues in honor of his promotion. The new general and his family sat at the head table with the other high-ranking officers and their wives. In the middle of the hall were the tables for the families and friends of the new officers.

A man in dress uniform escorted her to a table where the Van Horn family was seated. As much as she enjoyed being an independent woman for the first time, she was grateful that she sat with people she knew and liked. She was relieved that Tinie was sitting with her parents at another table.

When dinner was cleared away, the band began to play dance music. Mrs. Van Horn urged Ellie to join the other young girls who had gathered on one side of the hall, where the new officers sought out their possible dance partners. Somewhat like waiting to be chosen for a sports team, thought Ellie.

She stood next to Tinie who was waving to get Pieter's attention for the first dance. Pieter saw her and began to walk towards her. Just then, Tinie's father came forward and asked, "You know your mother hates to dance, so do me the favor, Tinie. Let everyone see you dance with the new general."

Without waiting for an answer, he whisked her onto the dance floor.

Pieter, already half-way across the open floor towards Tinie, decided to continue forward, and veered slightly towards Ellie.

"May I ask you to dance," he bowed slightly and held out his hand. Ellie gave a half curtsey and joined him.

"I hope I am up to the challenge," Ellie replied. "you really wanted to dance with Tinie."

"Perhaps."

As summer went by, Gran and Ellie fell into a comfortable routine. Days were for trips to Amsterdam, The Hague, Wassenaar, and Leiden for museums and shopping. Evenings were a rotation of dinners at the homes of their friends.

One evening they went to the Mulder's, friends whose home was in Leiden. It was a large house on a canal with a beautiful garden behind the house. The design of dwarf fruit trees and curved stone paths around flower beds made the garden look much larger than it was.

Pieter and his family were also there. He and Ellie sat next to each other at dinner.

"So, what do you actually do as a Professor of Chemistry?" Ellie asked over dessert. "It sounds very technical and serious."

"Research into paints and inks," Pieter replied. He saw the look on her face. She tried to remain serious. "Don't laugh, it *is* technical and serious. We're working on how to make paints and inks last longer. Not to mention ensuring that the actual colors of paints and inks remain the same from one batch to the next. We blend different chemicals to make that happen."

"It sounds like you're playing," Ellie giggled. "or cooking – mix this, add this."

"Not far off from the truth, actually. A large number of companies are interested – publishers, construction, clothing makers, and even the government. But I am more interested in your life, starting with England. If I ever go there, what should I expect?"

Evenings like that one flew by as Pieter and Ellie learned more about each other.

Ellie missed Maggie and Agnes. She wrote to them as often as possible. They were already in jobs or training. She wasn't sure about her own future. It was frustrating, but not to the point of worry. Yet.

Finally, Gran and Ellie hosted a dinner. The same circle of friends met again and small talk ruled the evening. During glasses of port after dinner, Pieter asked Ellie, "And, what's in your future? Embark on the English Season like your mother and grandmother?"

Pieter seemed genuinely interested. He was serious and quietly friendly. She certainly liked him, and he seemed to like her. Was this how romances started?

"Perhaps," mused Ellie. "My friends and I are waiting until next year because we were the youngest in our class. Too smart to stay with our age-mates but too young to be adults. To me, presentation is all about getting a marriage proposal, which I am not at all ready for. But if my friends do the Season, I might go along with it," Ellie replied.

She was surprised at what she admitted next. "My impossible dream is to be in the foreign service like my father. I doubt I can get a job like that, even with my father's connections. Maybe as a translator, maybe as a teacher. I do like languages. I'd have to go to a university for language classes. Honestly, I don't have much of a plan."

"I can help you with the university part if you're serious," Pieter offered. "I know someone in the Language Department. He likes to tutor new students. You could meet with him to see what you need to do."

"Really?"

"Let me work on it."

Pieter smiled warmly and a few days later, he called her asking her to lunch with Prof. Willems, a recently retired professor from the Language Department who still had an office on campus.

Professor Willems looked to be Gran's age. His office walls were lined with bookshelves that overflowed with books and memorabilia. More books were stacked under the window. The Professor began his interview in English, suddenly switching to French, and then back to Dutch again, all the while asking Ellie to describe her adjustment to living back home. At the conclusion of the meeting, he asked her to come in the next day for an official evaluation.

Her tests were written and oral. The questions were varied and Ellie felt off-balanced for most of the day. At the end of the day, the professor said, "Your English is excellent, no surprise, coming from an English school. Your

French is also very good. However, your Dutch needs work. Your vocabulary is adequate, but your spelling and grammar are atrocious. I think you can be admitted as a foreign student. I shall become your tutor and you could begin studies in Winter Term."

Ellie was excited. She shared the news with Pieter and Gran at dinner.

"Cheers! Let's have champagne! To the next professor in our midst?" Pieter then added that Prof. Willems had just called him. He considered Ellie one of the most naturally gifted language students he ever taught. Ellie was embarrassed. She never found languages to be all that difficult. Changing from language to language was like changing from eating the meal to drinking the wine and back to the meal again.

Lessons with Prof. Willems and time spent with Pieter made the weeks fly by. Gran was her main support and confidant, reminding Ellie to "Be prepared, and then you can adjust to whatever happens. Don't over-plan, just pay attention. Improvise as you go along. I am still doing just that, after all these years."

An interesting aspect of Professor Willems' life was his work as a prison tutor. By Dutch law, all prisoners were required to receive educational assistance. It was thought that if people had education, they would not return to a life of crime once they were released. Prof. Willems visited the local prison each week to work with the prisoners. He liked the challenge and the success that came when "his" prisoners were released, and did well in regular society. He thought that Ellie should join him, as continued education for her, and give her a chance to help others.

Prof. Willems introduced Ellie to the women housed in a separate wing of the prison. Until then, she had thought innocently, that everyone had opportunities like her, they just had to work hard. Now, she met people who really had no advantages, no choices. But with a little help, so much must be possible, Ellie, the idealist still believed.

Her favorite student was Dora Linden, a girl about her own age. She was thin, serious, and suspicious of Ellie's motives in helping her. Dora had only gone to school for a few years before she had to work. One day, she stole food from a market. When the grocer fought to keep his food, she grabbed a knife lying on the counter and stabbed him. It was considered a minor crime until the grocer died of an infection. Dora, as a young teen, was in prison for a minimum sentence for murder.

Ellie taught Dora reading, mathematics (a joke, as it had been her worst subject at school), and a bit of history. Dora taught Ellie how to sew and knit, and told her stories of survival. As they traded their skills and their stories, they became fascinated by each other's lives and worlds. Ellie hoped that when Dora was released in another year, they would keep in contact.

Professor Willems and Ellie were now close friends. She was rapidly growing from English school girl to a Dutch adult. He explained Dutch life to her, laughing with her over the difference in English and Dutch habits. She often invited him to dinner, which led to a friendship between him and Gran.

Ellie realized that she and Pieter were falling in love. She dreamed about life as Pieter's wife. She didn't want to, it might jeopardize the real relationship, but she couldn't help it.

She met Pieter and his friends at the university. Conversations ranged from work to theology, philosophy, jokes, and of course, just plain gossip. Throughout everything was a thread of politics, mostly centered on Germany's rebirth as a military power. Their small nation was vulnerable to whatever might come. What could they expect? What would they do?

One evening, as they were bicycling home after their time at the pub, Pieter stopped by a canal and became serious.

"If the Germans really get aggressive and take over our country, I will be called up from Army Reserve to Active Duty," he said quietly. "You know that, right?"

Ellie just nodded.

"I care deeply for you and want to make sure that you are safe," he continued. "You know that too."

Ellie nodded again.

"So, I am asking you to marry me. The life of a professor/scientist/reserve officer is not very glamorous, nor pay well, but we do have our wealthy families to support us. With that to consider as perhaps a warning, will you marry me?"

Ellie hesitated. Now that he was officially proposing, she wasn't sure that she was ready. Did she want a broader social life before settling down? She had only seconds to respond. *Am I old enough to make this decision?*

"Yes, of course, but can we wait a bit? I only turn 18 in December," Ellie replied, happier than she had ever been in her life. *How would she tell her friends? How do you plan a wedding? Where would they live? What would she do after they were married?*

Almost like he was reading her mind, he said, "Of course we can wait. First finish your classes. But we can find a place to live in town now, our own home. Something like the Mulders' house. I can start living there at any time. We can live there until we take over our parents' social responsibilities."

Ellie smiled, and said, "You have really thought this all out, haven't you? No, yes. I've been thinking about this too."

"Do you love me?"

"Yes. I guess I always have."

A long embrace later, they pedaled to Ellie's family home to announce to Gran the big news. Ellie thought to herself, *should I run to the church* and scream the news from the bell tower? Or should I keep this a secret, all to myself. Do I jump for joy, or act serenely like I am expected to behave as an adult?

At that moment, Pieter turned to her and kissed her. Oh, that's fine too.

"I'm curious," Ellie need to know. "What happened to you and Tinie?"

Pieter first stared at her, then laughed. He shook his head, "I turned out to be a total bore. I'm not the party type. She let me know that our relationship wouldn't work. I never knew we had a relationship."

"Boring! I guess I like the boring kind of man," Ellie smiled. "I mean, love the boring man."

Gran was not surprised to hear the news. She just wondered why it had taken them so long to realize what was obvious to the rest of their friends. She asked, "When do you plan to announce this? Christmas would be the right time, though that is still a few months off."

Upon hearing that they planned a long engagement, Gran relaxed. "Very smart to wait. Think about your own well-being before you start sharing your life with someone else."

Gran sounded like Miss Archer, thought Ellie.

Then her mind began to spin. Who do we tell first? When would they have the wedding? Where? She needed to make sure that Maggie and Agnes could attend.

CHAPTER 5
Early November, 1936, Agnes

Several calls came into the Emergency Ward at the same time. Emmy and Agnes were there for their third time. The whole day had been busy. Night was busier, due to the expected Guy Fawkes Day fireworks. They didn't expect the unrelated night calls to be high as well.

Emmy and one doctor were busy with a woman who had fallen on the stairs outside her house. She was pregnant and began to have serious labor pains when she lost her balance. There was no calling a midwife, she was rushed to the hospital. She had broken her leg, and now the baby was coming quickly. Emmy's head was spinning between what she learned in school and what her mother had taught her about delivery procedures, while the doctor studied the broken leg.

A man had been brought in with symptoms of a burst appendix. A surgeon from the operating theater was called in. The surgery happened right there in the Emergency Ward.

A motorcar accident brought in two more people; fortunately their injuries were minor. Stiches and wrapped sprains. Agnes and a third student nurse ran back and forth between the accident victims and the surgeon performing the appendix operation.

Between contractions, the new mother's leg was set in a supporting brace. After the baby was delivered, the mother waited for her leg to be set and put into a cast. Emmy brought the baby to the women's ward and was back in the

Emergency Area in time to bring the mother up to the women's ward to be reunited with her infant.

The accident victims were patched up and released to relatives who would take them home. The appendix operation was over, and the patient was sent to the men's ward for recovery.

Finally, a period of calm settled over the Area. The staff began to take their long-awaited tea breaks.

Agnes was about to go on her break when suddenly the door to the ward burst open. Two attendants brought in yet another patient.

"Knife wound!" shouted one of the attendants. Agnes ran over to see what she could do. The man's cheek was sliced from eyebrow to chin. She instinctively began to pinch his face together and press down on it to stop the bleeding. She called to an orderly to bring the doctor over as soon as possible. Dr. Beech, Head of Emergency Care, arrived. Agnes was cleaning the wound with one hand, while pinching the wound together with the other. He studied her without moving, making her nervous. Had she made a mistake? She just kept cleaning up the blood that was coming from the wound. Finally, Dr. Beech took over and she stepped aside.

"Well, Sister, we meet again," said the patient, disrupting her thoughts.

Agnes recognized who it was. "Hello Weejun. What happened this time?"

"Ah, a wee discussion about the English and the Scots," Weejun grimaced. "The other chap and I didn't agree on which folks were the best. You know, Lassie, I recognized your touch just now. You're looking as lovely as ever."

Just as before, Agnes was unsure what do say or do. She blurted out, "thanks, but just keep your private parts under control this time."

Weejun tried to laugh, then winced at the pain. Dr. Beech was trying to stitch the wound, and raised his eyebrows to study Agnes again. Pretty young to be teasing like that. And remaining that calm.

When the ward quieted down, the doctor asked, "How did you know the way to stop the bleeding?" the doctor asked. "You're a first-year. Have you had emergency medicine classes yet?"

"No, just Red Cross First Aid. They told us about applying pressure to stop bleeding. Did I do the right thing, Dr. Beech?" Agnes asked, not knowing if she had overstepped some rule about what she was allowed to do or not.

"You did fine. Just surprised that you didn't run down the hall in a panic to get me, rather than stay with the patient. You kept rather calm and professional. You might make a good operating nurse or member of the Emergency team."

Dr. Beech went off to see another patient, and Agnes walked back over to Weejun to check up on him.

"How are you?" she asked.

"I'll live, though I'll wind up a tad uglier after this," was Weejun's reply. "Just how old are you? You look a wee bit young for a Sister. More the age that my daughter would be."

"Nearly eighteen."

"I was right, then. And a bit posh. Even for nurses. What do your parents think of all this?"

"That doesn't matter." Weejun waited for more information. "I am a bit of a runaway. What about you and your family?"

Weejun sighed. "They all died in a house fire about 10 years ago. A bit of a runaway myself afterwards. I came down to London for a job and a new life, but the old life came with me, drinking and all. If you still have any family, my advice is, as someone old enough to be your father, stay with them."

Agnes sensed that neither of them wanted to go into any further details.

"Maybe someday we'll be together, but not yet," Agnes stated with an emotion she was surprised to feel. She did miss them. Instead, she told

Weejun, "Meanwhile, take care of that wound, like the doctor ordered. And stop fighting."

"Yes, Sister," he replied trying to sound meek.

The doors burst open again, another accident, this time a man whose hand was wrapped in a blood-soaked towel.

"You!" the man shouted, looking over at Weejun. "You'll pay for this if my hand is mucked up."

Agnes shouted out louder, "Stop yelling or you will be thrown out. Sit down and wait your turn!"

"No one else here, I'm next. And throw that bloody Scot out!" the man continued to shout. "Let him bleed to death, worthless scum like the rest of them."

"I said sit down and wait your turn. As it turns out, the doctor just left for a tea break – you might have a long wait."

The man sat down, grumbling and staring at Weejun, who lay quietly staring at the ceiling trying not to smile. When Dr. Beech returned from his break, he asked Agnes to assist in treating the belligerent man. He wanted to watch her reactions to assisting in an operating situation. Agnes tried to be gentle in washing his wounds, fighting off her anger at his bullying behavior. She concentrated on tweezing the many glass shards from his wound, causing continual mopping up of blood. It was a tedious procedure, but after half an hour of removing glass, stitching up, and bandaging, Dr. Beech sent him on his way.

Agnes returned to Weejun's bed. He was sitting up, waiting to be released. She asked, "Was that the man you were fighting?"

Weejun nodded. He asked, "Where did you learn that imperial voice? I wager it wasn't in some nice girls' school."

"My mother. I just act like she does when she wants to get her way. Surprisingly, it nearly always gets results."

"I imagine that's why you left. I'm thinking it has to do with two strong women in one house? Still, you might want to keep in touch with her," Weejun closed his eyes, a tear running down one cheek.

She didn't want to answer. He was too close to the truth.

"You really like Emergency work, didn't you," observed Emmy on their way to breakfast after their long night. They were both exhausted. "Let's just change our sad-looking aprons for clean ones. I think we can get through classes before changing over into clean uniform dresses."

"I do like Emergency," admitted Agnes. "I liked the high-speed action of everything. No time to think, just do. I want to see what surgery is like before thinking about a special area."

"I prefer the quiet bedside time with patients," Emmy became very serious and thoughtful. "You know Clive?" she asked. "The medical student?"

"Clive, who you are glued to at the Sickly Doctor? You two are quite the pair."

"We're getting married as soon as he finishes his program next year."

"Fantastic! Does anyone else know? The official engagement part? Everyone with eyes expects it is only a matter of time.'"

"Not yet. Thing is, Agnes, I'm not prepared to be a doctor's wife. I'm not of his social class. Can you teach me how to be rich? Or at least how to behave around rich people?"

In answer, Agnes invited Emmy to Aunt Charlotte's house for dinner on their next night off.

CHAPTER 6
Christmas, 1936, Emmy

"I told you Shellings was a grand house," Emmy whispered to Clive, stepping out of the cab in the Mayfair district of London. "It's been in Maggie's family for generations. It's like a living museum, but it feels more like home than you would expect."

"Don't get used to it, Emmy," Clive said as he studied the city mansion. The street lights gave him a view of trees and a narrow garden in front of the house itself. "Mum and Dad live well, and so shall we – but not this well. We'll visit folks such as these, but first as their doctor, maybe later as friends."

Mr. Bolton, the butler, opened the front door and smiled. "Good evening, Miss Emerald."

"Hello, Mr. Bolton. This is my fiancé, Mister Clive Raleigh," Ellie said.

"Sir," Mr. Bolton bowed slightly. "May I take your coats?" He looked over their shoulders. "Ah, and Miss Eleanor is arriving. With your permission, may I bring you all in together?"

"Absolutely," replied Emmy.

Mr. Bolton greeted Ellie and Pieter, and passed their coats and hats to a waiting footman. The four guests were ushered into the sitting room. Agnes and Maggie were already there with Lady Charlotte, who invited them to be seated. Clive looked around. Dark blue drapes hung ceiling to floor, the walls were pale blue, highlighting gilt-framed pictures. Oak and mahogany furniture was upholstered in greens and blues and large oriental carpets covered the parquet floor. Light came from electric lamps and candles. Nothing too new, Clive noted, and the old pieces were well cared for. Like Emmy said, comfortable. Better not get used to this, he repeated, this time to himself.

Mr. Bolton and a footman brought in trays of sherry and crackers with salmon and pate. Lady Charlotte lifted her glass of sherry.

"I am so delighted to have you all here for my early Christmas dinner, as Agnes, Maggie and I will be off to Oakstone for the actual holiday. Here's to a Happy Christmas and a wonderful 1937 to you all."

They lifted their glasses. "Now then," Lady Charlotte proposed, "Let's share our hopes and expectations for the new year. Clive and Pieter, we know only small pieces of your stories. Now we can hear from both of you in person."

Pieter began. "Hello, all. Thank you, Lady Charlotte for your kind invitation. I am a chemist at the University of Leiden. I prefer card games and puzzles over sports - which I play poorly. Like most Dutchmen I love to discuss politics, but perhaps, not tonight. I look forward to 1937 because Ellie and I will become officially engaged."

Everyone looked warmly at Ellie. "That's right," she said smiling. "The announcement will be at my birthday party, just after Christmas. I'm studying languages at the University. Dutch, French, and of course, English. Our actual wedding is far in the future."

Mr. Bolton sounded the dinner gong. Lady Charlotte led the group into the dining room. Mr. Bolton, with two footmen and two housemaids, began to serve the meal.

"One order of business," Lady Charlotte said as they were seated. "Please address me as 'Aunt Charlotte'. 'Lady' is for those outside the family."

Dinner began with a clear turtle soup decorated with triangles of toast and accompanied by white wine.

"I suppose I'm next," Clive ventured. "Along with Pieter, I thank you for inviting me to this wonderful evening. My father is a surgeon in York. I plan to join his practice when I finish school. I may try to practice another specialty later on, perhaps psychiatry. Like Pieter, I have never been very athletic. I do play cards, billiards, and oh, an occasional game of tennis. Also enjoy, politics, but not this evening."

"We girls are next," said Maggie. "I'm at the *Times,* at least through the coming Season. After that, I hope to move to regional news. It's much more interesting than the social pages. In honor of this evening, no politics or stories for the paper."

That last comment brought on soft laughter. Mr. Bolton and his team removed the soup bowls, refilled the wine glasses, and brought in the next course: *saumon en croute.*

Agnes, next to Maggie at the foot of the table, cleared her throat announcing her turn. "Well, 1937 will be the middle of my middle year of nursing school. It turns out I have the talent of 'bluffing'. One doesn't have to be totally sure of something to be considered the authority. One just has to *act* with great conviction. Has anyone else felt like this? It's crossed my mind that politicians might be bluffing at least half the time. Oh dear, have I crossed the line about talking politics?"

The group responded with laughter.

Clive responded, "We medical students learn that during our first year. You establish your authority and those around you accept it in some odd way. Agnes, you give yourself no credit. You don't need to bluff. After only a few months at St. Bart's, you are the talk of the place. People love you, but more importantly, they respect you. The Head of Emergency Services, Dr. Beech, is really impressed. Normally first year students don't get to do more than sitting with recovering patients or clean up after the rest of us. You are far ahead of that."

Emmy nodded, "You've even been asked on surgical procedures, something usually only third-year students might get to do."

"Well, I give you credit for helping me get used to it all," Agnes said. "Now, who's next?"

"Mr. Bolton, serving our Christmas turkey," Aunt Charlotte replied. On cue, Mr. Bolton and his team replaced the empty fish plates with plates filled with turkey, chestnut stuffing, and a mix of brussels sprouts, parsnips, and carrots. Another glass of wine, this time red, was served. There was silence as everyone enjoyed their meal.

As Mr. Bolton introduced dessert, strawberry and cream tarts, Emmy shifted in her chair.

"Last up," she said. "More than I can say, I thank you all for helping me prepare for my new role in life. It wasn't what anyone in my family would have expected. My grandparents were both in service, a footman and a lady's maid. They wanted my mother to have her own career. And now, my mother, a midwife, is just as determined to get us all into our own careers. She made us read, took us to museums, and showed us the nicer shops, but this is a jump higher than she ever expected. Again, thank you."

Aunt Charlotte spoke, "She did well. You're more prepared than you think. You will be a great plus for the people of York."

Maggie said, "Being in the upper classes is more than table manners and management of a city house. Country life is quite different. It's more relaxing and freer than city life, but there are extra duties like farm management, village social commitments, and the like. I doubt if you need to take on all of that, though."

Emmy began to panic. "That has to wait. I am curious about the rest, but not yet. Mostly I think we will be city folks. I merely wanted to know how to sit properly and how to eat with people other than my family and the rabble at the hospital. I just don't want to make too many mistakes, just be as presentable as possible."

Aunt Charlotte said calmly, "Of course."

This brought a sympathetic murmur to all at the table.

Maggie spoke first, "In truth, you're actually farther along than some of our classmates who only ate in household nurseries or school. They actually have to learn more than you ever had to. You are already more than just presentable."

Ellie sat very still. Well, Gran, she thought to herself, here we go. She said, "Emmy, we creative and devious girls can do more to make you comfortable in any social situation. In fact, you might *come out* of this as someone quite *presentable*."

Lady Charlotte was the first to respond. "Are you suggesting that Emmy be presented to the new King, along with the three of you?"

Polite coughing hid the inhaling, laughing, snickering, and gasping.

"Can we do that?" asked Agnes, catching on immediately. "Maggie and I qualify right off. Don't you have to have a sponsor? Maggie, you have been writing about this in the paper. Doesn't Emmy have to have a registered pedigree of sorts?"

"Not always," Maggie thought out loud, sensing the beginning of pre-prank thought session. "It seems that every year or two, there is a mystery girl who goes through the Season without obvious connections. Everyone does need a sponsor, someone who has already been presented. I think that's all."

"And I qualify as the daughter of a high-ranking diplomat. There is an allotment for families from 'favored' countries," said Ellie.

"So, it might work," Agnes said, with a grin. "How do we start?"

"I could be her sponsor," proposed Lady Charlotte, feeling energized by the creative way the girls were thinking. "I've been presented, and have the proper connections. All we need is a good story of why she's been invisible thus far."

"Wait just a minute," said Emmy. "You haven't asked me if I'd want to do this."

"Well?" They all looked at Emmy. Emmy looked back at Ellie, Agnes, Maggie, and Aunt Charlotte. They were not joking; they were genuinely and affectionately interested. Clive and Pieter gave her amused but confident grins.

"Oh, fine. Yes. Why not? Let's give it a go!" Emmy wasn't sure why she agreed. She knew it wouldn't work out anyway. This was one of those dinner conversations that everyone would forget by morning.

Aunt Charlotte rang for Mr. Bolton. She said to him, "We are going back to the sitting room for our cheese and coffee. And more wine. This is turning into a long night." She turned to her guests, "Now, let's get started. If the new King has Courts this year, we have roughly six months to get ready."

Aunt Charlotte spoke quietly to Mr. Bolton as they left the dining room.

The sound of the door opening woke Emmy up. A maid pulled back the drapes. It was bright outside, and December sunrises were around 8am. Where *was* she? Oh, Aunt Charlotte's house. Agnes had lent her a nightgown and some clothes for "tomorrow" and that was now.

"Good morning, Miss. Shall I bring you some tea?" The maid asked in a soft voice.

"What time is it?" Emmy felt as groggy as she did after a long night at the Sickly Doctor. Ah, all that wine last night.

"Nearly nine o'clock, Miss. Breakfast is being served until eleven."

"When did you get up?"

"Normal time, 5am, Miss. I light the fires in each room and help prepare breakfast. Then back up here to help guests get ready for the day. Would you like anything else, Miss?"

"Gosh, no," Emmy was now sitting up straight. She felt guilty about sleeping while someone else did nearly a full day's work. And her grandmother had done all this before electricity and modern conveniences. She answered, "Just the tea please."

"Yes, Miss."

Emmy washed her arms and face in the bathroom, hoping that it would erase her bleary look. Coming back into the bedroom, she noticed that tea was already set on the table next to the window. The maid had also laid out a skirt, blouse, and loose jacket from Agnes' wardrobe. Very quickly, she was ready to join the rest of her friends.

"Good morning," Emmy greeted Ellie in the dining room. "Ellie, last night seemed very unreal. Did it really happen?"

Ellie nodded, then giggled. "Yes, it happened. It's going to happen. There is food on the sideboard. It's a good thing that you and Agnes are free today – you don't look so well."

Emmy sighed. She didn't feel that well. But here she was. She looked around the dining room. "This room looks so different in daylight. I like how painting the walls makes the pictures show up better than in front of wallpaper. I need to remember this for our own house."

Ellie agreed. "Pieter has so many books, I doubt if it will make a difference if we paint or do wallpaper." She turned to face Emmy, "So, to the point, do you really want to do this, be a debutante, meeting the King?"

Emmy shook her head slightly, "It is a lovely dream, but I doubt even you three can make this happen. Though, I would rather curtsy to King George than his brother. What a surprise that King Edward plans to abdicate. I guess it was his only real choice."

They were eating when Pieter and Clive arrived. They chose coffee over tea, with an eye towards the eggs and bacon on the sideboard. Clive was wearing a cardigan obviously too large for him.

"Thanks for the loan of the cardigan, Pieter. It was very kind of Lady, er, Aunt Charlotte to ask the De Wevers to send over some clothes for today

– and to think of me, too," Clive lifted his coffee cup in thanks. Pieter returned the gesture.

"Sorry that it doesn't fit too well, I'm a bit taller than you," Pieter replied. "Good morning, ladies. It seems that we are in the midst of a great cabal."

"I would imagine that our gentlemanly role is to keep mum, and stay out of the way," Clive offered, as he sat down at the table.

"You would be correct, gentlemen," Ellie replied in a very proper manner.

Agnes and Maggie straggled in, and sat at the table while Ellie brought them tea and toast.

"Good morning everyone, I hope you are all well," Aunt Charlotte entered the room. She looked like a general ready to execute a battle plan. She opened a notebook and began, "I have been thinking about our talk last night and have some ideas."

She raised one finger. "I know that Lady Astor will present her niece this year. She comes from Kenya and her parents can't make it home. That's a plan we might follow. I can present Emmy as the daughter of an old schoolmate stuck in India or somewhere exotic. We can keep the details very simple."

A second finger went up. "With our third king in three years, there will be many distractions. The press will be trying to outguess the king on any plans he might make. Since each girl is usually more interested in herself than in any one else, very little attention should come our way."

A third finger rose. "Every girl goes to the preparation classes, (dance lessons, royal etiquette), so Emmy, you're not behind there. If you make mistakes, it's because you have been living abroad. School will always come first and your schedule will be our guide. So, what do you all think?"

"Well, I'm convinced," Maggie ventured. She looked around the table, and everyone nodded yes.

Emmy took over, "Thanks one and all. I don't want to ruin your big day. I can step out at any time, right?" Nods from the group. "Right. Also, I want to be fully active in this. And I want to bring my mother and sisters in on this. My sister Ruby is apprenticing to a seamstress and is working on my trousseau. She can make additional clothing as we go along. Also, for some of the events, I'd like it if they might be invited to enjoy the fun too."

"Absolutely!" cheered everyone. Too early they thought for more champagne or wine, there was a simple toast of raising tea and coffee cups.

Agnes remembered the agreement with her mother. She decided to be like Scarlett O'Hara in *"Gone With The Wind"* and 'think about that tomorrow'.

CHAPTER 7
Spring, 1937, The Season

"The Battleground Tea" was Maggie's first 'Eighteen' column covering the preparations for The Season. Lady Royd, who controlled the Season's calendar, and the Lord Chamberlain, who controlled the Royal calendar, needed to be contacted for a Court date. Only then could sponsors plan the rest of their celebrations. After getting their Court invitation, nailing down the desired date and place for the Coming Out Ball was a competitive challenge, the ultimate 'battle' between sponsors. Maggie was curious to see how her friends' mothers plus Aunt Charlotte would do this.

The night before their Battleground Tea, Aunt Charlotte asked Agnes, "How much do you know about your mother?" she asked, "I mean, really know."

"Not much. Just that she dislikes me enormously because I won't fit in her mold," Agnes replied.

"Hmm. Do you remember your grandfather?"

"No. He died when I was 4 years old. He wasn't very nice. He frightened me."

Charlotte sat quietly for a while. "You know that your mother and I were classmates at St. Martin's. You need to know her story:

John Fletcher was the tyrannical owner of Arrow Tea Company, a major import/export firm. Divina, Agnes' mother, was his only child. She was expected to be the best at everything. She was terrified of making even the smallest mistake, and so she avoided school activities like theater or sports for fear of failing. Charlotte and Jane were her best friends, but even they couldn't get her involved in school life or having a bit of fun.

When John wanted to take over a small competitor, Rose Herbs & Teas, he arranged the marriage of Divina to Kenneth Tripler, the son of the owner. It 'sealed the deal' like a medieval royal contract. Kenneth even agreed to changed his name from Tripler to Fletcher so that the name Fletcher would continue at Arrow Tea. Divina and Kenneth did grow to love each other. They worked hard to make both business and marriage work. Divina became a capable executive by copying the tyrannical style of her father. It was raising their active and stubborn daughter that nearly broke them apart.

Charlotte continued, "Your outburst made them realize how much they had changed. Ever since you left, they have been seriously trying to return to their original relationship. They are now more content with each other and less intense about business. You and your parents must reunite. At least be civil while we are at tea tomorrow."

Agnes wasn't sure. There was one issue that she couldn't confront. "I'll try," she said in a quiet voice.

Maggie privately asked Aunt Charlotte about Agnes and her mother. "We just have to wait it out," was the reply.

The four girls and their mothers met at the Ritz Tea Room; the mothers were armed with diaries and folders filled with papers. This might be the girls' celebration, but it was also a crowning moment for society mothers.

"So, we begin," Lady Divina started. "I had wondered if our new King George would even have Courts this year. King Edward's informal Courts were a disaster! How it rained at one of the garden Courts and everyone was drenched! Half the girls receiving notes by mail informing them to consider themselves done just for showing up. After all that preparation. Happily, George announced the return to evenings inside the Palace."

They all agreed.

"The Courts will be late in the year, though, with the King George's Coronation in May," Maggie's mother reported. "Lady Royd assigned us for the first Court on July 1, along with most of the St. Martin's girls. Our ball will be the week following, just as the Henley Regatta is finishing up."

Trays of savory and sweet foods were placed on the table. The old pot of tea was exchanged for a new hot one. Emmy, hypnotized by all the fuss, tried not to get fruit jam or meat pie juice on her new rust-colored suit. Ruby barely finished the skirt the night before. Suddenly she realized someone had asked her a question.

Aunt Charlotte saved her from answering. "Oh, Emerald is still adjusting to Mother England. She has only been here since Christmas, and before that, just a few times with her parents on leave."

The mothers finished checking their lists and signing on for various assignments – flowers, invitations, reception decorations and food, and transportation on the night of the Court itself.

As they left, Divina Fletcher whispered to Agnes, "When will I see you again?"

Agnes answered, "soon." She wanted to say more, but just walked away.

In May, Maggie left the actual coverage of The Season to experienced writers of the social pages. She was moving to the Oxfordshire regional news desk of the *Times*.

Agnes was finishing her first year of nurse training and getting ready for a practical term in the summer. Her classwork and her social life at the Sickly Doctor made her busy and happy. She chose not to worry too much about her mother, or see her outside dress fittings and presentation classes.

Ellie was going between the two countries every few weeks. She wasn't sure that she loved travel anymore; at least not this often. Classes at the university were taking a lot of time and she missed Dora and the other prisoners she taught. In England, there was the training in dancing and learning the insane traditions that went along with presentation. No time for Pieter or any of their mutual friends. Gran reminisced about her own debut and shared stories of a long-ago era.

Emmy was exhausted. The training was just as odd and foreign for her as it was for Ellie. They laughed several times about that, but only when they were alone. The dreaded curtsy, was a nightmare: face the King; lock one's knees; lower nearly to the floor while keeping one's back straight; rise; step back. Repeat with the Queen. Back out of the space (keep facing the monarch at all times) while managing not to trip on the train of one's gown. Emmy curtsied to her sisters and mother at home. They snickered affectionately.

She taught Clive the dances as soon as she learned them. It left her a small amount of time to rehearse her presentation story. ("Don't know much about India, we were kept inside the compound. Haven't been back home long enough to know much about England either.") At least her final year of school was easy. She was specializing in midwifery, and she knew much if it already from her mother.

Her wardrobe was also not a problem. Some items were bought on sale; Ruby made the rest. The other girls gave her a few dresses and gowns that Ruby altered and updated. And her white presentation gown would be her wedding dress.

Emmy had only one request. "I want to change my name to protect my family, should anything go wrong," she announced one evening. "And, I want to change my name to Emma Ventnor. Emma is an easy change from Emerald, and Ventnor is my mother's maiden name."

Aunt Charlotte agreed and a friend made the change quickly and quietly.

The First of July. Maids and hairdressers helped prepare everyone for the visit to Buckingham Palace. Fathers dressed in evening white tie, then stayed out of the way. After all, they were merely window dressing.

In early afternoon, the girls and their families took limousines and queued up on the Mall. The short drive to the Palace took several hours. The mothers brought knitting and embroidery to pass the time, and a picnic basket for each limousine. Agnes, her parents, Charlotte, and Emmy rode together. Charlotte and Divina chatted together, Emmy and Agnes played cards and watched people watching them. Kenneth sat in the corner of the limousine and read his favorite author's newest book, *Murder in Piccadilly*. Ellie and Maggie were in the other limousine with their parents, doing much the same. Maggie's father grumbled, "We could have walked this round trip three times over."

"Oh Father." "Oh Edward." The De Wevers chuckled and handed out small sandwiches. Photographers and bystanders peered at them along the way. Half-way through the ride, the girls switched cars so that they could sit with another group.

At 6:30, they arrived at Buckingham Palace. Dresses with trains, and hair with headdresses underwent final examination before the families entered the Palace.

The girls and sponsoring women were escorted to a row of chairs to wait for the call into the Throne Room. Mothers fussed with their daughters' appearances. Several of the mothers were quite plump. In white or pale evening attire complete with headdresses of the required three ostrich feathers, Maggie thought they resembled chickens in a farm yard. She commented on this to her three friends. Their giggles made the people around them turn and scowl.

Finally, it was time to be ushered into the Throne Room and seated in the order of their presentation. Fathers and dignitaries from across the globe lined the sides of the room. The Throne Room itself was awe-inspiring white, gold, and brilliant light. Everything and everyone glittered.

A herald called everyone's attention as King George and Queen Mary entered with their entourage in full court dress. King nodded to the audience and waved everyone to sit. Then it began.

The Lord Chancellor knocked his mace on the floor three times and announced Maggie's full name. Her mother stood behind her. Maggie came forward, curtseyed, the King said something (she never remembered what it was), then she backed away. She concentrated on staying upright. She repeated the whole procedure with the Queen, backed away again, and it was over. She breathed again. And so it went for Agnes, Ellie, and Emmy. They were now officially titled ladies of the British Empire.

After the last presentation, the entire audience erupted into singing "God Save the King." Then the King and Queen led the entire company to supper in the Banquet Hall.

Later, Emmy and Maggie along with Maggie's parents rode together to the De Wever's home next to the Dutch Embassy on Portman Square. Agnes and Ellie shared a limousine with their parents. Agnes told her parents the real story about Emmy. Were they smiling in amusement or just being polite? She decided not to ask. They did look less critical and stiff than she remembered.

At the embassy, the four posed with their own photographer, and shared a late-night supper with Pieter, Clive, and Emmy's family. They recalled every detail for them. Emmy had made it! It was like the triumph they felt after driving Headmistress Lattery's blue MG convertible onto the bridge.

Maggie finally drifted off to sleep as early dawn broke. She tried to make her tired mind work for just a few more minutes. Someone had been in the Throne Room, someone she should have recognized but hadn't. Perhaps it was nothing.

Their ball was the final part of their Season. The girls still wore long gloves and hair accessories, but those now matched a rainbow of colored gowns. Agnes chose pale yellow with brown trim for her gown, Maggie had on sage and dark green, Ellie wore her favorite colors of navy and pale blue, and Emmy's gown was mauve and deep purple. The mothers, along with Emmy's mother and sisters were equally elegant and colorful.

Lord Edward Shelford, Charge d'Affaires Albert De Wever, and Lord Kenneth Fletcher wore sashes and medals of honor, just as they had at Court. Clive, Pieter, and Maggie's brothers Herbert and Sam wore their white tie and tails. Their ball was held in the Dutch Embassy Reception Room, which was in the center of a traditional Georgian mansion. The sponsors decided that it was elegant enough on its own. The only added decorations were rose bushes in large urns on the floor and vases filled with several varieties of cut roses on tables around the room. "Classic setting, good food, and music from both a great jazz band and a small classic quartet, entertained a large group of classmates with their escorts, dignitaries, and extended families. Simple, fun, not over-the-top, and perfect for them" was the comment made by a reporter.

Maggie checked her dance card. Her brother Herbert came over to remind her of the promise made last summer. "Well," he questioned. "Whose card do I fill in? Anyone suitable?"

"Of course. Just don't be so demanding," Maggie laughed. "Now – that girl in pink. Babs Markley. Reading languages at Oxford. She was in our class at St. Martins last year. And that girl in light blue, Nell Grover. Finishing up this year, serious and smart. Shy, but you might like each other. Good luck."

Just then, Maggie froze.

Herbert saw her reaction. "What's wrong?"

"I just saw someone I think I should know and I can't place her. Oh dear, she's coming over here. Oh, God, it's Miss Archer and she's all dressed up!"

"The Headmistress from St. Martins? Wasn't she the terror you played your prank on last year?"

"No, this is the Assistant Headmistress. More the intimidator, demanding us to make something of ourselves. Never saw her warmer side, yet she's here, laughing and smiling. What is she doing here? She was at the King's Court last week! That's who I saw!" Maggie couldn't move.

"Here she comes," Herbert observed. "My cue to disappear. Thanks for the dance tips."

Miss Archer closed in and looked directly at Maggie. "The three of you, in ten minutes, outside by the fountain." With that, she turned away quickly, joining in a nearby conversation.

Maggie caught Agnes's eye and then Ellie's and nodded towards the ladies' powder room. Once inside, she whispered, "Did you see who is here? Miss Archer! She was at Court last week, too. She wants to see us outside."

"Why, I wonder," said Ellie, her eyes wide open.

"Is she still after us about the car?" Maggie wondered. "I know she was the one who found us out."

"She is rather more beautiful and elegant than I ever imagined" added Agnes. "You wouldn't guess that from the way she looks at school."

"Shh," Maggie said. "We're due in the garden."

"Actually, here in the powder room is just as good," came a voice behind them.

"Miss Archer," the three gasped and turned to see her standing in the corner.

"Lady Jane Archer, actually. And thanks for the compliment, I think."

Stunned silence.

"I have dedicated myself to encouraging and raising up women to lead this nation. I am happy to see I was correct in noticing your potential. Not only were you quite clever at school, you are also creative, imaginative, and brave. Be just as good in improvising as life comes along and you all will be just fine. Use all your talents wisely."

She turned to Maggie, "I penciled in a dance for you. Listen to what that man has to say." She looked at the other two girls. "By the way, my friends, Lady Emma is a most charming and worthy addition to the titled ladies of the land. *Very* well prepared."

With a wink and a half curtsey, Lady Archer left the powder room. As the girls, still stunned by the encounter, returned to the Ball, they saw Lady Archer briefly speak with an older man in full military dress. He crossed the floor and came directly up to Maggie.

"I believe I have the next dance with you, Lady Margaret," he said. The man was her father's age, heavily decorated with medals and gold braid. "Lady Jane Archer thought we should meet."

The music began. As they made their way around the floor, he explained, "My name is Air Marshall Dowding. You know that England is building defenses against a possible German threat of war?"

"Yes, there is a lot of talk at the newspaper where I work," Maggie replied.

"Yes. Well, I command a piece of that preparation. I am seeking people to work with me," he said as he led her in a circle of steps. "People with creative and open minds. Unconventional. I hear you might fit that bill. Ask your father about me, and phone me in the next few days."

He bowed slightly, thanked her for the dance, and escorted her back to her friends. Before she could say anything, she was pulled onto the dance floor again.

The ball stretched until 3 am and left them exhausted. Everyone stayed at the De Wevers' residence next to the Embassy, just as they had after their presentation.

Agnes, Emmy, and Clive took quick naps in the upstairs guest rooms before heading back to the hospital. When they arrived at the doors of the hospital, the entire school staff and student population had formed up at the entrance. Emmy thought, what did we miss? Not a bridal shower at this hour of the day. Did we do something wrong, Agnes wondered.

The Director of St. Bartholomew's School of Medicine and Nursing stepped forward, and in his loudest voice announced, "Ladies and gentlemen, doctors and nurses, students: I announce the arrival of Lady Agnes Fletcher, Lady Emma Manning-Ventnor, and the future Doctor Clive Raleigh. Welcome to our humble midst," he bowed. "Now, have a quick bite to eat before you go home to get some sleep."

Everyone clapped and roared with cheers and laughter. They went inside, pushing and singing a bawdy bar song. A small party had been set up in the canteen in their honor.

"How did you know?" Emmy asked one of her friends.

"Pictures in the morning paper about some great balls, easy to recognize the old gang. So, why weren't we all invited?"

"This is why," Clive replied through his laughter. "You rowdy lot are incorrigible. But thanks to you all. See you tomorrow."

Back outside, Agnes suggested, "Let's go back to the De Wevers' house. They're probably just waking up."

They arrived to find only the staff alert. Maggie was sleeping in a most ungraceful pose in an overstuffed chair in the sitting room, never making it all the way to a guest room. She woke when Agnes entered the room, sat up, trying to regain some of her dignity. Agnes asked, "What was all that about Miss – Lady Archer? She knows about Emmy and didn't report it to anyone.

She was rather nice. That's what is truly terrifying! Who would have thought she led such a double life! And that man, General Something?"

Maggie was still trying to focus. "I agree about Archer. The man? Something about a job in the nation's defense or whatever. I'm supposed to ask my father."

"Here I am," her father announced his arrival from another part of the house, signaling a servant carrying pots of tea and coffee. "What a marvelous affair last evening. You ladies were positively radiant."

"Father, who was that man I danced with? He said he knew you and that I should call on him in the next few days."

"Ah, Hugh," said Maggie's father, taking a cup of coffee from the servant. "Air Marshall Hugh Dowding, Commander of the Fighter Group of the RAF. He's upgrading our aeroplanes, airfields, and detection systems. He loves new stuff – tech and military. Dowding can be very stubborn, but he is a good man. If he fights an enemy the way he fights his superiors and the government, God help them. Definitely won't be boring working for him. Absolutely, go meet with him. Absolutely."

More coffee and tea, along with trays of eggs and ham, breads and all sorts of rolls arrived. The Shelfords and the De Wever family came into the dining room at the same moment as Aunt Charlotte and the Fletchers. No one noticed when Agnes' father nodded to the other two fathers. The three men stood together.

"Perfect timing," said Agnes' father. He announced to the gathering, "Before everyone settles in for breakfast, we need to go outside." The whole assembly followed him. Ellie was the first to react, shrieking with delight. She was looking down the street, then back at Agnes and Maggie.

Each of the three fathers stepped forward and handed their daughters the keys to the three blue 1936 MG convertibles parked in front of the residence.

CHAPTER 8
Autumn, 1938

The coast of Kent smelled of fresh grass, sheep, and cows, mixed with the salty air of the Channel. Pilot Officer Maggie Shelford turned at one of the many similar-looking farm gates, and drove into RAF Moore Hill Station. She checked in at a camouflaged guard hut. The military outpost was made up of newly built concrete huts and three 300-foot towers surrounded by a strong wire fence. She dropped off four men beneath the towers. She drove further to the car park at the main building before walking back to meet them at the tower.

After some discussion, they all headed back towards the central building. Three of them walked ahead towards the station headquarters, leaving Nigel and Maggie to trail behind.

"What do you think of our boss?" Nigel asked. "Dowding certainly lives up to his "Old Stuffy' nickname and reputation."

"I'm used to him," Maggie said, "He may be single-minded and stubborn, but he treats me exceptionally well."

"I like his imaginative and innovative projects. *And* how he mixes us inexperienced types with scientists and a few regulars to make the higher-ups consent to them," Nigel remarked, then asked, "By the way, how does a personal assistant get involved with this Radio Location thing?"

Maggie took her time replying, "Radio Detection Finding. It's officially named the Chain Home System, or CH. I'm one of Air Marshal Dowding's assistants, but I report just as often to Vice Air Marshall Park about CH. I often drive for both of them as an ATS chauffeur, like today. But with the five of us, a large car. With one or two passengers, something much smaller. I also take notes, do odd errand running. Help with polishing up reports and speeches. No specific duty, just everything. Never dull, never routine."

Maggie looked at Nigel. He remained rather casual, showing no true military bearing, and kept one hand in his pocket all the time. "Never dull indeed. Dowding expects a lot and I never know what he is thinking. I prefer working with Park. Great pilot, all business like our boss, but hands on, witty and good-natured. Typical New Zealander. They make a perfect balanced pair, those two."

Today's first stop was to check in on the operators of this Group 11 CH unit. Corporal Cotter was the technician updating the equipment connecting the tower to the observation building. After lunch, they would inspect Drummond's responsibilities: a new airfield runway and an underground telephone cable being laid all the way to HQ.

"Well, here we are," Maggie said, knocking on the door of the radio hut. A middle-aged woman in uniform trousers and light-weight jacket welcomed them.

"Good morning, Mert," Maggie smiled. "The bosses will be here shortly with Corporal Carter. He's working the tower before the system test. This is Flying Officer Drummond – working in airfield construction." Turning, she continued, "and this is Myrtle Fenwick, Chief Operator for this station."

"Come in. Tea all around?" Mert had hot water ready on her camp stove. "Happy to be back in uniform. Better than doing paper work after Ypres in the Great War. It may not be my place to say this, but I'm not sure if we'll have peace or war, what with the news from overseas, but we'll need to be ready."

"Well, ma'am, some folks hope for war, if only to prove that all this effort is worth it. But we saner folks just hope that our work will prevent the worst from happening," Nigel commented.

"Right. How was the drive here today?" Mert asked.

"Not bad – a few slick spots due to rain. A little longer than usual. Autumn is certainly here," Maggie replied.

"A few slick spots!" Nigel remarked. "We nearly skidded off the road a few times, but Officer Shelford kept us on the straight and narrow. Quite the driver, she is."

Maggie didn't think driving was so special. She felt like a simple farm girl. That's what her father had encouraged, "Just in case you need to know."

"Tea's ready, and here come the bosses," Mert noticed and began serving everyone. The two senior officers entered. Maggie and Nigel stood up. With a wave of his hand, Dowding gave them permission to sit. Cotter remained outside, talking with Mert's husband, Phil.

"Improvements installed," Dowding announced as he picked up his cup. After a few sips, he looked around. "Ready for the test?" He picked up a stopwatch with his other hand.

Park telephoned the local airfield to send a squadron into the air. Dowding started his stopwatch. Maggie took out her notebook. Mert spotted the planes on the screen in front of her. She called RAF 11 Group Headquarters at Uxbridge. The "enemy" squadron flew overhead a few minutes later. A second squadron from a neighboring airfield flew in to intercept them. Dowding stopped his watch, put it in his pocket, and set his cup on the table. Maggie closed her notebook. Dowding nodded, never changing his expression, and began walking towards their car. Time to go. The team trotted off to catch up with him.

"Thanks, Mert," Maggie called as they left.

Next stop was Nigel's airfield. They walked along the newly paved runway. It looked like a short road. Trenches were being filled in where cable had been laid. (Dowding insisted that every CH station and airfield be connected to

HQ, independent from overhead telephone wires, one of his more innovative ideas).

That evening, Nigel asked Maggie to dinner at the Martyr's Hotel, the most popular restaurant near Northolt and Bentley Priory.

"So," Nigel said, setting down his menu. "How did you make it into the 'Inner Family' that Dowding has created?"

"The Air Marshal asked me to dance," Maggie said with an enigmatic smile. Before Nigel could do more than raise an eyebrow, she returned the question. "And you?"

"Family connections. Second son, a bit wild, barely passed his engineering exams, no real direction." Nigel explained. He added in a false voice, "So Father says, 'Hugh, old chap, can you help a friend?'"

Maggie laughed. "Actually, same story for me – the family part. And I don't want to disappoint the Air Marshal or my father. I felt the same way with my first job."

"What was that?"

"Newspaper. Only 17 years old and straight out of school. No less than a social hire at the *Times*. After a few months as a copy clerk, I was given the chance to write a small column. A frivolous bit in the social pages – debutantes and other girls turning eighteen and learning about the world. It was called 'Eighteen'."

" 'Eighteen'! My mother and sister loved that column! They used it as a guide for her presentation this year. So, you were a deb. Shelford. Lord Shelford's daughter, I presume?"

"Guilty. Can still curtsey with the best of the lot," Maggie said, surprised that she was proud of her column. She doubted that anyone had read it. And suddenly, a compliment from an unlikely source.

The waiter brought their dinner, and the conversation slowed as they ate. Nigel ate with just a fork. His left hand, in a stiff glove that he wore all the time, remained in his lap. She was intrigued, but too polite to ask. They fell into a comfortable mix of chatting and silence.

"And now, what do you do for our boss?" she asked Nigel. "I only know it's to do with runways."

"The magic of turning grass into hard tops. Now that's exciting dinner conversation," Nigel answered with a chuckle. "Dowding finally convinced Air Command to construct paved runways after it rained for three weeks solid at Kenley. No planes took off or landed in the mud. And you know how many airfields we have, just here for Fighter 11 Group. Lots to consider – the type of ground underneath, what surfaces to use, how heavy are the aircraft, how long and wide. Also, the negative side – how to repair said runways as fast as possible, maintenance issues.

"Oh, and before you ask, my hand. Hard not to notice. Childhood accident, my left-hand fingers and thumb had to be amputated. So, lesson learned – no more playing with Guy Fawkes firecrackers. My palm works a bit, but this job is as close to flying as I shall ever be. Hence the Air Construction Service. Hope it doesn't put you off."

Maggie laughed. "Not at all. You seem quite clever at using one hand." She ventured a tease. "It doesn't seem to stop your ability to attract the girls." The women she worked with all gossiped about Nigel, and many of them had dated him this past year. He was good-looking, seemed nice, not at all like the image she expected.

"Ah, yes, my reputation as the 'Great Casanova.' And you, then," Nigel grinned, "are you attracted?"

Maggie avoided replying. The rest of the evening was an easy conversation between two close friends. It was nice to have a friend, like a brother to talk with.

Andrew Cashleigh was someone else in Maggie's life. He was a new pilot at Northolt Airfield. They shared common friends, ideas about life, and a sense of freedom after years of school. His family was well-known; his father was a high-level politician. Andrew sometimes acted carefree and sometimes he threw around his importance was too snooty. No argument that he would have a lot of responsibilities in the future. But not yet.

Maggie and Andrew had been seeing each other for several months, usually over a pint at the Flying Pig. They danced and shared stories about people they both knew. Although they had many mutual friends, they had never met. She was nervous about his status as a pilot. Here she was in the Air Force, nervous about flying.

He was getting more serious about their relationship than she was, though that might change. She set Andrew aside. That is, until Nigel brought him up.

"Your chap's a sharp one, Andrew is," Nigel observed. "Cashleigh's earldom is a bit higher up than either of our fathers, even if they are all Earls. Andrew and I went to school together. Likeable bloke, but competitive. Life with him will be demanding, political, public."

Maggie responded, "Rather ominous comment."

Nigel smiled, "Merely passing on information to a friend."

Maggie and Nigel rarely saw each other after that dinner. Nigel hopped from airfield to airfield. Maggie worked with the CH operators, juggled orders from Dowding, and drove frequently for Dowding or Park. News from Europe grew grimmer, making their work more urgent.

Maggie visited the Operations Room at Uxbridge whenever she could. It was fascinating. It was the converted ballroom of the old manor and was surrounded by observation balconies. An enormous table map of southeast

England covered most of the ballroom floor. The map was continually updated with sites of radar towers, airfields, and active squadrons of fighter planes.

The system seemed simple. Radio operators like Mert monitored CH radar along the coast and reported incoming planes to the Filter Room operators for their Group. The filter teams sifted out which aircraft were friendly or not, then sent that information onto the Controllers in the Operation Room. WAAF plotters placed marker blocks on the table map identifying the movements and locations of all the aircraft. Officers on the balconies gave battle orders to the Controllers who then directed the pilots to their targets. The system was not perfect, but improving every day. Maggie suggested joint meetings of Field Operators, Controllers, and pilots to build trust and a sense of teamwork. Park liked the idea and mentioned it to Dowding, and it happened.

Nigel had similar experiences with the airfields and their runways. Not perfect, but improving. Dowding accepted many of Nigel's suggestions, even when they were not yet tried and true. Maggie often wondered if the plane development and production was in the same "not perfect but improving" state. Not to mention pilot training and Andrew.

There was more to war than just fighting the enemy. She listened to Dowding's frustrations in getting financial support from the government. The politics of social rank over military rank, what made strategic sense over how much money went to favored companies. Dowding often simmered on his way to London, and boiled on the way home.

When they could, Nigel and Maggie shared their tales of joy and woe, and enjoyed relaxing with each other.

Meanwhile, her brother Herbert had signed up with the Army, and Sam was leaning towards Naval duty. Most everyone in Britain had a war-related volunteer position. It seemed that war was coming, whether England was prepared or not.

Agnes made frequent trips to Maggie, who lived in the officer section of the WAAF quarters at Northolt Airfield on the northwestern edge of London. There, life centered around the Flying Pig, a pub and dance hall near Northolt Airfield. Maggie made similar trips to Agnes in London, going to the Sickly Doctor Pub, and dining with Aunt Charlotte. Sometimes they treated themselves to a meal at the Café de Paris in the West End. Their lives were almost carefree.

They were also busy assembling Ellie's wedding gift: a professional sewing machine like Ruby used, and yards of blue fabric (Ellie's favorite color) that went into a trunk, along with other smaller treasures. November was quickly approaching. They were looking forward to seeing her again.

CHAPTER 9
Autumn, 1938, Ellie

Ellie's wedding was in early November. She was excited that her two best friends would be coming a few days before the actual Big Day.

Agnes and Maggie carried small overnight valises and had a compartment to themselves for each stage of the journey; their trunks were sent as cargo. They knew the journey well.

During the voyage, Maggie talked about Andrew and Nigel.

"Don't think twice about choosing between them," Agnes told Maggie. "One might be just your 'boyfriend' and one is your 'real deal.'"

Agnes explained. "You should have at least one boyfriend before you find your real true love. At least that's what Emmy told me my first year of nursing training."

"Do you have either of these?" Maggie was curious.

"No. Just telling you what I have heard. It seems true though."

"Oh."

Agnes sat quietly for a few moments. "Just think. Some of our classmates are already married like Emmy, or Ellie in a few days. Some already have a child. And we haven't even gotten engaged."

"Or had our 'boyfriends' yet."

Agnes continued, "Well, let's just see what 1939 will serve up. I already have my basic diploma, and will have certificates in surgery and emergency medicine by May. Then I need to decide where to go – stay at St. Bart's, go to a new hospital, or join one of the military nursing services. In any case, there will be more time for a social life. What about you?"

"Well, no big decisions or changes for now," Maggie answered. She thought of Andrew, then Nigel. Were they both 'friends' or was one 'real'? Andrew was determined and serious about getting married, even if it would be delayed until after the war. Nigel was such a good friend that she didn't want to give up that friendship, just because Andrew saw him as a rival.

Not the time to decide, she thought, drifting off to sleep.

They met the De Wever's driver in Hoek van Holland. He loaded the travel trunks into the family sedan. Their third trunk was missing. The port agent reassured them that it would be found and delivered to the De Wever's home within 24 hours, not to worry. Ellie's driver told them not to worry, this sometimes happened with the family's belongings and nothing ever went completely amiss. They remained worried – what was missing was their gift for Ellie.

Ellie was waiting for them at the front door of the De Wever's home. With their frequent visits on school holidays, they were treated as part of the family. Gran enjoyed being their extra grandparent. They began helping with everything from flowers to last-minute dress and gown fittings.

Ellie's brothers, still studying in England, would arrive just one day before the wedding. The girls were relieved by that. No chance of being annoyed by the twin boys, especially Ben. (Hopefully they had become more mature, but only time would tell.)

Ellie was radiant. She wanted to show them everything in her new life.

The next day, Ellie and Pieter introduced them to their world. They went to the university where Pieter taught and did his research and where Ellie studied. Leiden University was almost as old as Oxford. Old friends and new merged into one group at the university cafe. Stories about the engaged couple were exchanged, often to their embarrassment.

They ate lunch at the Van Horn's home and met Pieter's family. Again, Maggie and Agnes were warmly welcomed as members of the extended family. The Dutch upper class felt more relaxed than the English, which suited them perfectly.

After lunch, Pieter had to return to the university. Ellie wanted to show the girls around her new home in the center of Leiden.

"Pieter and I will eventually inherit his family home, but until then, we want to be independent," Ellie explained. "I hope you like our new house. It is quite small compared to how we grew up, but we find it rather charming."

It was charming. It was on the corner of a main street and a smaller side street, between a city park and a side canal. The area behind the house was a garden surrounded by brick walls. Trees had lost most of their leaves and flowers were no longer blooming, but Agnes and Maggie could see carefully laid out vegetable and flower beds divided by small gravel paths. Two storage sheds against the back wall were separated by a gate to the back alley.

The interior of the house was simple – a central entrance hall, staircase, and hallway straight through to the back. A small washroom was squeezed under the stairs. On the left of the front door were the dining room, pantries, and kitchen. On the right were a large sitting room and a library with two desks.

Upstairs were four bedrooms and a full bathroom (very modern). The top floor, just under the roof, had storage areas and a bedroom for live-in staff. Dora, now freed from prison, was the housekeeper and lived there already.

The furniture was a mix of styles from both families and articles they bought for themselves. A decorator used fabrics to bring everything together in a way that was magical. Perfect for Ellie.

Ellie was happy that her friends liked everything – not that it should matter, but it did. The girls took the chance to talk privately in the new sitting room.

"I am not the dreamer ignoring serious issues anymore, really," Ellie confided. "I have developed a serious side. The Dutch think war is a sure thing.

Pieter is in the Dutch Army Reserve and his background in chemistry will be valuable to the war effort. I am almost finished with my studies — maybe I'll teach. If war breaks out, I haven't decided whether I'll stay here or move back to England. No matter what, we should promise to stay in contact. Remember our secret code? We may need it."

"Enough serious talk, we are here to celebrate a happy wedding," Agnes interrupted.

The missing trunk was finally delivered the day before the wedding. It looked a bit odd. Even though Ellie knew what it contained, Agnes and Maggie hoped she would like the extra few things they added to their present. Ellie opened the trunk and gasped. Pieter gasped. This was not the reaction that Agnes and Maggie were expecting. They looked in — and gasped. It was not their gift! This trunk was filled with theatrical make-up, costumes, puppets, and props for a children's theater company.

Ellie and Pieter looked at each other and led the rest of them in wild laughter that went on until they were all in tears and stomach aches.

The girls tried to explain what must be a shipping error. They promised to send a replacement. Ellie shook her head.

"No, we love it," Ellie exclaimed. "You know I've always loved theater. I'll think we are back in school. I can perform plays and devise grand pranks. Wait, this isn't another one of those pranks? Are you sure?" Agnes and Maggie shook their heads. They wondered what they would do if the real owners came to collect and exchange trunks. For once, a prank had been pulled on them.

The wedding day was sunny and warm for November. Ellie, her mother, Gran, and the girls were helped into their dresses by extra ladies' maids. Mr. De Wever dressed in his best formal suit and sash. Pieter, in his Dutch Army uniform, came to Ellie's house in a horse-drawn coach. The wedding party followed in carriages and motorcars to town hall for the legal marriage license and registration. The procession then traveled to the Pieterskerk for the marriage ceremony. Ellie tried to concentrate on their vows and what the pastor said, but she was too distracted. She promised herself that the next time she was at a wedding, she'd listen more carefully to what was being said.

Church bells rang. People from the town and the nearby villages looked up and waved as everyone rode the carriages and cars back to the De Wever's home.

The reception guests included their university friends, as well as their families, family friends, and members of the diplomatic corps. It was a grand day.

At the dinner, Agnes and Maggie were seated between Ellie's twin brothers. Ben was just as annoying in his attempts to flirt as he had been with his teasing them when he was younger. He was turning into a sour young adult. Complaining about not being appreciated like his brother. He asked Agnes to dance, and of course she couldn't refuse. He tried to pull her against himself and she kept pushing him away.

"That's not a very good dance step," Ben remarked.

"I agree," Agnes said. "Let's sit down."

"Or we could find something else to do," Ben tried to make a meaningful smile. "Something more private."

Agnes tried not to laugh. "I know where you're going with that. And, no. Emphatically no. You will always be Ellie's little brother. And quite honestly, you're just not my type."

Sadly, it didn't stop him from trying his charms on her for the rest of the evening. Agnes just tried to ignore him and his silent fuming.

His twin, Theo, was the direct opposite. Kind, polite, and quiet. The girls accepted his dance invitations. Some of the university friends also asked the girls to dance and the evening went by swiftly.

During the meal, they were charmed by Professor Willems who sat across from them. The girls concentrated on him as he told one interesting story after another.

He told the story of his own marriage. His wife had died several years earlier, and he still missed her. "We overcame some serious problems," he shared. "We married too young. When we had been together for about five years, both of us found love outside our marriage. But we returned to each other. Trust was difficult to rebuild, but eventually, we did, and we were more loving than ever before."

Maggie looked at Agnes. She had suddenly turned very pale, and looked down. Was it the soup or the lovely veal dish that was being served at the time of their conversation? She was relieved as Agnes returned to active talking, so maybe nothing serious after all.

On their way back to England, Maggie and Agnes talked about Ellie marrying her first boyfriend and whether that was wise. Ellie, the dreamer, may not always be as happy as she was now. But Pieter was a 'real deal' type of man. They left it at that.

Agnes came out to Northolt soon after they returned to England, and went to the Flying Pig with Maggie. Nigel was there and danced with both of them. Just as the music ended, Andrew and another pilot, Dickie, walked in. Nigel waved them over.

Andrew was in a good mood. After giving Maggie a causal kiss, he ordered a round of cocktails for the entire group.

"They're the rage in London, I hear," he said.

"Only if we get something to eat at the same time," Agnes, said. They sat down, chatted, and began dancing again. They left when the pub announced closing time. Early for most pubs, but the RAF wanted their pilots to get their sleep.

"What a night!" Agnes said as she got ready for bed. "Did you pair me off with Nigel or Dickie so you can be with Andrew? Nigel is more your type than mine. I prefer the extroverted types, full of energy and action."

"You mean like Andrew?" Maggie wasn't sure if she was looking at a rival or not. She didn't want to think of defending her relationship. On the other hand, Agnes was right about Nigel, he was more her type. "Sorry, I was somewhere else. Back with Ellie. The dresses, the food, the parties. We were back in our old lives – no uniforms and nameless foods. What will that be like after what we're doing now?"

Agnes thought for a moment. "Not sure. Pieter's friends think that war is right around the corner. At the hospital, preparations vary from casual to serious. And here at Northolt, everyone is fully active in all of it."

Maggie was tired of switching from Andrew to Nigel and back, "Well, we can't do anything about anything right now. Go to sleep."

PART TWO

CHAPTER 10
May 1940 - Ellie

May 10th. Her mother's birthday. Ellie was at her party in London. But why was the celebration so noisy? Ellie came out of her dream. These were not party sounds; they came from loud engines. How odd, she thought, to have such heavy trucks out so early in the morning. The sun was rising. It must be around 5:30am. She turned over, waiting for little Wim to start fussing in his crib. The sounds outside were growing louder. No changing gears, no coming and going. Not trucks, then What was making all that racket? She got up and headed for the window. She saw shadows of fast-moving clouds, yet no evidence of wind, the trees were still. She looked up. There must have been hundreds of planes swarming overhead, the reason for the shadows and the noise. She was terrified.

She wished Pieter was still here, but two weeks earlier his Army Reserve unit had been called into action. The Dutch Army expected the Germans to invade any day. Ellie shivered as she stared at the planes. Where was Pieter?

The noise kept increasing and Wim began to cry. At nearly one year old, he could create a lot of noise himself. She walked into Wim's nursery and picked him up. She tried to comfort him, while trying to calm her own nerves.

"What is going on?" Dora came into the nursery, still in her nightclothes. "Why are there so many planes? Where are they going? Is this war?"

Ellie replied more bravely than she felt, "I really don't know. Let's get dressed, have an early breakfast, and find out."

Ellie threw on a cotton skirt and blouse and dressed Wim before coming down to the kitchen for breakfast with Dora – a simple meal of bread, cheese and jam, and coffee. Still early in the morning, even with the noise of planes, heavy trucks, and occasional explosions, people were leaving their houses and gathering in the streets. They left the house with Wim in his carriage, aiming for the center of Leiden. They joined an ever-growing group moving towards the town square near the canal docks. Curiosity won over fear in the hunger for news.

Karel, who owned the Centraal Tafel Café near the town hall and the newspaper offices, was talking with one of his frequent customers, a newspaper editor. The editor stood at the counter. He wasn't wearing a jacket or tie. His hair was a mess and he kept running his fingers through it.

He said to the crowd, "It's the Germans. They have invaded. Full attack. Planes, parachuting troops, tanks, infantry. The wire services are full of reports from all over. I needed a break from reading all the stuff coming in. So much for us trying to remain neutral."

"What should we do?" Ellie asked the editor. Several others gathered at the café looked to the editor as well.

"I don't know," replied the editor, downing the last of his coffee in one gulp. "It's easy to say, 'stay safe,' but I don't know what that means. Go home, check your supplies, your family. I just don't know," he repeated.

Ellie's mind went over the past year. England and France had declared war against Germany last September and the Dutch government announced that its military was on full alert. Every household was storing as many supplies as possible. The number of canals in Leiden meant that the water table was too high for creating waterproof cellars, but people found innovative ways to design secret storage areas. Valuable possessions were hidden; evacuation plans created.

Dora, her survivor instincts on full alert, interrupted Ellie's thoughts. She leaned over, "He means we're on our own. We need to get what we can as fast as we can."

With that, she strode off towards her favorite market. Ellie, with Wim in his carriage, followed. Dora took charge of the shopping.

The market was crowded. Each shopper quietly took what they could, while trying not to look too worried, too frightened, or too greedy. But there was a thin line of rising anxiety in many people's eyes. No one wanted to say something that might trigger a wrong movement. They bought what they could and left the market quickly.

"Well, until we know otherwise, I think we should treat today like any other day," Ellie decided when they arrived back home. "I shall go with Professor Willems to the prison and do my tutoring. You and Wim must go out after lunch to continue learning as much as you can."

Dora pushed Wim's carriage throughout the streets of Leiden that afternoon, but nothing she heard made sense. Police, firemen, and reporters were running everywhere at once. Confusion grew to open panic as the sounds of gunfire and explosions continued to come closer to the city, especially from the direction of The Hague. She heard reports of bridges being blown up, roads closed, paratroopers landing near bridges, fires and shooting going on in the fields. None of that was good.

The next few days remained tense. With news of the government's surrender, there was a small sense of relief that the fighting was over. Under that was frustration and fear for the future. Queen Wilhelmina and her top advisors escaped to England. Crown Princess Juliana and her children left for Canada.

BBC radio news was the only information that could be trusted. Queen Wilhelmina used broadcasts to tell her people to return to their normal routines. Roads, bridges, and damaged neighborhoods needed to be cleaned up and repaired. Farming had to be done, school and work schedules were reinstated, businesses reopened as soon as they could.

New rules were announced daily, some government offices closed, and every day, new shop keepers shut their doors when they ran out of things to sell and couldn't get more merchandise. Ellie thought that life was now like a ballet. Each step was very delicate; losing one's balance was costly.

Meanwhile, she was anxiously waiting for Pieter to come home. As part of the surrender to the Germans, Dutch military officers had been rounded up and placed in detention camps. After a few weeks, they were released and ordered to return to civilian life.

Pieter arrived home in late May. He was angry by how quickly they had lost the fight. He hung his uniform in the back of his closet, and said very little about his time in detention. He became moody and silent. Ellie tried to cheer him up with a celebration of his return with a small party. Gran and a few friends from the university were invited. Discussions were really just a list of everyone's unanswered questions. No one had plans; no one knew what to plan for. With a curfew in place, the party ended before dark, around 10pm.

"What happens now?" Ellie asked Pieter on their way to bed. "Do you have to report again to the Germans?"

Pieter nodded and spoke softly, "Probably. I'm going back to the university tomorrow to see what's happening. Tonight, though, I want to make sure we try to create more trouble for the Germans," he gave a sly smile. "Perhaps by increasing the number of Dutch citizens, we can tip the balance of power in our favor."

"Well, that's romantic," Ellie commented with her own sly grin. Pieter's presence was all she needed to feel safe again.

Pieter returned to the Chemistry Department and worked on routine projects. Many evenings, he came home just as curfew began, too late for a proper dinner.

He met with staff and students eager to resist German occupation. During his time in the detention camp, he met other officers interested in message systems and counterfeit document production. With his best students, he experimented on invisible and short-life inks. They worked on chemicals for specific inks, and tried to learn how to reproduce German printing techniques and supplies, like paper, ink, and cleaning agents. Another group worked on new technologies for invisible messages. Amusing twist, Pieter thought; his major research had been in making paint more permanent, and now he wanted them to fade or disappear quickly. Either way, his research might help the Germans. That could not happen. He began to plan his escape to England.

Ellie returned to her language studies. She nearly had her diploma in English, French, and Dutch when she discovered courses in Arabic language and culture. It might be fun to learn more about Arab culture as a distraction from being a mother and trying to survive German occupation. She could still call up a few phrases in Arabic from her early childhood in Bagdad. She promised herself to study Arabic *after* receiving the current diploma, only one month from now.

She knew Pieter was planning to escape to England even though nothing had been said. She couldn't share her fears of staying in Leiden alone with little Wim. She just treasured every moment she and Pieter had together. It was too late to think of going with him to England, especially considering Wim's age, and possibly leaving Gran behind.

Dora's routine was the same, whether it was war or not. She continued to take care of Wim and run the Van Horn household. She learned how to manage the food ration system that started in June. She listened for whatever gossip she could hear at the shops and markets and passed it on to Pieter, Ellie, and Professor Willems.

She adored Prof. Willems. He was so gentle and unassuming; you'd never expect that he was brave enough to enter a prison. In appreciation for his helping her and others, she cleaned his house every week. She was curious why such smart men like Professor Willems were so untidy in everything else. Did brains only have enough space for one thing, like either serious thought or practical things like 'street smarts'? Ellie had very little practical sense, not even enough to learn how to cook. And Dora had very little interest in dreams.

International news continued to get worse. By the end of June, the Germans added Belgium and France to their occupied lands. They heard about the heroic rescue of thousands of stranded English soldiers on the coast of France at Dunkirk. Then, when the Germans took over Paris, all of Europe seemed under German control. Pieter said that the only remaining hope was England. He wondered out loud if the Germans would invade England or not. He and his university friends developed stronger connections with Resistance leaders, and helped plot actions to thwart German rules.

Ellie and Pieter, along with their family, adjusted to Occupation rules. The safest way to live was to remain invisible and ignore the rules that didn't apply to them.

Gran came for weekly visits. She preferred being in Ellie's home in the city rather than sitting alone in the family's large country house. She loved little Wim, and she had too much energy to sit and chat with her neighbors all the time. It was getting harder to visit them in Wassenaar and The Hague. Streets were blocked by German traffic and several bridges were still out. Bicycles were wearing out quickly; people sat on cargo barges in order to move between cities when buses were full. Fuel for motorcars was becoming hard to find. And her favorite neighbors, Pieter's parents the Van Horns, were stranded in America. They couldn't get back home even if they wanted to. At least they were safe.

Ellie began a storytelling career at church and for children's groups around Leiden. She put her costume collection, wigs, and make up to good use. She wasn't using her newly received language diploma, but she was now part of the neighborhood.

Gran sat at a window in the sitting room. "Tomorrow is June 29th, Prins Bernhard's birthday. Don't you think we should join the celebration? The plan is to wear carnations like he always does. And fly our flag. I have one for our house." Gran surprised Ellie by wanting to be publicly active against the Germans while Ellie was trying to remain invisible.

"All right," Ellie said, unsure of what might happen. But the next day, she saw Dutch flags flying from many homes and shops. And like Bernhard himself, the people of Leiden wore carnations. The Germans weren't happy, there might be a punishment. But it seemed worth it.

The Germans fine-tuned their control and began to limit the freedoms of Jewish people living throughout the country. Men of all backgrounds, Jewish and Christian, were recruited to work in German factories. The complicated ballet continued. And the people adjusted.

Until late July.

"I've been evicted!" Gran shouted as she stood on Ellie's doorstep. Her motorcar was parked in front of the house, filled with suitcases and boxes. Ellie was startled by both the news and by the shouting of her grandmother. "I have twelve hours to leave the house. Help me empty the car. We have to go back and get more things from the house." Ellie followed Gran to the car. She began to carry boxes into the house. She called Dora to help them.

Gran's voice dropped to near silence as she continued, "The worst of it all is that I was told to go by your brother Ben." Gran had tears in her eyes. "He was dressed up in that awful NSB get-up. He said, that it was better for *him* to tell me to get out. He could make sure that a really high-ranking officer would take over our house and treat it well. If someone else handled this, we may not be so fortunate. I can't believe that he thought that made sense or that it would make me feel better. My own grandson! A traitor not only to his country but to his family!"

Ellie, carrying a box, couldn't respond. Ben had always been annoying, but this was more than she could have imagined. She knew he had joined the NSB, the Dutch group supporting the German take-over of The Netherlands. But turning the family home over to them! She wondered if her parents knew what was happening. She didn't know where her other brother was, probably still in England, but she knew that Theo was more patriotic than his twin brother.

There were two more round trips with the car to bring Gran's boxes into the house. Then they sent the car back to the house, drained of all but the smallest amount of fuel.

Pieter was furious when he came home that evening. Of course, Gran could stay with them for as long as she needed. That night in bed, they held each other tightly. They heard Gran crying softly in the guestroom next door to their bedroom.

Two days later, Prof. Willems arrived at the door, with two boxes and a suitcase at his feet. He said weakly, "Some vile German major just tossed me out of my house. He says that the new administrator for Leiden needs it. I have nowhere to go." He looked totally helpless.

"Come in," Ellie sighed. Prof. Willems entered the sitting room and saw Gran.

"Oh, hello," he said, taking off his hat. Gran stared at him. Ellie sensed something was going to happen. The Professor and Gran had become friends, but both were coldly quiet. Ellie and Gran instantly knew he expected to stay.

That cannot happen, Gran decided. He may be a very nice man, but she was already in residence. And that was enough of a burden for Ellie and Pieter. Ellie felt the tension, as the Professor also realized what he was hoping for.

"Where will you go?" Gran asked the Professor as politely as she could.

"I think he may need a place to stay for at least tonight," Ellie ventured. "Pieter might have some suggestions when he comes home."

Dora listened to this from the hallway and went into the kitchen. However this was to be decided, she needed to prepare a larger meal for this evening. She was certain that both Prof. Willems and Gran would both be staying for as long as necessary, even if no one else knew it yet.

Pieter walked in earlier than usual. He saw the group sitting stiffly and silently. "What now?" he asked as he kissed Ellie and picked up Wim. Gran and the Professor stared at each other – like fighters facing off for mortal combat, or in this case, a roof overhead. Every attempt at simple dinner conversation stopped quickly. Professor Willems was invited to stay in the second guest bedroom. Without speaking, everyone decided to go to bed early.

"Can we make this work? Can we take in both of them?" Ellie asked Pieter when they were alone later that night.

After a very long silence, Pieter said, "We have to. Our friends have accepted whole families and total strangers coming from bombed-out Rotterdam and the smaller villages in ruins. Not to mention those who were forced to evacuate their homes. At least these are people we know and love. I'm leaving for England soon, and we do have room for both of them. It will be good for everyone involved."

Ellie was relieved that she didn't have to choose between Prof. Willems and Gran. "I agree. Thank you."

Over breakfast Pieter announced their decision about taking in Prof. Willems. He could stay in the second guestroom. Boxes were unpacked or stored in the attic where Dora lived. In less than a week, a new social order was working in the Van Horn household. They all worked to adjust to the loss of privacy and space. And Dora now had five sets of ration cards to manage.

As this new routine was being set up, there was another adjustment. Pieter's parents in America sent letters to their household staff to not cooperate with the Germans, just leave the house and stay safe. The Brinkers, who had been their housekeeper and gardener, closed up the house. They asked Pieter for a place to stay. Meanwhile, Dora had been asking for help in caring for the enlarged family. Pieter welcomed them to the family.

The bedrooms were reassigned. Wim moved in with his parents. The nursery became Dora's room, and the Brinkers moved into the attic. Boxes were sorted and shifted again. Prof. Willems and Gran remained where they were.

Dora now managed seven sets of ration stamps and did most of the shopping. Mrs. Brinker helped with cooking and housework. She was very friendly inside the house, but she never ventured outside. (Some people are like that, Pieter explained.)

Mr. Brinker did the maintenance jobs and tended the large garden. He and Pieter converted the remaining flower beds into vegetable plots. They built secret storage places inside the house as well as enlarging the garden sheds to hold more food. Ellie's theater trunk became a traveling theater wagon with a seat for Wim and a small toy box.

The household established a set of public routines for their neighbors – and the Germans – to monitor. Dora always went to the same grocers and farmers. Mr. Brinker went to the same café every morning before coming back home to work. Ellie, Gran, and the Professor went to the same cafes most afternoons. They went to church every Sunday except for Pieter and Mrs. Brinker. Ellie and Prof. Willems continued tutoring at the prison twice each week. The family, in mixed groups, took walks in the local parks and maintained a social life with their neighbors. Shared ration tickets were the best way to entertain or have parties. Pieter became less visible.

"I think we can live like this, at least for a little while," Gran said. "But public life and the political situation are not improving. I'm restless just thinking about everything."

"Well, you could do something about it," suggested Professor Willems, as they strolled along one of Leiden's many canals. "For example, I teach in the prison system. The Germans are still going along with our civil laws."

"That is hardly suitable for me," Gran said. "But there must be some other useful work I might do. I wish we had left for England before this all started, but there wasn't enough warning. And Ellie insists on staying here. My son-in-law in London is still trying to get us out through diplomatic channels, but I don't have my hopes up."

"You're right," the Professor said. "The English have so far stopped the Germans from invading this summer, but there are a lot of bombing attacks on English cities now. You might be safer here than with your daughter in London."

"Still," Gran said, "I want to do something."

"Allow me to find you a suitable task," Dr. Willems said with a sly smile. "Meanwhile, try to maintain your social life. You say that a few of your friends live in their homes along with the German occupiers in Wassenaar. You might keep an ear open for information on the Germans during your visits. I can pass that on to the right people."

From a window, Ellie watched the two older people walking along the canal. Was that a budding romance? They were in deep, intimate discussion, reminding her of her first conversations with Pieter. How quickly that led to falling in love. Even now, even when they couldn't spend so much time together, their evenings were still very romantic. How would she cope with everything if he goes to England, or is captured, or killed? She couldn't speak of it, but the anxiety of missing him was always present.

By November, life was getting more oppressive. The Germans ordered the dismissal of all Jewish officials and professors at the university. Many departments lost their best teachers and students. It was so outrageous that open protest was the only response. At a special assembly, Professor Cleveringa, Dean of Leiden's Law School, gave a resounding denunciation of the German decree. The audience dared to stand and sing the Dutch national anthem. The speech itself was shared and published throughout the nation. Students across the country went on strike. The Germans responded by closing both Leiden *and* Delft universities.

"That's it," said Pieter. "I've got to go. I no longer have a job, and the Germans will be looking for me, either for involuntary labor in Germany or for being in the Resistance."

Ellie tried to protest, but Pieter waved his had to quiet her. "You know people who can help you. You can help the local resistance groups. You know where I have hidden chemicals in the house and how to use them. I feel certain that you will be fine. My false papers are ready, and I have the names of helpers who can get me to England. I'll find a way to let you know I'm safe. You just won't know exactly when I plan to disappear."

"I don't think I can manage without you," Ellie felt tears coming.

"You're not doing this alone. Everyone in our house is already helping out. Lean on them, learn from them. I can leave in confidence that all of you will be well, not that I want to leave, believe me."

That night, they held each other as tightly as they could, not sure if they would ever be together again.

At breakfast the next morning, Pieter spoke to Ellie while everyone was listening. "You know what I love most about you? Your smiling. Making people cheerful and hopeful. It strengthens their resolve. It lifts their morale in the darkest times. Promise me, you will always try to be a bright light for everyone."

"I'll try," Ellie promised. The household nodded in agreement. Was this his farewell speech?

Two days later, Pieter didn't come home for dinner. A former student came to the door.

"Prof. Van Horn left today."

CHAPTER 11
August 1940, Maggie

"Sergeant Cotter!" Maggie called out into the maintenance building. Cotter jumped to his feet. He was now a sergeant and a leading electrician in the Chain Home system.

"Collect 10 meal rations and your gear. And two wooden planks, eight to ten feet long. And wear a blue or red jacket over your uniform. You have twenty minutes."

Cotter saluted and ran off. He had been waiting for a ride. His repair kit, spare parts, and extra machines for the CH stations were at his side. He ran to the Mess Hall. Food was always available, especially when it was signed out to a personal assistant to the Air Marshall. Cotter knew Maggie and respected her. He would follow her regardless of her volunteer WAAF status. The planks were even easier to get than the meals at the Mess Hall. Construction supplies could be found all over RAF Northolt as teams of men repaired the runway and nearby buildings. Every day, after bombing attacks, repairs were underway somewhere on the Air Field.

In less than twenty minutes, he was back at the motor pool entrance. Flying Officer Maggie Shelford drove her blue MG convertible out of the garage, wearing a light-weight red jacket over her uniform.

"Your car?" Cotter asked, uncertain of what she was doing.

"Yes. It's small, civilian, and quite agile getting around the debris in the road."

"Your car." Cotter said, accepting her logic.

She nodded, "Civilian cover is better than official-looking staff cars or armored trucks for safety and quickly." She assessed Cotter's pile. Very soon, all was stowed in a large box tied to the back of the car or individually tucked into spaces throughout the car. The sergeant sat in the passenger seat, wearing a green jacket. His legs straddled the planks which rose up above the car, giving him no front view.

Maggie slid into the driver's seat and turned on the engine.

Cotter nodded. "I heard that in addition to the four radar station huts that were destroyed, some of the operators were killed or wounded."

"All the more reason why I'm making a personal visit. At least all the towers survived with only minor damage. All the stations have to be fully back up by tomorrow. Pevensey and Rye say they can fix the immediate problems themselves. But Dover and Moore Hill need those new machines," Maggie said. "Here we go!"

Maggie circled London and headed southeast through Kent towards Dover. She sped along the empty roads. Late afternoons were usually lovely in mid-August. Today, though, the loveliness was marred by craters scattered across the farmland. Smoke was visible where houses and vehicles still smoldered. Cotter had only side views of the landscape, but also saw the destruction.

The security guards at the Dover station were at first wary of the MG. When they recognized Maggie, though, they waved her in. The towers stood undamaged, but the concrete hut was destroyed. The local team was picking through the rubble around their station and starting to build a temporary wooden hut. Sergeant Cotter helped the operators set up a new radar unit, fondly known as the "fruit machine", on a table under a tarpaulin. Then he spliced new connecting cables from the new unit into the tower cables and the underground transmission cable. The local crew didn't need any meals; they hadn't suffered much damage to their homes. The camp stove was supplying mugs of tea to everyone, so Maggie gave them extra tea ration cards in thanks for their hospitality. Then the blue convertible sped off to the next destination.

"Moore Hill – my favorite station," Maggie said as she parked. "Hello, Mert. Are you and Phil all right?"

"Right as rain, as always," Mert said. "Time for tea?"

"First, what needs to be repaired?" Maggie asked. "I see that you have some folks rebuilding the hut?"

"Just a few walls missing. The crew is done replacing them with wood. They've gone home for now. We can use this tent and table set up for the machinery," a man's voice coming from behind Mert. "That old hut's gone the way of my leg, it has."

"Oh Phil," Mert said. "That joke is just getting too old."

Sergeant Cotter smiled at the older man, who was using crutches. Though he had lost his leg in the Great War, Phil was still eager to "fight for King and Country." He had been a radio technician back then and was one of the first volunteers in the new conflict. He and his wife became operators for this CH station, happy to do their patriotic duty.

Cotter finished the connection of the new machine to the underground cable that stretched all the way to Bentley Priory. Then, Phil pointed to the closest tower. Several support struts were bent, broken, or missing. ("flying debris from the bomb" he suggested). Cotter saw a break in the transmission cable, about 60 feet from the ground. ("easy splice" he judged.) He grabbed a coil of cable, wire, tape, rubber tubing, pliers, and wire cutters, and jogged over to the tower.

"Watch out for that hole!" The shout came at the very moment Cotter fell into it. A second shout came from Cotter as has he writhed in pain. Maggie and Mert ran to him.

"I think it is just a sprain," Cotter said between his clenched teeth.

Mert and Maggie helped Cotter limp to a chair. Mert began to wrap his ankle.

"We'll have to get someone from town to climb the tower," Mert said, showing more than a little concern for "poor Cotter."

"No time for that," Maggie heard herself saying. Turning to Cotter, she asked, "Can I do the repair? We have to get back to Northolt before black-out starts."

Cotter studied the broken cable and the tower. "Maybe a temporary fix. The cable snapped right next to the tower ladder, and the ends are still attached to the tower above and below the break. Just two wires inside the tubing, not like a complex telephone cable," finishing his assessment.

Cotter quickly showed her how to make the splice. With no time to think, Maggie started up the ladder. Heights were her private terror. At home, she barely managed to climb into the hayloft of the horse barn, and that was only a 9-step ladder. It must be over one hundred steps to the broken strut. To make it even worse, she asked herself, what if there were still stray enemy planes in the air, what if I fall, what if, what if. She shut off her mind and concentrated on what needed to be done.

All the way up, she kept repeating, this is for you Andrew, this is for you. Oh, and the rest of the pilots as well.

She was there. She reached the higher dangling cable. Grab it, trim away the old outer tubing. Twist the old black wire with the new black wire sticking out of the cable tucked in my belt. Wrap the twist with tape. Repeat on the red to red. Tape over the whole repair. Go down the ladder to the other end of the break. Do everything again.

Done. Maggie began backing down the rest of the ladder. She kept whispering Oh God, Oh God, Oh God, until she reached the ground.

When she stepped away from the tower, her knees didn't want to work. She just stood there for a few minutes, pretending to study her handiwork until she regained the use of her muscles.

"Right. Time for that tea. And perhaps a quick bite to eat, and then we're off," It wasn't as casual as she wanted it to sound, but her three comrades stared silently at her and nodded. They opened some of the meals they brought and ate quickly.

Phil asked as he ate, "Do you still drive the Air Marshall? That, and CH communication – a big load."

Maggie replied, "Well, we all do what we can."

Phil continued, "It's rather worrisome that we have so few fighters up against the enemy every day. The Huns come in such big numbers."

Maggie thought a minute. Phil was a military history enthusiast. "You never heard this, Phil. It is rather hush, hush, and causing a major row among the top brass folks. Air Marshall Dowding uses an unorthodox plan that doesn't require many planes. A full-out offensive would just about end the RAF right now, so, he uses small squadrons that meet the enemy right away. They annoy and distract the enemy until the rest of the squadrons arrive for the main battle. I heard him say that we don't have to win every fight; we just can't lose them."

"Classic. Small groups of insurgents historically mess up the grandest of regimental battle plans. The unexpected often holds the day." Phil winked, "Not a word of it shall leave these lips."

Maggie and Cotter promised to send a welding crew out the next day to repair the broken struts and make a more permanent repair to the wire. With that promise, they began their return drive to Uxbridge, Northolt, and Bentley Priory.

"Raids every day, repairs every day. Do you have enough equipment and electricians to do that?" Maggie asked Cotter.

"I think so. We'll see soon enough," Cotter said. "Do you think we can keep up? The bombing is getting heavier every day. Where do they get all those planes? I have to admit at times, I get a bit nervous about our chances."

"So do I," Maggie admitted. "But Luftwaffe losses are higher than ours. That will only get better as we get more planes delivered and more pilots trained. Just have to be patient."

She suddenly slammed her foot on the brake. Once stopped, she opened the door and walked ahead of the car. Cotter saw nothing because of the planks.

"Cotter, can you limp over here? And help me with those planks?"

"I think so, ma'am," was his reply.

In front of the car was a small stream. The bridge over it was now rubble in a mid-sized crater, too big to drive over or around. Maggie set the planks across the crater, crouching and eyeing the car several times. She shifted one plank a few inches to one side.

"Hop in," she finally said. Cotter obeyed, and she casually drove across the planks and they continued their drive. The sun was low in the sky.

"How did you know what to do?" Cotter asked in wonder.

"Past experience," Maggie smiled. "Sergeant, how is your family? I'm sorry, I don't even know where you come from."

"Just south of London, near here," Cotter replied. "between Kenley and Biggin Hill. They have a nickname for the area now – Bomb Alley. So far, the family is still all fine. They have an Anderson shelter in the garden. The metal arch of the top is supposed to allow bombs to roll off of them. Seems to be working." Cotter was feeling bold. "And your family, ma'am?"

Maggie answered. "They live in the country west of Oxford. Too far west for most attacks. My parents opened their house to some children and mothers from London. They are as safe as can be." She paused. "How's the ankle?"

"After that bit of walking, it hurts more than I would admit to the lads," Cotter said.

"Straight to the Station Hospital at Uxbridge then," Maggie said.

She picked up speed, swerving to avoid more craters and tree debris scattered in all directions. She took corners of the unmarked roads like a race car driver. Cotter guessed that the she had memorized the routes before signs had been removed for security reasons. He held his breath several times during the ride, almost regretting that he could finally see the road ahead.

When they got back to Uxbridge, Cotter exhaled in relief and joined several men who were waiting for treatment at the hospital. Maggie drove her car into the motor pool garage and went to the HQ to report in. She looked at the Northolt runway on her way. It was well camouflaged – the runway had been painted to look like grass with a stream crossing it through the middle. Repairs were finished for the day. Nigel mustn't be getting much sleep these days. She wondered where he had been this day. There had been several big attacks on air fields all over southeast England. He'd be quite busy.

She passed by the security guards at Bentley Priory and walked through the Filter Room. During the day, this room was a scene of organized chaos. Right now, all was quiet, with only a few staff on duty.

The Command Room itself showed a different story. Colored pins on a large wall map showed which airfields and radar stations were damaged. Maggie gasped. Every installation had damage pins, many labelled 'high damage.' The faces of the people in the room were drawn. All day, calls had reported loss after loss. The CH stations gave the flyers the advantage against the much larger German Air Force, but the loss of runways, pilots, and planes (even temporarily) were reaching not just critical but tragic levels.

"Ah, Shelford," the chief of Chain Home radio operations commented. "Nice work today."

"Dover and Moore Hill are operational, though further repairs will be needed. By now their requests are probably here," she reported in her most official, calm voice. "And we need to train up some new operators." Her voice cracked as she thought of the people who had died at their stations.

"Also pilots," was the reply. She thought of Andrew.

"We heard that you 'saved the day,' Officer Shelford," remarked a bemused senior officer, trying to lighten the grim mood. He annoyed everyone with his attempts at being cheerful. "And taking a jolly romp in your MG convertible. I'd like to have your assignments."

"You might find it not to your liking," Maggie replied. Military humor was often ghoulish, but right now, she was too tired to put up with it. She looked around the room. "This office reminds me of my father's game room. He plays the Battle of Waterloo with little toy soldiers. You play with these pins in much the same way. If you'd like to be target practice for the Germans, sir, I suggest you do it in a military vehicle like the ones we saw flipped over on our way. At least I wasn't an obvious target, and I didn't wind up as a casualty of war."

With that, she left. She had gone too far, losing her composure in front of the brass. My less-than-brilliant military career is certainly over Maggie thought as her feet carried her across the inner yard to the officers' mess hall. She saw a few pilots sat in small groups, talking softly. Most of them had flown two missions that day, and their faces showed exhaustion and sorrow as they looked for their missing friends to enter the room. Each time the door opened, all eyes turned to see who might be coming in. Then the eyes turned back to the companions who were there. Andrew's whole squadron was absent. They were probably already sleeping. She left without sitting down or eating.

She had one more stop – reporting to Air Marshall Dowding.

"Ah, Maggie, well done," he said as she entered his spartan office. "I heard that all stations are running again, with no small credit to your own personal action."

"Oh?"

"Moore Hill called in as soon as you left. Chief Operator Fenwick gave us the story of your marvelous repair job. Bravo." He gave an unusual and brief half-smile before becoming serious again. "Right. On the other hand, it is a serious breach of military conduct for a low-ranking, volunteer officer to berate any officer, especially of senior rank. Well deserved, perhaps, but not acceptable. Meanwhile, I need you early tomorrow. Drive to London."

"Yes, sir, sorry sir," Maggie replied. Still in uniform then. Twelve hours from now. She started to turn around to leave.

"Another thing," Dowding's face was without expression, "Find a way to wear trousers from now on when you're in the field."

She left in complete embarrassment, but also with a smile. She headed back to the officers' mess. As she started up the steps, a hand shot out in front of her and stopped her from going in.

"You need a real meal. I know that I do," Nigel Drummond said as she turned around. "Martyr's Rest?"

"I'm too tired to think or eat," she said. "And it's late."

Nigel replied. "Agreed. Shall we?"

By the time they arrived, most of the local diners had left.

"How are you? We only see each other at command briefings," Nigel began. "How's the social life? Still with Andrew, as all can see." He made her feel instantly comfortable, like an old friend or brother. Even so, Maggie was visibly surprised at his comments, and at feeling slightly defensive. She nodded.

"Ah, yes. Hard not to notice. He's become quite the flying ace, he has," Nigel leaned in as if to share a great secret. "No ring yet? You two should be getting close to the altar by now." He waved his hand in the air, as if reading a big headline, "Highbrow wedding cheers up a nation at war."

"Put that way, it sounds awful," Maggie put down her soup spoon. "Seriously, I just can't get beyond his being a pilot. In case you haven't noticed, they tend to have a short life span. And he's one of the daring ones. Not sure I could handle the loss."

"Sorry, a sensitive point to be sure," Nigel sat back in his chair. "Meanwhile, my lady-killer reputation has faltered. First, the girls I attract are not interesting enough, and second, the interesting ones require too much time and effort. You're in that second category by the way."

"Such a compliment," smiled Maggie. "This whole conversation is taking a strange turn. It's this stupid war."

"Stupid war indeed," replied Nigel. "Anyway, tomorrow night, there's a new local band giving a dance at the Flying Pig. It will go on past the bedtime of the flying crews, but we can stay up a little later."

"If I get back from London in time," Maggie accepted.

Maggie thought of Andrew and his tendency to be jealous. Well, let him be. Nothing is tying her to him, yet, and he shouldn't be so possessive.

Maggie met Andrew the next night at the Flying Pig. She danced with Andrew and members of his squadron. The squadron was a family of its own, tighter than brothers, looking out for each other. Several pilots from other countries made it an interesting party. Andrew was cheerful and full of energy. Nigel came in and sat down with them.

"I just flew the newest Spitfire – right out of the factory. One of the first of the new model. It flies like a dream come true," Andrew announced. Nigel responded with questions about take-offs and landings, and airfield conditions.

Maggie sat there, not interested in what they were saying. She let herself sag into the chair and nearly fell off when she began to doze. I guess I am more tired than I thought.

The two men realized that she was there and that she was most likely bored. They changed the subject to include her. How sweet they both were, really.

After Andrew and most of the pilots left, Nigel and Maggie stepped onto the dance floor where they stayed for the rest of the evening. One or two of Andrew's mates defied curfew. She knew they would report back to Andrew, but she wasn't concerned.

Andrew did find out and was furious.

"I thought we were an item," he said angrily. "What is it? Are you with me or not?"

"There isn't anything to decide," Maggie felt cornered. "You're you, and Nigel is just a friend. We hardly see each other, and then usually just for business."

"Yea, well, my mates said you two really liked dancing together," Andrew said.

"I like dancing – with you and with Nigel. It's the dancing, not the partner," Maggie regretted that as soon as she said it.

"Fine, dance with a floor mop then," Andrew stomped out of the room.

CHAPTER 12
August, 1940, Maggie

"Maggie! Wake up!" Maggie's eyes popped open. Was that Andrew? Was he still upset about my dancing with Nigel a few weeks ago?

"Go away," she called back. She turned over under her bedcovers. Not time to get up yet and sleep was precious.

"I'll give you ten minutes," Andrew called back through the door. "The weather is positively awful. That means no flying, and that means we can get away from this miserable place. Besides, our squadron is being rotated off duty for a few days of rest. Pack a bag for a couple of days and I'll be back to pick you up. No argument. I've even arranged leave for you with Dowding himself. Okay?"

Maggie was now fully awake. She needed a break and this might be the best chance she'd get for a while. She decided to go along with Andrew.

"Okay."

Andrew was standing outside Maggie's door when she opened it fifteen minutes later. He took her travel case and guided her to a Bentley. A driver in full livery opened the back door for her. Andrew joined her.

"We're going to my parents' house in Kent," Andrew explained. "Middle of the Weald, all farms and orchards. Not far, but far enough away from Northolt. You shall love them – my parents and Tarnsham Crossing."

The countryside was usually beautiful even in the rain. Since she wasn't driving to the CH stations, she could enjoy looking at the scenery. There were areas that were dreary, ghostlike. Ruined buildings in the towns and bumpy roads. The trees and grass fought hard to look greener and more alive, the rain having washed away the dust and dirt of the summer. What a difference sun and rain make to a landscape, she thought.

By the time they arrived at Tarnsham Crossing, Maggie had nearly forgotten all about the war, and was reverting to her pre-war life – except that she was still in her uniform.

Andrew's parents stood at the front door to greet them and the house staff lined up in the entrance hall. He was, after all, the heir-apparent of the family.

Maggie remembered to curtsey to the Earl and his wife. And so it began - the rituals, the small talk expected during a visit like this. Lady Cashleigh led her into the house, suggesting that she might want to freshen up before lunch, (meaning, please change out of that dreary uniform and into an acceptable frock). A lady's maid, Sandra, escorted her to a guestroom upstairs. Maggie assured her that the room was just lovely, and that she had the right clothes for her visit. Maggie's travel case arrived, and Sandra hung her evening dinner dress and her day-time outfits in an armoire. Was there anything else? Sandra looked so eager to please, Maggie felt that she needed to give her a task.

"Just shake out my things and set up toiletries," Maggie said. "Oh, and my hair. It's due for a trim, so it doesn't look quite right. Can you help?"

Sandra smiled and began to fuss, and Maggie caved in to the pampering. It was like being back home, or at the De Wever's during Ellie's wedding. It felt wonderful after two months of non-stop German air attacks, losing friends to air combat, and driving senior officers to and from intense high-level meetings. That was all very far away, at least for a short time.

She changed into a yellow linen summer dress with matching jacket and floral-print scarf. Andrew met her outside her door and escorted her into the main hall. Very relaxed in his country jacket and open shirt, he was a different person. Not the swaggering pilot, more the man at home with himself. He gave her shoulder a reassuring squeeze as they walked into the dining room.

Conversation over lunch was the expected interrogation, though friendly. Maggie kept her answers as general as possible. She knew what ladies were supposed to say, especially careful to keep her opinions to herself. She reached for a biscuit, surprised that it was from Shell's Bakery, and not one baked by the cook of the house. Because of the war, there were very few biscuit varieties left on the open market, Shell's being one of the only biscuit producers left. What lovely gesture to acknowledge Maggie's family, especially on such short notice of her visit. She looked up at Lady Cashleigh and they both smiled in recognition.

Andrew and Maggie escaped for the afternoon. They took umbrellas and wore boots (Maggie and Lady Cashleigh had the same shoe size). The grounds were wet and muddy, but the rain had turned to mist. Andrew described the areas that they couldn't see – the outlying areas of the grand estate.

"Don't' fret," Andrew said. "You'll be seeing them often enough in the future."

Maggie felt nervous. Was he about to propose? This was the life she grew up with, the life she had put on hold for the duration of the War. What would it be like to live here, be in charge of this place? The house and estate were larger than Oakstone. It would be a challenge. If she could only hold off the decision to be married until this war and its dangers were over, including Andrew being a pilot.

He was eager to overcome her indecision. He wanted her to like Tarnsham. He wanted her to love him. And she had to admit to herself, her resolve was weakening.

"What are you thinking about?" Andrew stopped walking and turned to her.

"Just taking in all of this," Maggie answered, trying to be neutral and casual.

"I wish you would take me more seriously," Andrew said. "I know that you like me, but why are you so hesitant to let your feelings for me to show?"

"I need a little more time, that's all," Maggie responded.

"We've known each other for a while now," Andrew left his comment hanging in the air. "How much more time do you need?"

They continued walking around stables, barns, a tennis court, and a large Victorian era greenhouse. The settings were familiar to Oakstone. She ventured to think how she might change things if she had her way. Andrew was getting harder to refuse. She liked him very much, and, that was turning into love.

That evening, Sandra did wonders to her hair using hair clips and bows that matched the rose-colored gown she brought for dinner. Maggie had an amusing thought as she sat at the dining room table. The custom for this kind of visit was that the formal inquisition happened during a casual lunch, then the casual conversation occurred during formal dinner. Now it included how the two fathers knew each other from the House of Lords. Then talk shifted back to Maggie herself.

"How is a lady's life in the RAF? Quite a change from how you were raised, I imagine," Lady Cashleigh asked. Maggie weighed the tone of the question. Her tone was not condescending, but rather genuinely interested. Keep it light, she reminded herself.

"Oh, it is a bit like being in school. Uniforms, taking care of oneself without help, common dining facilities, and everything done in groups. Wouldn't you say that, Andrew?"

Andrew nodded, "Mostly correct. No real privacy. And, for me, I get to fly, which I love."

Maggie hoped no one saw her shiver.

After dinner, the family listened to the latest BBC news and a classical music program. The sitting room was filled with the history of a family that stretched back to early England: portraits, Oriental rugs and furnishings from all over the British Empire.

By the time she went to bed, she was ready to admit to loving Andrew. As long as he didn't try to control everything without her consent. She thought she could be happy at Tarnsham. She would say yes when he proposed. She surprised herself that she could change her mind in less than a day.

The next morning, Sandra mentioned that the rain was over and the weather was clearing. Maggie thanked her, and took her time getting ready for the day. As expected, yesterday's clothes were clean and ready to wear again. She put on the only other clothes she had with her, a white summer blouse and light blue skirt, covered with a navy cardigan and yellow scarf. After Rosie gave her hair a vigorous brushing, she went down to breakfast.

She slowly went down the grand staircase, pretending to be the lady of the manor. Andrew was waiting in the hallway below, and they walked into breakfast together. Half-way through the meal, they heard a low rumble of thunder. Rainstorms again, thought Maggie.

Andrew reacted immediately. He stood up so quickly that his plate of eggs flipped over on the table. "It's Messies – we have to get back," Andrew turned to his parents. "We have to go, Mother. Father, get Victor to take us back to Northolt. Maggie, grab your uniform – we can change in the car. By the time we leave, the bombers should be just past here. We can get to Northolt between in and outgoing fire. I'll have to fly the second round this afternoon, even if I am on leave."

Andrew bolted out of the sitting room and ran up the stairs to grab his uniform. Maggie looked at his parents, who were looking at her.

"Thank you for everything," Maggie said to Lady Cashleigh as she set her teacup on its saucer. She ran up to her room, scooped up her uniform, and ran back down the stairs. What did he mean about changing in the car?

Victor drove the Bentley up to the entrance as Andrew and Maggie ran out of the front door. The incoming bombers were overhead.

"They're too intent on their targets ahead to worry about us," Andrew tried to reassure Maggie and Victor. "Let's go!"

Andrew directed Maggie to sit in the front seat with Victor, and he jumped into the back seat. Wrestling under a car robe used to keep passengers warm, Andrew changed from civilian to pilot. The skies overhead grew quiet, though the rumble of air warfare could be heard in the distance.

"Time to switch places," Andrew said. Victor stopped while Maggie and Andrew changed seats.

Maggie slipped her trousers on under her skirt and wiggled them up past her hips. She changed her shoes (no socks, she noted to herself), then pulled her skirt off over her head. Then under the car robe, the blouse came off easily. Putting on the uniform shirt was harder. Too bad I don't have Sandra now, Maggie thought. Finally, she emerged from the car robe, tucked in her shirt, and began putting on her tie, jacket, and belt.

Halfway back to Northolt, the German bombers flew over them on their return to Germany. This was a time of the greatest danger. As the bombers ran low on fuel, they dropped their remaining bombs randomly over the countryside to lighten the weight of the aircraft. Andrew directed Victor to pull off the road to wait for the planes to fly on.

Suddenly there was a loud noise and a huge gust of wind. The world spun in a million directions.

Maggie opened her eyes to a cloud of white. She went back to sleep. Later, she woke up again, and the white cloud held shapes. She forced the shapes to take on some detail. Bed, table, walls, windows. Still all white, but window panes were defined, and there were shadowy skin-colored faces and hands. A hospital? Why was that? She tried to turn her head but stopped, it hurt and made her very dizzy. Her second attempt was slower and more successful. The rest of her body refused to move.

"Well, hello there," a familiar voice spoke. "It's about time."

"Agnes, why are you here?" Maggie asked, her own voice sounding dry and hoarse.

"I'm a nurse, why else?" Agnes replied. A voice behind her chuckled. Nigel.

"And what are you doing here?" Maggie asked Nigel. "Is this a hospital?"

"Do you remember what happened?" Agnes asked gently. Maggie slowly shook her head. "It's all right if you can't recall, it is quite common for memories to be blocked after something like this happens. You were in a car accident. You're in Station Hospital at Uxbridge."

"An accident?" Maggie tried to concentrate. Tarnsham, the drive, changing her clothes. Then, nothing. "Where is Andrew?"

Nigel and Agnes remained silent.

"He died in the accident," Agnes finally said, as softly as she could.

Nigel gently added, "It seems that a German bomb exploded near the car. A shock wave flipped the car into a drainage ditch. The driver and Andrew were thrown into the windscreen when the car hit a tree head-on, killing them both instantly. You were tossed about inside the car as it flipped."

Agnes continued, "Your lower right arm is broken and you have deep bruises and cuts on your face and leg. Hence you being wrapped like a mummy.

The doctors think that you might have a concussion, but Nigel thinks you are merely exhausted and need a good night's sleep."

"Oh," Maggie murmured, and went back to sleep.

Agnes turned to Nigel, "She'll be fine. Right now, I have to return to London." Nigel nodded. She gave Nigel a hug. She wanted to stay with Maggie. In emergency and surgery work, she didn't have to get to know the patients. Just treat them and hand them over to recovery nurses. It was harder with friends, especially Maggie.

Nigel stood by Maggie's bed for a few more moments before going back to HQ to let the Air Marshall know her condition. Her arm and various cuts and bruises would heal in a short time, but it would take longer for her to work through Andrew's death. He promised himself to help her recover, however long that might take.

"Good morning," Nigel said in a cheerful voice. "You look as lovely as ever."

"Not true," Maggie woke slowly to his voice. "First, it is dark out, so not morning. Second, I must look awful. Give me a mirror. I want to see what I look like."

"Okay, but be gentle with yourself," Nigel smiled as he warned her. "Have you been awake for long?"

"In and out," Maggie replied. She held the mirror in her left hand. Her right arm was useless in its heavy cast.

Her head was wrapped in a white turban of bandages, in the middle of which was a large brooch. Her facial bruises made her look like a Middle Eastern chieftain with black eye makeup. She laughed, which made instant pain attack her entire body. "Oh Agnes."

"Spot on," Nigel agreed. "She sends her love, by the way. You'll be liberated from here tomorrow. Doc says most of your bandages will come off before leave. This is actually your third day of incarceration."

"Three days? What have I missed?"

"Winnie and The King have been out to Uxbridge to view the fighting from the Operations Room. We're sending everyone up at once now," Nigel informed her. "Including Mallory's Big Wing. His usual delayed response is a second punch that the Germans don't expect. Short version of the story: larger numbers of fighters and bombers going up every day to meet larger numbers of fighters and bombers. New planes and even newer pilots filling the gaps. Runways hit and repaired by local maintenance teams. CH getting info to HQ so that we know when and where to send everyone. We are holding onto a slight advantage."

"I've been remembering more about the accident. The noise and a big shove – a shock wave?" Maggie lowered her voice. "When is Andrew's funeral? And for the driver?"

"Three days from now, at Tarnsham. The driver in the morning, Andrew in the afternoon."

"I need to be there," Maggie struggled to sit up. "For him and the family."

"Really? Did things go that well on your little trip?"

"No formal engagement," Maggie said. "But very close. I feel I do need to be there. The only survivor," she let her thoughts trail off.

"I'll go with you," Nigel stated. "You need someone to help you through it, I assure you."

With that, he bent over and gently kissed her on her unbruised cheek. "I'll always be there."

That's nice, Maggie thought, as she drifted back into sleep.

Nigel took her to a new restaurant after the funeral. She was exhausted from both her injuries and the emotions that went through her. All the thoughts of what might have been. The family was kind, even in their grief. That made it harder. She had no idea what to do next.

She sat silently at the table. She didn't remember ordering anything, but the waiter brought her a plate of fish and vegetables. She stared at her food. She dropped her fork in anger.

"What's wrong?" Nigel asked. "Are you all right? Not hungry?"

"How am I supposed to eat?" Maggie exclaimed, being both frustrated and emotionally drained. She waved her right arm in its cast. She paused when she realized that Nigel had but one hand all the time. She dropped her voice in total embarrassment, "Sorry. How do you do it?"

"First," Nigel grinned, "one cannot just stab the meat with one's fork and chew around it like a giant lollypop. That gets one into a lot of trouble with one's mother. Second, accept as much help as is offered. Enjoy being spoiled and don't let on what you can do without help."

They both laughed as he demonstrated. "Just cut with the side of your fork, like this." He demonstrated again. "And order soft foods like this fish."

"For the rest of your temporary one-handed life," Nigel continued, "ask for help with food, underclothes, and your shoelaces. You don't have to learn coping skills. You'll be fine. Meanwhile, let's try this." With that, he pushed his chair as close to her as he could. He tucked her right arm behind him, supporting her cast with his left arm. Using their 'good' hands, she put her fork into the piece of beef on her plate, and Nigel used his knife to cut it. Then they moved to his plate, finishing it with a flourish. By the end of the meal, the entire restaurant had been entertained with their efforts. They left to a round of applause. (And the waiter forgot to collect their ration tickets or payment for the meal.)

CHAPTER 13
Christmas, 1940, Agnes

Maggie, arm recently out of its cast, was on Disabled Leave. Air Marshall Dowding had retired and was waiting for a new assignment. She didn't mind leaving the airfield with its memories of Andrew. She visited Aunt Charlotte and Agnes in London before Christmas.

The De Wevers invited Agnes and Maggie to the Dutch Embassy for Saint Nicholas Day. Queen Wilhelmina herself hosted the event for the exiled Dutch families in England. The reception hall was hung with patriotic orange banners, and large red, white, and blue flags. Plates of *spekulas* cookies, sausages, and cheeses were served. Seasonal songs and the national anthem were sung, and the mood was cheerful. The children happily received small presents from Saint Nicholas.

The De Wevers gave the girls personal packages with cookies, photos of Ellie and the Van Horn family, and a letter from Ellie. It was written carefully (censors read everything), hoping that they were all doing well, while making light of her own situation. Typical Ellie. The De Wevers told the girls that life in Holland was now much more constricted and dangerous than Ellie let on, both because of censorship as much as her own tendency to make light of difficult situations.

The Sunday before Christmas, Agnes and Maggie had tea at the Ritz. Maggie and Aunt Charlotte were having Christmas at Oakstone with her parents. Agnes was planning on Christmas with her parents in London.

Maggie waved her thin arm, "It is still so stiff after three months. It's painful when I try to stretch it, reminding me of stretching before doing sports at school. I can't feel sorry for myself when I see how severely others are wounded."

"Well, that's normal. How are you dealing with the rest of your healing?" Agnes asked as the waiter served them weak tea and chicken sandwiches.

Maggie reported, "There is a long scar on my arm, and a small scar on my face close to my hair line. I'm just letting my hair grow longer and no one should see anything."

"I meant Andrew."

Maggie took time to sip her tea. "It frightens me to say this, but he is fading from my memory. We saw each other nearly daily for two years, and yet he's drifting away so soon. Was he a 'boyfriend' after all, and not the 'real deal', like Emmy describes? I was truly convinced that we would get married by war's end after our visit to Tarnsham. I may not be as healed as I thought. The accident, though, is still fresh in my mind. I still over-react when I am startled. I have a quick flash of memory and chills at sudden sounds or being jostled in a crowd. And now, what about you? Any 'love' interests?"

"No boyfriend for me. There are three men in my life, but none of them are in the eligible category," Agnes replied. She counted them on her fingers. "Dr. Beech, the doctor I work with. He helped me when I was a student and after I was finished, he appointed me to Surgical Assistant, a big promotion. He's nearing 50 years old and happily married. Weejun. He's also nearing 50. He's a former patient. He's a butcher from Smithfield Market who used to drink and fight a lot. He credits me with his change into a gentler sober person. Not sure if that is true. He thinks he is my substitute father and I am his substitute daughter after his own died in a house fire. He recently became an Air Raid Prevention Warden. Then there is my father himself, who I see often for lunch. So, no one begging for my attention."

"How sad we sound! Especially with so many military men and doctors around us," Maggie sighed. "What about that med student, Nate 'something'?"

"Very old news, there," Agnes replied with a sneer. "Thought he was God. He thought we would be the perfect team. No mention of romance. Really! There has to be at least a cuddle now and then. On another topic. Did your letter from Ellie have any coded messages? Mine seems just straight forward."

Maggie answered, "Perhaps she has forgotten it. Though she was the one who reminded us back of it at her wedding. Mr. De Wever said we could send letters through the Embassy and the Red Cross. I think I shall write to her after Christmas."

"Good idea," Agnes agreed. "This will be a strange holiday season."

Maggie nodded. It would be strange. She was going home to Oakstone and had never celebrated Christmas anywhere else. Her younger brother Sam would be home from Oxford, having just finished up. Herbert would not be there. He was stationed in Northern Scotland. All over the country, families missed someone because of bombings, evacuation, or being on duty. A very strange Christmas, indeed.

Agnes let her mind wander. It was noon, Christmas Eve. Another night and morning had passed by without a bombing. How long would that last? How did it feel to sleep at night? She doubted if that would ever happen again, now that night duty was the norm at St. Bart's. Since September, London had been under nightly attack. If the summer months had belonged mainly to Maggie and the RAF fighter squadrons, then autumn months belonged to Agnes and the cities. Daylight raids over airfields became night attacks on urban areas.

When London was spared, German planes targeted other cities or randomly hit the countryside. Hospitals like St. Bart's, took on increasing numbers of patients. There were always the expected workplace injuries, household accidents, and illnesses. Becoming more normal were war injuries. Hospital staff learned on the spot how to treat burns from explosions as well as injuries from flying shrapnel, collapsing buildings, fires, breaking glass. A third group of injuries included tripping and falling because of blackout conditions, plus stress-related illnesses and accidents. After being treated, most patients were sent home, if they had one. It wasn't the volume of cases that was exhausting, it was the constant switch from one type of patient to the next with no gap in between. Even Agnes was getting weary.

Dr. Beech, Chief of the Emergency Services, gave Surgical Nurse Fletcher as much responsibility as he could. He had watched her as a student and admired her quick mind and instincts. She might become a doctor someday, he thought. She was still young, but she was respected as a leader, good at triaging patients, and directing staff to the right place to give the right treatments.

Life was surreal.

Nights were surreal. By December, blackouts began thirty minutes after sunset (5:00pm) and lasted until thirty minutes before sunrise (8am). Darkness was dark. People stumbled and bumped around, using small handheld torchlights or candles. White lines down the middle of roads helped people from wandering completely off track. Doors opened briefly, shedding dim light on small areas of sidewalk. Small curbs on roads and pathways helped as well.

Then, when everyone was used to the dark, there would be an air raid. Suddenly, searchlights blazed through the sky, reflecting off the huge silver barrage balloons floating over the city. People were nearly blinded by the brightness and then thrown back into the pitch blackness again after an air raid was over. Many people couldn't sleep due to eyestrain headaches caused by switching from dark to light to dark conditions.

Noises were surreal. With people remaining inside and no real light outside, London was eerily quiet. Until the sirens of an incoming raid filled the air with sound: anti-aircraft guns, bomb explosions, buildings collapsing, fire sirens and fire units racing through the streets, together with the sounds of the fires themselves. And planes roaring overhead. Everyone ran for shelter. Auxiliary Fire Service, Air Raid Precaution wardens, and other emergency crews were on standby, listening for alerts and meeting the needs in their neighborhoods.

Through it all, Londoners tried to make sense of life, insisting on keeping daily routines at all times.

Agnes and the hospital staff were always on alert. If a siren sounded, tea breaks were over. Leaving the patients and staff because it was the end of one's shift was not done.

There had been a truce of sorts with no bombing for the past week, but everyone knew that the war would come back after Christmas.

Christmas itself was surreal. Not many decorations or special foods were to be found at any price. Gifts were hard to find, even with ration tickets and money.

This Christmas was to be Agnes' first official visit with her parents. She had seen them at social occasions since her court presentation. She had been to lunch with her mother and father separately and felt comfortable with them for short times. This was her first full family visit in nearly four years. There was no way to predict what would happen.

In the late afternoon of Christmas Eve, Agnes stood in front of her old home, looking at it almost for the first time. The stairs leading to the front door of Natterbourne House, the Fletcher home, looked intimidating for a few seconds, and then so inviting. She knocked.

"Welcome home," Mr. Leo, the Butler, beamed as Agnes entered her old home. She couldn't help but beam back. He led her into the sitting room. Mamma sat in her favorite chair; Poppa sat in his. She looked around. Nothing had changed. The room was a museum Display of English Life. She scanned the scene swiftly and memories sped back as she looked at the pictures and furniture. She had forgotten so much after making Shellings her home. I wonder where I really belong, she thought.

Her parents both stood up to welcome her as if nothing had happened. Well, Agnes thought, let's see how long this will last.

"You have changed, and so have we," her father began, while they enjoyed a glass of pre-dinner sherry. "You have become a wonderful young lady, even if it wasn't what we expected."

Her mother added, "You are very much like us. Strong willed and independence are traits you received from us. And that is a compliment."

"I'm not sure if everyone thinks that is a compliment. I have often gotten into trouble for my strong will both at St. Martins and at St. Bart's," Agnes admitted. "If I remember, I was often in trouble before you sent me off to school. Too independent and too headstrong, I keep hearing. Most often right now, I pretend to know what I'm doing, even if I am unsure. Sometimes that backfires. Is that a family trait?"

"Possibly, as long as you can figure out how to follow through," smiled her father. "It is a matter of learning the timing of your challenge and which battles to fight. Rather like playing cards."

Agnes remembered what Charlotte said about her mother afraid to try new things, and yet she stepped into the role of director of her family's tea company. Strong will may sometimes take a little longer to emerge, as well as how to use it wisely. Independence? Probably her father accepting his domineering wife by keeping his own interests was his form of independence. She also noted that both of her parents were trying very hard to bring her back into the family. She noted that she was trying as well. It just might work out. She was hopeful.

"And now, Mrs. Millie and Mr. Leo have dinner waiting for us. Not the usual Christmas fare, what with rationing, but I'll wager still up to par."

"Anything is better than eating at the hospital canteen," Agnes said lightly. "And I remember Mr. Leo's cooking. He's a magician."

"Thank you, Miss Agnes," Mr. Leo said as he led them into the dining room. Agnes wondered about Mr. Leo for the first time. His accent sounded Slavic. He and his wife Millie had been the family's servants all her life and yet she knew nothing about them, not even their last name. She was determined to find out about them.

The Fletcher family chatted over a dinner of vegetable soup, fish (not rationed), turkey (her family could afford the luxury), and an apple sponge cake. The supply of tea from their own import company and the wine from their cellar helped everyone relax and share stories. Her parents were genuinely interested and entertained by her life as a nurse. She felt that she was a child again. They had been close as a family, especially when they traveled together each summer, and that feeling was returning.

At 10:30 pm, they walked the few blocks to St. James Church for the midnight Christmas Eve service. Blackout conditions made them walk slower than usual. They were glad that they knew the streets as they went.

The church was very drafty. Not everything was fully repaired after a bomb hit the church in October. That didn't stop the people in the neighborhood from gathering on Christmas Eve. People needed the security of unfailing tradition. They craved the gift of tradition, the familiar scriptures, music, and the message of peace. Agnes thought about the people throughout the world who were at similar services and praying for peace. How sad that it was only a hymn and a dream.

The congregation listened with one ear attentive to the service, the other ear half-waiting for an air raid siren. "Silent Night" was sung as a heart-felt prayer. At the end of the service, the worshipers wished Happy Christmas to each other and walked away in silence.

Back home, Mr. Leo had cups of tea for them before they left for bed. Agnes stood in the middle of her room. She was in a time machine with dolls, picture books, ribbons from school for sports, photos of family holidays. How much of that little girl was still inside her? Did she ever expect to be washing her own soiled nurse's uniform each night?

"Are you alright?" It was Mrs. Millie, her mother's lady's maid and housekeeper.

"Oh, Mrs. Millie," Agnes said in surprise. "I'm just remembering things. It seems so long ago. And I missed you more than I realized."

"We missed you too," Mrs. Millie said. They hugged each other for the first time since Agnes had been very young. "Your mother was so sad – it was as if you had died. She was sure it was something she had done."

Actually, it was, Agnes thought. "Well, I'm here now," said Agnes. Mrs. Millie helped Agnes out of her dress. She didn't really need the help, but welcomed the feeling of being a spoiled little girl again. As Mrs. Millie reached the door, Agnes asked, "I am curious. Where are you and Mr. Leo from?"

"Russia, a very long time ago."

"I don't even know your last name," Agnes confessed. "Until very recently, I just thought you as part of our family."

"We feel like a part of your family too. Our name is impossible for the English to pronounce. That is why your family calls us by our first names – it is easy. Ready now? All right then, good night."

Christmas morning was cold, even with the luxury of central heating and the fire set in the sitting room. Agnes dressed quickly in her best casual clothes – thick sweater over a woolen skirt and heavy woolen stockings. Her parents were already in the sitting room with a cups of strong tea ("as long as India is still under British control, we shall have tea," her father, the owner of a tea company once remarked to the newspapers as reassurance of one English tradition not to be lost during the war.)

She put the presents for her parents under the tree. Mrs. Millie brought her tea along with a plate of eggs and toast.

"Time to open presents," her father proposed. He moved the presents to each person's chair.

"First, Mother," Agnes announced. Her mother opened her present: a lace shawl. "It's from Belgium," Agnes said. "I've had it since Maggie and I were in Europe for Ellie's wedding. I hope you like it."

"It's lovely," her mother looked genuinely happy.

"And Father," she said. He opened a heavy box. It contained the latest recording of his favorite opera, "The Magic Flute".

"Wonderful!" he exclaimed, also genuinely happy. "You remembered!" (As if she could forget his continual humming of his favorite arias, including 'Papagena'.)

"And now your gifts, my lovely daughter," he continued, pointing to the largest box by her chair. "Perhaps not the most exciting gift, but one you need to receive."

Agnes opened it. Inside was a ledger and a pile of very official-looking papers. She looked blankly at her father.

"Your trust account and its ledger," he explained. "The rest of the papers are a collection of estate and company details, and a document stating your appointment to the board of directors of Arrow Teas. You are twenty-one, and as the heiress of the company, and you need to start taking part in the management of the business. You can continue your nursing career while learn your role in the business."

Agnes took a deep breath. Some Happy Christmas, she thought. I should have expected this. She was sure that she would never be ready to take over the business, but held back any thought of saying that to her parents. "Thank you, Poppa."

Her mother waved dismissively. "You have always known that someday you will be the head of the company. There will be plenty of time to work out details. Now, for a more appropriate gift for Christmas. I think you will like this a lot more than a stack of paper," she added. Her mother pointed to the smallest box.

It was a jewelry set once worn by her grandmother. Earrings, a necklace, a brooch, two bracelets and a ring. Pearls with diamonds and rubies, set in swirls of gold. Agnes saw her grandmother at once, in a brocade dress and fur cape, waiting to go to a grand ball somewhere. She looked up at her mother. Nothing but affection.

"It might be time to have a jeweler redesign the whole set for a more modern look," her mother suggested. "And the last gift," she added.

Agnes opened the remaining box. It was a photo album of the family's last holiday together when Agnes was fourteen years old. A happy time in the Alps in an open motor car. Learning how to echo in the mountains. Swirling long pasta with a fork in Naples. The Venetian Canal gondola ride. Paris and the Eifel Tower. New dresses from fancy French shops, and the surprisingly rough Channel crossing to get home when she was terribly seasick.

"Thanks so much for all of this," Agnes found her voice full of emotions she hadn't felt for years. "I guess the family is back together again."

After a late lunch, Mr. Leo and Mrs. Millie drove her back to St. Bart's. In her room, she opened each present again, looking slowly at each photo, business document, each piece of jewelry. As she placed everything back, the shift bell rang to begin night duty. She prayed for a normal night, no bombing tonight, please.

CHAPTER 14
December, 1940, London

Four days later, December 29th, 1940, was a Sunday that no one will forget. Sirens wailed to alert Londoners of an incoming German attack. People scrambled for shelters, rescue and response teams gathered at their posts, and the holiday break from attacks was over.

In the hospital, Agnes started the checklist. Patients were moved away from windows. Supplies were readied in the emergency rooms and surgery wards. There was one final chance for a sandwich and a trip to the toilet.

At first, the bombing noises sounded normal (Agnes thought, rather an odd concept, normal bombing). This raid, however, was longer and louder than most. There were shouts that fires were breaking out "everywhere". She heard glass shattering, bricks and rocks hitting the outside walls of the hospital, and bomb explosions echoing between buildings. Fire sirens went off from all directions. The bombing seemed continuous. Casualties were coming in a constant stream, some on foot, some in various vehicles. More burn injuries, more people with smoke inhalation, more everything. Patients sat or lied on the floors waiting to be helped.

Agnes took time between attending each patient to see which people needed the most urgent help. She had devised a colored ribbon system, but that didn't last very long with the number of people coming in. She paired people together, one serious injury with one not-so-bad. With quick instructions, she had the 'not-so-bads' help with first aid on the serious ones and alert the medical staff if the 'bad ones' were getting worse. She had no idea if it would work, but busy people don't pay as much attention to themselves, so fewer complaints from the 'not-so-bads' for a while.

On their way in, ambulance attendants reported, "Hamilton's Printing office just collapsed," "A tube shelter just got hit," "No more water for the firehoses until the tide comes up the river – the pumps are too high to work until then." "They got a bomb in the roof of St. Paul's Cathedral." (Now that *was* a scare, St. Paul's was only a few blocks away.)

Around eleven o'clock, the skies became quieter. The fire trucks, ambulances, made their way through the city and rescue teams worked frantically. One fireman came in and couldn't breathe without coughing for almost an hour. Between coughing spasms, he spoke of fires that were gathering together. "Those incendiaries. You watch two or three small fires grow into one huge one. They suck up all the air in one big wind storm, and the noise is so bad, we can't hear each other."

Agnes listened to all this without raising her head from the stitching she was doing. At that moment, she had no idea if this leg belonged to a man or a woman, only that it needed to be closed up. She no longer was afraid of air raids; they were too frequent. She could only continue to work, removing glass shards, cutting away the worst of the burned flesh, bandaging, calling orderlies to bring more supplies, and listening without responding to the stories each person told.

When morning finally came, and it did come, Agnes went outside the hospital to see for herself what had happened. For the first time, she heard that there had been two separate raids. She was so busy that she never realized that there had been a small period of quiet.

The streets were filled with smoke and dust. It was as warm as a summer's day, with the fires smoldering on every block. Firehoses crisscrossed the streets. Men were coated in ash and looked like ghosts. Civilians helped uniformed men trying to control or douse the remaining fires. Air Raid Precaution Teams were searching wreckage for survivors. Groups of ordinary people searched for loved ones or salvage or loot what might have remained in the rock piles that were once homes and offices.

"Sister! Lassie!" called out a familiar voice.

"Hey, Weejun," Agnes replied. "Good to see you came through last night. It was a rough one for you too, I gather?"

Weejun, in his Warden's coat and helmet, just nodded. He was weary and it showed. "You need to come with me, right now," he said. Agnes didn't have to think twice. She trusted him completely.

"What happened?" she asked.

"Your parents," he said quietly. "They live around St. James Square? Fletcher's the name, right? That area got hit last night, and I think you might want to go 'round to check up on them. I'll come with you."

Agnes saw agony on his face. He knew more than he's saying. She felt a weight in the bottom of her stomach. She was no longer weary, she had to go with him. She nodded, and the two of them set off. Could what he said be true, that something happened to her parents?

It took them two full hours to cross the city. The block where Agnes grew up was not just unrecognizable; it was gone. A few badly damaged buildings remained, no trees, just piles of rubble. Fire trucks and teams of rescue workers led by the local Warden searched for buried survivors and bodies and helped families begin claims of damage and other official reporting.

"I think that's our house, over there," Agnes said very weakly, hoping to be wrong, even while she recognized where they were standing.

Weejun put his hand on her shoulder and led her very slowly to where she had pointed. In his softest voice, he asked, "how many people might have been inside last night?"

Agnes answered slowly, "My parents and Mr. Leo and Mrs. Millie. Four."

"Wait here." Weejun walked over to the local Warden, spoke to him, and pointed to Agnes. They came over to her. Weejun said, "They found three bodies in your house. The Warden needs you to identify them if you can. Are you up to it?"

Agnes nodded, not sure she could. They walked over to a bakery van that served as an auxiliary ambulance. She stepped into the back of the van and held her breath. There were three litters covered with blankets. The Warden slowly lifted the middle of each blanket. Agnes gasped and immediately said, "That's my mother's hand – I know her watch." Then at the second litter, "And that hand is my father's – it's his ring. Do I have to see their faces?"

"No," replied the local Warden. "Now the third?"

"I'm not sure," Agnes said, wondering if it was Mrs. Millie or Mr. Leo. "Mr. Leo, the cuff of his jacket. One person is missing, a woman. And I don't know their full names. Just that they were Russian. I'm sorry." Where is Mrs. Millie, she wondered.

"That's fine, ma'am. We can do the rest. Sir, since you are a Warden, you can help her with the rest of her paperwork. You know what I need."

Weejun nodded. Agnes and Weejun began the long walk back to St. Bart's. London was already picking up where it had been the night before. Fire trucks and hoses were tidied up, men and women were sweeping the streets to make them passable again. Newspapers had been printed overnight and were on stands along the streets. A photo of St. Paul's Cathedral wreathed in smoke was on the front page of the newspaper. That the famous church had been spared was a beacon of hope for the city. Agnes barely noticed.

Weejun broke the silence, "Did you ever make peace with them, your parents?"

Agnes nodded, "Just five, no four days ago, over Christmas. It doesn't seem fair. It was so nice to be together again. Now all I have left are three presents."

Weejun sighed, "I didn't even get that when my family died in the fire. Be glad your last memories are good ones." Just before Agnes went inside the hospital walls, Weejun asked, "I'll tell Dr. Beech if you want. Can I take you anywhere? Anyone else need to know what happened?"

Agnes mentioned Aunt Charlotte and Maggie, their Oakstone and Shellings addresses and telephone numbers before slowly going inside.

"I'll call them to take you home."

She made it to her room and cried until Aunt Charlotte and Maggie, also red-eyed, came all the way from Oakstone to take her home. They would be back at Shellings a few weeks later. She was given two weeks off. Weejun helped her with the official reports of death, property damage, and next of kin for the government officials.

Emmy was in London visiting her mother and sisters for Christmas and announced her pregnancy. Maggie and Agnes come to the city to see her. They celebrated and mourned over lunch at the Sickly Doctor. The normally cheerful, crowded pub was quiet, as everyone tried to recover from the latest round of air raids. The pub itself was damaged, but like all of London, defiantly open for business.

For small talk, and a change of mood, Emmy asked if either girl had any "social prospects." Maggie mentioned her time with Andrew, with its sad ending. And perhaps that he had not been the 'real deal'. Emmy recognized her term for judging the chaps they dated.

"Having a 'boy' or 'girlfriend' is not new. My parents had them," Agnes took a deep breath, "only they had them after they were married."

"What?" Maggie and Emmy sat up.

"That's why I left my parents. On one of our school holidays, I went into my mother's bedroom as I usually did. Only this time, she was absolutely naked, with a naked man (not my father) in a very affectionate embrace. She didn't see me.

"I knew that my father spent time with other women. Doing what, I didn't know. I was just so overwhelmed at what I saw, I couldn't say anything to anyone. Not to them, not to you or Ellie. I just knew that it was terribly wrong, that my parents must only be pretending to love each other."

Agnes continued, "'Friends.' Their marriage was arranged when they were very young. So, they dated after they got married rather than before. Like Ellie's Professor said at the wedding. I was too young to understand any of it. It took me until recently to get over it all. I finally forgave them and was nearly at peace with myself for creating all those years of sadness. Sorry, it's just so awful right now."

Emmy and Maggie then wrapped her arms around Agnes. It was all they could do.

"What's Clive up to?" Maggie asked Emmy. "Has he been called up for duty yet?"

Emmy answered, "Not yet. In addition to his general practice, he works with veterans who are in rehabilitation, especially the mental aspects of their war experience. What they call shell shock."

"What is that, actually?" Maggie was finding herself being once again a curious journalist.

"Long-term problems as a result of war or bad events. Anything from recurring nightmares or headaches to unexpected physical reactions to normal sounds and situations. Guilt at surviving an assault that killed your mates. It's not the same for each person, and most people get through their lives without any real problems at all."

Maggie shivered, thinking of Andrew and the accident.

"How do you treat it?" asked Agnes the nurse.

Emmy thought about what she learned from Clive. "Each person needs to tell their story, and work it into their lives. Agnes, you see some of that. Each person suffers differently. It's not just soldiers. Even just witnessing continual death and destruction, or the continual fear of being next."

Agnes nodded. She thought about losing her parents, and Maggie losing Andrew. Maggie spoke for both of them. "I guess that would us. What should we do?"

Emmy replied, "Share what happened. If you can't resume normal life or absorb normal stress in a reasonable amount of time, get help. Your mind should heal like a physical scar. Memories still there, but faded, not crippling or obsessive."

Maggie and Agnes returned to Oakstone for the second week. Aunt Charlotte remained at Agnes' side. She had been Agnes' substitute mother for the past few years, and now that was no longer temporary. They walked on wintery garden paths daily, silently working through what had happened. (Aunt Charlotte hadn't walked this much since her nature-loving husband died.)

Just before returning to London and St. Bart's, Agnes asked Maggie, "Would it be out of order for me to want to go to the Flying Pig with you?"

"Not at all," Maggie replied. She was happy to see Agnes was to showing interest in life again. "It's been a while for me too. Maybe Nigel will be there to cheer us up."

CHAPTER 15
April, 1941, Maggie

In early April, Maggie and Agnes met again at the Sickly Doctor. It looked like the Sickly Something. The pub was being rebuilt after a nasty incendiary bomb hit the neighborhood. It was too popular with the local population to be destroyed. In fact, it was more popular than ever for a community that wanted and needed to stay together. The barkeeper and owner accepted volunteer help to rebuild the pub while continuing to pour weak pints every day.

"We are all incredibly connected to each other," Agnes shook her head in disbelief. "How many other girls like us are being followed by Lady Archer? There must be more, not just St. Martins' girls."

"I really have no idea," Maggie answered. "She knows positively everyone. Lady Davids once said that there are less than a thousand families in the Debrett register. Calculating the number of individuals in any given age bracket, we probably know most of our age-mates in some way. What makes me curious is how many more 'Lady Archers' are out there helping girls with their connections. It makes sense that these ladies would know so many people. We are merely their latest project."

"Well, it is nice to know that someone is watching," Agnes said. "Lady Archer visited me after my parents died. She was in school with my mother and Aunt Charlotte and wanted to do something personal. 'Any help I might be able to render' were her exact words." Agnes set down the chipped mug with more glue than pottery on the table with more nails than wood. "I'm using that connection. Why not? I can't manage all the legal work I've had since December. The solicitors suggest that I have a male advisor (read uncle or husband, I think) to do the thinking for me. I want someone who takes me as a serious and intelligent person, capable of making my own decisions. And I do want to ask your father to be one of my trustees."

"I'll talk with him. His legal advisor is very good," Maggie suggested, adding, "in addition to Lady Archer."

At the Ritz Hotel two weeks later, Maggie waited for Nigel. She wore her uniform with a skirt, which she disliked immensely. Stockings were rationed and impossible to find, meaning that cold bare legs were normal. She preferred the trousers suggested by Air Marshall Dowding, but this evening at the Ritz was special.

Nigel arrived in a new uniform. He looked incredibly handsome and healthy compared to most of the people around her. His normally blonde hair was nearly white. She stared at Nigel's tanned face. She was happier to see him than she realized.

"Where have you been?" she demanded. "You look like you've been on holiday to some tropical beach. I thought you said you've been working extra hard. Did I waste my time worrying about you? I could have been out dancing or living a carefree life. Well?"

"Such accusations! Work, seriously," was his reply. "North Africa since Dowding retired in November. Hence the tanned face. And arms. Fighting in Africa requires lots of tanks and lots of air support. Therefore, lots of airfields are in order. (Sorry, locations cannot be disclosed.) So, you needn't accuse me of irresponsible behavior. It's war, you see. I'm innocent of all charges, except for living outside most of the time."

"Sorry." Maggie tried being contrite and happy to see him at the same time. Happy? More like contentment that all was well with Nigel at her side.

The waiter approached. No need to look at a menu. Rationing had cut choices to two main courses even at the Ritz. Rather dull. And payment included money and a ration ticket. But the Ritz was still one of the best places in London.

"Soup, please, and the duck," she ordered from the waiter.

"Soup for me too, and the fish," Nigel said. He then turned full attention to Maggie. "Now, what is Flight Officer Shelford doing for King and Country? You didn't tell me anything very specific on the telephone or in letters, which by the way were gratefully received."

"Big picture first. As of last week, you know that we women were finally admitted to full status in the Royal Air Force. I couldn't write about myself for a while because there was nothing to write about. I only got my new assignment a few weeks ago. I am a reporter again, in the general pool of the Military Publications Office, specifically on the staff of the *Union Jack,* an Air Force officer at an Army paper.

"I was on Disabled Leave for my arm, and then, after Christmas, I stayed in London to be with Agnes. One evening in January, we went to the Savoy for dinner with Aunt Charlotte, my old boss from the *Times,* Lady Davids, and Lady Archer from our old school. I simply sat there while they discussed my future. They decided that I should continue a career in journalism and arranged my appointment to the *Union Jack*. And so it happened. How that worked out with the RAF is beyond me."

"Anyway, there are three of us chief reporter/editors, one each from Navy, Army, and RAF, doing and collecting stories about the Home Front for those stationed abroad. I'm doing a new version of 'Eighteen,' interviewing girls in factories, Land Army, Home Guard, volunteer organizations like the Women's Institute, and even those at home who knit hats, socks, bandages, and the like. There you are – new job, and new military rank as well. No sun tan working here in England."

Waiters arrived with a bottle of wine and the soup (broth with a few vegetables floating in it). Two triangles of toast rested next to the bowls. In a hotel like the Ritz, a meal was served as attractively as possible, making rations look edible. The taste wasn't too bad, either, Maggie mused.

"Ah," Nigel began. "Well, connections again for me, too. Air Vice Marshall Park suggested me to Air Marshall Harris of Bomber Command. Bigger planes need bigger runways. We all had shady reputations having been with Dowding, but Harris needed someone with my qualifications. I went to Africa with an inspection team and stayed on. I studied the terrain, decided on what will work, started projects, and then trained local units to do the work. They promoted me to Squadron Leader so that I could look and sound more commanding."

"And here we are," Nigel concluded. "Two vagabond RAF officers, roaming all over the map."

"And here we are," Maggie echoed.

The soup dishes were cleared away, and dinner was served. Maggie stole glances of Nigel. She had to be honest, he was not just a 'brother.' Not just a 'friend.' He was moving into the 'real deal' category. They were just so comfortable together. It was as if they had never been apart, certainly not for five months.

She studied how Nigel used his fork for cutting and eating his fish. He was so agile at scooping up potatoes and sauce, she hardly noticed it at all. She found herself laughing as she remembered their "team eating" adventure when her arm was in a cast. It wasn't that long ago, or was it?

"Share the joke?" Nigel asked.

"Our last dinner together. We were quite the spectacle." They tried to retain the appropriate behavior for the Ritz Hotel, but kept laughing at odd times through the rest of their meal.

An American reporter sat at the table next to them. He kept one hand in his lap, being the correct manner for someone from 'across the pond.' That didn't help Nigel and Maggie who were laughing at their own behavior, and kept seeing the Yank out of the corner of their eyes.

They left the Ritz in a good mood and strolled towards the banks of the Thames. The sound of the water was their guide. A new moon meant that it was less likely that there would be a bombing raid. They wanted to enjoy the calm and peaceful evening for as long as it last.

They reached the river. Nigel broke the silence. "Is there a chance that you can get away so soon in your new job? I'm going to Manchester to work on the Ringway Aerodrome. I'm leading a crew to start construction of a paved runway. I'll be visiting my family and I'd like you to meet them. What do you say?"

Maggie froze. She thought about the visit with Andrew Cashleigh and his family. She tried to convince herself that it couldn't happen twice.

"When are you thinking of going?" She tried to keep her voice calm.

"In a week's time," was the reply. "We'll go by train. I can explain my family to you. Or is it too early for you to take on another trip like this?"

The smile in his voice was so inviting, and his concern so evident, she didn't have to see it. They continued to walk along the embankment in silence. It wouldn't be like her visit to Tarnsham, she kept thinking.

Agnes knew immediately why Maggie was nervous about the visit. Aunt Charlotte agreed.

"Go. Otherwise everything you do, see, hear, will remind you of your experience with Andrew," Agnes insisted. "Remember what Emmy said. Experiences come back as terror moments if you don't work them out. Besides, Nigel knows the whole story and can help you through anything that might happen. And Nigel might be the 'real deal.' Concentrate on that."

Maggie's leave was contingent on bringing back stories for the *Union Jack.,* which made her ask Lady Davids for a contact at the *Manchester Guardian.* She packed a full week's civilian daytime and evening wear for her introduction to the Drummond family. It was a new adventure, although much of it would be back in the familiar territory of great houses, servants, and the appropriate behavior.

They wore their uniforms for the six-hour train ride to Manchester, ready to put them away as soon as they arrived. The countryside rolled by. She had vague memories of family vacations as they rode through the Peak District. The hills became more pronounced, the farmland more rugged, the towns further apart. Her father liked the hunting; her mother liked the rigorous hiking paths. Nigel pointed out the city of Stoke-on-Trent where most of the country's porcelain and chinaware were made. War destruction was everywhere. She saw damaged buildings, factories, and bridges, and the land itself showed craters and fire damage. At least it was less than around London.

Nigel interrupted her thoughts, "I am guessing that we were raised in much the same fashion. My parents took time to be with us, played games, and taught us practical skills."

Maggie nodded. Father taught her as well as her brothers about farming, driving farm vehicles, sports, and hunting. Their mother insisted that they all know how to cook, mend and clean their clothes, and pick up their own room. ("How else will you know if your staff is doing a good job, or needs training? You also should know how to do things, just in case you're on your own.")

Nigel continued, "As the second son, I was expected to have a career along with my family allowance. Then, with no fingers, I became the family project. In order to survive boarding school, I was taught how to eat, dress, play sports, especially self-defense and brute force fighting. All done with lots of humor and very little sympathy. I qualified for our school's teams for cricket and tennis. And, I kept the school bullies under control. I didn't do much classwork, but I survived. Never praised, achievements were expected with an occasional 'well done' but that was all."

"My experience, exactly!" Maggie realized. "I always felt the need to work hard for compliments. Not that it mattered, but it would have been nice. I didn't know anything I did was of merit until I went to school and work."

Nigel and Maggie were met at the railroad station. Robbie, the driver, and Nigel exchanged news as if they were best friends. Quite unlike Andrew's driver Victor, who had remained formal to the end. The memories made her heart race. Not the same, not the same.

Manchester was scarred by heavy bombing raids, a little less than Central London. They headed south of the city through moors and small wooded areas. Within fifteen minutes, they turned on to winding gravel road to the family home. Shrubs and trees were decorated with the early spring leaf buds; apple and cherry trees were in flower. The house sat in the center of a great lawn, surrounded by evergreen trees on three sides. It was a great 'Victorian pile" of stone. Nigel explained that it was the restoration of an older home razed by fire in the early 1800s. Maggie suddenly felt uncomfortable in her uniform.

Lady Drummond greeted them at the door. After a brief side-kiss to Nigel, she said, "You must want to freshen up before tea," she said as Maggie gave her half-curtsey. "Rosie will take you up to your room, and we'll see you in a few minutes."

A few minutes! Do I get completely changed out of my uniform, or just fix my hair and make-up? Rosie led the way to the second floor, and opened the door to a room that was a contrast of pale green (drapes and light sage colored walls), and dark brown (ancient wooden furniture). It was very lovely. The door remained open as a servant entered with her luggage.

Rosie spoke up, "Pardon me, miss, but we don't have much time before tea. Shall I put away your clothes or help you change first?"

Maggie was still coping as the greeting "to freshen up" had been the same at Tarnsham. (She didn't even know what Nigel's home was called. How strange that she hadn't learned it.) She must pay attention to the present. "Thank you, Rosie. A quick face wash and I'll have the gray trousers and that blue sweater for over the shirt I am wearing. That will have to do right now. And let's trade out this uniform tie for that red and blue scarf," Maggie replied. "Are we that late in arriving, or is there some rush that I don't know about?"

Rosie laughed, "Oh no, miss, it is just that Lady Drummond would rather spend time with her guests than have them fuss too much."

"Oh," was all Maggie could think of as an answer.

Back down stairs in the sitting room, she saw that Nigel had also changed out of parts of his RAF uniform for a civilian look without changing into a completely new outfit. Well, this will definitely be a new experience.

Nigel guided her around the house, explaining the history behind the paintings and statuary, and the history of the Drummond family. He talked about his family with a sense of humor, not really dismissing them, but not letting their story be weighed down with importance.

When she asked about his father, he merely said, "You'll see tonight."

CHAPTER 16
April 1941, Manchester

Casual dress was announced for cocktails and dinner. It still meant changing into something nice. Hotel or private club dress were the code words. Maggie chose a mid-length woolen dress with matching hem-length scarf. At dinner, she went through the traditional 'interrogation.' The scrutiny was far less grueling. This time she was with a second son, not the future 'Lord of the Manor.' Still, she remained on her best behavior, keeping sharp attention to what was happening.

Saturday was a work day for both of them. Nigel had a military car take him to the Ringway Aerodrome. Mr. Philips from the *Manchester Guardian* arrived at the house with a list of women for Maggie to interview. Four seemed best suited for the *Union Jack*.

A few phone calls later, she and Mr. Philips were on their way to meet with a woman at a silk mill. The mill once produced everything from drapes to evening gowns; now the workers were mostly women who sewed parachutes and other military items like ammunition bags, flags, and jacket linings. "After we cut the parachute patterns, the left-over scraps get used for the rest of the items. Some scraps get sent to a small clothing company that makes underwear," she said with a smile. Maggie wondered what the censors would do with that information. How Emmy's sister Ruby would love to work with these bits of silk in her new dress shop!

The afternoon interview was at a farm, asking about the Land Army girls who were cleaning up last year's fields and beginning the spring plantings.

Dinner that night was again club dress. Maggie chose a soft gray wool dress trimmed with matching beads and a large mauve silk scarf over her shoulders. She needed a minimum of jewelry, and asked Rosie to concentrate on her hair.

The family talk ranged again from the day's activities to Nigel's view of post-war air travel and Maggie's interviews for the *Union Jack*. There was concern about Nigel's older brother, Alfred, whose battleship had just left for Australia.

Lord Drummond gave Maggie a brief history of Manchester, including the rise of the textile industry. He mentioned his work as a banker until Lady Drummond changed the subject with some success ("too tedious for dinner, darling," she remarked.) Even with additional talk of war and general politics, the evening remained enjoyable.

Sunday was not a day of rest. A great noise woke the household at 7 am. It came from the direction of Ringway. Fire sirens were heard in the distance. Sheer reflex made Maggie and Nigel jump up, dress automatically in uniform, and go down stairs. They surprised each other by arriving in the front hall at the same time. Now this was a reminder of Andrew, the early morning, uniform, quick leaving the house.

"Let's go," he said, pulling her outside. They ran to the garage filled with cars, trucks, and farm vehicles. "Pick something to drive. I'll tell you where to go." He paused. "It isn't a bombing raid, just a single explosion – likely a crash on take-off or landing."

She chose a Ford Estate Wagon and started the engine. Nigel jumped in and gave her directions. As they drove off, she became familiar with the car itself.

"What made you take this car?" Nigel was curious.

"We have a Ford like this at home. They were made in Canada and shipped here well before the war. My father made sure I could drive it around the estate," Maggie said, turning where Nigel pointed.

Within minutes, they were at the airfield. They showed their identification cards to the guards and entered the military installation. They followed the plume of smoke to the end of the runway. The wreckage of a mid-sized plane was surrounded by fire equipment and a crowd of people.

Ambulances were being loaded, litters held additional injured people waiting for a ride to the hospital, fire hoses were still dowsing smoky areas around the wreckage, and a group of officers were conferring at the edge of the scene before them. Nigel and Maggie joined them.

Maggie thought back to the bombing raids at Northolt a year ago, except this was a one-plane accident. Then she saw that some of the injured people were women in combat uniforms and boots. Nigel said something about this being a training site for parachute jumping. But women? They were part of the group of injured jumpers, still with chutes strapped to their backs. She filed that away as a question to ask later. Part of her wanted to react, to do something.

"Do you need more transport?" she asked an officer standing near her. "That Ford over there can take a couple of litters."

"Who are you?" asked the officer, suddenly aware of her. "How did you get here?"

"Flying Officer Shelford, here with Squadron Leader Drummond," she replied. "I want to help."

"Take those two ladies to St. Luke's," the officer said, pointing to two litters on the ground near them. "And this airman. He knows the way."

"Sir," she answered. She backed the Ford into an open space, while the injured women were helped out of their parachute packs. Other airmen carried the litters and slide them into the rear of the car.

"We're ready!" The airman called out as he jumped in, and they drove away. One woman was unconscious, the other groaned in obvious pain. Maggie concentrated on the driving directions from the airman.

At the hospital, the airman and three orderlies brought the litters inside. Maggie saw Mr. Philips standing at the entrance of the hospital, notepad in his hands. She walked over to him.

"Too bad about the accident at the aerodrome. No one will ever know it happened," he said without any emotion. Maggie looked at him.

"Pardon?"

"Hush, hush. You saw the women? Jumping is part of their training before being dropped into Europe as spies. Mustn't let the Huns know about them, must we? I shouldn't even know about them, but I've seen and heard enough to figure out the real story. Censors can only cut what they see and read."

Mr. Philips saw her quizzical look, and explained, "My real passion is history. I keep a private file of what I see, so that future historians will have a full picture of the war," Mr. Philips waved the small notebook that he stuffed into his satchel. He then waved a small pad of paper with more writing on it. "For now, officially, nothing happened."

Maggie talked a little longer with Mr. Philips before returning to Ringway with the airman. No work for Nigel until the next day.

After telling the family what they could over lunch, Maggie and Nigel changed into outdoor clothing. They spent the afternoon walking through the forest that surrounded most of the house and stretched farther to the east. Tall trees towered over moss-covered rocks and a carpet of leaf litter. To Maggie, it was the enchanted forest of the books she had read as a child. Nigel explained that the land was a game preserve for hunting and just enjoying nature. Therefore, the name "Elk Tree Park." They sat on a bench along the path, enjoying the complete silence of the forest.

Maggie reminisced. She chuckled, "When we were on our basic training, we had a sergeant who taught us 'outdoor skills.' He actually said that we could always find North without a compass, because moss grew on the right side of a tree."

Nigel laughed along with her. Without any warning, Maggie began to cry. He held her until she was too tired to cry any longer. The plane crash of the morning brought a mix of memories: Andrew and their car accident and the plane crashes she had seen at other airfields last summer become one giant horror. How much more of this could she take and still behave calmly? Nigel put his arm around her shoulders and she leaned into him.

She didn't want to move. She was safe inside Nigel's embrace. They were one person, one body. She couldn't imagine being without him. They remained in silence for a while longer, then continued their walk. A family of deer crossed their path.

Maggie thought, this is lovely. It's perfect.

"Isn't this perfect?" Nigel said in the quietest voice. Maggie nodded. The deer seemed to nod as well. Neither of them wanted to break the silence as they began walking slowly for the rest of the way towards the house.

"This is what we shall be doing for the rest of our lives," Nigel said as he opened the door to the house. "Walking together until we are so old that our nurses shall push us in matching chairs."

"Of course," was Maggie's response.

The peace of the forest was replaced by a new form of energy in the house. Nigel's younger sister Chloe and her two young boys had arrived. Her husband was at sea with the Royal Navy, so she came home to visit as often as she could. This time it was because she was curious about Nigel's new 'friend.' The boys immediately ran to Uncle Nigel.

Dinner this time was full formal dress, pre-war style. Rosie showed Maggie a closet of dresses that guests had left behind (common for people with large houses). She chose instead to wear her own dark blue silk dress, with pieces of a set of family pearls that she had received for her court presentation. Rosie fixed her hair again, automatically knowing to hide the faded scar from last year's accident.

Chloe was thrilled to meet the author of the 'Eighteen' column of the *Times*. Although a few years separated them, she and Maggie shared stories about girls they knew. The boys, two and three years old, began to play with the fire poke and were quickly scooped up by Nigel. A new game was played far away from the flames until dinner was announced and the boys were sent to bed.

Dinner was sumptuous. Rationing was the talk of the table, but there was generous meat (venison from the forest didn't count in the ration), vegetables from last year's garden (also didn't count), and baked goods (sweetened by jams made by the Women's Institute and therefore acceptable). Rations didn't include wine and was poured generously. Maggie found that most of the noble class often just did what they wanted, war or no war. That made dinner at the Drummond family interesting.

"All of us must be compliant with rationing," explained Nigel's father. He looked at Maggie, "It is bad form for a member of the House of Lords to break the law on rationing or anything else. Your father and I have pushed hard on what should be expected of us peers. Alas, not all are complying."

"You know my father well?" Maggie asked. She didn't remember the Drummond name coming up in conversation at home.

"Our committee memberships are separate, but we overlap on many issues. A good man, your father."

"Thank you," was all Maggie could say.

As she went to bed, Rosie confided, "I hope you like his Lordship as much as you like Sir Nigel. He is a very popular man. I got my job as a favor to our family. He does that a lot, help people."

"Oh?"

"He led the soldiers from Manchester in the Great War. Afterwards, the men asked his banking advice on starting their own businesses or help with fixing up their farms. His bank gave out a lot of loans. He's tough on repayment, respecting and understanding the men who didn't want to be in debt in the first place. My father had a hard time of it, so his Lordship took us all on here at Elk Tree Park. We got good incomes and skills to help our family get back up and running. I still work here, mainly because I like it."

Very interesting, Maggie thought. Nigel made his father sound like a know-it-all telling everyone what to do. The same man, but seen from a different eye.

Monday. A work day. Nigel returned to Ringway. Mr. Philips took Maggie to her third interview in a porcelain factory in Stoke-on-Trent. When war broke out, only a few factories sill made fine dinnerware, like Wedgewood. This factory began making only serviceable items. Maggie interviewed a woman whose original job was painting the decorations on dinnerware, but her current duty was to check the quality of the sinks and toilets made to replace those destroyed in the bombing raids. Some of the sinks and toilets were being sent to military camps. She was just as proud of her new work as with her old. Maggie's views on toilets would never be the same.

The final interview was with a welder. She had replaced her brother in the family owned business, a repair shop that worked on all variety of 'injured' motor vehicles. Very important, now that no new civilian cars were being made or imported. Who else would hire a woman welder but a father who wanted to keep his shop open? The burn scars on her arms were a bit off-putting at first, but Maggie loved her sense of humor. She deserved a good life after this was all over.

Maggie used Tuesday, Wednesday, and Thursday for writing-up days and leisure. She sat in the library of Elk Park to read a novel for the first time since the war began. What a treat! On Thursday evening, Nigel declared that his work was done. He turned the project over to the local unit of the Air Construction Service.

On Friday, Nigel introduced his city to Maggie. Robbie drove while Nigel gave her a guided tour of the to the important sites of Manchester. They visited to several shops in the smarter part of town, with packages handed to them for various members of the family. Maggie was surprised at the friendliness towards Nigel as they walked along. Lunch at a private club was just like London, again with warm welcomes given to Nigel, and therefore her.

Their last evening at Elk Park was formal again. Maggie let Rosie pick out a forest green gown from the dress closet. Its draped effect hid the fact that it didn't fit exactly. She still wore her own jewelry. She asked Rosie to style her hair in a way that didn't hide her scar. The past was definitely in the past.

Nigel greeted her at the top of the central grand staircase. He noticed her new hair style immediately and smiled. They came down the staircase acting like Clark Gable and Vivian Leigh. Whether that was a scene like it in the movie or not, they couldn't remember and they didn't care.

Chloe and the boys were still there, the boys wiggling in their sailor suits. Cocktails would be brief, and dinner was simplified, allowing the two boys to sit at dinner with the family. Formal dinners and manners had to be learned, and formal for the Drummonds was not always that formal. Again, very similar to the Shelfords. Chloe wanted to hear more about Maggie's interviews. At that moment, Maggie was inspired.

"Chloe, may I interview you?" Maggie asked. "You're involved in charitable work, aren't you?"

"Well, yes," she replied in a surprised mix of shyness and honor. "Our local ladies do quite a bit. I am the honorary chair, but I try to do my part of the real work."

"It may not be in the *Times*, but I'll make sure you get a copy of the paper when it is published. We can do an official interview tomorrow before we leave."

Chloe was thrilled. The boys sent to bed and dinner over, the family went back into the sitting room for a glass of port. Nigel walked around the room, stopping behind Maggie's chair. He had his good hand in his pocket. Something dropped on the floor and he knelt down to retrieve it. He turned to Maggie, still kneeling, with his hand out, and asked, "Well?"

Maggie saw a ring in his hand. In the center was a small oval ruby, surrounded by tiny diamonds. "Well," she said, "if we are going to be walking around the forest together for the rest of our lives, we ought to make it official. Yes."

"Hurrah!" exclaimed Lord Drummond. The rest of the family joined in toasting, clapping, talking all at once.

"Only," Maggie interrupted, "only being official after asking my father of course! And this is too beautiful to wear all the time. Besides, I'd be out of uniform."

"I guess we need to go to Oakstone as soon as possible, then," Nigel said. "and by the way," he took something else out of his pocket, "I already have a solution to the ring."

He handed her a small jewelry box. It held a miniature version of the ring, set as a pendant on a chain. "You can safely wear this necklace under your uniform. The ring is my grandmother's. The jeweler made the duplicate pendant for you."

Somehow, she interviewed Chloe on Saturday. Somehow, she and Nigel took the train back to London on Saturday afternoon. But she had no memory of those things.

Sunday came, and a few phone calls later, Nigel and Maggie met Agnes at the Sickly Doctor for a light supper and announcement. Agnes and her friends from the hospital were the perfect end of a perfect week.

CHAPTER 17
Summer, 1941, Agnes

In a curious twist of fate, Agnes was back at RAF Northolt. Actually, RAF Station Hospital at Uxbridge, a few miles away from the airfield. The last time she was here was in January, just after her parents died, a lifetime ago. She was officially back as part of a military/civilian nursing exchange organized by Dr. Beech.

Agnes followed Sheila Hargrove, a nurse in the Princess Mary's RAF Nursing Service into The Flying Pig. It still looked like a typical English pub — dark wood-paneled walls, brass taps and bar railings. The walls and the bar itself were filled with dents and scratches from fist fights and arm wrestling competitions, and holes left by darts and wood-eating bugs. The surfaces remained smooth only through constant polishing by elbows raising pints.

The pub sat on the edge of Northolt Airfield. That made it an unofficial extension of military life. A full year into the war, however, created many changes. Military flags, photos, and posters hid the original walls. A corner of the room stood empty so that local bands could come in for dance nights.

Men and women in uniforms from many nations mingled on their off-time. As a nurse, even off-duty, Agnes noticed the visible scars on most of the bar's patrons — mostly facial and hand burns and glass lacerations. Gaunt faces expressed the story of more invisible wounds.

Sheila guided Agnes through the crowded pub to a small table. Several men watched them make their way. Two pilots, a bit braver than those who merely ogled them, approached the table carrying two beers each and pulling up some empty chairs with their feet.

"Hello boys," Sheila said with a cheerful smile. "Right on time to meet our Agnes. She's part of the exchange between the St. Bart's in London and our own Princess Mary's at Uxbridge. That's why no uniform."

One pilot looked vaguely familiar, but Agnes couldn't place him. His shoulder patch was Polish, but the chest badge was RAF. He smiled at her, and seeing her confusion, introduced himself.

"You do not remember me, I think," he said. "Jan Novak. Andrew Cashleigh was my good friend. One night we were here all together. You, your friend Maggie, and another chap." He wiggled his left hand in a way that Agnes recognized as meaning Nigel.

"Oh, right," Agnes said. "Sorry, a lot has happened since then. Including the fact that Maggie and Nigel" she wiggled her left hand in the same way, "are getting married."

"Ah, I thought so," mused Jan. "Andrew was crazy about her, but I think it was not mutual. I am glad that she is happy. Is this a good thing? It is a short time after Andrew died. Andrew was a good friend to us Polish flyers. He got me into a regular squadron, not the separate one for Polish flyers only." He paused, "Shall we dance when the music starts again?"

"It is a very good thing. And yes, let's dance," Agnes said, studying him over her beer. Jan was attractive, and his English was far better than many of the foreigners she had met. He also turned out to be a great dancer. Nice, interesting. Her warning signals went up – he is a pilot. They have very short lifespans. She and Maggie shared their concerns about dating pilots, but she decided just to enjoy the evening.

Later, back in the barracks used by the Nursing Service, Sheila asked Agnes about Jan. "You two seem to know each other. What's the story?"

"I came here a few times last year with my best friend," Agnes answered. "She used to work at Bentley Priory. One time, her boyfriend and Jan came and we all sat together, that's all. Why? Is he taken?"

"Actually, no," she answered. "He and his brother sit with either the English pilots or the Polish, uniquely comfortable with both squadrons, in the air and on the ground. He's popular with everyone. Sometimes though, he just sits here alone with his own thoughts."

Another nurse walked by their beds and checked the blackout curtains before turning off the lights. "Tomorrow starts the civilian rotation into our unit. Be ready. Our patients are young, strong, and very impatient to get back to the fight. Not willing to rest up and follow directions."

"So I've been told," added Agnes. "The reason for the exchange is that Dr. Beech wants me and some of the other sisters to think about military service, now that women are being called up. He worked this out with an old mate from the Great War. From what I've heard, I don't think I'd like military regimentation – medicine is already regulated enough. Is there any room for initiative?"

Sheila nodded. "You'll see. Primarily in the theater itself, we're like any other medical staff in the world. Outside though, it can get silly. We put up with it and laugh when we can."

It proved to be true. For normal illnesses and accidents, treatment was straight forward. She knew as much about burns and accidents as some of the military nurses. Nightly bombings were enough experience. The sequence of care was different, though. There were small hospitals at the battlefront airfields for triage and first aid. 'Patch them up and send them on their way.' The more seriously injured went to field or general hospitals, like Uxbridge, where major treatments began before shipping the men to recovery centers.

Some Princess Marys were assigned to transport care. Nurses served on evacuation flights to monitor and tend to patients from the time they left the fighting front until they reached full hospital treatments.

Sheila was right. The doctor/nurse relationship was the same as in a civilian hospital. Everywhere else on the air base, including the dining areas and the nurses' quarters, protocols were rigidly military. Really, Agnes thought, was it that important that my personal locker and trunk were "properly" arranged, with clothing folded just so? And who could talk to whom, officer or non-officer made such a difference. In all, civilian life remained far more appealing. If she joined, *if,* she'd try for a unit in the first or second step of the process, where work was faster and less routine.

"Ah, you're back," Jan observed when Agnes and Sheila returned to the pub two nights later. "This is Stan. He is my brother and best friend."

Stan nodded, smiled, and waved the girls to their table. "My English not good like Jan. I try. Jan is very good with language. I am good with planes." Stan is the fun one, Jan is serious, Agnes observed.

"Hello," said the two girls at the same time.

Stan worked up his courage to speak again. "Do you come here too often?"

Sheila, and Agnes began to laugh. Stan looked down. "More mistake?" He looked at Jan for help. A few words back and forth in Polish and Stan blushed. Then he got up, smiled sheepishly, and left.

"Sorry, he is trying very hard," Jan explained. "I went to the university in Warsaw for languages, history, and literature. Stan studied engineering, and only learned Polish and German. He listens to the enemy pilots on their radios, and tells us Poles what they are doing. That is one reason the Polish Squadron does so well in the air. Stan sometimes shouts orders to the Nazis in German to confuse them. Sad for the English though. I listen to Stan, translate commands to the English pilots and make my squadron follow me. Sometimes it works.

Last summer it worked very well. Now we do more escort duty. Sometimes we are attacking, not only defending like last year."

Sheila got up to use the ladies' room at the back of the pub.

Jan leaned forward, "You have a very interesting face. You are always studying what is happening. I don't know if I should seduce you or tell you all my problems."

Agnes drew in her breathe. Not a pilot, not a pilot. "Well, start with your problems, and we can go from there," she offered.

Jan laughed. "That is a relief. I don't think you would be easy to seduce. That is a compliment. I am too serious for being in pubs. I would rather be alone than go to parties. But being alone is also not very good. Memories come back. We lost everything – family, country, friends. So, I come here just to be with people. Not to talk, just not be alone. It is difficult to explain."

"Oh, I understand. I'm the same way!" Agnes said in surprise and relief. "I've lost family and too many friends as well. Though I still have my country, I think. I have become afraid to get close to someone anymore."

"Yes. And here, in war, everything is too fast. Friendships usually take more time to grow than we have. The girls here in the pub usually only want to be one-night friends. I like to take time to learn about someone. Can we be good long-time friends?"

"Sounds fine," Agnes replied.

The month of the nursing exchange went quickly. Uxbridge Infirmary was merging with a WAAF hospital. The military nurses were involved with the merger even after their shifts were over, leaving Agnes with more free time. She spent that time with Jan and Stan. She didn't want to say that she was falling in love, she just knew that she wanted to be with Jan all the time. There was always something to talk about, to share. They focused on the present; the future was not discussed. It seemed too superstitious.

Returning to London was more difficult than she expected, but at least she was back in her familiar world. On the first day back in London, she signed papers making Arrow Tea Company into a trusteeship under the management of the Shelfords. She would remain the head of the company without needing to run it. Most of the business was suspended by war (importing anything was minimal, what with disruptions in shipping as well as rationing), it seemed an easy thing to do. Tea was still being bought and sold, with India and Ceylon still in British hands, and the company was doing well.

That night she and the Shelfords had dinner at the De Wever's house. Both families had 'adopted' her as their extra daughter. The De Wevers had a letter from Ellie.

"It took six weeks to get to us, but at least it got here," Mrs. De Wever said. "Those censors must be working overtime. Anyway, she says that her household is quite large, but adjusting to Occupation. Your wedding gift helps her put on shows at schools and church, telling stories and fairy tales in costume. And Wim is growing quickly. We miss them so much."

"I remain surprised that with all her language studies, her Dutch writing is still very poor," commented Mr. De Wever.

"May I see the letter?" asked Agnes. Something he just said triggered a thought.

Mrs. De Wever handed her the letter. "It's in Dutch."

"That's all right," Agnes said, taking the thin sheet of paper with its very small handwriting. Then she took a pencil and paper. For half an hour, she sat in a corner and just studied the letter and scribbled.

"Sorry, but this is important," Agnes finally stood up and said. "She used a code we devised while we were in school. That's why her writing seems odd. She says that her brother Ben is NSB, and that Allied agents are being caught because they have the wrong clothes and papers. Can the Dutch people here do something about that?"

Mrs. De Wever, stunned, looked at the letter. "What code? How did it get through?"

"Perhaps because it is so simple. It is in English inside the Dutch letter. Maybe we can continue to use it," suggested Agnes. "I'll help you form a reply, if you want."

"Absolutely," Mr. De Wever said. "We can tell her that her information will be passed on. Can we do that?" Mrs. De Wever wrote a draft letter in Dutch, then Mr. De Wever and Agnes put the code in the text. It was sent the next day.

There was a strange wartime normal in London and all of England. Germans were bombing English cities, and the Allies were retaliating with raids over Germany. The bombers ruled the skies, fighters escorted them every day. Agnes thought of Jan every time she heard planes overhead.

Jan came to London with Stan whenever they were free. Aunt Charlotte was eager to see Agnes' new friends; Agnes was returning to her normal self with them around. Grieving for her parents, but that was moving into the back of her mind.

Agnes, as tour guide, took the brothers around the city. They went to the noonday concerts at the National Gallery. They ate at restaurants where the RAF Polish uniforms made the brothers into heroes of the Battle of Britain, as it was now called. Agnes was happy to be with Jan. Stan came as their self-appointed bodyguard and chaperone. He insisted that it was to improve his English. And he found humor wherever they went.

When she was off-duty, Agnes often went out to Northolt and the Flying Pig. She had made several friends among the pilots and the nurses. While there, she stayed at the women's barracks, which began to feel like another home.

She could relax and be almost carefree. At St. Bart's, all was serious. She was promoted to shift matron, and continued to act like her domineering mother. She got away with it because she was good at emergency care, and because Dr. Beech gave her the freedom to do so. It didn't help her make friends, though.

Dr. Beech kept up his push for military nursing. But then, quite suddenly, he switched his approach. "Why not medical school, right here at St. Barts? You could probably teach some of the courses." It wasn't a question; it was a challenge.

"Thanks, but no," Agnes replied.

Jan met her at the Sickly Doctor. The pub now had half-stone, half-wood walls, a metal roof, real tables, and an odd collection of chairs. The floor was as smooth as dirt can be. All of the construction materials came from local piles of rubble, costing the pub's owner virtually nothing. The labor had been donated by pub regulars.

Jan agreed with Dr. Beech's idea. "If you are already doing a doctor's job, why not?"

"Just no," Agnes said. "Besides, after this war is over, I might have to give up nursing entirely to run my family's company. I don't need more choices."

"Well, I am asking you to make a choice right now," Jan said. "Would you be my guest at a special dinner next week? It is given by the Polish Government here in London. It will be a combination debutante ball and awards dinner. Very formal. We need a break from all this."

Agnes, thought, no harm in that. Besides, it might be fun after all this time to get dressed again and see what a wartime ball might be like. "I would love to," she replied.

Now, what to wear – maybe I can borrow something from Maggie that Emmy's sister Ruby can alter at her new shop. A new dress to celebrate the opening of the new shop was ordered, and included a matching hair piece. Simple, wartime chic.

CHAPTER 18
July, 1941, Agnes

The Polish banquet transported Agnes to another country. It was on a par with English royal events. She wore a rust-brown chiffon gown with some of the jewelry that her mother gave her. She sat with Jan and Stan Novak and some other pilots with their dates. Their blue RAF uniforms were professionally cleaned, with added braided shoulder cords and medals received from the Polish and British governments. She realized that Jan and Stan were well-known and well-respected by their countrymen. Jan was considered special and several people wanted to talk with him. Most of the conversation was in Polish. That was fine with her. She liked watching other people and their body language.

Dinner was very tasty, though according to Stan, "not like home. Rationing is bad for parties. Someday, you come to Poland for real food."

Then came the speeches. Agnes sat there politely dreaming, quietly thankful that there was a break in the nightly bombing. Suddenly, Stan poked her. Jan was standing up and walking towards the head table. There was a speech that seemed to be about Jan, who remained standing at attention. The room erupted in clapping and a large blue sash was placed over Jan's shoulder. More clapping, and a medal cross hanging from a purple ribbon was pinned to the sash. The same medal was awarded five more times to Stan, the other pilots, and two civilians, though without the blue sash. Now came more cheers and a standing ovation, followed by the singing of the national anthem. Agnes felt overwhelmed. "He is now national hero, very special," Stan explained proudly.

"Well, so are you," Agnes pointed to Stan's medal. He shrugged.

The second half of the evening allowed the younger generation a chance to have some fun. The older couples danced a few stately waltzes; the young jumped up for jazz and fox trots. Some couples, like Jan and Agnes, stayed on the dance floor for the whole night. The next day would be hard for both of them, but they didn't care. Tonight was a time to celebrate. She was not sure how much longer her 'no pilot' philosophy was going to last.

A few days' later, Maggie called. She wanted to see Agnes and tell her something important. They met at the Ritz, their favorite restaurant, for afternoon catching up. Agnes assumed that it had to be about Nigel.

"So, when's the big day?" Agnes asked.

"In four weeks," Maggie beamed. "We have been trying to find the date ever since he proposed and we finally got leave at the same time. Mid-August, I know, the worst part of the summer. But we have enough time to plan for it. We shall use the Hillford village church, then reception at the house. Hubert's wife Alice and my soon-to-be sister-in-law Chloe are to be attendants, and of course you will be my maid of honor."

"What do we wear?" asked Agnes. "I really don't have many outfits. Between the bombing of our house and wearing only nursing uniforms or street clothes, I'm a bit challenged."

"Well, what did you wear to Jan's big dinner? Maybe Ruby can make you something new or alter one of my dresses," Maggie said.

"Another new dress from Ruby, I think. Meanwhile, is Nigel in town?" asked Agnes. "Jan and I want to take you two for dinner in celebration. And Nigel has yet to meet Jan," Agnes added.

"Next week, then," Maggie answered. "Jan is your 'real deal', then?"

Agnes just gave her a look as she raised her tea cup.

The middle of August was tropical. Agnes dreamt that she was in the film "The Road to Zanzibar." She woke up in a jungle, wishing for a winter day. She lay on top of the thin sheet, her blanket tossed on the floor. Today, she was traveling to Oakstone for Maggie and Nigel's wedding. Her small traveling case was packed. Her new peach-colored evening gown, a new pastel linen dress for the wedding, plus hats and accessories had been sent ahead. After a quick breakfast, she called a taxi. London had been hit again by a night of bombing, but she and the taxi driver hardly reacted to the sights of destruction. Weaving through rubble was normal. When she reached the train station, she was ready for a bath.

Jan was waiting for her at the Northolt train station. He jumped on the train heading to Oxford. She waved and he found her, quickly sitting as the train began to move. She was euphoric. Nigel and Jan had enjoyed each other, meaning that she and Maggie would continue seeing each other. And, Jan was taking an assignment as a flight instructor, which would remove him from the battle line.

She pointed out landmarks along the Thames River Valley as they travelled westward. The Shelfords' chauffer was waiting for them at the station. They rode through Hillford to Oakstone.

The large arched gate in the driveway and flowering shrubs framed the house from a distance. She could sense that Jan was impressed by the beauty of the place. And, Agnes thought, just wait until you meet the family themselves, my family too.

Lady Shelford looking amazingly composed and cool as she welcomed them. "We have lovely electric fans in each room to keep the air moving," she directed them into the sitting room. Maggie came into the room just minutes later, as did a maid with tea and shortbread.

"Lunch in about an hour, but have something right now. Then off to your rooms to freshen up." Maggie realized that it was her first time saying this, just as it had been said to her before.

A parade of guests arrived throughout the day. Additional maids were hired to attend to the guests, and Agnes was grateful that she had some help. Her hair, always impossibly curly, was totally out of control because of the hot and humid weather. Fortunately, her temporary maid was a wonderful hairdresser, as well as good with other wardrobe matters.

Dinner was casual, adapting to the heat. Day dresses and skirts were acceptable, and everyone was grateful at that announcement.

Agnes' hair was pinned back and somewhat tamed by a large bow. It reminded her of her nurse's cap, but was far lovelier. Jan wore a borrowed civilian suit that made him look even handsomer than ever.

At the end of dinner, Maggie's father announced the wedding schedule. "The church service tomorrow will be at eleven, then a leisurely procession back to the house. Local weather promises to be cooler tomorrow." (That brought a great sigh of relief.) "The wedding breakfast, and later Tea, will be served on the side lawn where you see those tents on the side lawn. Then, afternoon free, evening formal supper, with dance music to follow. The bride and groom will leave early the next day.

"We will follow the war-time rationing to the best of our abilities. I give special thanks to Lord and Lady Drummond for graciously bringing venison and wild boar meat from their hunting park. Most of the fowl, fruits, and vegetables are from Oakstone and the village of Hillford. Our neighbors, Lord and Lady Forsworth, supplied most of the milk, cream, butter, and cheese. And of course, Shell's Bakery provided the breads and cakes. And of course, the flowers were grown and cared for by the Oakstone gardeners."

Applause followed. Lord Drummond offered a toast to the bride and groom, after which the guests broke into conversational groups over sherry and port.

Agnes and Jan mingled with the other guests, listening and telling stories, and meeting new people. Some old family friends offered belated condolences to her about her parents. She leaned on Jan during those moments. So many people had died in the war, she had put her own personal sadness behind her, especially for Maggie's joyful celebration.

I wonder what my own wedding will be like, Agnes thought. It might be hard to put together a grand party with no parents and no home. For the time being, that was far off, not even a fiancé. Well, not yet. The casual chatter brought her back to the present. After a last glass of sherry and a late evening stroll with Jan, she went to her room and slept soundly.

Agnes woke up late the next morning. Her maid had to work quickly. Between bites of toast and sips of tea, Agnes washed and dressed in a mid-length rose-colored linen dress. A wide pre-war headband held her hair in place. The other members of the bridal party wore similar summer dresses and headbands. Chloe's boys hadn't decided yet how to behave. Their grandmother and a nanny would figure out what to do with them after the ceremony.

Agnes arrived downstairs after breakfast had been cleared away, but did get a quick second cup of tea. She nodded to the gathering of last night's guests, and watched those who were arriving barely in time for the service. She saw the De Wevers arrive and went over to them.

Mrs. De Wever spoke to Agnes on the way to the church. "Thanks for breaking the code. We didn't know about it and Ellie has been using it since Christmas. Nothing urgent or dangerous, but it is a wonderful extra line of communication."

The wedding service at the church was shortened due to the continued heat and the crowd took their time strolling back to the estate for the afternoon's reception. The people in the village wanted to greet the new couple and offered everyone a drink of water and best wishes. A light breeze arrived at Oakstone just as the first guests stepped back onto the lawn.

Agnes and Jan walked through the estate gardens later that day by themselves. Jan was wearing his dress uniform just as he had for the Polish celebration. He took off the blue sash with its medals and gave it to her.

"I don't want this at Northolt. Please keep this safe for me," he said. He put his hand in his pocket. "And I'd like you to wear this whenever you can. I got the idea from Nigel."

It was a pendant copied from the design of his Polish Medal of Valor, together with a thin gold chain necklace so she would wear it under her nurse's uniform. "I know what you think of being attached to a pilot, so this is a 'best friend' gift. Perhaps more someday, I promise."

With that, he gave her a kiss that made her nearly too weak to stand. It wasn't like any kiss they had exchanged before. She allowed her emotional wall to dissolve, as she accepted both the ring and the kiss. She was filled with feelings of great fear, and even greater feelings of love.

Agnes felt that she was perhaps one of the happiest people in England. Sure, the war news was dismal. Greece and Yugoslavia had fallen to the Germans. Japan was taking over big areas of Asia. Yet, Nigel and Jan saw hope in the progress being made by Allies in North Africa. Jan was sure that the Germans couldn't conquer the Soviet Union. It was clear that the United States would enter the war soon – too many of their merchant ships being sunk by German submarines. None of that was important to Agnes. At least when she was with Jan.

Back in London, Agnes tended to her patients with their normal complaints and injuries from the never-ending bombing. Her nursing colleagues were joining military units and going off to Singapore, India, Africa. Well, she had her taste of military life and was happy to remain in London at St. Bart's. Jan's transfer to the training squadron was only two weeks away. Seeing each other after his transfer needed to be worked out. It would be at least three hours away by train, if the trains were running.

She was talking about some of those things with Dr. Beech over lunch at the hospital canteen. The doctor glanced up as the door opened. He stood slowly, his face going rigid. Agnes looked at him, and turned to see Stan.

He stood there, his eyes red from crying. Jan. Stan moved forward just as Agnes crumpled. He knelt down to her, and they held each other and cried.

"When? How?" Agnes finally asked.

"Early this morning," said Stan, accepting a glass of water and sitting down at a table. "Squadron went out last night, protecting bomber mission. Then, on return, Germans attack. Jan and three other Spits hit, but come home. Planes all crash, pilots all dead. No chance to save."

Dr. Beech went over to a telephone and talked with someone. He came back, calmly saying, "Sir, take Agnes to the airfield now. ARP Warden MacFagin is waiting outside for both of you."

Stan and Agnes nodded, and left, supporting each other. At the entrance, Weejun stood next to an ambulance. "Oh Lassie, here we are again. We have no luck, me and you."

"Thanks, Weejun," Agnes managed. "This is Stan, Jan's brother."

Weejun nodded before driving them to the airfield. He recognized Stan from times Agnes brought the two brothers on a tour of the Smithfield Market. He went with them directly to RAF Station Hospital where a small morgue was set up. With her experience with burn patients, she wasn't sure she wanted to see Jan. Stan went in first, came out, and said quietly, "It is ok, not bad to see."

He was right, Jan looked more asleep than dead.

"What killed him?" she asked an orderly. "He wasn't burned?"

"No, either smoke or a sudden altitude change," the orderly said. "Lack of oxygen either way. I'm really sorry, he was one of our best."

Stan nodded. He took Agnes and Weejun over to the officers' quarters. Some of the squadron pilots were carefully packing Jan's trunk. They asked Stan what to do with it.

"I'll take it to my friend's house," Agnes heard herself saying. "It's not far from here, and we can look through his things later."

Stan nodded. Weejun nodded. The men carried the trunk to Weejun's ambulance. Then the three of them and the squadron's pilots went to the Flying Pig for a beer. They wanted to stay together. At this time of day, the pub was quiet.

Stan asked the next question. "Where we take Jan now?"

Agnes thought for a moment. "We can ask the Shelfords if the Hillford village church is available for a funeral. There is a cemetery there, too. Oh, but he is – was – Catholic?"

"No problem," Stan said. "Not too Catholic. It is okay I think. Do you stay here tonight? More men are back and want to say something. We want to be together when we are sad."

Agnes nodded. "I can stay at the nurse's barracks."

Phone calls to the barracks, the Shelfords, the church, and Dr. Beech were made. The funeral could be the next day at the village church. Agnes was wearing pendant. She vowed never to take it off.

Weejun waited for Agnes. "Do you want me to stay? You know I'll do anything for you. You helped me turn my life around. Whatever you need, you know I'll do."

Agnes looked at him, "No I'll be fine. I'm in your debt, too, really. After my parents and now this."

Weejun looked lost, "We're both on our own, Lassie. We'll have to take care of each other. I'll leave you now and come back tomorrow for the funeral." With that he touched his hat and left for London.

One week later, Agnes entered Dr. Beech's office. He spoke softly, "Well." He paused. "Well? Do you want to come back yet? Or at all? This is rather difficult for you, and I am truly sorry for all you have lost. We've been here before, haven't we?"

Agnes thought how hard it was to tell him her decision. He had been a rock she leaned on. He had encouraged everything she had done, including her appointment as Night Matron 'at her young age.' He knew before she did how she felt. He had been her acting father for five years.

"I'm leaving. I just signed up with the Princess Mary's."

"Air Force, then. Too bad for the Queen Alexandria's, and the WRENs." He didn't seem surprised.

"I have more connections with the RAF: Maggie, Nigel, and Jan for starters. I feel I owe them in some way." She ventured a joke, "and besides, the Army has all that mud, and I rather dislike being seasick."

"We'll miss you, but you will always have a home here at St. Bart's. I'll make sure that you get a good assignment with the fly boys."

"Thank you, Doctor."

She packed her spartan quarters, called a small delivery company, and sent her belongings out to Oakstone. Her body did all this without thinking, but then, there was very little emotion left for her to do much else. In fact, as she touched pendant, she decided never to get close to another person, loss was just too hard.

CHAPTER 19
October, 1941, Ellie

They had their system to surviving Nazi occupation. Multiple systems. Every household had their own. It was important. Systems and routines kept people disciplined and sane in an insane world.

On this day, Dora was the first to leave the Van Horn household. She was an expert at getting food, using the seven ration books allotted to them as a start. She tried to be in the first group of shoppers at any store. She paid, bargained, and traded for whatever was available. A very serious and tough dealmaker, she made sure that her family was fed.

Today Dora was lucky. She brought home a whole kilo of pork. Some of it was fat, but that was as valuable as the meat. Most of the meat would be in today's meal – the remaining meat and fat was for tomorrow.

When she first came out of prison, she hardly smiled. Now she cheerfully went marketing and made friends among the other shoppers. She listened to each day's gossip – who was taken by the Germans, which areas were damaged or destroyed by bombing raids, what were the latest rule changes. Of course, the Van Horns listened to the news on their hidden radio, but Dora never let on that she knew anything. She usually traded fluff information, but it was enough to keep her in the loop for more important news. She passed on everything to the Professor. Today, the 'friendly' policeman warned the shoppers of a *razzia*, a round-up of members of the Resistance or any men left in the city who could be sent to Germany for factory work. One would happen this evening.

The second person out of the house was Ellie. She placed Wim on the seat of the theater wagon. She was grateful that Pieter and Mr. Brinker had transformed the trunk into a wagon. She pushed the wagon around the city to wherever she performed. She was famous for her presentations of fairy tales, folk stories, and short plays. Everyone enjoyed the escape from the harsh realities of German occupation. Plus, the wagon reminded her of Agnes and Maggie. Today, she planned to tell the story of Cinderella, handing out the roles of fairy godmothers and dancers at the ball to the children at school.

No one suspected that dreaming, sweet, always smiling Ellie also did minor work for the local resistance movement. She passed information from the school parents and teachers to Professor Willems, and supplied some of Pieter's chemicals to his former students who created inks for counterfeit documents. Working with the chemicals made it feel as if Pieter was still around. Her memories of Pieter were contained in their wedding album and two small photos on her bedstead. One photo was taken during their first summer together when they took a family holiday to the islands in the Biesbosch region of the Maas River. The other was taken at a birthday party for an old friend. A third photograph was the family portrait from Wim's Christening that was displayed on a table in the sitting room.

Professor Willems was the third person to leave the house. Three days each week, he rode the bus to the prison where he gave his 'required educational lectures' to the prisoners. He tutored a few men who were working towards school certificates while he exchanged information with the resistance leaders being held there. He sent on the information from them, as well as Dora, Gran, Ellie, to the next level of people. The kindly, genteel retired professor was not part of the local Resistance – he had other ways to get news to the right place.

He spent his afternoons with Wim, who was nearly two years old. He played magic tricks with Wim who loved watched things disappear and return from thin air. They took long walks along the canals to watch the birds, plants, and fish.

Mr. Brinker, left to have morning 'coffee' with friends before starting his never-ending daily chores. The root vegetables had to be stored in the garden sheds, along with the clean-up from the summer, and the planting of winter crops. Not forgetting continual repairs of the house and tools. Always something, never the right supplies for the jobs at hand.

The fertile Dutch soil provided farmers with great harvests, only to have them whisked away to feed Germany. Every Dutch home had a *moestuin*, or vegetable garden, a necessity with the slim ration allotments. Mr. Brinker was using every bit of his knowledge and skill to keep his family fed. He was a quiet man, listening intently, rarely contributing to a conversation. People were complicated. Animals, plants, and machines were simple. His friends could rely on his help when they asked, he asked for help when he needed it, and that was that.

Mrs. Brinker stayed home, enjoying her solitude as she straightened up the house. She didn't like going out. Outside was too open, no security, no place to be comfortable. Inside the house, she was secure enough to be chatty, relaxed, and good company for the other three women living in the house. She started making a soup made from last night's leftover vegetables, hoping that Dora would find some meat. She talked with her neighbors while shaking out the carpets on the front stoop, letting them come to her, of course. Her friends understood, and visited her often.

By lunch, Dora, Ellie, and Wim were back home. Mr. Brinker came inside from the garden with a couple of apples. They all had heard about the *razzia* planned for this evening. *Razzias* filled everyone with fear that loved-ones might be swept up and never seen again. Mr. Brinker and Prof. Willems were too old to be taken, but they knew several men who would hide or try to escape for England. Luckily for most, the word went out early enough for people to go underground, at least for a short while.

Gran arrived late that afternoon from her regular visit to Wassenaar. Her friends tried to meet every two weeks to stay in touch. Two had been forced to evacuate their seaside homes because the Germans were building shore installations. They moved in with relatives who lived further inland, a few kilometers nearer to Leiden. Two, like Gran, saw their grand homes used by German military officers or bureaucrats, and chose to move in with family. One still lived in her house after the Germans took it over. That is where Gran had been on this visit. Smiling at the German occupier and going about their own time together, chatting and playing cards. They missed their previous social life, but had created a new one. Gran was determined to carry on a normal life. At times, she even walked the ten kilometers. Four hours in each direction in good weather, not difficult. She didn't think of herself as too old for the exercise. Besides, she loved trading the gossip at each end of the trip.

Mrs. Brinker and Dora started the evening meal, saving a small piece of meat for tomorrow's lunchtime soup. They gathered a few potatoes from the garden's autumn harvest. Tomorrow the whole family would work on preserving another batch of root vegetables for the winter.

Just as the family sat down for dinner, there was a knock on the door. Too early for the *razzia,* and too late for friends and neighbors to stop by. Mr. Brinker opened the door. In walked – no, paraded – Ben De Wever. Ellie looked at her younger brother in disgust. His NSB uniform was so out of place in her house. How he could be a member of the Dutch pro-Nazi paramilitary was shocking, sad, and fearful all at the same time.

"Hello, dear sister," he beamed. "I'm in town and thought I'd stop by for a bite to eat."

"Hello," she said in her most proper manner. "We don't have much, due to the rationing imposed by your friends. In fact, our best produce, I hear, has been stolen and sent to Germany. But since you are family, we'll give you something."

Without so much as a thank you, Ben sat down at the head of the table. Gran said nothing, but was visibly angry. No one said anything to him or dared look him in the eye.

Ben carried on a one-sided conversation about all the wonderful things the Germans were doing. He tried unsuccessfully to make friends with his nephew, little Wim. The meal, though meager, dragged on seemingly for hours. No one responded to him with more than two or three words at a time. To his credit, Wim sensed the mood in the rook and didn't react to Ben. The atmosphere was tense.

"I think you three," Ellie said quietly and nodded to the Brinkers and Dora, "should take Wim to visit the Poldermans. They might have some extra fruit we can use for dessert." They nodded, stood up, taking Wim by the hand, and left.

"Why are you really here, Ben?" Ellie asked after they left, both hands flat on the table.

"There is a *razzia* tonight, and I thought I might warn my favorite sister," Ben offered. His friendliness was obviously false. Ellie was very close to losing her temper.

"Well, we should all be safe," Ellie replied. "No one here is eligible."

"What about Pieter," Ben's smile was fading. "I would think that he might be worried about being picked up."

Ellie's hands became fists which she slammed on the table as she stood up quickly.

"That is enough!" she said loudly. "We haven't seen Pieter for a full year now. You know that. I have asked you to use your connections to find him. And the authorities in town. A lot of good that has been. Fine and marvelous German administration! A year! And still no news. He is lost in your bureaucratic system that is supposed to be so great!"

The room was silent. Ben had never seen his sister this angry. He ventured, "maybe he went underground and escaped."

"Pieter?" Ellie looked bewildered and her voice was high pitched. "Pieter, the non-adventurous professor? Taking on such a daring trip? Hardly! He couldn't remember to put money in his pocket for lunch." Ellie's voice grew louder, her face redder. "He went missing the day that the university was shut down. How many people were sent away that day? How many have still not been accounted for? Ben – think – hardly anyone was even planning to leave back then. We were trying to adjust to occupation and live day by day, just like now. Admit it – your German friends lost Pieter in some paper jungle. You want Pieter? You have him! You find him!" Ellie was shouting without taking a breath.

Gran, Professor Willems, and Ben stared at Ellie. This was not the Ellie they knew. She was always so sweet, seemingly out of touch with the real world. At best, she tried to lighten a heavy mood with a smile or a rosy comment. No one had never seen her lose her temper, or even show angry. She had never raised her voice, let alone shout.

Ellie herself was surprised at her outburst. She used her total concentration to stay calm for the sake of all the rest of them. Then, out of the corner of her eye, she felt like she was on stage at school. Lady Macbeth's mad scenes all over again. Well, she thought, my real emotions are better than Lady M's, whose evil and guilty words came from a very different set of emotions. I'd better speed this up. Ben has got to leave, and fast, before little Wim and the others come back.

"Get out of this house now, Ben, and do not come back. Ever." Ellie walked towards him and got as close to him as she could. She was nearly hysterical (really) as she added, "Go back to your new friends. No wonder they took you into the NSB. You aren't even civil to your own family. Do not ever come back here. This is not your house and you will never be welcome."

Ben was so startled that he backed up in fear that she might do herself (or him) some harm. He tried to regain his composure, looked at Gran who was equally angry, turned, and left the house. "Just be careful, all of you," he said reining in his anger and discomfort.

Ellie stepped forward and closed the door. She paused, her head leaning against the wooden door frame. She turned around, visibly shaken, and said, "I hope he got the message. I can't ever do this again. Well, maybe for Pieter." She gave them a weak smile. She walked slowly over to a chair and fell into it.

Gran came to her and gave her a hug, Professor Willems patted her on her shoulder. No sooner than they began to breathe normally again, the door opened, and Dora, the Brinkers, and Wim entered. Dora noticed the contorted faces of the three people in the sitting room. Unsure of what had happened, except that Ben was gone, Dora asked, "We waited until he left — what happened?"

"Not tonight," Gran answered. "Just know that Ben is now longer welcome here."

Mrs. Brinker and Dora cleaned up the left-over dinner dishes. Dora bravely asked. "Is he disowned because of his politics?"

"Something like that," Gran suddenly looked and felt far older than ever before. She ushered Wim and Ellie to bed before going to her own room. To her, Ben was dead. Worse, he was alive and no longer family.

Ellie didn't sleep. She missed Pieter so much. As much as she was utterly exhausted by her outburst, she heard every sound that night: planes overhead, traffic, the whistles and shouts of the *razzia*, Gran's muted crying, and finally the delivery people at their early morning rounds. She knew that nothing would be totally right again in her world.

Dora came in to get Wim dressed and bring him down stairs for breakfast. Ellie pretended to be asleep with her back to the door. By mid-morning, Gran came into her room. "Time to get up. Now." Ellie barely moved as Gran helped her get dressed and brought her downstairs. The blackout curtains in the sitting room were pushed back so the light from the street shone in, brightening up both the room and the mood of those inside. Mrs. Brinker handed Ellie a cup of treasured real coffee as she sat down in her chair by the window.

"I guess I ought to apologize for my behavior last night," Ellie offered, "but I didn't realize how angry I had become. Oh, and Mrs. Brinker, incredible thanks. You were very brave to go out last night."

Mrs. Brinker nodded.

"You just said what we all felt. I was actually rather proud of you standing up to Ben. He has always been such a bully," Gran said gently, and then added with a chuckle, "He couldn't get a word in. It was well deserved."

"He'll be back — and he'll be vengeful," Ellie looked out the window.

"We'd better be ready," Gran reassured her. "We have some time before he or any of his cronies come by again. Your normally sweetness, plus the potential of another tantrum, will make him think. And word will get around. We just keep to our regular routines. I think I heard the King or Churchill say, 'keep calm and carry on.' Exactly what we must do."

"Maybe, but," Ellie hesitated.

"No buts," Gran said. She realized that they had just broken their promise only to speak in Dutch. It would not be good if Wim started to talk in English until the Germans were out of their country for good.

Just then the postman arrived. There was a letter from Ellie's parents in England. It was dated two months ago, and was in an envelope from the Swiss Red Cross agency that handled overseas mail. She opened it and read her mother's report of Maggie's wedding, waking up and shedding the remnants of last night's outburst. The letter that both Maggie and Agnes sent their regards, particularly Agnes, remembering their school year promise to stay in contact with each other.

Ellie wondered if that meant that the letter might have a coded message in it. They hadn't used it up until now. She found a pencil and a scrap of paper. She copied the important letters from the original message. She read her new message over several times, not ready to believe what it said. She jumped up, shouting and dancing in circles.

Dora, Gran, and Mrs. Brinker came running. Had Ellie really lost her mind after last night?

"Pieter is safe!" Ellie shouted as she hugged all three women. "He's in London. He got there in July. Our code works! Agnes broke it, so they all know that Ben is, well, Ben. They just started using it now with this news. And everyone else is fine."

There was a great sigh of relief at the news, especially after the previous evening. Pieter was safe, the De Wevers were in good health, Maggie was married, and even Agnes was moving up in the hospital's nurse's ranking order. There was a future to look forward to after all.

Mrs. Brinker brought them back to reality. They had to plan for the next visit from Ben or any of his colleagues.

"Where should we hide the radio?" Ellie began the conversation. "And what should we do with the chemicals that we use for cleaning paper that gets used to create forged documents?"

"My theater props should be handy," suggested Ellie.

The Professor smiled, "I can revert to my youthful career as a magician and create double containers for the chemicals. It's time that we make those chemicals less tempting for little Wim anyway."

Mr. Brinker offered, "I can make a few more hiding places in the sheds or maybe even here in the house. In fact, Mr. Pieter and I started doing some of that before he left."

Dora spoke with total honesty, "Our true personalities are so strange, we can use them as they are – no one will believe them anyway."

All done in three days. The family earned a good night's rest.

A week later, a pair of German soldiers (without Ben) came to the house to question them and search the house. General inquires, they said. Ellie continued to insist that Pieter must be in German hands.

Ellie proudly showed them her theater wagon. Her theater performances were entertainment already sanctioned by the Occupational Government. Would they like to see her legal permits and look through her wagon of props, makeup, and costumes?

Gran showed them the start of her "latest" knitted scarf. (Her first lesson had been just one week ago from Mrs. Brinker). Would they like to see the rest of her collection of used wool yarn, rewound and ready for new projects? He basket was overflowing with balls and wads of yarn. The soldiers never found the crystal radio hidden in a hollow ball covered with glued-on wool at the bottom of the basket.

Gran's upper-class friends? Really, none of us know or care a wit about politics. We just gossip and play cards like the old days. My room? Overflowing with clothing and pictures. She had jars of make-up on her dressing table that no one expected were actually containers of inks for document forgery. Cup of imitation tea downstairs?

Professor Willems. Ah, the prison teaching. The Occupation officials said local and national rules still apply. Teaching in prisons is required. Education gives criminals an honest path to good careers. Being retired, I no longer have contact with many people in society at large. Besides, the university is closed and any students I knew went back home or are working in German factories. I don't do anything much, just read and lecture about reading. If you would like to create a group to discuss German literature, I can help.

Dora simply said nothing. I never went to school, can barely read anything. Yes, I was in prison, and was taken on as help here when housing was too difficult to find. The Van Horns felt sorry for me. My work is non-stop, so no time to do anything but what they ask.

The Brinkers told much the same story, their employers were in Canada leaving them without work. Ellie was kind enough to give them work and a home. Let us show you the kitchen and the gardens as they are. All inside space is being used by the large family in smallish quarters. Sure, lots of jars of spices. The family was used to foreign foods, and the spices helped them eat the poor food they got on ration tickets. The sheds just held vegetables, like everyone else's sheds. Fertilizers and seed boxes contained just those things. By then the soldiers were bored and left, uncovering nothing.

With that, the Van Horns returned to their daily habits. The following day was just like any day in wartime Holland. Waiting for food, chatting with friends, helping neighbors where they could. While their radio continued to report grim news in whispers, Ellie wrote carefully coded letters to her parents.

Meanwhile, Pieter had arrived in England just after Maggie's wedding. He went to the offices of the Dutch government in exile to report his appearance. The Queen invited him to her office; her custom was to welcome her subjects individually as they arrived in England. After the initial paperwork was filed, the De Wevers were called. They had an emotional reunion, questions and answers tumbling together.

The Shelfords plus Lady Charlotte and Maggie, Agnes, and Emmy (Clive was now an Army doctor in Scotland) were invited. Pieter told them about his journey.

When the Germans took over The Netherlands last May, the Dutch military officers were placed in detention camps, and later released. Back at the university, Pieter secretly taught some students about special processes to make ink invisible and visible again. In November, after the university students went on strike, the German response was to shut down the university.

"I had to escape before I got rounded up," Pieter continued. "A friend of mine and I became 'divers' or 'England-travelers'. We had false papers. I became Andre Perrin, a French pharmacist. We stuffed money and other necessities in the linings of our clothes and used makeup and wigs as disguises. Thanks to Ellie, I had a bit of theater training. We traveled by train out of The Netherlands through Belgium and France with the help of friendly railroad workers and other underground networkers. Not too much trouble. We were given one contact name at a time along the escape route. We slept in convents, empty houses, city parks, churches, and small farmhouses. All along our papers were accepted. And when they weren't, we outran the officials.

"We made it to Switzerland. I signed in with the military attaché at the Dutch Embassy in Bern. The Swiss wanted to remain neutral, so all of us foreigners were placed in work camps. Not more than simple necessities, but safe. We were allowed to go to the local university, and I studied English. We dug drainage canals and did other hard labor, waiting for the time to leave. We finally got the chance to cross the Alps back into France, then across the Pyrenees into Spain. That wasn't so easy. There were fewer secure routes, and the mountains were a challenge in themselves, with pockets of snow still in late Spring. We were caught immediately after we crossed the border and wound up in a Spanish jail because we didn't have the right papers.

"Fortunately, the British in Gibraltar made regular visits to the jails to find people like us. We were brought to Gibraltar, given uniforms and some money. We waited for a ship to England. After landing here, we were sent to a British military camp. We were checked for security reasons and waited for assignments. I'm currently a civilian worker with the Defense Department working on code and message techniques. I do hope to get a military assignment soon."

"And Ellie?" Maggie asked.

"Your news is more recent than mine," Pieter replied. "All I know is that she has a houseful of fine people – her grandmother, Prof. Willems, Dora, and a couple who kept house for my parents. Most houses are filled with evacuees and other strangers and it isn't always friendly, so it is good that in our house, they all know each other well."

He added, "And, the theater trunk you gave us for our wedding is being put to good use. Ellie has a traveling children's show that she brings to schools and churches to tell folktales. Very entertaining. And a great public image to protect her and the family."

Pieter decided not to tell them that when he was in Switzerland, he had made two trips to The Netherlands on secret missions ordered by the Dutch Attaché in Bern. He brought information and spare radio parts to the Resistance in Amsterdam, and escorted people out of the country who needed to get to England. It was painful to be so close to home and not visit, but the risk and the emotional stress was too high.

He also didn't tell them of being shot, dislocating his shoulder when he jumped out of a train, the number of cold, hungry nights along the journey, or the exhausting nature of living in constant fear of being caught. The war was still a long way off from being over. Everyone needed good news, he thought, not reminders of pain and suffering.

PART THREE

CHAPTER 20
Early August, 1944, Agnes

Agnes was barely listening to her companions. They were having dinner in an orchard by a half-ruined farmhouse in the middle of Somewhere, Normandy, France. Summer in the pastoral countryside of Normandy should have been delightful. Quaint, with apple orchards, peaceful farms with cows and sheep. Villages with cafes. Wine and cheese. The dinner in her mind had dance music in the background, people in typical French regional costume, and abundant food and wine.

But that wasn't this Normandy. The orchards had been shredded by artillery shells, paths and roads had more potholes and rubble than smooth spots. Music was replaced by the sounds of metal – big tanks, trucks, jeeps, cannon, and smaller metal things like rifles, helmets, hollow gun shells. Virtually no life, no farm animals, nothing pleasant at all.

Farmhouses and entire villages were now merely broken walls poking out of piles of rubble and dust. Local people and animals were either exhausted, missing, or dead; many bodies and animal carcasses were lying unattended. If that wasn't enough, there were the smells – burning wood, rotting animals, gas and fuel fumes – if your nose hadn't become numb along with the rest of your senses.

And yet, local farmers like Renee and Pierre Dumont invited Allied soldiers to share meals with them as thanks for being liberated. Part of liberation was that RAF hospital stations were expected to help locals whenever possible.

Pierre and Renee were grateful to Agnes and her friends for treating Pierre's broken leg. When the roof of their house collapsed inward during one battle, Pierre was trapped by falling beams. The Dumonts were so welcoming that a friendship developed with the nurses. Agnes wished now that she had studied French with more interest, though sign language worked pretty well.

This evening, Agnes and Vera brought their new boss, Matron and RAF Squadron Leader Philippa Rangleton with them. They donated a sack of sugar and some tea to their farewell dinner. The hospital station cook was happy to give them the sugar after they treated him for a knife wound sustained in a fight. He would have been sent home if the brass found out about it. He added extra fresh fruit and jam to their package, which the girls passed along to Renee and Pierre.

Agnes turned back to listen to Vera. They had become good friends back in England where they had trained together in a medical unit to be sent with the Allied invasion forces. "Well girls, please explain what's been happening – from the beginning," Nurse Squadron Leader Philippa demanded, stopping their general dinner conversation. "You two! Nurses trained at St. Bart's and St. Thomas! You would think that the premier nursing schools in London would have produced better qualified professionals. For the two of you to get this far, really." She gave a snort.

"Sorry," was all the two could utter.

"Oh, I'm not finished. I was transferred to this medical unit after being with the same hospital team from England to Africa to Italy, and I was ready to go home. But the brass said you needed experienced leadership. They said your unit was new to battlefield conditions and needed a veteran after your commanding officer was killed in a German attack. I can see why," She ran out of breath.

Agnes spoke up, "Our supplies ran out and we needed to do something. We had these boys to take care of. When that last convoy was destroyed by the Germans, we had to improvise."

"What will happen now?" asked Vera.

"First, no more taking table legs from civilians for splints. That is stealing from the locals, even if they have no use for table legs without a table. Same with bed linen. Second, no more leaving wounds open to the air – or covering them in tea bags. Third, no more brandy used as disinfectant. I daren't go on," Philippa continued to snort. "Even in Africa, we could find decent and proper supplies. Well, other than water."

"Ma'am," Vera said with quiet confidence, "growing up as a Girl Guide in Canada, I learned a lot of forest survival skills, including first aid. I searched for anything that was the right size for splints. And the bed sheets we found were used to tie the splints, not close to any open wounds. Agnes knew about tea used in preventing infection, so we used some of her collection of tea bags. Keeping wounds open until proper surgery could be performed was our choice, based on what was happening."

"We had to consider the high risk of infection," Agnes ventured, "because a farmer had hidden those soldiers in his barn before they came to us. The dirt floor was, well, not very sanitary, what with cows and horses standing by. I didn't want to close the wound while it might be so unsterile. I wrote that on the airman's tag, so that the docs back home would understand."

"And your attempt at being me? Pretending to be a full commanding officer matron by taking and wearing my jacket?"

"Fully guilty," Agnes admitted, head down. "I was just so angry at the whole war, and not getting our supplies when the first convoy got hit though," She raised her head, looking defensive but not contrite, "Nevertheless, it worked. We had the supplies by nightfall."

"Be that as it may, it was totally irregular and impertinent. A punishable offense, impersonating an officer above your rank."

And here in comes – our trip back to England and return to civilian life, thought Agnes. Just a well, at this rate.

Their boss sat up straight. "If you think you will be sent home, forget it. We're too short-staffed as it is. But take this reprimand as it is given."

"Yes, Matron."

"Now, in your favor, both of you are quite calm under stress. I guess working in London made you both more battle-ready than expected. And your creative skills, regardless of how you got them, are, after all is said, quite useful in wartime. We nurses often ignore military protocols to get on with the job at hand. On-the-spot decisions are more the norm than standard procedures. I can totally overlook your first aid approach if seen as having no choice, and that bag of sugar, and the reason you have it, as well. Honestly, I might have done the same in both cases."

"With no further bother, therefore, I am making battlefield commissions – promotions – for you both. Flying Officers Agnes Fletcher and Vera Bartonsmith, you are now Flight Lieutenants. Rather funny, that the very reasons for your reprimands are the very reasons for your promotions.

"Now, the overall plan is that a small medical field station will stay here by this airstrip, but the full hospital station moves on. The next location will be the more permanent step in the evac system. Bartonsmith, you are taking over surgery theater. Fletcher, you'll have the triage and emergency area. You will continue forward after setting up the hospital station. Your promotions begin when we move out. I am finally going home. You two will be on your own."

"Yes, Matron," the two girls said, looking at each other and Philippa.

"Now, back to a growing friendship and enjoying our dinner. After which we shall find that pub that the Yanks have set up down the road. And please, call me Philippa," she rose carefully from her wobbly chair. "Let's celebrate those promotions and my escape from the Front."

The three nurses lifted their nearly finished glasses of wine. Pierre and Renee, who knew no English and were watching the entire conversation, sensed that something serious had been discussed. It was now resolved, so they lifted their glasses and joined the toast. Vera used her schoolgirl French to explain what had been discussed. They all felt at ease. Hugs all around as they said their goodbyes.

"Time for the pub," announce Philippa as they started walking. "Question for you Vera. How did you get into this? And what was that about backwoods scouting?"

"My brother and I joined up in Toronto," she answered. "He wanted to be a pilot in the RAF, and I came along to see what I could do. We were both Scouts and did the mandatory summer camp in northern Ontario. Rather tame, actually, but we thought it was a great adventure. My brother went to flight school at Duxford, so he was one of the first pilots to fly a Spitfire. I went to nurse training at St. Thomas. Then, with several of the girls in my class, I went into the Princess Mary's. That's why we're with the British, not the Canadian troops."

"And you, Agnes. Dr. Beech said that you were an excellent nurse with very high-grade instincts, as well as having quite a demanding presence. I have to agree. Where did that come from?" Philippa paused, "And why do you keep used tea? I realize that you have quite a stash of loose tea in your kit, so why the keeping of old tea in bags? We don't seem to be short of that elixir."

"My mother," Agnes said simply, with no emotion. "She never wasted anything and knew tea could still be brewed from the old gatherings. Most people find that a horror, but there it is. She told me about tea as an antiseptic.

"My tyrant side comes from her as well. It's how she directed the family business – and my upbringing. I vowed never to be like that. I was young when

I entered nursing, so her act became rather handy. Dr. Beech loved it when I bullied patients and staff into submission." Agnes had brief loving memories of Weejun.

Philippa nodded. "Dr. Beech loves to single out promising nurse and doctor students. Pushing and guiding at the same time. That's why I am here. Yes – also a St. Bart's nurse, encouraged by Dr. Beech. Soon I'll be back home, training up more girls for the front."

With that, Philippa walked into the pub. Funny, thought Agnes, the men still stand when we women walk in. Chivalry isn't quite dead.

The pub could have been anywhere. Here in the destroyed village, Agnes was reminded of the Sickly Doctor pub in London after the Blitz – half-bombed out walls, a few shaky tables, and a tarp for a roof. But as with all pubs with young patrons, it was loud, boisterous, and welcoming. The Allies were moving through the Normandy countryside and on toward Germany. The momentum of the war was shifting very subtly. Everyone knew that it wouldn't be any easier for a while, and both sides sensed it. Germany was slowly retreating, but not giving up. Pubs and partying in those conditions were a serious and necessary ritual.

"I hope we stay close to the Canadian Army," Vera tried to shout over the music and laughter.

"You might see some friends?" Agnes shouted back.

"Sure, and they have more food and supplies than the English, but --" Vera shouted over her shoulder as someone grabbed her hand and led her to the quickly cleared dance floor. Agnes felt someone tap her on the shoulder for a dance and there was no more chance to talk. The nurses were in great demand and stayed until closing time, dancing with as many of the men as possible. It felt good to have a few minutes of being carefree. The men under Allied Command – Dutch, Polish, Czech, Australians, Canadians, and of course

British. All had different ways of dancing to the same music. Keeps one alert while you unwind, she thought. Alert in a good way.

On their way back to their tent, Vera continued their last chat. "I think I have a boyfriend. We met back in England. Sam's part of the supply corps and travels around a bit. I get letters from him from all over. At first from England, now from southern France. He may come here. He is rather cute and very funny. Sometimes I feel guilty about dancing with total strangers instead of being true to Sam. I doubt if he would mind, though. He is enough of a flirt to be dancing with other girls. As long as we wind up together, we should be fine."

Agnes smiled. She was glad that Vera was happy. Inside, Agnes was still thinking about Jan after three years. She fingered the pendant he gave her. Modeled after his Polish medal of Valor, she touched it whenever she needed strength or courage or valor. She was determined not to have any more 'loves' in her life – she felt like a bad luck charm. First her parents, then Jan. Not to mention the men she had met either at St. Bart's Medical College or at the Flying Pig near Northolt Airfield. So many had died. Too many. Despite all that, she realized that she was finding more happy moments each day. Maybe her heart was finally healing.

"Changing the subject, I'll miss Pierre and Renee when we move on," Agnes said. "They have been so nice to us. Can we leave anything else with them when we go?"

"How do you begin to return their generosity of sharing their wine and fresh bread with us, especially when you know how dear it is to them?" Vera said. "Our own offerings are so minimal, and no one recently has asked for 'private' help like the cook. Our access to extras is rather limited."

"Except my unlimited tea supply. We could get something from the Canadians or Americans. They always have cigarettes and chocolate," Agnes thought out loud. "We'd better move fast. I hear that the Yanks are splitting off from us and moving south while we stay with Dempsey along the coast."

Arm in arm, the two girls continued into their tent for another night of exhausted sleep. They were so used to the constant noise of battle and planes overhead, they slept soundly.

Their RAF unit moved on to another location within the week. They were considered part of the Front Line battle groups. And the Front kept moving. Planes brought in supplies and ferried severely wounded soldiers back to England. Airfields and medical stations were required to keep moving with the line of combat. Soldiers with minor injuries went from battle-site first aid stations to recovery areas and back to the front line. The more seriously injured were stabilized and went to general hospitals in the region, well behind the fighting.

The very seriously wounded were sent home by train to hospital ship, or flown back to England from units like Agnes'. Medical teams like Agnes' worked a mix of advanced first aid and emergency surgery that helped the wounded men survive the half-hour flight to England. She liked the fast pace of patient care, the continual movement of the front line, and the rapid-fire thinking without waiting for routine to set in. All this in tents or temporary huts, making things happen with or without proper equipment. She had to constantly be creative, like using worn-out stockings or knitted pullovers to make slings for blood transfusion bags or filter bags for water to be boiled for drinking. Not quite pranks, though pranks had been good training.

Agnes decided that there were two things she still needed to do soon. One was that she should learn how to drive. The other was to get a seat on a plane. She heard so many stories about how grand it was to be so high up in the sky. Well, someday, for both.

Two days later, the medical unit squadron broke down their own tents, counted and sorted supplies, packed trucks already numbered to match the loads they bore. The new unit replacing them would bring their own equipment and gear. Agnes and Vera took up their new duties, checking off the packing up of their hospital; they wanted the unpacking at their next location to be well-organized. They walked around checking on everyone's individual jobs, while seeing to the final line of patients needing emergency help. Philippa left with the patients on an evacuation flight. The dirt and grass runway and the empty buildings were all that remained. Planes needed to have emergency landing spots at all times.

Vera and Agnes found and delivered one more gift of Canadian chocolate and cigarettes to the Dumonts.

CHAPTER 21
August, 1944, Agnes

Agnes started to climb into the lead jeep in the convoy. Suddenly there were loud female screeches followed by equally loud male laughter. Agnes turned to see what was happening.

The canvas "Privy Tent" had just been collapsed so that it could be rolled up and taken to the new location. No one thought that the tent was still in use. The dropped canvas revealed three nurses sitting awkwardly on camp toilets for all the world to see. After the initial silence while everyone tried to figure out what happened, the laughter had begun. The girls remained frozen where they were. They were looking around for some cover and the men just watched with varying amounts of amusement.

"All right," Agnes heard herself shouting, "Men – dismissed. Back to your duties. And don't forget – we see more of you in our surgery than what you see of us here."

The girls remained in their half-squat. She turned to a couple of nurses who had been waiting to use the toilets. "Make a tight circle around the ladies to form a privacy wall. Girls, finish up what you're doing and let's get on those trucks."

Agnes walked inside the circle and added quietly, "Listen, laugh it off. Don't let them know how embarrassed you are. If you show any sign of discomfort, you'll never hear the end of it. It was not malicious, it just happened. It wasn't that bad, just naked bums. At least it wasn't the shower tent. We all needed a break in tension. Next week the story will be great, and none of you will be personally remembered. Carry on!"

Vera agreed, "Years from now, we will be telling this story and laughing too." The girls were still unsure about their reactions, but more relaxed as they got up and joined the trucks in the convoy.

Vera climbed into the jeep with Agnes. "The girls really respect you and listen when you speak."

"You realize of course, a lot of that has to do with my accent." Agnes offered.

"Oh. London, right? I love learning the different accents from all over England," Vera said.

"London, yes, but my accent isn't regional," Agnes said. "It's what they call 'posh'. Sometimes people find it a bit intimidating, and I absolutely use that to my advantage. I use it heavily when I need to make people obey me. Then I switch back to a more common way of talking."

"Oh, no wonder," Vera smiled. "Well, it works. You have the reputation of a 'woman made of steady, unshakeable steel.' Do you have a title? Do I need to curtsey, or call you something?"

Agnes laughed. "Not here ever. But in the right places, you would address me as Lady Agnes. Here, just plain 'Agnes' is fine. Anything else seems ridiculous, right?"

Vera was interested. "In Canada, our family would be considered posh. My father owns a big food company. I was supposed to have a debutante ball and marry someone who might take over the business, but I came over here instead. I don't think my mother or my father will ever forgive me."

Agnes nodded. "Oh yes, parents – mine had the same expectations. Funny, we've been together for two years, and we know so little about each other. My parents owned a tea company – import/export. Hence, my large stash of tea. They wanted me to take over the business eventually. Not that I want to. I can't imagine sitting at a desk all day."

Agnes added after a few moments of daydreaming, "We do need to think of a way to get back at those boys for the Privy tent. I really don't believe that story about it being an accident."

The convoy began to move. The three-hour ride to their new location ten miles away was a somber reminder of the ruins of war. The roads were hardly more than dirt paths or crumpled asphalt. Mud rarely had the chance to dry, and when it did, it became hardened ruts and potholes. The volume of traffic made pre-war London look and sound like open countryside. Agnes never imagined how many types of vehicles existed. Specialized transports, military tanks and troop carriers, normal automobiles, and still in use, horse-drawn wagons of all sizes.

Still, it was better than the first month in Normandy. The Army was moving faster, less was being destroyed. Was that a positive? Even so, there were countless demolished buildings, ruined farms, and dead animals wherever Agnes looked. Pulverized rock and concrete dust and powder gave the sunniest days over to haze. And when it rained, the mud might hide anything. Yet the French people like the Dumonts were happy to be liberated, even when there was nothing left of theirs to celebrate.

When the convoy finally stopped, the Chief Engineer directed the first crew to mark out the future landing strip. Agnes wondered if Nigel Drummond was doing this sort of thing wherever he was.

The planned permanent buildings were marked on the ground with stakes. Tents and temporary paneled structures were set up next to the construction sites. Signs directed drivers to each location. The loads of equipment and temporary housing hopefully wound up in the right areas. The airfield command hut, kitchen, and hospital went up first, then living quarters. Finally, the piles of supplies and equipment were moved into the various structures.

The hospital that would be larger than the one they left, with over one hundred beds for the military wounded and the local population, plus a holding area for evacuation. The operating room was planned with 4 surgical stations.

Even before all was ready, Agnes, Vera, and their teams were tending to the first wave of incoming wounded soldiers. Jeeps and ambulances (covered jeeps, really) were arriving over a grassy field; the access road wasn't even ready. And they could hear the first planes landing on the half-done runway. They knew that at dinner later, the pilots would complain about a half-paved, half-ground landing. Wait a day or two was always the reply of the ground crew working at top speed.

As soon as possible, the next most important structure was added: a pub. It opened within two days of the new mesh runway being completed. A time to celebrate. There must always be time to celebrate.

Agnes admitted to Vera that ever since entering nursing school, life had been one long hop from pub to pub. Under normal circumstances, she might never have entered even one pub in her entire life.

"I would have been hopping from tearoom to tearoom," she laughed.

Vera laughed, "Probably a mix for us in Toronto, but where's the fun in tearooms?"

"The Beer Spitz is here," went up the shout that interrupted their chat. The men cheered and ran towards the runway.

Agnes looked over at the air strip. There at the end of the runway, turning around to set up for the return flight, was a Spitfire Supermarine. The pilot got out, as a crew stopped the propellers and set chocks under the wheels. Refueling wasn't needed for such a short turn-around flight, but the reloading from a supply flight to courier service began immediately. A man in a tan Army uniform stood ready to board. He stepped back when he realized that there was some time before take-off.

Meanwhile, the real attention remained focused on the plane. Under each wing, strapped securely next to the fuselage, was a large keg of beer. Agnes had heard of this, the British military's officially "unofficial" ration of grog or beer, delivered to the battle front. She suspected that most of the beer was delivered by truck. In France they were using planes, but she had never actually seen it until now. The ground crew detached the kegs and rolled them towards the new pub.

The pilot began to walk over to the command hut to talk with his passenger. Then he and the soldier started for the pub while the support crews finished their work.

He took off his leather helmet and Agnes stared in disbelief. It was Stan Novak. She slowly walked towards him in a trance, not wanting to take her eyes off him. She was afraid that he might disappear. Soldiers and airmen swarmed him, the hero of the day. They backed off to give him some room to walk to the pub. Just before he entered, he turned his head and saw her.

His reaction was the same as Agnes' – he froze and stared at her. His face was hard to read, but he slowly turned his whole body and started toward her. They met and stared at each other for a moment. Then they hugged each other.

"I can't breathe," Agnes gasped as she tried to get released. When she stepped back, she saw that Stan was crying, just as she was.

"Hello," Stan mumbled.

"Hello," Agnes mumbled back.

"I don't know what to say."

"Neither do I."

"Okay, okay," called one of the pilots standing by. "So you know each other. Now, as Delivery Pilot, tap our lifeline here so we can quench our thirst.

These are our first wooden kegs and what they contain has to be better than what's been coming out of those cleaned out fuel tanks." It was as much a threat as it was a prayer.

The movement of the crowd pushed them both into the pub. Stan stepped forward to do the honor of tapping the keg. Traditions, no matter how new, had to be followed, and the pilot or driver of the beer delivery was supposed to open the latest arrival. An appreciative roar went up with the discovery that the beer was really beer. Now that the RAF was delivering beer in wooden kegs, life for the military was looking up.

Stan then took Agnes' hand and led her out of the pub, looking for somewhere private. They found a stack of unopened crates, and sat there, not ready to say anything. Too many memories and emotions, where could they even begin?

Finally, Stan spoke. "Why are you here?"

Agnes explained that after Jan died, she thought the best way to live up to his name was to become involved with the Air Force Nursing Corps, the Princess Mary's. It was good work, she was too busy to think about anything, and she felt like she was doing her part to help in the war effort.

"And you? No more fighting?"

"Temporary duty," Stan replied. "Punishment. I am veteran pilot, not many like me after five years in sky. I am now Squadron Leader. Mix of Polish and English. We speak good English now and fighting in same squadrons. Then Group Captain gets married. We have big party. We fly low over church and house to celebrate wedding. Group Captain likes, but his boss very angry. He demands all squadron is two days in jail, then off normal duty for one month. Pilots still needed, so we fly not so important missions, like beer. Jail also for Group Captain, no honeymoon. So, I deliver beer to Army and RAF. We have longer runways, so next time in bigger planes with more supplies that change to hospital evac on return. I qualify in all planes now."

He was trying to be funny and serious at the same time. Agnes had to laugh. "Your English is much better. I am so happy to see you."

"I am too. You still miss Jan?"

"All the time." She pulled out her necklace with Jan's pendant. Stan nodded in approval, smiling and serious at the same time. "So, now what?" Agnes asked.

"Get through war, then see," Stan shrugged. "And you?"

"Get through war, then see," Agnes echoed with a smile. "Let's go back in the pub for a pint. Are you staying long or do you go back right away?"

"I have half hour, I think. We fly between German and Allied raids. Time for one pint." He rose and courteously offered his arm as an escort. Agnes accepted and into the pub they went. The time went quickly and Stan had to return to his plane.

"Now I know your unit, I check flights to bring next beer," he said giving her another suffocating bear hug. "But soon I go back to fighting."

And he was gone with a wave.

"Who *was* that," Vera was full of curiosity. "I'm guessing a brother, cousin, or former and still friendly boyfriend. Intimate but not sexual."

Agnes wasn't sure what to call Stan. 'Nearly brother-in-law' came the closest. "I was seeing his brother Jan until, well, his last flight."

"Oh."

"This is a replica of his Polish Medal of Valor. It's all I have of him," she really wanted to be alone, but knew that wasn't possible. "He was pretty high up in Polish society and in their Air Force. His brother, Stan here, is also a pilot — they both flew that first summer of the war. Stan seems to have a charmed life."

"I think you need each other," Vera observed. "Emotionally, not romantically."

"Agree."

"Meanwhile, I have just the distraction for us. I met a chap in the motor pool today. He showed me a map," Vera said with a sly voice. "We are moving closer to the Belgian border. If that's the case, we are near some very old towns that have been making lace and tapestries since the beginning of time. Do you want to see what's left of those towns and maybe find some souvenirs?"

"Sounds good," Agnes. "Just hope we have the time to find out."

They found the time. With map in hand, Agnes and Vera found a sergeant with free time and a permit to drive a jeep. They signed one out of the motor pool with a driver.

Vera sat next to the driver, Sergeant Croyden, "Can you find," she looked at a crumpled bit of paper, "Pont Saint Denis? I was told it was near here. This is an old map, but from what I heard, so is the town."

Croyden looked at the map. "I know we are here," he said, pointing to a blank section of the map. "And here are some larger towns. If we follow signs to them, we should find what we're looking for."

"Thanks," Vera said as she sat back in the rear of the jeep.

"Ma'am, beg your pardon, what are we looking for," he asked. "A chemist shop? Something for the hospital station?"

"Oh, nothing quite that official," Vera leaned forward again. "Croyden, are you married?"

"Yes, ma'am."

"Good. We are on a personal quest, looking for souvenirs. Lace to be exact. If we are lucky, you can bring home something for your wife. The bayonets and other stuff the men scavenge or loot don't interest us, but this does. Will that be okay with you?"

"Quite, ma'am," Croyden smiled. He was a middle-aged man, thinking that his daughter, now sixteen, might also appreciate a lady-like present from him.

They drove away from the main traffic of the war onto smaller farm lanes. Croyden checked the map several times as the lanes grew narrower. Then one lane again as they approached an actual village, one without too much war damage.

"We're here, I think," he announced.

Vera hopped out of the jeep and spoke to the first person she met. It wasn't the first time that her Canadian French had proved useful. She turned around and nodded to Agnes and the sergeant.

The village of Pont Saint Denis was one main road, three blocks long. There were a handful of shops and a café lining the street. It didn't take very long to walk the entire village and return to the jeep. No lace. And the café served a very thin soup with an equally thin slice of bread.

"Where to now?" asked Agnes.

Vera replied, "I did get a suggestion from the waiter at the café. There are lace makers in the area. They stay in their houses and haven't sold any lace since the war began. But if we come back tomorrow, he shall have them and their wares here on display. What do you think?"

They finished their soup. Croyden surprised them with an answer. "Come back and bring lots of money. Buy up everything they want to sell. I'll wager that you'll have many customers for the lace back at the base, women for themselves, men for their loved ones back home. I want to return to buy some presents for my gals."

Agnes was taken aback. Vera caught on. "A little side business, Croyden?"

"Up to you, but in your honor, I'll keep this exchange on the up and up."

Vera nodded and decided for them. "Tomorrow then. Let's go back and see how we can do this." She told the waiter who smiled and bowed to all three of them.

A pair of jeeps drove the same route on the following day, carrying two more nurses and another driver. Lunch at the café was more generous, a small sandwich with a slightly thicker soup. Space on the café tables was made for the display of lace items. Table cloths and runners, collars, shawls, handkerchiefs, and doilies were in piles and spread out everywhere. After much back and forth bargaining with the lace makers, a deal was made for the village's entire stock of hand-made lace. Agnes was silent on the way back to base.

Vera looked at Agnes, "You're very quiet. What's on your mind?"

"I can't take any of this lace."

"Memories? Like with the Polish fellow? This stuff is simply gorgeous. Especially the shawls."

"Especially the shawls," Agnes replied. "And yes, memories. My parents died in the beginning of the Blitz, December 29th. My Christmas gift to my mother was a lace shawl that looks very much like those we have here. I just can't."

"Oh. Sorry," Vera and Agnes reverted to silence.

Back at the base hospital, the lace was sold to everyone who was interested. Vera and Agnes watched Croyden, making sure he didn't try to make too great a profit from the adventure. A few handkerchiefs remained, and Agnes decided to keep them. Maybe she could give them to Ellie, Maggie, Emmy, and Aunt Charlotte. As she was tucking them into a corner of her belongings, Vera bounced in.

"If you don't want lace, how about the bags they came in?" Vera tossed two large carrying bags on Agnes' cot. "They are absolutely the most beautiful tapestry I have ever seen. Any memories attached to tapestry?"

"None whatsoever," Agnes replied. They were beautiful. "Thanks."

CHAPTER 22
Early August, 1944, Maggie

Maggie, in her RAF uniform, met Lady Jane Archer and Lady Davids, both in pre-war linen suits of quality. Were the two older women treating her as an equal or as their protégé? Both, thought Maggie. Lady Davids, her first boss, and Lady Archer, ever her teacher and mentor.

"You are doing quite well for yourself," Lady Davids said, pouring tea in her new residence, having been bombed out of her old home. This was a newly remodeled suite near the newspaper offices. "RAF Squadron Leader, and about to be Chief Press Camp Officer in France. Quite the success story, I must say."

Maggie was caught between being humble at their help in making this happen, and wanting to be seen as a competent and independent adult. "Thanks to you both for opening all those doors for me. I am truly grateful. I did enjoy working at the Military Newspaper Unit. I'll miss the hands-on editorial work, but I look forward to giving daily briefings to the war correspondents in the field, where the news is being made. Civilian reporters don't mind women journalists – unlike the English and American military, who follow the opinions of Monty and Patton. 'Women don't belong at the front,'" she quoted.

The two older women laughed quietly and lifted their tea cups as a toast.

"Your last interview did the trick. We merely suggested to a few officers that they review you fairly. They admitted you deserved the new posting. What exactly went on during that last interview?" Lady Archer wanted to know.

"I made the best of bad timing. I went to interview Rear Admiral Carrington, who had just been appointed commander of one of those naval bases sending troops and supplies to Europe. First, he grumbled about speaking to a WAAF rather than a naval reporter. I told him that I was a last-minute replacement. We couldn't delay our meeting; it was the duty of the press to be up to date. I promised to be brief, so that he could inspect the damage from the previous night's bombing raid. I offered to fill in the background details when I got back to the office. As I put away my notes and pencil, he asked me about myself. I said that I had been with the *Times,* then an early volunteer with the RAF, and now in the military communications unit. He suggested that perhaps I couldn't keep a steady job ('because I am a woman' was implied). I told him that the RAF decided to use my journalism skills after my boss retired and didn't need his staff any more.

"He continued to grumble. I think he felt put aside by the Navy, being assigned a port command that he felt was less status than commanding a ship. I switched topics by suggesting that I join him on his tour of the base for a photo opportunity. I found a few good locations and angles that made the base look quite secure (as well as making him look – commanding). He tried both smiling and serious poses. His appreciation at my choice for the final photo won the day, I think. Especially when I told him that the article would run in both *Blighty* and later in the *Union Jack,*" Maggie concluded.

"Well done," Lady Archer smiled. "What then?"

"He finally looked pleased when I told him that all the British military would see it. Such an ego," Maggie dared to voice criticism. "That's when I told him that the original reporter was on personal leave to tend to his family who were bombed out by the same raid that hit the naval base. And by the way, my first boss had been Air Marshall Dowding during 1940, so I could sympathize with his bombing incident. He was a bit more charming and apologetic after my remarks. Fancy that!"

"Well, here's to you, my dear, and *bon chance*" offered Lady Davids.

"I echo that – combat zone work will not be a lark, but you shall fair well," was Lady Archer's assessment. "Finally, are you finding girls to 'bring up the ranks'?"

"My assistant will continue in my place here," Maggie said. "A Land Army girl with some newspaper knowledge. Very sharp. She will be promoted to sergeant within the month. Maybe get into the officer corps if the war goes on long enough."

"Very good," Lady Archer said, as she stood to leave.

Maggie planned to walk from Lady Davids' place to Shellings. It would take perhaps an hour, time she wanted to take some photos of London and see her favorite sights once more before leaving for France. Whole city blocks were continually being cleared of rubble, some were to be used as parks or community vegetable gardens. Many buildings she passed were skeletons – two or three walls with square holes where windows used to be, joined at odd corner angles. Single walls were torn down each day – declared hazardous, as people climbed through the rubble to scavenge what they could. The same destruction was evident in Manchester and every city. She noticed tiny plants growing between the stones and bricks in the worst of the city's devastation. Hope and defiance. She didn't need a camera to remember what she saw.

The other memory that she would take to France was less tangible: the spirit of London. The city lived on two separate levels – the street-level mess, and the lively underground world of basement bars, dance halls, and shelters people used each night to escape being bombed. Like the plants growing in the rubble.

Her thoughts were interrupted by sensing someone coming up next to her.

"May I walk with you?" Lady Archer asked. Maggie slowed her step as she nodded.

"Congratulations on your discretion just now," Lady Archer said. "I know what else happened at that interview, the part you didn't mention."

Maggie's face turned bright red. "Pardon?"

"You saved Carrington's life. I heard that a live bomb was found at the port during your visit. That during its defusing, you saw it explode. That you pushed the Admiral under the window ledge in his office before the window blew in and scattered glass everywhere. That you carried on with the interview as if nothing had happened. That those actions were the real reason why he supported your new assignment in Europe."

Maggie was speechless. How did she know this? She needed to find out who Lady Archer really was.

Maggie replied as she always did, "I just did what I could. And the bomb part of the story would be censored anyway, so it didn't happen."

Lady Archer's smile was very cold. "Exactly."

Less than two weeks later, Maggie was on a transport vessel, crossing the English Channel to France. There were other women on board the ship: nurses, low-ranking office staff, and Red Cross hostesses. Among them were a few wearing military uniforms with shoulder patches bearing a large "C" for Correspondent on them – the civilian and military war correspondents, warcos. Those women kept to themselves until they spied Maggie as an officer not affiliated with any other group. They invited her to join them in trading stories during the crossing of the Channel (calm), riding jeeps into Caen (jarring), and waiting for their assigned quarters at the press camp (otherwise tedious).

Maggie's first morning in the Caen Military Press Camp began with an official 8 o'clock briefing for the radio and print reporters. She had done briefings before. She expected the waving and attention-getting behavior, but felt the sudden fear of being in the wrong place. These journalists were experienced in war conditions. She was the raw recruit, yet in charge of the place.

"We are setting up our military newspaper printing operation here in Caen," she began. "And this press camp is the first of the permanent ones set up as the front continues towards Berlin. We will offer the usual services – office space, some supplies, official censors, mail pouches for quick shuttle service to London, and shared time on wire services – all limited as you would expect. Everything will be available on a first-come-first-serve basis. No assistants camping out to wait for you to arrive. Questions?"

It seemed like all hands went up. "Miss, Miss," a man called from the middle of the pack of reporters. Maggie ignored him.

"What about jeeps?" a familiar voice blurted out. She looked out at the group. It was Max Howard, the ambitious flirt who had left the *Times'* mail room (and dark room) for the *Daily Express.* He was kitted out as a photographer. Well, he made something of himself after all.

"First come, as I said," Maggie replied with a smile. He smiled back.

A few questions later, she acknowledged a woman who was lounging in the back.

"Martha Gellhorn, *Colliers,*" her accent was obviously American. So was the way she made sitting in a folding chair look comfortable. "What about getting women some of those jeeps and a bit of wire time?"

"If you're here first," Maggie smiled. She knew that women warcos usually had no support from the official press offices and had to wait longer for everything. They didn't even have equal access to the battle front or the outgoing mail pouches.

"And by the way," she sounded as casually as she could as she turned to the first reporter, "I am Squadron Leader Drummond, or Major Drummond, if you need me. That is all, everyone."

She walked to the canteen. She needed to have a break before starting her work in helping with the setting up of the newspaper production area.

"Well hello there Margaret Shelford," came a voice. Maggie turned to see two familiar faces. Max Howard and Olivia Portson-Drake. She hadn't thought about Olivia for over ten years. Their families were close friends, but Olivia was at least five years older than Maggie. "You recognized me, how nice after all these years. Where did you pick up 'Drummond'? Married?"

"Hello Olivia," Maggie said. "Nice to see you again. And yes, married."

"Congratulations. After-dinner drinks tonight? Max, Marty and I shall be at the Lively Bar after we write up and send our stuff. See you there after the 8pm briefing?"

The bar was crowded, mostly with warcos. The fighting troops were already bedded down in a camp across the main road. The Lively Bar was make-shift – a ruined building as its core. The usual dirt floor, tarpaulin roof, partial stone walls with roll-down canvas sides, and minimal furnishings. The patrons looked worn out – all dust, smudges of oil, mud, and sweat marks on their uniforms. The odors matched the uniforms.

"Welcome to Europe," Olivia spoke first. "Max says you already know each other from another world." (Max nodded and lifted a chipped glass of something.) We're both freelancers for the Independent News Service. By the way, I go by Ollie Drake in the field."

"And I'm Marty Gellhorn, Yank, and known as a total annoyance to all bureaucrats. Hope you're not one of *them*," Marty said.

"Hello," Maggie said, trying not to sound awed. "I'll try my best to fit in." She had thought Ollie Drake, a well-known English writer, was a man, not the glamorous debutante she remembered from her childhood. And Martha Gellhorn was the famous warco extraordinaire. She had covered the Spanish Civil War, and had stowed away on a transport ship on D-Day plus 2. She went to France as a stretcher bearer before she was discovered and sent back to England. And here she was!

Max joined in, "So, since you will be our shepherdess for the duration of whatever, we want to give you a quick orientation to being a warco. How about tomorrow? Can you get a jeep? I'll drive. Make sure you are properly kitted out. We can leave tomorrow right after your briefing."

As early as she could, Maggie signed out a jeep, aware that her desk was filling up with paperwork on only her second day on the job. She had a helmet in one hand, her small personal camera in the other, food rations and a notebook in a backpack. The others strolled out of the briefing tent. Max threw his camera gear into the back of the Jeep, then sat in the driver's seat. Maggie sat next to him. Marty climbed in next to Ollie in the back, with a very abused Michelin map of France. Marty looked at Ollie and Max, "Let's see where we can go to get our fill of daily carnage. Any ideas?"

"The Falaise business is over but gives an example of what we're up to. Word is that you and the Yanks are about to head south, splitting off from us Brits and Canadians," Ollie said. "Falaise may have been the scene of one of the biggest battles before the end run to Berlin. We haven't been there yet. Let's see if there is one more story around there before Marty leaves us. I rather think you like solo work, Marty, so thanks for putting up with us."

"Even back in Spain, we often worked in groups," Marty said with a sigh. "as long as we didn't compete for the same deadline. Solo work just makes it easier to slip in and out of situations. Right now, I also need to find Ernest, though I think our marriage is over. He's probably with Patton or one of the other colorful generals. I just have to find the biggest *real* bars in the biggest towns."

Max started the jeep. Maggie remained quiet, trying to figure out her relationship to Max. Would he bring up what happened back at the *Times*? She listened to her two writing idols while she took in her surroundings. An hour later, they came to a stop. They were at the town of Falaise. A major crossroads, therefore, a major strategic goal. The Dives River itself was barely a stream. Until both sides of the war wanted the crossroads. The battle, horribly long, was won by the Allies. At enormous expense.

The Dives River had backed up. A huge dam blocked the river's flow, made up chiefly by the stampede of retreating Germans. The stampede began with horses and supply wagons falling over each other into the river. Then the German soldiers being pushed from behind with a wall of horses and wagons in front of them, followed by motorized vehicles. All piled up on top of each other. The inevitable happened, they toppled over each other like a pile of toys, or a heap of coal just emptied by a delivery lorry. The stench of decay was overwhelming, otherwise it might have been a fantasy drawing of Breugel having a nightmare.

Maggie lost her complete sense of reality when she reached down to pick up a German helmet, only to see a head still inside it. She was violently sick and needed to be helped back into the jeep.

CHAPTER 23
Mid-August, 1944, Maggie

At the 8pm briefing that night, Maggie looked as if she had fought the entire war single-handedly. She read the day's briefing without any emotion. Then she looked out at the faces in the room.

"Well, Pygmalion stands before you, transformed from new recruit into war veteran in one day. I worked at Uxbridge and Bentley Priory with the fighter squadrons during the summer of 1940. I went in and out of London during the first winter of the Blitz in 1941. Death and destruction are not new for me. Even so, I was not ready for what I saw today. All my senses are numbed, no, they're gone.

"Sight, at the enormous damage to buildings, military vehicles, horses, and dead men not yet collected for burial. Sound, much more pervasive more than what I have become accustomed to, constant gunfire from ground and air, the screaming and moaning of the severely wounded. Smells of burning fuel and buildings, rotting animals, gunpowder, dust, body odors. Taste and touch, just gone. How you continue to remain calm enough to report all of this every day is a wonder."

The warcos, some of them veterans of five years or more of witnessing combat, listened intently. They had heard of her tour of Falaise that day. For some, it was a reminder of how hardened they had become to the details of combat. For others, it was confirmation of their own changing feelings about war in general. They remembered their first days of reporting and how it affected them. The most cynical warcos were placing bets with themselves on how long she would remain, or how quickly she could build her personal shield to the horror around her.

"And yet you are expected to write your reports of heroism and positive wins, a bright future, and high morale. And that is out there, the spirit of the troops. There is optimism, and that is what our office will help you send to your readers and listeners. Next briefing is tomorrow at 8am."

Max was staring at her. So were Ollie and Marty. They took her by the hand and led her to the Lively Bar.

"I can't believe you pulled that off, that report of what you saw today," Max said. "Are you okay? I think you are still in shock."

Ollie added, "We did this to you too quickly. Sorry. Oh, and you didn't eat or drink anything all day. Hold on, I'll get you something. The primary rule of warcos in the field – eat when you can, sleep when and where you can, write when you can remember the details." She shoved her plate of bread and unidentifiable tinned meat at Maggie. Maggie shook her head and left the plate untouched.

Marty added, "Well done, tonight, by the way. More of us feel the way you spoke than we care to admit."

Maggie wanted to push the food away, but realized she was hungry after all. She nibbled while she accepted the large glass of wine, which turned out to be calvados brandy, given to her by Marty.

Two hours later, her new friends half-carried her to bed. She didn't remember very much of the evening other than crying as much as any human could. The next morning, Ollie was at her side as she got up for the 8am briefing. Washing her face quickly, in the same clothes as yesterday, she set off for the podium. She had never felt so hungover in her life. She could barely see the typed paper in her hands.

"Business as usual," she announced at the briefing. "Thanks to all of you who made me feel welcome yesterday. It won't make me play favorites, but I do feel a bit more like a veteran." There was a soft noise of sympathy and acceptance by the group. She read the briefing and went to her office.

As she passed Ollie on the way to her office, Maggie said, "Thanks for yesterday, really. Don't look so concerned. I'm told that I am pretty resilient. I react once to something new, sometimes really emotionally, then I'm okay the next time it happens. I might still cry about it, feel it affecting me, but I can get going again. I'll be fine, just no more calvados for a while. I'll be in my office today."

Ollie smiled, waved, and headed for a jeep with another warco. "Adjusting to this is a challenge, and there is no time to process any of it. Just keep going. Today, as a break, we girls are off to do 'women's' reporting – the 'behind the front' stuff we are actually allowed to do. It's off to a local hospital. See you tonight."

Two days later, Marty bade her farewells as she joined the US Army heading south and west towards Brest and Paris, talking about a return to Rome. As a parting gift, Marty handed over her Michelin map of France to Maggie. She passed on the same advice that Mr. Philips gave her in Manchester. "Write what is expected in one diary. Keep another one that tells the rest of the story. That way the censors are happy now, the historians later on."

Maggie continued to drive around the battlefields with warcos from several broadcast bureaus, as well as the BBC. Her first day was in fact her worst of the war. If she survived that and stayed on, the veterans consoled and encouraged, she was able to stay on for the rest of whatever more may happen.

Some days she went with Ollie or Max or both. When they teamed up, Max and Maggie took turns driving. Some days like today, the three had a driver,

Kip. Max sat in the front. There was an agreement that jeep conversations were never about the war.

"Where did you go to school?" Ollie asked as she stared at the dusty landscape of farm land left fallow because of the war. The hedgerows, known as *bocage,* were simply gone, giving them a wide view of the land. This land was grazing area for the dairy cattle that produced the creamiest cheeses. Today, though, now cows were to be seen.

"St. Martins School for Young Ladies," answered Maggie.

"So did I. Ah, and you said something about Bentley Priory. Dowding's territory, right?"

"Yes, but not right after leaving school. First a short time at the *Times.*"

"Lots of name dropping there. Let me guess – a bit of assistance from Lady Jane Archer?" Maggie whipped her head sideways to look at Ollie.

Ollie laughed. "I knew it! What did *you* do to get her attention?"

Maggie said, feeling strange about the new connection to Ollie. "My friends and I parked the Headmistress' motorcar on top of the walls of the foot bridge near the stables. The tire span and bridge walls were a perfect match."

"Brilliant!" Ollie howled. Max had been daydreaming and woke to the two women laughing hysterically. He was instantly alarmed and looked around to see what was happening. No, nothing. He returned to his half-wake state. Kip drove calmly and said nothing.

"What about you, then?" Maggie was now very curious.

"Climbed the bell tower and wrapped the clapper in cushion stuffing. The next time the bishop visited the school, his bum made a paper-crackling noise as he sat on the cushion during Vespers."

"Brilliant!" Maggie echoed. "I often wonder, though, who is Lady Archer? She is quite good at connecting people. And she seems to be everywhere."

Kip stopped as a British Army convoy approached. The lead jeep driver shouted to make them pull over. Kip drove onto the nearest field. Ollie stood up in their jeep and shouted, "Where are you going?"

"Berlin, or Amiens, or Rouen, or as far as we can go. Germans and fuel permitting," the answer was shouted from the lead tank.

"Who's your commander?"

"Dempsey".

"Let's follow them," Ollie sat down. While they waited for the convoy to pass, Max pulled out his 'Reporters Notebook', a pocket-sized hardcover diary and scribbled a few words. Ollie started typing on her portable Hermes typewriter, always ready in her backpack. She didn't waste time with first writing notes. Maggie sat patiently watching the traffic. It was all flat trailers loaded with tanks, cannons, and other large equipment. No tents and personal gear. Was the front really moving?

Kip finally turned back onto the road, following the convoy at a distance to allow the dust to settle. As the noise of the convoy diminished, a new sound was heard. Airplanes. A mix of fighters and bombers. From which air force? It wouldn't matter, but Kip automatically steered the jeep back into an open field. On the road, they were a target. In a field, the assumption was that the jeep was inoperable from war damage. Bodies may or may not be alive from a pilot's perspective.

Kip parked just as the planes came overhead. Luftwaffe. Maggie recognized that they were Messerschmitts heading home. She heard the strafing come nearer and saw a thin line of dust racing towards them.

Then she then she found herself lying on her back in the field. Why was she out of the jeep? Had she passed out? Before she dared get up, she slowly checked her arms, legs, and back. Everything seemed in order, no pain, so she sat up. Ollie and Max were standing up and looking around. They walked over to Kip, who remained lying on the ground. They looked so serious, Maggie thought. Kip must be dead.

Maggie began to shake all over and then she broke into a cold sweat. She put her head between her knees, trying to shrink into an invisible ball. Was this Tarnsham all over again? No. Think rationally, this is not Tarnsham. She slowly unwound, stood up, regaining a semblance of composure. She inhaled deeply several times, trying to convince herself that she was fine.

Max looked closely at Maggie with a questioning expression. Not as composed as I thought. "I'm fine," she said. "Kip?"

"Didn't make it. Let's take him back to camp. Forget the convoy," Max decided for the group. With that, the three picked him up and placed him in the back of the jeep. The jeep was battered with grass stuck all over; it had flipped over completely. Max sat next to Kip's body, Ollie and Maggie sat in the front. Ollie was more emotional than Max and Maggie had seen before. And yet, Ollie was a true veteran.

Ollie offered to drive, but after a few hundred feet, she stopped. "Sorry. Maggie, you have to take over. I'm too upset about Kip."

She didn't want to right now, but there it was. The shaking was over, but she was chilled from sweat. "All right then. I drove the car onto the bridge, I can drive us back to camp. Just keep talking, you two. Keep me occupied."

She turned the car around and headed for the press camp. It was like Southern England with potholes, ruts, and hidden rocks. She tried to get up some speed. Maggie wasn't sure that driving would take her mind off the memories that kept flashing up.

Ollie began, getting her emotions under control, "Right. Lady Archer, our beloved nemesis who keeps turning up. Short version. Early member of the Girl Guides, friend and associate of Lady Baden Powell. Girls should be self-sufficient. One of the millions of widows from the Great War. Became a suffragette at war's end. Women must be self-sufficient. Prepared to lead the country and the world, with real educations and real professions. Back to girls being self-sufficient. Her connections? A not too distant cousin of the King. Social ties beginning at the highest level. Wiggling in and out of many circles. Working at a school helps her find the 'perfect future leaders' – she collects those with the combination of intelligence and creativity. *Et voila,* girls like us."

"Good God," replied Max from the back seat. "What a manipulator. Though, the lady behind the wheel here has the reputation of someone determined to succeed. Saved the day for some friends. At the *Times* she taught herself how to type in record time while writing her *very* popular column. Oh, you thought you went unnoticed?"

Maggie felt her face get red and hot with embarrassment.

Ollie turned to face Max. "Do tell."

"Don't you dare," Maggie warned. "I'll toss you out."

Max ignored her. "Ever hear of a fluff column in the *Times* called 'Eighteen'? Betty Bonder? Yes? Well, allow me to introduce Miss BB!"

Ollie was for once speechless. For a minute. Then a burst of outrageous laughing, "On the surface perhaps fluff, but an amazingly good social study of class in England. Even better when she – you – expanded to other girls. Kudos! Is that the origin of the 'Women on the Home Front' sections of the *Union Jack*?"

Maggie just kept driving. "Now written by a whole new group of writers, but yes, I suppose so. I haven't done a Bonder piece in a few years. *And* I think it is also the origin of BBC's 'Women in War' program. Just don't tell darling Dimbleby. He always wants to take the credit. But, by the way, Max, I thought you were going to be the next great crime writer."

"My pictures of crime were better than my pen, that simple," Max said. "Now photography is my beat, like Capa or Bourke-White, I hope. Clark was an excellent instructor, once I took him seriously. By the way, I am a bit more respectful of people now than I was earlier on, especially women."

Maggie wondered. "Was that why you left us?"

Max chuckled. "No, just perfect timing with the new job opening up. Letty just disappeared."

They drove on, until Maggie announced, "We are lost. I see some undamaged houses just ahead. Ollie, can you find out where we are?"

"Will do, BB." She grinned with her new knowledge and jumped out of the jeep.

Within a few minutes, Ollie returned. "Only the main road is officially liberated and there are pockets of Germans on both sides of the road, who want to stay hidden. Here is our way out." She pointed to places on the map. As they finally turned back on to main road, Maggie spotted an Allied airman walking alone in the fields. She pulled over.

"Need a lift?"

"Yes, please," he answered. "It seems my unit forgot about me." He was old for a Flight Officer. He had what Maggie's father would call 'the look of unsuccess', someone likely to be forgotten in a field. He got into the jeep next to Max. Kip was propped up between them. "Oh, my," he remarked when seeing Kip's body.

Ollie demanded, "what's your story?"

"I'm Flight Officer Peebles, former landscaper from the National Trust. Surveyor for an RAF landing strip. Between the convoy and the strafing that just happened, they forgot that I was measuring the field for an ALG."

Maggie went on high alert. "What sort of field? Long or short?"

"Under 4000 ft long, PBS."

"Short landing strip for reconnaissance, emergency landings and refueling, suitable for small transports. Prefab Hessian rolls, so temporary?"

"Yes ma'am," Peebles answered, surprised at her knowledge.

"That means Airfield Construction Service? Who is your commanding officer?" she dared to hope.

"Wing Commander Drummond," he replied.

"Is he right- or left-handed?" Maggie continued.

"Very right-handed," he replied uncomfortably. "He is all over this region setting up a series of airfields at the front. We're moving fast now."

With that, Maggie sped towards camp. (Sergeant Cotter now had new comrades in the small club of terrified passengers who survived Maggie's skilled combination of speed and maneuvering.)

At the Lively Bar, Ollie explained her reaction to Kip's death. "He was the son of one of my family's household staff. I promised to keep an eye on him. I hadn't seen him for years, and we kept our previous relationship private. I guess I need to write a letter to his folks. Maggie, your turn to cheer me up."

That night, Maggie dreamt of Andrew Cashleigh and their final drive. Andrew's face faded into Nigel's. Where is Nigel tonight? Nigel, Nigel, she hummed. The drone of the nightly planes was as familiar as a lullaby.

CHAPTER 24
Late August, 1944, France

Maggie sat in her temporary Press Camp Office looking at a mass of paperwork. She gave a pile of administrative files to her aide. The remaining pile demanded her immediate attention. News releases waited for censorship reviews, and Maggie had a hand in keeping the correspondent submissions flowing to the newspapers and magazines headquartered in London. At least the radio broadcasts were not her concern; they were sent to London to be censored there. Most writers knew what to say, making her work go much faster.

She paused before reading and marking up the releases. She looked at the newspaper photo glued into her 'real history' private diary. It showed a beautiful, clean street with lovely buildings on one side of the street, trees lining the other side. Well-dressed and well-fed French people were running towards the photographer and cheering their liberation. The caption read Falaise. Her own memory of that city was quite different, and included that head she found in a German helmet. Censorship in a nutshell. Mr. Phillips, Marty, Ollie, and she were among those who would make sure future historians had a full picture of what happened. But not today.

"No interruptions for ten minutes and I'll be done," she called out to her aide. Sergeant Garrett also heard her, eager to get away on his motorcycle.

She initialed the last releases and sealed them in envelopes for each publisher. She stepped outside and gave them to Garrett who put them in his satchel and sped off to the airfield. He imagined himself on the Pony Express routes of the American Wild West, like the cowboys in those adventure films.

Maggie walked over to the van that served as a storage unit. What did she need before the next move forward? At this point, probably only her desk and chair, and a few desk supplies. For her aide as well.

The war was changing. The larger body of the German Army might be retreating, but smaller divisions and individual soldiers were fighting back block by block in each city, with snipers in any tall building or tower. The bigger towns were the major battle sites for both sides, the surrounding villages were more likely to remain intact. Warcos now found their own lodging and food or were settled into military units that adopted them and took care of all their needs. It meant that she had some time to work as a preliminary censor, along with her job of daily briefings, arranging interviews, and occasional news reporting behind the front lines.

Maggie heard a commotion at the gate to the camp. Curious – midday was normally quiet. The only sounds should have been the low rumble of gun fire, planes, and tanks in the distance. She went out to see what was happening.

A thickly-built woman in a uniform was harassing a young sentry. She had one hand on her hip, the other waving papers wildly in the air.

"I can't understand why you are incapable of answering the simplest questions, my dear child," the woman was saying loudly. "I repeat, where *are* we?"

The sentry caught Maggie's eye, pleading for help. He may be a hardened veteran, but this woman was intimidating.

"Perhaps I might help you? I am Squadron Leader Drummond, the commanding officer of this camp," Maggie intervened. The woman wore the civilian version of an Army uniform. Her insignias indicated that she was with ENSA, the agency that brought entertainment to the troops in the field.

The shows had a variety of singers and dancers with a few famous performers thrown in when they were available.

Maggie thought that they were very brave, putting on shows close to the front, and willing to perform under ever-changing circumstances. This woman must be either the director of a show or head of a whole touring group. At any rate, she was very dramatic. Her heavy use of makeup didn't match the uniform.

"OH! Well," she paused long enough to gather more breath so she could begin another tirade. "Our ENSA troupe is just outside this – this – this camp, and we have *no* idea where we are. Our drivers have *useless* maps. We are *hungry* and *tired*. And we have performances *tonight*."

"Where do you have to go?" Maggie asked politely.

"Some place called Ahmen, wherever that is," was the reply. "But what with not finding any food or lodging around here – this is *far worse* than *all of Africa!* Not even a *town* nearby for shopping. There might not even *be* a show!" The woman pawed through her over-sized handbag, found a bright lipstick and added another layer to her heavily made-up mouth. That done, she looked around. "Do you have a decent toilet here? I am *so tired* of these camp things. And another thing, this guard is *so* impolite. *Never* answered my questions and was *so terribly and visibly RUDE!*"

Maggie wanted to be rude, but held her tongue. "He is our sentry, keeping our place secure. We are strictly ordered not to reveal our location. Perhaps you do need to know, and I can make sure we tell your drivers how to get to Amiens. The hotels near the city will be fine for your troupe, I am sure."

"*No* one treats us with the respect we deserve for putting up with these conditions while we try to do our professional best," the woman's rants slowed to a mumble. "I could be doing *far better* if I had stayed home, but we all have to help the war effort," she sighed. "Just where is everyone right now?"

"This is a Press Camp, and the correspondents are with the troops are in the field. And if you want to get to Amiens, now is the time to go, before the troops return to camp and the traffic becomes worse than central London."

"Well, if you can get me a small glass of water. I am *so* tired of all this." She dropped onto a folding chair near the entrance of Maggie's tent. She took of her wide-brimmed hat – and wig.

"Agnes!"

The two girls began to laugh and dance with each other. Although they had been writing to each other constantly, it was something else to be face-to-face.

"There is an ENSA troupe near here," Agnes said. "I made friends with the Assistant Director, Gertie, who lent me this costume. She is rather large. The extra padding I have on is awfully hot. I really do need that glass of water."

"You will be the next actress among us," Maggie laughed before becoming serious. "I haven't heard from Ellie for a while, or the De Wevers. What about you?"

"No, but I'm not worried, yet." Agnes wiped the excess lipstick and powder from her face. "Anyway, I have a few days off while we wait for the next hospital station to go up. Any chance you can get away?"

"Probably not. We are also in the process of moving. Where, I don't know."

"We're like frogs or toad, you know – work here, move on, jumping over other units, and they jump over us," Agnes said. "Our unit is called the Hopping Toads. It's fun to be on the move. Dr. Fitzgerald, and my co-matron Vera and I are called the Head Hoppers."

Maggie thought about it. She and the warcos were also always on the move, keeping in touch with the front. She was reminded more of locusts, grabbing food (or stories) as they moved along, the army destroying everything in its way. What would it be like to stay in one place for more than a few days?

"I had wondered what it would be like once we reached the bigger towns," Agnes said for both of them. "With troops moving so fast, there should be less destruction. We are starting to use actual buildings for hospitals – convents, large homes, even real hospitals that we find in bad condition. Fewer tents, more like normal medicine every day."

"My job too," Maggie admitted. "Your letters give me a good idea about what you all do – you could be a correspondent. Your letter about the Spit flying in the beer was fantastic! Have you seen more of Stan? What is he doing now?"

"Testing new planes for the RAF, less actual fighting," Agnes shook her head. "I've only seen him twice since then."

"What was that like? Bringing back ghosts"

"A bit like that. We both miss Jan. We cry and laugh together without being embarrassed. Like long lost relatives. It isn't romantic, just nice to be with someone who knows my whole story, including Jan. What about you? You said that you were in a jeep accident that reminded you of what happened with Andrew."

Maggie hesitated. "It felt like a total repeat. I think I was unconscious for a short time, but only bruised. I woke up shaking and perspiring. I had to drive us back to camp which kept me distracted long enough to calm down."

"Remember what Emmy said – that might be a form of shell shock. Did you get help?"

"Not yet, but if it happens again, I might. Ollie reported that our accident was her seventh near-fatal event (along with avalanches, car wrecks, sinking boats, and being shot). She taught me how to separate events, so I don't relive them exactly. Did you ever go for help?"

"Not yet," Agnes admitted. "I just keep pushing the memories that pop up to the back of my mind. Don't allow myself to think about any of it. Stay so busy that there is no time for grief. I like surgical work because it is very detailed, mechanical in a way, ignoring the patient as a person. Then, socially I can concentrate on personalities and emotions. I expect that some day I won't be able to keep the ghosts at bay. 'I'll think about that tomorrow', as Scarlett O'Hara would say."

Silence.

"Do you think Nigel is near here?" Agnes asked.

"We write all the time, but I haven't a clue where he is," Maggie said. "Why?"

"Have you looked at a map? We are very close to the French-Belgian border. I hear we're heading for Antwerp. A huge port that is perfect for getting supplies in. And Brussels is near too. Main roads to everywhere. If the airports are not badly damaged, we'll be setting up evacuation places in existing locations. I wager that Nigel is starting to think about the repair work. He might be very close to us right now and we don't even know it."

Maggie's mind began to spin. Flight Officer Peebles. Why hadn't she registered his answers to her interrogation? He confirmed Nigel's presence. Had she been so addled that she hadn't processed that information?

"He is near," Maggie said with a start. "I just have to figure out who can help us find him. Military secrecy is so insane, sometimes I don't even know where *I* am."

A warco will know how to find out. Ollie. After the evening press corps briefing, tonight with its medal ceremony for three soldiers, the girls went to the newest warco hangout with Ollie. They presented their problem. Ollie was ready with the solution.

"Perfect timing! You'll never guess that tomorrow I have an interview with a Group Commander to go over the role of air cover here in France," she exclaimed. "I can direct some questions to airfields, steer Nigel into the conversation somehow."

Agnes stared at Ollie as she left. Like Maggie, she thought that Ollie Drake was a famous male writer. Her connection to Lady Archer and St.

Martins' was amazing. What a different world here with the press corps – living history as it happens, Ollie had said. Funny, thought Agnes, I was never interested in history at school, and now I am living it. And working with Maggie's romance as a part of it. Grand!

The next evening, Ollie reported back. "I did the entire day in an American accent, my warco uniform looks like all the others. Good thing, too. The Group Commander was a sweetheart. He was so charmed by a woman who was interested in airfields, that he took me to a field being built. I began my interview as we rode.

"We arrived at the field, and, instant success – the Wing Commander in charge of the construction was Drummond by name! As you said before, very right-handed. Interviewed him in my American accent – told him I was with *Life Magazine* but working the British angle.

"Maggie, your spouse may have a sweet smile, and may be a real flirt, but there's no interest in a follow-through. Believe me, without going into details, I know plenty of chaps – and their signals. He is devoted to you. When I told him that I was a warco, he immediately talked about his wife, you, and that I would like her, you. I should try to look her up.

"Two-hour drive from here for a normal person. You should make it in far less." Ollie shuddered. "Here is a map with directions. I'll navigate if I can get a story out of it." She waved Marty Gellhorn's battered Michelin map of France.

Agnes was ready to start planning. She smiled, "Shall we see what additional costumes our friend Gertie has in the ENSA closet?" "We'll go together. Besides, Nigel may be building my next field hospital station. Shall we?"

After the next morning's 8 o'clock briefing, Ollie, Agnes, and Maggie set off on their adventure. Maggie drove, wearing a wig and an ATS motor pool uniform. Ollie wore a civilian man's suit, Agnes wore her clothes from Gertie. Agnes was now a member of Maggie's terrified passenger club as they raced to the new airfield.

At the airfield entrance gate, Agnes got out and repeated her performance. Ollie stood next to her, hat pulled down to her eyes. Maggie stood behind them, also head down. There was a slight nervousness when they spotted Flight Officer Peebles. He didn't recognize them.

"What *are* we to do?" Agnes ranted. Wing Commander Drummond approached them, not sure what all the commotion was about. He didn't recognize any of them.

Agnes brazenly looked him in the eye. "I have a whole ENSA troupe trying to get to Ah-meen and our maps are *useless*! What *are* we to do? We might have to do our show here if we can't go further!"

"I doubt if that could happen," the Wing Commander replied with a smile. "We are in a place that doesn't exist yet."

"Alice in Wonderland, wonderful," Agnes said sarcastically. "Now what?"

"Oh, bother," Maggie said as she moved forward, tossing wig and hat aside. "We're here!" Mindless of what the airfield crew might see, she wrapped her arms around Nigel. He held her and what followed was a kiss like those seen in great films.

Agnes and Ollie revealed themselves during the embrace. Nigel brought them all into his tent, similar to Maggie's and ordered refreshments from his aide.

"I think we need to cool off, we were getting carried away out there," Nigel remarked.

"Where have you been since we last saw each other? Your letters are so vague," Maggie asked.

"As were yours," Nigel replied. "South Europe – Greece, Crete, Malta, Southern France, and now here. Now it's repair work of installations that the Germans have abandoned. Agnes, you're getting hospitals in much the same way."

Agnes nodded. "What's next? I hear Antwerp and Brussels. Maybe even as HQ for the winter if we can't break through."

Nigel nodded. "If we do make it that far, we might be able to live together for a brief time."

There was the sound of gunfire in the distance. "Well, we're still at it." Nigel said. "Were you the ones who picked up Peebles a few weeks back?" Maggie nodded. "I rather expected it was you, the way he said the woman drove him back to the press camp. You do have a certain reputation as a driver. Safe but daring. I wasn't sure of how to get to you."

All too soon, the group had to leave. The promise was made:

"See you in Brussels!"

CHAPTER 25
November, 1944, Ellie

Today is Wim's fifth birthday. And tomorrow is our sixth wedding anniversary. She rolled over in the dark, aware of being alone in the bed made for two. We spent only two of those years together. What will it be like when the war is over and we're back together? I love the man in my photos, but will he have changed too much? I know that I have changed. Will we still love each other like before, or as new people, not the people from our photos? I wonder if...

"Breakfast in ten minutes!" came the call from Mrs. Brinker, downstairs in the kitchen. With a sigh that came out as a groan, Ellie came out of her thoughts. She quickly washed her face in the basin against the wall of the bedroom. She slipped into a summer dress that now acted as an undergarment, then pulled on a thick sweater and woolen skirt. Everything seemed to be a size too large, but the layers kept her warm. She brushed her hair and checked herself in the mirror. She didn't feel very attractive, she was too skinny.

She helped Wim into his own "new" clothes for the second time this week. He wanted to wear them all the time. They were long pants and a matching vest she had altered from the trousers from one of Pieter's old woolen suits. She pulled a sweater knitted by Gran over his head and fed his arms through it and the vest. They met Gran in the hallway, also dressed in layers.

"Your new sweater is lovely," Ellie noted as Gran twirled around in it. Gran was now an accomplished knitter. She had pulled apart an old knitted cape to make a navy pullover with a matching scarf, plus Wim's sweater. "You and Wim look like matching school boys, though the scarf turns yours into French *haute couture*. You've become quite the knitting genius in only a few years.

Gran smiled, "Thank you. I am rather proud of my newest creations."

Professor Willems and Mr. Brinker were already at the table. Mrs. Brinker and Dora presented the family with a special treat – a seven-egg omelet. A half loaf of dry bread, sliced and toasted was made edible by a thin layer of butter and jam made with pears and sugar beets. It was an amazing feast. No wonder the meals lately had been rather lean.

"Happy birthday!" they all sang to Wim.

Gran smiled, "Plus remembering your anniversary, of course. These little celebrations are so helpful in breaking up our dismal routines, and St. Nicholas isn't due for another month. So here we are."

The family, including the Brinkers and Dora, lingered over the morning banquet, savoring every bite. Outside the house there would always be the distinct separation of employers and servants. Inside this house, though, everyone was more or less equal. Affection and concerns were shared, jobs were shared, respect for each other was shared.

Slowly, each one stood up from the table and started to go in separate ways. Professor Willems went to the prison, Dora left for the bakery, Mr. Brinker walked to his favorite café, Gran packed her bag for her monthly overnight visit to Wassenaar, and Mrs. Brinker began her routine cleaning. Ellie took Wim to school.

"I like my new clothes," said Wim as he looked up at Ellie. "The teacher said I look very grown up. I told her that they were my papa's trousers, and so they really are grown-up clothes. Did he wear them in that picture you always look at?"

Ellie nodded. "I think so. Mrs. Brinker helped me make them for you. You grow so fast that the measurements kept changing. And then Mrs. Brinker altered the suit jacket for Mr. Brinker."

Wim declared. "I want to see Papa for real, not just in a photo, don't you?"

"Of course, and it will be soon," Ellie said. Little Wim could be so serious. What a childhood! Being in a house filled with adults might be part of that. The teachers told her that he was kind and helpful to everyone and a natural leader in the few sports that four and five-year old children could play. At home, Professor Willems was encouraging him to be curious.

Seeing war all around the city had to be part of that childhood too. At least Leiden had beeen spared from the heavy bombing so far. Ellie tried to be cheerful and creative around Wim so that he could be a playful child. It was hard, when she was aware of the dismal news of the last month.

Belgium, parts of France, and some parts of the Netherlands had been liberated and were now under Allied control. It had to be soon for the rest of us, she tried to convince herself. Even with the recent set back at Arnhem a few weeks ago, surely the Allies would free us before winter. What was taking them so long, she wondered.

"Okay, Little Man," she said at the gate in front of the school, "I'll see you at lunch."

She bent down to kiss him. Then he ran through the gate and into the school. She waited a minute, turned around, and headed back home.

"Mrs. De Wever?" a soft voice behind her asked. Ellie turned to see two young men approaching her. One was Simon, one of the local resistance group members who made false German identification papers. She was alarmed that he contacted her in open daylight.

"What do you want?" she asked, trying to see if they were being watched.

"Gerrit and I need your help right away. It can't wait until tonight," he said with deep concern and urgency. "We have the correct paper to do the job. You just need to clean it up and give us new ink. Please."

Ellie hesitated. "All right, but go around to the back alley. I'll meet you at the gate." She was more nervous than usual, being seen with them in the middle of the day. She couldn't refuse to help, though. Many people risked so much; it was the least she could do. She knew that Pieter would never refuse to help, and therefore neither could she.

She entered the house, went down the hallway and through the kitchen where Mrs. Brinker was sweeping the floor. Ellie continued out through the garden to the back gate and let the two men in. They all kept their coats on since the kitchen was cool now that the stove was not in use. Ellie stood on a chair to retrieve a jar with a black lid labeled "syrup" and handed it to Simon. (Black lids indicated chemicals for the Resistance, not what the jar itself said.) Gerrit placed two sheets of paper on the work table in the middle of the kitchen. Ellie looked at the printed sheets as she took the jar and twisted off the cap, placing it carefully next to the jar. She poured a few drops of liquid into a glass of water and set the jar on the table. Then she took a dish towel, dabbed it into the glass, and began rubbing the ink off the paper.

"What is that stuff?" Gerrit asked. "Not syrup, I assume."

"Caustic soda," replied Ellie. "Very dangerous stuff. Don't touch it, it burns your skin badly if you do. Stand back, just in case. This is the best at dissolving inks, especially these new ones being used by the Germans. There, I think that does it. Give the paper a chance to dry." She took the towel over to the sink and began to rinse the caustic soda out of the glass and towel.

Suddenly, there was very loud insistent knocking at the front door. Mrs. Brinker opened the door and was pushed aside as two German soldiers and a third man entered the house. Before the two men in the kitchen had time to escape, the soldiers had run down the hall and grabbed them. Ellie looked at the third man.

"Ben!" cried Ellie, greatly alarmed to the point of terror. "What is going on?"

"That's what I want to know," Ben said grinning in an evil way. He stood in the doorway between the hall and the kitchen. His para-military NSB uniform insignias showed how high he had risen in the Nazi Occupation Government. "We have been following these two suspected criminals for several days now. They have avoided recruitment for work in Germany several times, they have been seen in the company of known resistant leaders, and have recently stolen valuable government documents. And here they are! And what looks like the documents are here too. I wonder what is going on? Your position in this is very suspicious!"

"What are you doing?" Ellie felt, rather than heard, Mrs. Brinker quietly leave the house. She, Gerrit, and Simon were alone with her brother and the soldiers, and he was about to turn her in as a spy or worse. What would that do to the other people living in this house? The thoughts sped through her mind. "You would turn in your own family? How can you even think about that!"

"*That* is what *you* should have been thinking about before helping the enemy," he continued to smirk at her. He had the upper hand at last. His family had always treated him poorly and now was his chance to get back at them.

"The enemy?" Ellie thought back to their last encounter. "*You* are the enemy. And you are losing the war. Don't you see that what you are doing is futile? You will soon face charges yourself as the enemy."

"Excuse me Sir," interrupted the soldier holding Gerrit, "what should we do with these two?"

"Bring them to the police station. I'll deal with this one," answered Ben, reaching to take Ellie's arm. With that, the two soldiers wrestled Simon and Gerrit out of the house. Ben moved into the kitchen. He saw the blank papers, still damp, lying on the table. He saw the "syrup" jar and held it up to examine it.

"So, actively working with the enemy," Ben continued. "Really, even though you are my sister, you expect me to let you go? You turned me out of this very house, told me I was *not* family. And now you want me to be loyal and kind to that same family? I do have to laugh. Especially with the evidence that Pieter is still here with these chemicals around. At least in spirit if not in reality.

The only sad part of all this is that none of your other co-workers is here to defend you. I'm taking you to the station now. Let's get this over with."

"Don't come near me," Ellie stood still. "Don't come near any of us."

All this time, Ellie had been trying to think of how to escape. How to protect the rest of the family. She was only half-listening to Ben. She heard the front door open. Please be the Brinkers, she prayed. Meanwhile she remembered the spot on the counter behind her where the meat knife always rested. Ben stepped nearer, still holding the open jar. She retreated, slowly put her hand behind her back to keep her balance and feel for the knife. She found it and grabbed it tightly, still keeping her hand behind her back.

No one recalled exactly what happened next.

Ben heard Mr. Brinker behind him. He tried to turn, but lost his balance as Mr. Brinker tried to shove him aside. Ben's arm jerked upward, the contents of the jar of caustic soda in his hand flew into the air as he fell into Ellie. At the same time, Ellie brought the hand with the knife in front of her for protection. Ben continued to fall forward into Ellie, then twisted sideways to the floor. Ellie started to scream. And continued to scream. Mrs. Brinker began to scream, louder than Ellie. At first Mr. Brinker stared at the scene, unable to react at all.

Then, they all moved at once. Mrs. Brinker ran to Ellie. She had her head in the sink, trying to rinse her eyes clear of the caustic soda that had splashed into her face. Mr. Brinker rolled Ben over. He was unconscious, bleeding heavily, either dead or nearly so.

The Brinkers looked up at each other, totally blank of all expression. The front door opened again. They stood frozen on the spot, Ellie still crying and moaning over the sink, Ben no longer moving on the floor, the kitchen knife visibly embedded in his stomach. Breaking the spell of shock and panic, the front door closed.

"What happened?" Dora asked, dropping her shopping basket on the hallway floor. Both Brinkers started to speak at the same time, with Ellie crying and making noises behind them. Finally getting most of the story, Dora then asked, "What are we going to do now?" She realized that she needed to take charge.

The soldiers and resistance fighters were gone and had nothing further to report. That was good. Ellie needed to get medical care immediately. That was bad. Ben. That was the worst of it. His body needed to disappear. Quickly, before he was considered missing. And how were they going to explain the loud cries and Ellie's injury to their neighbors or anyone else?

"All right. Hugo. (Dora used Mr. Brinker's name for the first time – she needed his attention.) Let's hide Ben in the shed. We can deal with him later. I'll take Ellie to Doctor Karel's office in the theater wagon. Petra, (again, first time she called the older woman by her name) make this kitchen look like we had, um, a grease fire. A bit of charred wood and smoke damage around the stove. That will be the official reason for Ellie's injury."

Dora looked at both of them. They seemed to understand. "Oh, and I'll get Wim from school on my way back from the doctor. Just make sure that the place looks close to normal when we get back. The Professor will help us figure out the rest when he gets back."

With that said, Mr. Brinker took Ben by the shoulders and Dora lifted his legs. He was heavy, but they had a surge of extra energy and moved quickly. They dragged Ben to the back shed, and shoved vegetable baskets aside. They laid the body down and covered him with the baskets.

Mrs. Brinker helped Ellie to a chair, relieved that her coat had protected most of her body from the acid. Ellie's eyes and face looked terrible. Her skin had already puckered in places, had been melted away in other places, and the undamaged places were a bright sunburn red. Ellie was shaking and whimpering. Mrs. Brinker tried not to look at the burns or make any comments. She just wanted Dora and her husband to come back quickly and help Ellie to the doctor.

Mr. Brinker rolled Ellie's theater wagon out of the shed into the alley, then around to the front door. Mrs. Brinker led Ellie out of the house and down the four steps to the wagon. Then she went back to the kitchen to clean up Ben's blood and figure out how to create the 'grease fire.'

Dora and Mr. Brinker saw very few people on their way to Doctor Karel. Word was already out that there had been police activity in the neighborhood – that always convinced people to stay inside and away from the windows.

The doctor saw Ellie immediately. He was skeptical of the grease fire story, but knew better than to ask for details during wartime. It was his part of the subtle resistance that most of his countrymen practiced. Don't ask too many questions. He wished he could send her to the local hospital, but knew that it was safer for her to stay in his office at least overnight. Treating the burnt skin and tissue could begin immediately. He wasn't optimistic about her sight returning, especially when she confided that the burn was actually caused by caustic soda.

"You couldn't find something less dangerous?" was his comment. "My report shall just say what you originally told me – grease fire in the kitchen. No one needs further information. My nurse will stay here with you for the next day or two."

Dora and Mr. Brinker left Ellie at the doctor's office and picked up Wim from school. Meanwhile, Professor Willems came home for lunch and was told about the whole incident by Mrs. Brinker. Over lunch they told Wim about the grease fire and that his mother had hurt her eyes. She would be staying with the doctor for a few days. After a brief lunch, Wim went up to his room for a nap.

During Wim's nap, the group whispered earnestly. Dora reported that Ellie may be permanently blind. Then there was Ben. The Professor considered what to do next. "Ben's body can never be found. Reprisals from the Germans, grief for the family, let alone Ellie's own mental state all have to be considered.

First, what do we do with the body? Second, what do we do with his clothing and uniform? And third, what will be our story about Ben's disappearance?"

Dora spoke up first. "People who cannot afford a funeral or a proper burial often just wrap the body and let it sink in a canal."

She felt their stares. "I heard such things in prison, but I thought they were just stories. Ben doesn't mean anything to me. Sorry, but since I have no history with him except his behavior in this house, I am not feeling very kind towards him. I have a hard time considering him as a real person."

The Professor spoke next. "Yes. We agree on his behavior. It's just that dealing with a dead person isn't something any of us thought would be our duty. Even in wartime."

Mr. Brinker offered, "I saw burials at sea during my navy days in the Great War. We can wrap him in a bed sheet. And get stones from the garden to sink the body in the canal."

Mrs. Brinker shuddered, "I can't think about all that. Too much for me. I shall concentrate on taking care of Ellie. And that may not be easy. How much do you think she will remember?" The others shrugged.

Dora again, "Shall the two men start in the shed while we women make the house safer for a blind person?"

Just at that moment, Wim came down from his nap. "Can we walk out to the canal? Our teacher says that some birds are flying home for winter. We are supposed to look for them."

The Professor looked around. "Wonderful idea. We have a few hours before darkness and curfew." They got up and left together. "Not much to do until later anyway."

Dora volunteered, "Then I shall help Mr. Brinker in the garden."

After dinner and Wim going to bed, the rest of the family went into action. In the back of the garden, Ben's body was undressed, and the clothes hidden. Three large stones were placed in the wagon, an old bedsheet, the body, and several strips from an of extra sheet to be used as ties. Dora and the two men used all their strength as they worked in silence. Then, well after curfew, they made their way to a canal two blocks from the house. The night was cold, but thankfully, no rain. For the first time in the long war, they welcomed the continual sounds of airplanes flying from both sides of the war going on round trips overhead.

They reached the canal. Ben's body was placed in the center of the sheet. Mr. Brinker startled himself. He remembered that for a sea burial the body had to be cut open to allow for gases to escape so that the body could sink. He thought, that's how Ben died, we don't have to do more than one or two more cuts. He asked the others to gather more stones, while he quietly and privately made the stabs with a knife they had brought to cut up the ties. The stones were tied in place at Ben's head, feet, and waist before the sheet was tied for the last time. Then the body was slipped as quietly as possible into the water. It sank quickly. They stood for a moment of silence, feeling the need to give some respect to the dead person, before returning home as quietly as they could.

Inside the house at last, Mrs. Brinker served them each a large glass of jenever gin, emptying the bottle. No one spoke. They went to bed without any further words or eye contact.

"Breakfast in ten minutes," called Mrs. Brinker like she did every morning. Strange noises came from the second floor. The Professor and Mr. Brinker were already at the table. The only person upstairs was Wim. When he came into the dining room a few minutes later, he was limping and trying not to cry.

Wim sat without saying a word. The Professor asked, "What's wrong?"

"Mama can't see," Wim said. "That is hard. We have to see for her."

"Yes," the Professor agreed gently. "But she will still be able to do many things for herself. And we must encourage her. We shall all help her when we can."

"I'm scared," Wim began to tear up. "I tried to be blind this morning and I couldn't do it." At least that answered the question of strange noises coming from upstairs.

"We are all scared," the Professor said kindly, "but your mama most of all. So, we must be brave and strong for her. Now, eat up so you will be strong, and I shall take you to school."

They continued the conversation of what Mama might be able to do all the way to the entrance of the school. The Professor told Wim's teacher about the 'grease fire' accident, just to be alert to Wim's behavior over the next few days.

Gran came home from Wassenaar to a household filled with chaos. Each person was working at being busy. She couldn't tell what they were thinking, but the mood was very somber. Ellie's blindness was only part of the atmosphere, but it was not the time to question anything. She decided to switch bedrooms with Wim, so that she could stay near her daughter at all times.

It took only a few weeks for Ellie to learn how to navigate her way around the house. She could even find stored-away items, if they had been returned to the same places. All of Pieter's chemicals were hidden in the garden shed or given to members of the Resistance. Her role was over. With their own version of military discipline, the family kept drawers closed, tables cleared, and sharp knives and scissors safely put away after every use. Neighbors were aware of the fire that Dora blamed on fatty pork and offered help if needed. Friends stopped by to visit.

The nurse and doctor were pleased at her physical healing. First degree red skin was now tan, like after a summer vacation, secondary blisters were closing and leaving minimal scars. The third-degree deep burns were also closing, and the doctor was removing old skin to allow new tissue to grow and keep the larger scars from forming. No one discussed the possibility of the recovery of sight.

Dora and Mrs. Brinker worked on the disposal of Ben's uniform. Each morning, a small piece of his clothing was tossed into the kitchen stove, each evening another piece went into the sitting room fire. The odd odor of burning cloth was explained as coming from the strange bits of wood they were forced to use as fuel. They were still working out what to do with the metal and hard leather parts, but figured out that a solution would be found. Dora treated the task as one more daily chore on a par with dusting the bookshelves. No emotions left for the incident at all.

Gran took on the role of running the household. She almost forgot to pass on some new information to Professor Willems. She had returned from her last visit to Wassenaar two days after the accident, and all had been set aside to take care of Ellie. When she finally unpacked her overnight bag, she saw the envelope with papers gathered by her friends and gave it to the professor.

"Rita is one of the most observant people in the world. She has to be, with Germans living in her house with her. She described something quite odd," Gran apologized for the delay. "First, German soldiers closed several blocks from all traffic, vehicles and pedestrians. Then, a very large truck, carrying a long tube, like a metal tower on its side, drove towards the city center. The tube was set upright. A huge explosion happened at the bottom of the tube, and suddenly the tube was gone, into the sky. The trees around the truck were charred from the explosion. And with that the truck drove off and the streets were open again."

Professor Willems listened intently. These rockets were the newest development in technical warfare.

"It sounded so ridiculous that I asked her to help me with finding documents if she could. Last month I left my camera-purse with her. She gave it back to me on this visit, along with those papers." Gran said. "Oh, and there were some additional papers left on a desk at Rita's house that I photographed for you. I think the film is good."

The Professor nodded. She was the perfect secret agent. Her friend Rita's house was occupied by a German general who had allowed Rita to stay on as his hostess. Rita's friends were allowed to visit regularly. They often asked the General – if he had time – to join them for dinner or a game of cards. He thought they were sweet old ladies.

Gran learned how to use a microfilm camera and designed a purse that looked like a simple silk bag with chain handles. Drop the handles and the sides fall down, revealing the camera attached to the bottom of the bag. 'Lady items' covered the camera until it was needed.

The General caught Rita and Gran in his study. Gran said that she had been asked to look at the portrait of the man over the large desk, a former mayor of Leiden. She was interested in bringing it to the town hall in Leiden if it would fit on a specific wall. She needed the dimensions. Could the General help her do that? He agreed. Like Ellie, a born actress, and far braver than she had even been before.

Meanwhile, Ellie was growing restless. Even though she was still in pain, she wanted to walk outside as often as possible. It was mid-November, but it was getting colder than a normal winter. Dora took Wim to school each day before shopping, and Ellie and Gran brought him home at lunch. The distance was only four blocks, but the uneven cobble streets were a challenge. Gran described each street, and Ellie memorized the locations of the stores on each block. She learned how to judge traffic from its sounds. Now the way was often slippery because of frequent autumn rains.

At home, Mrs. Brinker and Gran were teaching Ellie how to knit. Dora had tried and failed when they first met. Now it was a good way to pass the long days, though the only product of the work was a daily round of laughter. That was fine; no argument, laughter was sorely needed. Ellie had always been hopeless at handwork. At least now she had an excuse.

"I want to start storytelling again," Ellie announced one day over breakfast. She didn't see their faces, but she felt their awkward and negative silence. "I know someone will have to be with me, but I desperately need to be doing something. I can wear a scarf or hat, and let my hair hang down so no one should notice my scars very much."

Gran spoke up. "It doesn't sound like a good idea, but we can at least try. Sinterklaas Day is only a few weeks away, so there is no time. But you might be able to do something at church for Christmas. We'll talk to the pastor." (A 'no' from someone outside the family would be better than the family itself continually restricting her movements.)

The next day Ellie and Gran walked to the church through a drizzly rain. Ellie knew where they were as they walked. She knew each bridge that arched over the canals, the bakeries and butcher shops gave her familiar smells to follow, and the sounds of varying traffic helped her figure out some of the larger and smaller street intersections. Ellie's confidence was growing.

"Oh," shouted Gran. Ellie felt Gran's guiding arm suddenly pull her down onto the street.

"What happened?" asked Ellie as she fell to her knees along with Gran. Gran groaned.

"I slipped. I don't think I can get up. I think I twisted or broke my ankle. You need to get help."

"How?" Ellie crumpled to the ground next to Gran. They sat there shivering from the cold and the helplessness of the situation.

"There is a shop over there," Gran pointed, only then remembering that Ellie couldn't see where she pointed. It didn't matter. The shop was closed. She finally howled as loudly as she could, hoping it sounded urgent enough that people might help them rather than think it was a police raid.

It worked. Strangers came and picked them up and helped them to the church which was only a block further down the street. The pastor took them inside.

"Sorry, no heat in the church or the office," he apologized. "But I can call to get someone to take you to Dr. Karel."

Dr. Karel was surprised to see the two women, especially when it was the older woman who needed to see him, not Ellie.

He began by filling out some papers for her visit. "Name?"

"Granada Eloise Turner Smits," Gran answered.

"I had forgotten your full name," Ellie said. "That's why everyone calls you Gran, not Oma."

"Your great-grandparents lived in Spain and loved the city of Granada," Gran reminisced. "When your mother was born during our time in the United States, we decided to name her after a place there. And that is why she is Carolina, not Caroline. Oh, Ellie, you know all this."

"Yes, but I wanted you to be distracted from the doctor working on your foot. He's doing an examination or treatment of some kind?" Ellie asked.

"Yes," said the doctor, "and thanks to you, I am finished. It's a bad sprain, not a break. I've wrapped it as best I could. Keep your foot up as much as possible and watch for swelling. If the swelling doesn't decrease, let me know. No walking for a week or two, and then use a cane. I shall come to you. Do you need a ride home?"

"Yes please," Ellie and Gran answered together.

They were wet and cold through to their very bones. Mrs. Brinker quickly gave them a hot drink and a dry set of clothes. They had soup for lunch and spent the rest of that day and night in the sitting room sleeping in a cocoon of blankets and every spare garment in the house.

It was clear that both Gran and Ellie would be housebound for several weeks. No chance for Ellie to be part of the upcoming holiday celebrations. Never had Ellie felt so helpless in her life.

Dora had never felt so helpless either. It was obvious that she would run the house for a while, make most of the decisions, do the shopping, and help Mrs. Brinker slowly destroy Ben's clothing and uniform. Mrs. Brinker did her best to keep up household morale with creative meals, songs, and light chatter.

Mr. Brinker was the quiet strength that supported the family, silently filling the needs of the family. He was busy with maintenance and gardening, finding wood, harvesting food. Professor Willems tried to help everyone, running himself into exhaustion.

A severe winter was predicted. Rationing was now a joke – nothing seemed available, what with the railway strike that didn't show signs of ending. Postal service was nearly non-existent. The Allies slowed their advance through Holland, and the idiot Germans acted like cornered animals by striking out randomly at everyone.

Even Ellie, the dreamer, the actress, the one that people looked to for a moment of escape or entertainment, was struggling to keep a positive attitude. It was exhausting, but she hated being a burden on those she loved – it was already so hard for everyone.

CHAPTER 26
November, Belgium

One ring, then soft footsteps on the stairs. The door opening as quietly as possible. Albert De Wever was immediately awake.

"Excuse me, sir," the servant bet to whisper. "Her Majesty just phoned. She wants you at her office at once. She didn't wait for an answer. Shall I help you with anything, Sir?"

Albert was now fully alert. "Thank you. No. I'll be down in fifteen minutes and in her office in less than half an hour," he responded, with one foot already on the floor.

Caroline De Wever turned over, now awake. "What is it?"

"Queen Wilhelmina wants to see me, now. Yet another crisis. Just my luck to be acting Ambassador right now. It will be fine, love. Just go back to sleep." He went into the bathroom, splashed water on his face and picked up his razor, concentrating on being both fast and careful. He ran wet fingers through his hair. Not bad, he thought, when he looked in the mirror.

Fortunately, his clothes were laid out every evening for the following day. He dressed, checked himself again in the dressing room mirror, and went downstairs and met the chauffeur waiting for him. It was a short drive this early in the morning, from his residence next to the Dutch Embassy, along the exterior fence of Buckingham Palace to Stratton House. The guard at the Queen's residence recognized him and waved him in.

"Your Majesty," he said. Queen Wilhelmina was sitting at her desk. She waved him over to a chair near her. No matter what time it was, she was dressed and ready for a full schedule of activities. Her official office was next to her living quarters so that she wasted no time traveling between the two. Albert wondered if she ever slept or took time to relax. It was public knowledge that Churchill himself wondered the same thing.

"This morning I received a message from one of my personal agents in Holland. So far no one in my personal network has been captured, and their information has always proved very accurate. This last message is about your daughter. As far as I understand, she is fine. But, she is in danger and we are being asked to rescue her. It is a highly unusual request. What do you know of her involvement with the Resistance Movement?"

Albert was alarmed. Ellie, his Ellie? "Nothing at all."

"Do you know Dr. Matteus Willems?"

"Yes, he lives with my daughter in Leiden. His home was taken over by the Germans back in 1940."

"Ah," the Queen nodded. "Willems is one of my people. I'm guessing that his group is centered in or near your daughter's home. Who else lives there?"

"Her five-year-old son, my mother-in-law Granada Smits, Ellie's house-keeper Dora Linden, and the Brinkers, a married couple who originally worked for the older Van Horns."

The Queen paused, then up her hand to count on her fingers. "It is possible that your daughter's home is more central to my network than I thought. In the greatest of confidentiality, I will share with you what I know. Professor Willems volunteers at the prison. He gathers and exchanges information with the political prisoners there and has escaped German scrutiny thus far. He sends us information from the prisoners as well as from other sources as well."

Albert nodded. He knew of the Professor's work in the prison.

"More of his intelligence comes from townspeople perhaps connected to your daughter and the people living with her. Your mother-in-law frequently travels to the outskirts of The Hague and his messages also include happenings there." The Queen tilted her head to one side. "I'm sorry, I thought you knew this, or at least part of it."

"Oh God," was all Albert could say. Ellie's whole household is involved, and he is only hearing about it now? "What can I do?"

"Willems sent this message last night. It says, "evacLnu" (your daughter Ellie), then "inforkt" (information about the German rocket program). The 'nu' or 'now' is the urgent part and is hardly ever used. Imagine, ordering a queen to act on behalf of just one citizen during wartime," she ventured a chuckle.

"So," she continued, "we need to plan a rescue. It will take a unique team to do this. The southern part of the Netherlands is now liberated, but as you know, Leiden is still under German occupation. We need official Allied cooperation, but the rescue cannot be an officially acknowledged operation. Think, who do you know who might be able to help?"

While Albert sat in silence, the Queen reached for a bell on her desk, rang it, and when the door opened, she calmly said, "Bring us a bit of breakfast and a large pot of tea. Coffee later. We shall be here for a while. No visitors, unless I ask for them. Wait, get Leenders."

Albert was still stunned by what he had heard. As logical as it sounded, he was trying to absorb the enormity of what he had heard. He sat back in the chair, and thought of who he knew after ten years of working in London. So many people came to mind, but none, not one, seemed suited for what she was asking.

As breakfast arrived, a name popped into his head. Not someone he knew very well, or who did anything directly, but possibly had the connections they needed: Lady Jane Archer, from Ellie's old school. He mentioned her to the Queen. He answered some questions about her. He couldn't say why her name came up, just that it did.

The Queen rang her bell again. A senior aide entered. The Queen looked at Albert. "Do you know how to contact her? Or find out where she is?" Albert nodded, giving the name and location of the school to the aide, along with the possibility of a London address.

"Get her here." The aide nodded and left.

Lady Archer turned out to be in London. By midmorning she was in the office with Queen Wilhelmina, Albert, along with one of the queen's chief military aides, Major Arie Leenders.

Albert and the major recognized each other from previous meetings. Leenders was physically fit, someone who could be anywhere from thirty-five to fifty years old. He moved gracefully and economically; even the way he stood at attention was not rigid, but merely his comfortable stance. Without being obvious, he was on constant alert, intense and strong. Albert wouldn't want to cross him.

Lady Archer radiated her own kind of intensity and assurance. What a pair! Albert dared to feel more hopeful if they were in charge of whatever was going to be done.

Maps were now laid out on a conference table in the center of the room. Well-used maps with markings all over them. "I think I can help," Lady Archer smiled after the hour-long discussion of what and how a rescue operation might work. "But you must trust me, without knowing what I have in mind."

Albert nodded. "I can. Ellie and her two best friends often tell us how you show up at surprising times and connect them with all kinds of people and opportunities. You have my utmost trust and support."

"Well then," the Queen used her professional judgment of character, "if Mr. De Wever vouches for you, I add my support. Major Leenders will assist you with whatever you need. Here is my private telephone number."

With that, the conversation was over. Albert was unsure what he could tell Carolina, who was certain to ask what had happened.

Lady Archer returned to her London office and cancelled all of her appointments for the next two weeks, and phoned one of her friends, a certain military officer, to get a seat on the next flight to Melsbroek Airfield outside Brussels. She had dinner with Major Leenders to describe her first set of ideas.

The major was not entirely convinced, but at least it was a starting point. He contacted his own list of people and started to arrange his own plans. Working with people not trained for combat or military operations was an enormous gamble. But Lady Archer was incredibly convincing. He would agree with her for as long as her plan worked, but was ready with his own alternatives. Even the best military operations never worked out the way they were envisioned.

In Brussels, Maggie was deciding on the lead article for the Union Jack. The newspaper presses were now printing in Belgium, and she was an editor once again. There were enough 'raw' stories, but few would pass the censors before press time. She moved a few articles of "Ongoing Fighting in the Forests/Jungles/High Seas on the Front in Such-and-such a country" to the middle of the page and inside next to the advertisements. She decided that "Increased Torpedo Production" was today's headline.

Forget that Allied debacle along the Rhine River near Arnhem. Forget the completion of the Scheldt Estuary clean-up so that the Antwerp harbor could now supply the troops. Those were the real news stories. They might run in American papers, but the British military press was still held to very stiff rules. She was feeling increasingly restricted by her job, both by censorship issues and being back in a permanent office. Still, editor of a newspaper did sound impressive to those who didn't know better.

The best part of the job was that she and Nigel were together, living in a small cottage near the airfield. Nigel traveled most of the time, but when he was home, married life resumed in all its passion and glory. She remembered her family's cook teaching her how to prepare a few dishes and they hadn't starved or burned the house down yet. Having no military aides or servants, it was almost romantic to lead such a common-place married life. Maggie mused that it was the first time they lived together in their whole marriage.

"Ma'am, there is a troupe of ENSA performers waiting to see you," her secretary said.

Not again, thought Maggie. Well, these might be the real thing, not Agnes in costume. "Let them in," she said, standing by the layout table as two women and a man entered the room.

"Getting right to the point," said the man, "how do you want to announce our shows? We are accustomed to putting up stages in fields, but now we have what looks like unlimited theater venues to choose from. Do we buy an advert or can we get a regular article in the paper?"

"Maybe both," Maggie offered. "Let's figure out what works. The rocket attacks can still be a bother when they come down near a building, especially a theater. What shows do you have?"

She ushered them into her office, an inside room, more protection from bombings which still happened on a regular basis. The rocket attacks were truly terrible, both in Brussels and Antwerp. So, away from windows.

As the ENSA officers left, her secretary came in holding a calling card. "A woman came in with this. Didn't want to stay or bother you. She was, well, one of those 'in charge of everything' types. I'm surprised she just didn't march into your meeting."

Maggie took the card. The engraved side bore the calligraphed inscription, "Lady Jane Archer." She turned the card over to read, "Café de L'Opera, Brussels, 1800 hours." Not knowing how to react, she quickly stuffed the card in her pocket.

In Antwerp, Agnes swept up the shards of glass by the recovery room windows of the hospital. She hated, really hated the rocket bombs. Not only were they very destructive, they didn't even have the decency to make a noise as came down. Work in Antwerp was not like the four months in open-air field stations. Now, many of the severely wounded men barely received any care at all in the convent hospital where Agnes worked. Most were sent directly to England by ship or plane. The medical teams, though, still worked around the clock on a variety of military and civilian injuries.

Agnes couldn't get over the irony of finally having real hospital conditions, with beds and supplies, just when they no longer were as desperate for them.

The military thought so too. The hospital units from all over France were converging in Belgium where they waited for orders sending them to more active parts of the war. They expected to be deployed to eastern France and ultimately Germany, or countries in Asia, like India, Burma, or Australia. Agnes had mixed feelings of going that far off. There would be some exotic adventures to be had. Maybe. Let the RAF decide.

An orderly came in as Agnes set the broom against the wall. He held something in his hand, a calling card. One side read, "Lady Jane Archer," and on the other side, elegant handwriting invited her to "Café de L'Opera, Brussels, 1800 hours".

The orderly looked concerned. "Is something wrong, Matron?" he asked.

"I'm not sure how to answer that," Agnes stared at the card. All she knew was where she would be at 6 o'clock that evening.

Maggie and Agnes arrived at the same time. Their looks of surprise and curiosity were followed by resignation. Here we go, they sent a silent message to each other. The restaurant, one of the more elegant ones left in central Brussels, was crowded. The waiter expected them. He ushered them to a small table in one corner of the room.

"Right," said the graceful woman walking towards their table. "Let's get down to business." Lady Archer rarely wasted time on greetings or small talk. "Ellie is in trouble and you girls are the key to getting her rescued. With help, of course."

While the two girls stared at her and each other, Lady Jane continued. "I'll tell you what we know. And then we can figure out what to do." She turned to the waiter, "Three of the best drinks and meals you have on hand. We are on someone else's budget, so spoil us with your best."

Three hours later, they had the outline of a plan. The number of steps for the plan seemed to multiply with each suggestion, but they created smaller lists for each of them to work on, and additional people to contact.

Their part was of course, nurse and driver for the actual team going into occupied territory. The real reason Lady Jane wanted them to go was to convince Ellie to leave. She expected that Ellie would want to stay with her household. Her friends might be the only ones who could get her to leave.

"Two days tops to contact everyone we need and do the first round of work," Lady Jane announced. "Clear your calendars for the next few weeks. Maggie, your office is the most central for our work. Hush, hush, of course, and I have no doubt that you can figure out that part. See you in two days."

At six o'clock, after most workers had left, Maggie opened the door to the layout room. Seven men and women in a variety of uniforms and civilian clothing entered, eyeing one another for how they were to work together.

"Right," Lady Jane used her favorite conversation starter. "Let's get going. A simple rescue behind enemy lines. Introduce yourselves with what skills you bring, and where you are in the plan. To begin, I am Lady Jane Archer. My talent is bringing the right people together, I sincerely hope I've done that."

"Maggie Shelford Drummond. RAF. Journalist, skilled driver, generally handy. As Chief Editor, I closed the layout room to all personnel until this is over. Claiming 'hush, hush' is quite common in war. Right now, I am waiting for further orders."

"Nigel Drummond. RAF Airfield Construction Service. Leading airfield design and repair engineer. Knowledge of airplanes, airfields, and aerial map reading. Right now, studying the landings spots nearest to Leiden and searching for a plane."

"Cody Smith. Canadian Air Force. Air traffic controller, radio specialist, wireless operator, former pilot. Fluent German. Right now, creating an information stream to put on German military radio about an incoming VIP, and working with Allied Command on permitting an unauthorized plane in their air space."

"Agnes Fletcher, RAF Princess Mary Nursing Service. Surgical and Emergency Medicine Specialist. Setting up and running field hospital stations. Worked the London Blitz and northern France. Actress when necessary. Right now, assembling a medical kit."

"Stan Novak. RAF and Polish pilot. Can fly most planes, but best in Spitfires. Helping to look for plane. Fluent German, English okay."

"Arie Leenders. Netherlands Air Force. Pilot. Commando. Assistant Aide de Camp for Queen Wilhelmina. Right now, I am letting our ground contacts know that we are coming and what we need. I speak Dutch, German, French, and also okay English."

"Gertie Roundtree. UK Civilian. Assistant Director for ENSA in Brussels. Also, vetted by OSS to supply costumes, make-up, and acting lessons for folks like you."

"Right," Lady Jane said. "First round of reports and comments?"

Maggie ventured, "It sounds so simple, too simple. Fly in, drive to Leiden, pick up Ellie, back to the airfield, and fly home. Almost too simple."

Lady Jane agreed. "Just so. We still need to find the right plane, know the weather, and figure out a few backup plans for 'in-the-field' circumstances. But if you all have the skills and the character that I think you have, we will be successful. Can we be ready to go in two more days?"

Nigel spoke for them all, "It is a rather tight deadline, but if we must, we can be ready."

Major Arie Leenders was always ready. As a commando, he could be called to action at a moment's notice. He began to move his equipment into a hangar at Melsbroek Airfield as soon as he arrived in Belgium. His own ground network was alerted. Messages were already on their way to Prof. Willems and a few other people. The information that Lady Jane received was passed on to him, the official leader of the operation. His biggest concern was working with a team of 'unknowns.'

The men passed his first test. Military men, used to quick commands, no questions asked, yet willing to go beyond blind orders if necessary. A rare combination in Arie's mind, but present here. He just hadn't worked with them yet to find out the team's strengths and weak spots.

The women were the real worry. Not knowing them at all, he had to go by someone else's recommendations and instincts. They appeared to be capable and serious. Again, how will they work in this team? He'd wait to pass judgment.

Nigel, Stan, Arie, and Cody had the aviation part of the rescue. They chose Ypenburg, an old civilian airfield on the outskirts of The Hague. It looked unused, but Nigel asked for new aerial views. He also wanted to check the length of the runway. That would determine the aircraft to be used.

Cody sent out messages announcing the arrival of a new general in charge of Ypenburg. "The Germans are going to activate it after all – honestly!"

Cody found out that they were planning to use it in the near future, purpose not yet known.

Gertie measured the four team members for clothing, make-up, and wigs to match their roles. Maggie, as a young male from the German motor pool, needed a small Wehrmacht uniform and a way to pin her hair under her helmet. She was taken to an empty hangar where she learned how to drive a Horch, a mid-level German staff car. It was big and heavy, but could carry several passengers.

Agnes was a 'cheap date' for the General. She wore another one of Gertie's oversized dresses and a wig that was curlier than her own hair. In the afternoon, she put the compact medical kit in one of her tapestry bags. The more utilitarian bag contained additional makeup for the team plus a possible extra costume for Maggie or Agnes.

Stan became a German general. Arie would be an SS officer and escort for Stan.

All four practiced gestures that would help them pass German inspection. They also tried to guess what size would fit Ellie – they decided to take both a uniform and a dress for an extra date for the General. Extra padding was in the bag, for warmth and to fill out the costumes.

Stan grinned. "I like being general. Two arms, two women."

Lady Jane was content. She liked having short time lines in projects and operations. It left fewer opportunities for leaking information, plus it maintained concentration solely on the mission. Her favorite quotation came from Martin Luther. "Sin boldly," she remembered. There was more to the quote, but it wasn't important. The braver and bolder you are, the more likely it is that people accept what you say and do. Well, let's be brave and bold.

CHAPTER 27
November, 1944, Leiden

Maggie and Nigel stayed home both evenings before the rescue mission. They pretended that all was normal and quiet. And failed miserably. Dinners were half-eaten, but the wine bottle each night was emptied. The love-making was intense.

"That Lady Archer is exactly as you described her," Nigel said over breakfast. "She combines intimidation and encouragement. Hard to refuse. She demands loyalty, makes you want to push through, for her as much as for anything else. I actually like her in an odd way."

"Exactly. Honestly though, I'm actually more than a little frightened," Maggie finally admitted. "I think we're in over our heads in trying to go through with this. Are we at all prepared for such a daring rescue? I think we're all insane."

"My thinking too," Nigel said. "I wish I could go instead of you. It's times like these that I really hate my hand. Everyone else is doing so much, while I sit by."

"At least you got that warning to Arie and Stan about the new construction going on at the base. That's something that could have really gone wrong. So, it turns out, a *real* new general is coming. Besides, everything you do, wherever you happen to be," she swept her hand in the direction of their bedroom, "is perfectly fine."

Agnes and Stan went out for dinner both evenings. They remained in Brussels near the airport. The first evening was a return to the Café L'Opera. They ate quietly. They drank quietly. Smiled back and forth. They began to talk about the rescue. Agnes was anxious. She described as the adrenalin rush that the body uses to prepare for action. Stan described it like the feeling pilots get just before a big raid.

"It is a mix. First, you are feeling big. You shall be next flying ace, biggest winner in sky. Come home big hero. Then you remember all heroes do not come home. And you feel almost dead before you start. That is bad. You must put bad thoughts away, like garbage, before getting into plane," he tried to explain. "Same for us now. Bad thoughts are garbage."

They walked towards the bus that would take them back to Melsbroek, telling stories about Jan. They ignored the bus stop, turned onto a side street, and entered a small hotel. Nothing was said, no invitation, no suggestion, just a natural movement. Stan registered them at the desk, and they went to a room. Between laughing and crying, they held each other tightly, moving slowly, becoming more intimate, trying to make the night last forever. Agnes was full of wonder. What had taken her so long to join her love-making friends? Ah, the right guy and the right moment, silly. Her 'serious' side reminded her that Stan is a pilot. Who cares, said the new 'happy' Agnes.

They woke the next morning, wondering if life would ever be the same. Although they had been seeing each other ever since the summer, neither wanted to proclaim undying love. But there was more to their night together than being close friends. This was a dramatic change from whatever that relationship had been before.

"Last night was for memory of Jan. Next time we do this," Stan said, "we make memories for us."

Agnes agreed as they put on their uniforms. They went back to the hotel on the following night. It was both more relaxed and more exciting, even if the thoughts of the rescue hung in the air. They woke up very early, smiling and laughing. By the time they were dressed, however, they were intensely serious and quiet.

"Time to throw out garbage," Stan said.

The rescue operation was ready to go. The whole team met at Melsbroek Airfield in the early morning. Arie, Stan, and Maggie wore bulky German Army overcoats on top of their other clothes. Maggie was General Stan's driver, on his way to take command over Ypenburg Airfield. Arie was in full SS black, complete with motorcycle pants and high boots. Agnes was in a heavy fur coat over her padded brocade dress, not complaining about the extra padding on this cold morning.

The mission was going in full daylight, not sneaking in. It was threatening to rain; visibility was marginal. As bad as the flying might be, ground movements would only be expected from people who had to be out. That might be good.

Cody sat in the Melsbroek Air Control Tower, ready to direct the pilots. According to Cody, the German forces expected 'the new general' to fly in after inspecting the Maas River border (hence the approach from the south) and were ready to welcome him.

The girls saw the plane for the first time: a Junker Ju-52. It was a utility plane that could be used either as a bomber or transport. Many countries used it for commercial passenger travel. The Germans had discontinued using it as a warplane, but it was still a common sight throughout Europe. This one was camouflaged, but had no national identification or number. Cody received permission from Allied forces for the Junker fly over 'friendly' territory of Belgium. Maggie stared at the plane. Something looked odd. It had three motors. Was that a good or bad thing? She'd ask Nigel later.

They boarded the plane and took off, never gaining much altitude. Maggie wasn't sure that they could clear the tops of the trees they flew over. The distance of the whole flight was only eighty miles, maybe thirty minutes. She worried about what she overheard Nigel say about the landing. "Approach as low and slow as possible, in a controlled stall. The runway is officially too short for this plane." She had an image of the plane crash in Manchester with the parachute trainees on board.

For Agnes, it was her first flight. Here she was, a Flight Nurse, having never flown. She didn't have time to think about what Stan might really mean to her. She didn't have time to think about anything before she realized they were landing.

The pilots brushed the trees that lined the airfield and touched down on the front edge of the runway. There was less than ten feet left of pavement when they came to a complete stop at the other end. Stan and Arie exhaled loudly. Oh, thought Maggie, it *was* a close call. Well, first step done.

A few soldiers and airmen circled the plane, mostly out of curiosity.

"Well," boomed Stan's voice in German as he stepped out of the plane. "Seen enough? See how great our pilots are? Even a big plane can land here. Why are you all just standing around? Where is my greeting committee? Where is my staff car? I have no time to review this place right now. I must first do some personal errands before taking over this place. Move!"

And move they did. Arie nodded to a few airmen in the background. They came forward and talked to him. One brought over a motorcycle with a side car, another gave him some folded papers and pointed at places around the airfield and beyond.

A Horch staff car drove up to them. Stan continued to be pompous and in command. "My own driver will take over," He pointed to Maggie who changed places with the driver. She was nervous about her short training in a Horch in Belgium, but at least it felt a bit familiar. Stan and Agnes got in the back seat. Arie finished the loading of four crates of equipment into the rear of the car. He then climbed onto the motorcycle and casually tested the motor. He nodded to Maggie who nodded back, adjusted his helmet and goggles, and led them out onto the road to Leiden.

"I don't think we are followed. Arie is like race car driver," Stan said. "Can you keep up?"

"We'll find out," Maggie stared through the drizzle. The car responded like a mid-sized truck. With the streets full of mud and potholes (or bomb craters, who cares which), keeping up was going to take all her concentration.

"I'm looking forward to seeing Ellie and Gran again. And Wim for the first time. How will we get Ellie without Wim? Can we take them both?" Agnes wondered aloud.

"Of course," Stan said in surprise. "We talk about that back in Belgium. I'm surprised you not know. Wim is small, not take up space, so not part of official plan, just understood."

Without road signs, Maggie only half listened to the conversation. She was glad that Arie knew where to go. Her curiosity was mounting when he slowed down for a hitchhiker. It might be a man or woman in a heavy coat. Arie stopped long enough for the person to get into the side car, and then sped up again.

They drove into the center of Leiden. Maggie recognized the church where Ellie and Pieter were married. Then a few blocks later, the motorcycle pulled up to a house on the corner of a street. Ellie's house.

Arie's passenger got out of the side car and went to the front door. It was opened by a young woman, not Ellie. It must be Dora, the housekeeper. Dora let the passenger in, but froze when she saw the German soldiers exiting their vehicles. The passenger waved to the rest of the group to come in. A few heads peaked through curtains in neighboring houses and immediately pulled back in when they saw the *razzia* taking place. An SS motorcyclist and two soldiers entering the De Wever's house. Not good.

Agnes and Maggie pulled off their caps and wigs. Gran recognized them immediately and stood, opening her arms to welcome them. The hitchhiker had been Prof. Willems. Another couple came into the sitting room and joined in the reunion. The little boy who was following them must be Wim, thought Agnes, and the couple must be the Brinkers.

Arie in the SS uniform terrified them, until they realized that he was really Dutch and a close friend of the Professor.

Where was Ellie?

"It's okay, Ellie," said Gran. She looked at Maggie and Agnes and motioned them to remain quiet. Ellie entered the room, and for the first time, it was obvious that she was extraordinarily thin, and most obviously, blind. Nothing had been said to prepare anyone for that. Arie inhaled quietly and stared. His mind was racing. Adjusting plans, making new plans.

Both girls, quickly overcoming their initial shock, went to Ellie. They held each other tightly.

"And now what?" Ellie asked, after the initial excitement slowed. "What made you come here? This is really dangerous." She was unaware of Arie and Stan who stood at the side of the room.

Arie spoke up in Dutch. "I am Major Arie Leenders, aide to the Queen in London. We are taking you and your son to London. We know that this is a big surprise to you, but Professor Willems has explained everything to your household and they agree that you should leave. It is dangerous for you here, and you have information that will be very valuable to us in England. And, we have to hurry."

Professor Willems explained further, "The people who will take you are Maggie, Agnes, Stan, and Arie. I am giving them a packet of information to take to Queen Wilhelmina."

"I can't go," Ellie began to weep. "I am needed here."

Gran laughed, "If anything, you are a hindrance, and you know it. Now, we have already packed a small bag for you and Wim, including a few small toys."

Ellie answered, "I can't go without you, Gran. You are in bad shape as well. We can't all seven of us make it through the winter, can we?" She turned her head, waiting for an answer. "Can Gran come too? Is there room?"

Everyone in the room looked at Arie. First change of plans was not being able to return in the Junker, just not enough runway. Now, the rescue is for a blind woman, and then adding another passenger, an older woman who walked with a cane. The risks were adding rapidly. He was not happy. After a quick survey of the room, he decided, "It must be fast. We are supposed to be taking you in a *razzia*. Can you pack quickly for the lady?" Dora nodded.

Arie ordered, "Do that while we get everyone into the staff car. As slowly as we can to give you some time."

Translations back and forth to the housekeepers and all was done. Gran and Ellie were the only ones who understood all of the conversations. Wim stood silently, too confused and frightened to do anything. He held on to his stuffed bear, which felt strange, and watched what was happening around him. Tears flowed as farewells began. Leaving for safety, staying in mortal danger, separating after being so interdependent.

Gran turned to Professor Willems. "What about you? Can't you come?"

"Alas, no," he replied. "I need to manage the rest of my network from here. Besides, we will be fine. Mr. Brinker and Pieter built all that fancy molding around the ceilings of the main rooms, remember? Well, they are storage areas filled with tinned food. With fewer mouths to feed, we can make it through the winter. And the molding can be used for fires to keep us warm. The war cannot last much longer. And then, Granada, we will be together, hopefully in a home of our own, by ourselves. Yes?"

"Yes," Gran suddenly looked like a little girl with her first proposal. It might be her role to lift everyone's spirit, rather than rely on Ellie. Her granddaughter was too wound up with her sudden kidnapping to make much sense. She felt a surge of energy come from the people around her. She stood up using a cane. Looking around at the group, she said, "Then let's get going. I promise to keep up with you all. Do I get a costume too?"

CHAPTER 28
November, 1944, The Maas

Arie took the lead again as they left Leiden. Maggie tried to stay close behind him. Stan now sat in the front seat with Maggie. In the back were Ellie and Gran, each in wool coats with thick mink collars, and Agnes in her ENSA fox fur coat. Stan thought they looked like the mammal exhibit at a zoo. Wim and his bear were wrapped in a woolen blanket on Ellie's lap. He was quiet, bewildered by what was happening. There was no time for a last view of Leiden, or farewells, or a chance to adjust to their sudden departure.

Gran was reeling from what was happening. She first heard about the rescue two days ago. The whole household did. Except for Ellie, of course. Professor Willems wrote a note which he silently passed around to the family advising them of the plan. Gran let Dora pack small overnight cases for Ellie and Wim while she and Ellie were at Doctor Karel's office. Wim's bear was stuffed with some of the secret documents and recent films that the Professor gathered from his network.

Gran was prepared to see them leave. She wasn't prepared to leave with them. Now, with a proposal from Matteus, she wanted to stay behind with him. She struggled with the logic that Ellie needed her more, and that she might be a liability to those left in the house. She felt powerless and grateful at the same time. She hoped not to be a liability as a last-minute burden. At least her sprained ankle was healing quickly.

Conversation was in English, as friends caught up on their news. Ellie described her blindness due to a grease fire. Gran kept her eyes closed during the story. It had never sounded right, but there was never a way to find out anything more. Wim fell asleep, bored and unable to understand any English.

Agnes related her adventures of hospitals in tents and the improvising she had done, emphasizing the funny bits. Ellie talked about her storytelling career and using their trunk as a wagon. Maggie concentrated on driving.

"I guess we've all be improvising one way or another to get through all this," Ellie said. "Our lives haven't followed any of the paths we thought they would. We've really had to stay rather creative, haven't we?"

As the initial catching up slowed down, Agnes offered, "I want to give you a medical examination when we stop. You'll get some great specialists in England, but I want to check on your progress so far. One good thing about war – treatment of burn injuries has gotten a great leap forward. I also want to see your ankle, Gran."

Gran came out of her private thoughts. "Thanks, but I am nearly healed. If you wrap my ankle a bit tighter, I can walk unaided. I do around the house. That cane is more a psychological crutch than real support. But check-ups are always a good idea." She added, "I have to be in good shape. I suppose I need to start planning my wedding as soon as we are in London."

Arie sped through cities and towns at a dare-devil pace. Maggie's passengers found Arie's lead and Maggie's ability to keep up equally terrorizing. No one stopped the two vehicles; Arie as an SS escort to a German staff car didn't raise much curiosity. Gran tried to identify the towns to Ellie, but couldn't figure out why they were heading towards Dordrecht.

"Where are we going?" Ellie asked. "This is a strange way to get back to the Hague."

"We don't go back to airfield," Stan said. "Landing was very dangerous. Runway is too small. Take-off uses more runway. Arie has new plan with friends to cross river through Bee's Bush. Is that right?"

"Biesbosch," Ellie said. "Pieter and I went there when Wim was a baby. It is a beautiful area of islands in the middle of the Maas River." She paused, "Is that how we will get to Allied territory? The Maas is the border between the occupied and liberated areas. It must be heavily guarded."

"You sound rather nervous," Agnes said. "What is the Biesbosch like?"

"Well the whole area is very low ground, marshy in many areas. There are some higher grounds, a few islands with bushes and trees. There might be fishing huts there too. I remember thinking that the waterways were like a maze. That might help. But there are so many of us."

"We work out plan with local help," Stan tried to be reassuring.

Maggie listened as much as she could, but concentrated on driving. She hoped Arie was having fun. Did he think this was a game, zipping around road hazards on the motorcycle? Was he showing off? Or testing her? The car was heavy even without passengers and crates. He should take that into consideration. This is insane, she thought, both the demands on her and the car, and she was insane for going along with it. At least the rain remained a misty drizzle, not a downpour. The streets were wet and slippery, but she kept her eyes on Arie as she swerved around another crater.

They left the last city. She stole glances to the side and saw windmills in the mist and isolated farms in the distance.

With no real warning, Arie stopped. Maggie had to hold the car steady as she braked hard, trying not to hit him. A farmer had flagged them down. He got into the side car and Arie began to move again, much slower this time. Maggie followed him onto a side road, really a sand and gravel lane. There was a small cottage with an attached barn in front of them. The oversized barn door opened, they were directed in, and the door was quickly closed behind them. The farmer and another man took a horse-drawn wagon across the lane several times to hide their tire tracks.

The group followed Arie into the adjoining one-room cottage. There were a few chairs and a table in the center of the room and a pile of blankets in one corner. Stan brought in two crates from the car. They contained food, wine, and side arms with ammunition.

The farmer came in and talked with Arie over a bottle of jenever gin and shared cigarettes while the rest of the group huddled in a corner and watched. Maggie thought back on a photo she saw of a refugee family, huddled under blankets. This was not much different from the photos. We have no power over what happens, just like that family.

Wim and Gran stayed in a corner, talking quietly. The conversation grew from friendly to heated back to friendly. Deep silences followed each interaction. Ellie whispered her translation to Stan and the girls. "They're talking about boats. It seems that they can't take all seven of us in one crossing. They're deciding whether to take some of us now, or wait until we can all go tomorrow. Arie insists that we stay together. Wait. Now it looks like all of us tomorrow. Something about tides, and food, and being too late to call up more help today."

Stan observed, "Ah. Well, we have more of that gin, water, and tinned goods. For helpers and for us too."

After the farmer and Arie shook hands, the farmer left. Arie addressed the group.

"It is nearly dark and we must eat. No fires, no lights. Stan and I will each take two-hour shifts through the night to watch for any Germans in the area. Stay dressed so we can leave quickly if necessary. You must try to sleep. If you can't sleep, at least stay in restful positions with your eyes closed. Partner up to stay warm."

Stan chose to take the first watch.

Wim, who up until now had been invisible to everyone except Ellie and Gran, crept up to Arie, who invited him into his lap. "Are you very brave? Have you killed a lot of people?" Wim asked.

Arie smiled in the dim light. "I have killed people, yes, but only because they tried to hurt my friends. I am not sure if that is brave or just what people do when they have no choices."

Wim thought for a moment. He whispered in Arie's ear. "I have to be brave for Mama. Professor Willems said that even if we are sad that Mama can't see, we cannot cry. Just help her and pretend that we are all right."

Arie agreed. "Well tomorrow, we all have to be very brave. No crying, of course, but also no noises at all. We don't want to scare the animals in the Biesbosch or let the Germans know we are here. You can do that, right?"

"I can do that," Wim promised with great solemnity. "Do you have a family?"

"Not anymore," Arie said, glad that it was now dark and no one could see his face. Wim sounded like an old man. He decided to be open, something most of his comrades never heard. "Our house was bombed one night and no one was left. I was in the Air Force in England, so I couldn't help them. It made me angry, then sad. But when I help people, I feel good again."

"It is sad when people die. They go away and don't come back. That happens sometimes at school. I like helping my friends at school. What can I do here?" asked Wim. "I am five years old, you know, not a baby." He was quiet for a while.

Arie gave Wim, too old and wise for his age, a squeeze on his shoulder, "Don't worry Little Man, everyone on our team here will have something to do tomorrow, even you. You'll see."

Wim left him and crawled back over to Gran and Ellie. "Tell me a story, Momma." Ellie wrapped her blanket and arms around him. They found a way to nest into each other.

"I was remembering my room when I came home from school. It was filled with flowers – wall paper, fresh blooms in a vase. The bright colors. They reminded me of a folk tale I heard first in Bagdad."

No one understood Dutch except for Gran and Arie, but the soft voice of a trained storyteller relaxed her, her son, and her very tense and tired audience.

Stan came in from his watch. "Your turn, Arie." He crept over to Agnes. "Let's go out to garage. We can rest in private."

"Do you think that's okay?" Agnes asked.

"We make Arie jealous, that's all," replied Stan. "What are we fighting for? Only to protect people in love."

"Arie reminds me of a cat waiting to jump on a mouse," Agnes said. "Enormous energy waiting to be released."

Stan let out one little laugh. "Waiting for action. Always ready. Always on alert. Now for us, no alert, only ready for action. Come on." There were numerous challenges: finding the car in the dark, opening the door quietly, fumbling through layers of clothing, remaining silent while wanting to scream out in delight, fumbling to get dressed again, the car door again, all during Stan's two-hour 'rest'.

Arie's final watch was over. He woke everyone at the first light of dawn. "Time to go. Sinterklaas came last night." Wim looked up at hearing the name of his favorite saint. "He left us some eggs. I will leave some jenever and food as thanks. Did any of you get any sleep? No? Don't worry, today you can sleep on the boats."

He put on his knee-high leather boots and overcoat. "Here's what is happening. We are in luck. The tides will be going out, increasing our speed down the main part of the Maas as it goes towards the sea. There is also a heavy mist covering the river that will keep us invisible during that part of the trip. And, with daily bombing missions going in both directions, the sound of the small boat motors will be covered. The whole trip should be about four or five hours long. First part is getting to the boats. Ready? Let's go!"

Maggie couldn't believe that this was only the second day of their adventure. Everyone moved exactly as they were ordered. No complaints. She wished her warcos were as cooperative.

The farmer from the previous evening came as they piled into their 'assigned' seats in the Horch. He spoke quickly to Arie and opened the barn door for the motorcycle and the Horch, shutting it quickly before erasing their muddy tracks again.

Maggie followed Arie as though this was what she did every day. The rain was over, but there was a fog surrounding them. The roads were becoming smaller, less used. Arie stopped suddenly. What else is new, she thought. Arie waved her to stay in the car. He looked around, studying the land ahead and to both sides. When he walked back to the car, he looked grim.

"We have a problem, "he said to Maggie as everyone listened. "There is a stream ahead with a very narrow bridge over it, only for horse carts, and we are still several kilometers from the boats. Plus, even if everyone could walk the distance, we don't have the time according to the tide schedule."

Agnes, hearing this, wiggled out of the back of the car and trotted over to the bridge in her dress shoes. She grinned all the way back to the car. "No problem," she laughed. "Maggie, Ellie, we are back in school!"

Maggie stepped out and saw the "problem". It was a small stone bridge, the walls forming arches that sloped down to the land on each side of the bridge. She laughed along with Agnes.

She called out, "everyone out of the car." Ellie was eager to know what is happening. It was hard to wait for an answer. Gran explained what she saw. Ellie smiled.

Agnes paced the road behind the Horch several times, then went to the bridge and paced from one side to the other. She pushed on the stone sides of the bridge walls, only a foot high.

"A few rocks on either end should do it." She waved Stan, Wim, Gran, and Arie to join her in shoring up the ends of the bridge walls.

"Perfect!" Then she herded everyone including Ellie across the bridge. She crouched down and began to direct Maggie over the bridge. The tires of the Horch rode the top of the walls across to the other side. Gran described the whole scene like a radio reporter. Ellie wished she could see the latest version of their school time prank. She suddenly wondered where their MG's were. Hers was still in London.

Gran, who knew the original story, enjoyed seeing it in action, and it was obvious from how she described it. Bravo, she thought. Stan and Arie could only stare at the feat. Maggie crossed the bridge, more amazed than her audience that she actually did it. She pretended that it was routine, what else could she do? Agnes led Ellie over to Maggie who had gotten out of the car. They were school girls again, standing in the barn looking at the Headmistress' car.

Very few people impressed Arie. Maggie was now one of them. She didn't need encouragement or praise, a true professional. But it was time to go. "Nice job. Let's go. No time to lose."

The mood back inside the car was joyous and confident, but Arie and Stan were on high alert. The farmer had told Arie, who shared the news with Stan, that the Germans were looking for them. The real 'new general' arrived at Ypenburg to start the recommissioning of the airfield. Time and speed were now crucial for the escape to be successful.

They still needed to cross the wide river with its heavy shipping traffic and even heavier military surveillance. The Germans were retreating and trying desperately to hole on to what they still had.

Arie stopped the motorcycle very suddenly again. Would he ever learn to slow down gradually and warn her what he was doing? Probably not. Arie ordered everyone out of the car.

CHAPTER 29
November 1944, Brussels

They stood on the banks of the river. They could barely see the two men who greeted Arie, and the pair of shallow-draft boats tied to a tree stump.

After some pointing at the group, shaking heads and nodding heads, Arie turned and announced, "The three De Wevers and Agnes in one boat, leaving now. We three will get rid of the car and motorcycle and join you in the marshes with the second boat."

Maggie watched Agnes and the boatmen take Gran, then Ellie into the boat along with their first aid kit and travel cases. Wim climbed on board by himself. Waterproofed canvas lined the bottom of the boat, followed by a layer of wool fleece.

The passengers were directed to specific places to balance the boat. They were covered by heavy blankets. A final layer of canvas was laid over them, propped up at both ends to allow air into the middle of the boat. The boatman lifted his hand, signaling that he was ready.

They pushed off into the river, where they disappeared quickly into the mist. Arie was happy to hear planes overhead; no one heard the low hum of the boat's motor.

Arie turned to Maggie. "Can you do it again? That bridge thing?"

Maggie was unsure, but heard herself say, "Yes."

She turned the car around and followed Arie back to the bridge.

"You really like Agnes?" Maggie asked Stan. "She has been through so much. I want to make sure that you're the right one for her."

"Yes. You are friend and sister for her," Stan replied. "Agnes and I are alike. Too much sadness. We finally leave memory of Jan behind and now I think we can say I love you without thinking of him in middle. Agnes will not always be nurse. She also has tea company business."

Maggie nodded as she drove. "She said that your family also had a large business in Poland."

Stan explained, "All is gone, but yes it was big. After war, I want to stay with planes. Russian man in America is making helicopters, new design. I am interested. But I stay in England and work with him here. And be with Agnes."

Arie stopped at the bridge, which stopped Maggie and Stan from any further discussion.

"Okay. Ready?" Arie called.

Stan got out of the Horch. He and Arie crossed the bridge, Arie crouching like Agnes to guide her as she lined up with the side walls of the bridge. She couldn't believe that she had to make the vehicle and the bridge cooperate again.

"Drive the car halfway across, turn, and have it nearly go into the water."

Maggie tried to figure out how that would work. She watched Arie's hand signals and brought the front of the Horch onto the walls of the bridge. She held on tightly and abruptly steered to the right. The car jammed into and down on the stone wall, settling at an odd angle. She forced open the left door and slid across the side of the car and onto the road. That movement threw the car completely off-balance and it landed in the water upside down, taking the side of the bridge with it. Was this what he meant? She hoped so.

"Just in time," Arie said as he looked down the road. "Here they come. Stan, ready?"

Stan nodded. Maggie's heart sank. She stood there watching.

272

A Kubelwagen approached. A German officer and an armed soldier got out. "What is going on here?" the officer asked as he studied them. Arie's SS uniform made him nervous and unsure. Arie and Stan walked towards the Germans.

"What luck," Stan the 'general' took the lead. "We need your Wagen. As you can see, I need transportation and I am short of time. Stupid driver, really too young to be driving me around. But they are drafting everyone these days, even children. And now *this!*"

"But you could ride with your aide," said the officer who looked at the SS uniformed man and his motorcycle standing behind Stan. Arie glared and began to laugh.

"You must be mad." Stan turned around to head back to the Horch.

Arie sensed that the German officer doubted their story. Was he looking for them? Behind the officer, the soldier moved. Arie saw him reach for his rifle. Arie moved his own hand to the pistol at his hip. Stan saw Arie move, and spun around with his own handgun. Maggie crouched down to be as small a target as possible.

With the speed that happens in such situations, a gun fight started and ended. Arie was still standing, Stan was on his hands and knees. The two men from the Wagen were flat on the ground. Maggie stood, having been ignored by everyone. Then she moved.

"Stan," Maggie ran to him. "What's wrong?"

"Shoulder," he grunted.

Arie called Maggie, "Can you drive the Kubelwagen? They got me too." He pointed to the blood beginning to come out from a point of his thigh as he walked towards Stan.

Maggie stared at the Wagen. It looked like a jeep. Easy enough, hopefully. This was getting silly, all this driving. I am not in the ATS, I am a – what? I don't know any more.

Arie tied his belt around his thigh, then helped Maggie get Stan into the Wagen. She drove directly through the shallow stream above the bridge without any problem. The bouncing over rocks and tree branches that had floated downstream made Stan groan. Maggie apologized but just drove faster to get that part over with. The return trip to the boats was short. Arie told the local men what happened and one of them promised to drive the Wagen back to the bridge. They were helped into the remaining boat and pushed off.

"You're lucky," the boatman said to Arie, who alternately limped and hopped into the boat. "The river is at full ebb tide, so we can go full speed all the way to the turn into the marsh. The mist is still in our favor, though not as thick. Now, down under the canvas you go."

Arie grunted, "No, not yet. First we have to help Stan. He is bleeding a lot." The boatman saw that Stan was badly wounded as he turned up the motor.

"We have nothing," Maggie said, not sure of what to do. "Agnes has the medical kit and the rest of our supplies in the other boat."

Arie looked at Stan who was in obvious pain, his shoulder getting bloodier by the second. "It isn't an artery," Arie said, "no pumping going on. We must try pressure and try not to move him too much. Leave his jacket on. He needs to sit up to keep his heart even or below the wound."

Maggie nodded and helped Arie move Stan into a sitting position. Her look questioned Arie's decisions.

"All commandos get medical training just for this type of event," he explained. "Trust me." His own leg was still bleeding slightly as he moved next to Stan on his other side. He took out his bag of cigarette tobacco, shook out a handful of crushed dried leaves and handed them to her. Then he took a handful himself, emptying the bag. "Now, put it in your mouth and chew until it is paste. Then spit it out in my hand."

A few minutes later, Maggie gave Arie a wad of tobacco that looked as disgusting as it had tasted. He placed it in the hole of Stan's jacket, and pressed down. He released his belt from his leg and wrapped it across Stan's chest to hold the compress in place.

He rolled over Maggie to balance the shallow draft vessel. He leaned back. "Tobacco and tea are known for helping to stop bleeding."

"But now we have neither."

"In about an hour we will meet the other boat with Agnes and the medical kit. I can make it without too much trouble. Stan, not sure he can, but we have done what we could."

Stan was now wedged between them. He was in obvious pain, holding his breath for long periods of time to keep from making any noise. Arie, too. Soon, she stopped paying attention to them and allowed the rocking of the boat and the hum of the engine to put her into a deep sleep.

She woke with a start. The engine had stopped, the boat was no longer rocking, and the men were stirring. Agnes was there to greet them.

"Oh my God! What happened?" shouted Agnes, her smile changing to horror. Maggie sat up and realized that all three of them were blood-stained.

"We were shot as we left. Stan is worse off than Arie. I am fine, this must all come from them," she saw her own gray uniform with red blotches on it.

"Well, get them out of the boat now!" ordered Agnes. She and the boatmen pulled Stan out and laid him on the ground. Arie waved off assistance, then accepted a helping hand to limp off the boat. "Stan first," he grunted. "Then we have to keep moving."

"Not until you are both stabilized," Agnes said, taking over. "Pull that canvas cover over here and get the two men on it. Maggie, find all the alcohol we have – the gin, wine, whiskey, whatever we have. Ellie, tell Wim to get my medical kit. Gran, bundle up a blanket and make a hard bundle about the size of a bedroom pillow. Ellie, sit here and translate to the boatmen for me. Ask them for a knife."

One nodded and Maggie followed him, used sign language to get a good-sized knife, and then, with more sign language, made both of them stand as guards over the landing site. They wanted to leave as soon as possible, but Maggie made it clear to them that they must wait.

As Maggie collected the 'alcohol', she realized that the mist was clearing and that they needed to be sheltered. Just off the water's edge was a flat area half-circled by bushes dripping with moisture. She shook the branches violently to get rid of the water. They were a perfect water-level screen. She ran to the first boatman, motioning him to help her. He and his friend understood what she wanted. The three of them pulled the canvas from a boat and draped it over the bushes to create a roof. Then they dragged the canvas with the injured men on it under the make-shift roof. Agnes knelt to begin her work.

She undid Arie's belt and removed the compress. She looked at Maggie.

"Tobacco," Maggie said.

"Oh, okay. Almost as good as tea. For small bleeding at least. Not this."

She used the boatman's knife to cut away a large part of Stan's jacket. Where was the bullet? What was its trajectory? It looked like a very bad location and angle. Stan's skin was white and cold. He wasn't dead, but this was critical. The wound was close to his heart and lungs. He was so pale. Could she find the bullet *and* stop whatever was bleeding so much? Only one way to find out. She turned him on his side. The bullet had gone through his whole body. So, now it was a matter of bleeding. She would have to make a large incision to find its source. Gran came forward with her bundle. The two women rolled Stan onto his stomach over the bundle. With his back stretched like that, it would be easier to work, she could work through his rib cage.

Maggie brought a bottle of gin and a half a bottle of brandy.

"Drink as much gin as you can, Arie," Agnes ordered, taking the brandy. "We have no anesthesia and it looks like your leg really hurts. Gran, you hold the rolls of bandages. Wim, take all the white cloths out of the kit, all of them, and fold them into squares about this size." She showed him what she meant. Ellie translated and Wim went to work with Gran's help. "Be ready when I ask for them."

Agnes made the bullet hole in large and splashed the brandy on the incision. He groaned loudly without waking up. Now, Agnes took a deep breath. She opened the bullet hole and saw very little that would help her know what to do. She was desperate to help him, but didn't see where the bleeding could be coming from. Just compress the wound at this point, she told herself. A little more brandy and she covered the wound with the cloths. Gran and Wim kept handing her cloths as she asked for them.

"Maggie, look in the travel cases. Pull out a blouse or shirt. Fold it up. Put it over Wim's squares and press it against the wound. Gran, remove Stan's belt and strap the cloth tightly across his body. Then you two, roll him over. Cut the hole in his jacket a bit bigger, splash around some of the brandy, take another piece of cloth and do the same thing I just did. Use some of the bandage roll to cross over his body to keep it all in place."

She watched as they began to follow her instructions. She picked up Arie's belt and turned her head towards him. "You're next."

Arie winced and nodded.

"Are you properly sloshed?"

"Doesn't matter, does it?"

"Here we go," Agnes said. She turned her whole body towards Arie, still crouching. Together they tightened the belt around his upper thigh. The same procedure for a bullet wound, though Arie had already cut his trousers open with his own knife. He had been studying her procedures and figured out how he could help her. She looked at him and nodded.

She found the bullet in the center of his thigh muscle without having to cause him much extra pain. "Souvenir for you," she said as she handed him the bullet without looking up.

"I'll add it to my collection," Arie gritted his teeth. She used the last of Wim's bandages to press on Arie's leg, using up the remaining bandaging to wrap his thigh.

"Can we go now? We really need to be on the move."

Agnes was torn. Moving was so dangerous for Stan. But not being able to do any more where they were, she agreed. Agnes and Maggie changed places in the boats so that Agnes could take care of the two men. Stan was totally unconscious from losing so much blood. Arie was weak from losing blood and now very drunk from the heavy intake of gin. The girls rolled up the two canvases and hid them in the thick bushes around their surgery site. The boatmen started up their motors.

Everyone finally back in the boats, the boatmen set a faster pace. They explained through Ellie that they were fairly safe now. The Germans didn't like the marshes; they were constantly getting lost in the maze of streams. They were also far enough from the main river channel that they shouldn't be followed. Still, they were on the edge of German territory, and needed to remain very cautious. Ellie tried to remain calm along with Gran, singing softly with Wim, while listening to the world around her. It was frustrating not to see, to know where they were, to help.

"Welcome to Drimmelen. You're in Allied territory," the first boatman said an hour later. It was late afternoon, and the sun was low in the sky. They pulled into a small harbor. Two bakery vans were parked at the land end of a short dock. One driver helped the boatmen tie up the boats.

Arie woke up and tried to focus on the next steps of their travel, but was barely on the edge of consciousness. He wasn't even at the start of a hangover yet. Luckily, he had told Maggie, Ellie, and Agnes the rest of the plan.

Ellie, Gran, and Wim got out of the boat. Ellie, speaking Dutch, used the code words to connect with their rescuers. Maggie went over to Agnes and the men.

"I hope you have some purple nail polish," she said to one of the drivers. She kept her face hidden behind her loose long hair.

"We do, we just got a new shipment, it is in the vans. Let's go."

"That won't be quite as simple as you think," Ellie said. She translated what she could into English, then directed one driver to help Arie in his tattered SS uniform, who staggered and limped with help. He reeked of alcohol. The driver was disgusted until he saw the dried blood that went from the mid-thigh bandage to the toe of his boot. Arie said a few words before he fell into the van and continued his sleep. The drivers then carried 'General' Stan to the van and placed him next to Arie. A No one wanted to determine his status. A woman in an evening gown and fur coat stayed with them.

A woman dressed in a man's Wehrmacht uniform acted as though she was in charge of the group. She ran back and forth helping settle the men into the van along with the dressy woman. The drivers looked back at the lady who first talked to them. She held onto a small boy with a stuffed bear and an elderly lady with a cane, and they suddenly realized that she blind. A strange group to rescue, even in war, the drivers mused.

"We will travel all together in one van," Gran said in a very command-ing voice. The drivers both responded to the upper class accept and imperial manner instinctively. Gran as lady in charge. "And bring our three travel bags, if you don't mind."

The final step in the adventure was an anti-climax. The van drove through Breda to Agnes' hospital in Antwerp. Stan was declared dead on arrival at the entrance. The doctor tried to assure Agnes that no matter how quickly or how professionally he had been treated, Stan would not have survived. She wasn't convinced. Her heart slammed shut, as dead as Stan. She agreed to go with the rest of the team to Brussels, but didn't say a word. Ellie was now taking care of Agnes. She didn't know what to say or do, so she just held her limp hand. The group crammed back into the van and rode in silence.

Maggie directed the drivers directly to the Melsbroek Airfield, where the rest of the team was waiting. Lady Jane and Nigel sorted everyone out. Phone calls to London were arranged. Cody ordered dinner to be brought to the hangar. Nigel brought clothing for the women from Maggie's closet. Arie, now awake and feeling the beginnings of a vile hangover, allowed the airfield medics to look at his leg, but only after reporting to Queen Wilhelmina.

Lady Jane sat down next to Arie and asked, "Well? How was it, really?"

Arie took his time, "Amateurs, no training in ops, we shouldn't have been this successful. Your girls, something else again. Even by my standards, solid professionals. Stan was a bad one to lose, though. One of a kind."

Over their late dinner, they told their story, details getting jumbled as questions kept interrupting them. Although they were hungry, sleep was what they really needed. Lady Jane saw that and decided to save the debriefing for the next day.

"We'll be going to London in three days," Lady Jane announced. "Maggie, tomorrow you will write up the official brief version of the mission and also a detailed version for me."

"What? So soon? I feel like I have been up for months," Maggie stared at no one in particular. Nigel looked as tired as she felt. He probably worried the whole time she was away. Lady Archer and Cody looked like that too.

Arie spoke for the group, "Right now we all need to rest. Also, we have to plan a funeral for Stan."

Agnes lifted her head. "In England, next to Jan." Her head dropped back down.

Wim saw how sad she looked. He heard the name Stan. He was the man who died and was Agnes' best friend. He moved over to sit next to her to make her feel better. He held her hand but she hardly felt it.

Gran watched Wim and held back her tears until she went to bed.

CHAPTER 30
December 1944, London

On their first day in Brussels, the De Wevers had gone shopping for new clothes. After four years of strict clothing rationing, they were overwhelmed with choices. Wartime sill meant shortages, but they hardly noticed. Gran described each garment to Ellie, sales clerks determined the sizes for both of them. Sized meant nothing, they had lost too much weight during the Occupation. New clothes for Wim, too, and a few toys.

Gertie from the ENSA troop also helped them. Gertie studied Ellie's face with the burn scars that were slowly healing.

"No makeup yet, of course," was Gertie's cosmetic diagnosis. "But in a few months, look me up in London. I'll be off tour by then. We can help you look lovely. Meanwhile, use tinted glasses, sunglasses, not the black 'blind people' lenses. They're way too obvious, darling."

The entire team had two days of rest and good food. They were almost ready to go back to their 'real lives', except for Agnes. She had huge mood swings. There were times when she retreated into her own world, unwilling to communicate with anyone. Then, she would be overly attentive to the people and issues around her. She enjoyed the shopping, then claimed to be too tired for dinner. Mostly she remained passive, going along with the group on whatever they were doing.

Three days later the six survivors of the Purple Nail Polish Operation arrived in London. The whole team, including Wim, was driven directly from Northolt Airfield to the offices of the Dutch government in exile at Arlington House, to meet with Queen Wilhelmina. Joining them were Albert and Carolina De Wever.

The Queen stood as they entered.

"Major Leenders has given us a brief version of what you did to accomplish this mission. I doubt if you know how valuable this operation was. The plans of Ypenburg show the start of a permanent launch site for the rockets. That, and other details in Matteus Willems' reports will help us finish this terrible war more quickly. But the best part of this is the happiness in reuniting the family of personal friends.

"Our country will be forever grateful for what you have done. Please accept this medal of recognition and membership into the Order of Orange-Nassau." At this point, the Queen stood and presented to each one of them a bronze medal hanging from an orange and blue ribbon. Each one was recognized for specific acts of courage, including Wim.

The Queen especially acknowledged Wim's sacrifice of his bear who carried war secrets to England and would be repaired. His citation noted "his bravery and self-discipline in time of danger, and his help assisting in emergency surgery."

Arie, in full uniform, was already wearing a slightly larger version of what the rest received, but a newer, larger one in silver was put into his hand. One more was awarded and saved for Matteus Willems.

"We were sad to hear of the death of Wing Commander Novak," she added. "Is there anything we can do for him, other than acknowledgements and condolences to the Polish Government here?"

"It is our wish to bury him next to his brother in Hillford, your Majesty," Ellie spoke for Agnes.

"Then so it shall happen, with our government's highest honors," the Queen proclaimed. She looked at her aide, Major Leenders, who nodded. He would be in charge of making it happen.

Agnes barely moved. Ellie wouldn't leave her side, hoping to raise her wounded spirit. Agnes thought it was because Ellie needed her help to walk safely. They gave each other what was needed at the time. Maggie stood next to them, waiting for her turn to help them both.

One week after the members of the Purple Nail Polish team arrived in London, Stanislaw Novak was laid to rest next to his brother, Jan with full military honors. The day was cloudy and cold. Arie (painfully, but without the cane he inherited from Gran) led three color guard units, one for each country that Stan had served, through the village of Hillford. The church was filled with official representatives and soldiers from Poland, The Netherlands, and the United Kingdom. The De Wever family, the Shelfords, the Drummonds, and Lady Jane Archer with Agnes and Lady Charlotte squeezed into the front pews. Agnes almost didn't come. She had been ill for several days, most likely exhaustion. She came with Ellie, each relying on the other. She received Stan's medals from all three countries. She would put them in a small box with her own medal from Queen Wilhelmina and Jan's sash. The box would then sit in the back of her closet at Shellings.

Lady Archer helped in demobilizing both Agnes and Maggie from military service. Agnes moved in with Aunt Charlotte at Shellings. Charlotte was alarmed. Agnes' personality had changed since her return to England. It looked like the 'shell shock' of the previous war. Lady Archer reminded her that Emmy's husband was working with soldiers experiencing this. It seemed that Emmy had become one of Lady Archer's girls.

Emmy and Clive came as soon as they received Charlotte's request for help. Clive's diagnosis was that Agnes finally succumbed to the combined grief of losing her parents and two near-husbands, plus the continual experience of the Blitz and wartime service in France. He recommended long-term quiet and getting her to talk with people who had similar experiences.

It wouldn't hurt all three girls to spend time together. They were the best support for each other that could be prescribed. Maggie and Ellie had shared so much with Agnes over the years that they agreed to be with her and be part of her recovery as well as their own.

Maggie was glad they had the time together. She still had troubles with concentration, plus nightmares of Andrew, Falaise, and Ellie's rescue. Nigel's gentleness could only comfort her, not heal her. Besides, he had his own war memories to deal with.

Emmy pulled Maggie aside. "There is one person who I think can help Agnes."

The next day, Maggie and Emmy set out for Smithfield Market. It was early morning. The bus across London was filled with people, even though there were still daily bombings and war conditions to deal with. They stepped off the bus near St. Paul's Cathedral. They reminisced as they walked the rest of the way to the Market. The neighborhood blocks were being rebuilt by weekend amateur construction crews, knowing that they might be bombed out again and replaced later by something more permanent.

They entered the market area and began to ask for Brian MacFagin. At the tenth stall, a man finally recognized the name.

"Hasn't been here for a long while, being an ARP Warden and all," a butcher told them. "You might try the local school a few blocks that way – he's doing a lot of work with the boys around here."

At the school, they were directed to police station. "Yes, Mr. MacFagin. He leads a football team most afternoons in that park over there. He doesn't take nonsense from the boys. And they can get pretty rough. They've become quite feral, trying to survive the war. Pardon me, ladies, but it is a tough place we have here. You might want to have an escort."

"We'll be fine," Maggie answered. The area was familiar. St. Bart's and the Sickly Doctor were only a short walk from where they were. The pub was as good a place as any for lunch, she thought. Emmy and Maggie had a good chat.

"I'm still in debt to all of you. Our whole family is. Especially Ruby and the shop she was able to build up. And of course, my 'ladyship' title has come in rather handy," Emmy said. "I have become a community organizer, and as silly as it might seem, people take my word seriously. I'm using that to my advantage to promote health care, especially for young mothers."

"See? Not silly at all. It's the proper use for the title. Has Lady Archer been around?"

"Actually, yes," Ellie smiled. "Rather good at setting me up with the right people to get what I need for the mums and babes."

They went to the park and found a group of boys kicking a ball around a few obstacles. A large man watched and called out various warnings, encouragements, and instructions. They walked over to him.

"Mr. MacFagin?"

"Yes?"

"I'm Mrs. Raleigh and this is Mrs. Drummond. We're friends of Agnes Fletcher. A Sister from St. Bart's. She needs your help."

His reaction was instant. "I remember you both. Show me the way." He shouted to an older boy to take over the practice and waved his arm to let them lead the way.

On the bus back to Shellings, Maggie explained how Agnes was not recovering from her grief and war experiences. Weejun, (he asked them to call him that) kept nodding.

"So, her ghosts caught up with her then. It was just a matter of time. Poor Lassie," Weejun hung his head.

"She told me something about you, that you were the ARP warden when her parents died, and that you helped her with Jan's death as well. And that you were a patient of hers early on."

"All of that, eh? Short story on my end is that she reminded me of my daughter. They'd be the same age. When I realized that, I took her on as my own child and vowed to take care of her, as penance for not taking care of my own daughter."

"Oh?" Maggie asked.

"My family all died in a house fire a long time ago. It was my fault. I shouldn't have ..." Weejun paused, "never mind."

They arrived at Shellings. Agnes saw Weejun standing in front of her.

"Well, Lassie, here we are again," Weejun said softly. They held each other in a long embrace. He took her out into the garden for a walk that lasted well into the darkness of winter. When they finally came inside, both of them looking exhausted from a long crying spell.

He stayed for dinner. The meal was stretched from a stew for two into a hearty soup for five. Weejun thanked them all for their hospitality and promised to come back every week, with a contribution to the meal and no more crying.

Maggie now lived at Oakstone and visited Ellie and Agnes in London as often as she could. Nigel was being transferred to Asia, creating new airfields in the Far East as the war continued. Brussels was just a memory, their second honeymoon. She planned visits to her in-laws in Manchester. Northern England was still new to her, and her sister-in-law Chloe promised to show her new places each time she came.

Ellie, with Wim and Gran, stayed with the De Wevers in London while she received burn treatments. They worried about how Dora, the Professor, and the Brinkers were surviving. Every day, they listened to the news and followed what was happening back in The Netherlands.

She felt creative again, not having to worry about surviving day to day. She gained twenty pounds and finally looked like slender Ellie again. Ellie wanted to study languages again. When her burn treatments were finished, she hoped to start studying to be a translator. She began doing informal translating for business and state meetings at the Dutch Embassy. Meanwhile, she and Gran taught Wim how to speak English. He made friends with the children from the Embassy community and the neighborhood. Soon he would be starting school.

The 'team' (Maggie, Agnes, Gran, Ellie and Wim) went on trips to museums and concerts as well as to restaurants. They described everything to Ellie. They shared reading magazines and newspapers. When the weather was good, they walked through parks around London. Winter threatened to be extremely cold, but that didn't matter.

Bombs still fell around them, the planes still flew overhead, fighting in Europe and Asia continued, but their part in all that was over.

Pieter came to England on compassionate leave at Christmas. He was very nervous at first. So was Ellie. They were on their first dates again, getting to know each other. Ellie's blindness was new, having a five-year-old son was new, figuring out Pieter's part in a family that had worked well in his absence was new. They barely had time to mention all these things, let alone work out any solutions. But their intimacy returned. Pieter, ever the observant scholar, reminded Ellie that love was usually by touch anyway, not by needing to see. They knew that they could have a good life together soon.

Pieter served with Ellie's brother Theo in the Princess Irene Brigade of Dutch soldiers under Allied Command. They followed the Brigade in radio broadcasts. The main concern was that no one knew where Ben was. Ellie and Gran told everyone about Ben's actions in the NSB, including his last visit, but they had no idea where he was now. Pieter promised to search for Ben and check on the rest of the family if he could.

Arie was invited to dinner with Ellie's family. It was his new family after losing his own early in the war. He admitted to them that he was seeing a widow who worked in the code room who might be interested in him. Publicly, he announced that he wanted to give up smoking. Secretly, he thought it was still a handy, if bad, habit.

In January, Maggie received a call from Aunt Charlotte. "Agnes is pregnant. And she doesn't care. She wanders from room to room, fixing flowers, fiddling with jigsaw puzzles and not finishing them. I know you were just here, but after finding out that she is pregnant, she has stepped back into her shell."

Maggie came right away, bringing Ellie with her. Agnes smiled and talked with them, more cheerful than they had seen her in a long time. They could tell that it was a false display, but they played along as much as they could.

"We heard that you are pregnant." Ellie finally had enough of the small talk.

The cheerfulness dropped like a stone. "I don't want to talk about it."

"I don't think you can ignore this," Maggie said softly. "You have to make some decisions."

"I can't take care of myself, let alone someone else," Agnes said. "I just don't care anymore."

"Is it, was it, Stan?" asked Ellie.

"Of course."

"Then you must love the baby as a final gift," said Ellie.

"No, I don't want to love anyone anymore. My love is a death sentence for those I love. I can't go through any more losses."

Maggie gambled on being tough, "Well, you have three choices. I doubt if you want to end the pregnancy. So that leaves two choices. Keep the child or have the child adopted."

"Number three, I guess, but I do want to know what happens to it."

Maggie, not holding back her tears, knelt before Agnes. "There are many war orphans. A lot of families are looking to adopt them." She swallowed hard. "Agnes, I just lost a pregnancy. One I think began in Brussels around the same time you and Stan, well…"

Agnes looked up, her eyes focusing on Maggie as a patient as well as closest friend, "Oh? How are you feeling?"

"Not all that well, but that's not important right now. I just wanted you to know that there are places near here that are helping families right now. We are looking at one ourselves."

"I'm not, not, not sure. This is so ridiculous. So unfair. I can't do anything."

Ellie, ever the dreamer of new adventures, voiced the decision as a done deed, "Why can't Maggie and Nigel adopt your child? You can be the doting aunt or godmother! You'll still be around, just not all the time."

"What?" Maggie and Agnes were stunned. Could that actually work? Maybe. Nigel was in Australia with their old boss Keith Park fighting against the Japanese. He would agree. What about her parents? Or the Drummonds? Not everyone would need to know the origin of their adopted child, only accept the adoption itself. Maggie didn't think that anyone would object. How would she share parenthood with Agnes? Ellie's idea was insane. But.

"Oh," Maggie said. "Of course, provided that Ellie is the other doting aunt and godmother."

Agnes sat very still. She inhaled deeply, put a hand over her abdomen. "It would seem that we are about to cross our most challenging bridge."

Charlotte, who had been listening unseen in the hallway, smiled and exhaled. Those three always worked things out.

EPILOGUE
November, 1945

Lady Archer found herself watching the three girls again, and assessing them. She couldn't help the tear that escaped. It was quickly dabbed in case it should smear her perfect appearance. Next to her stood a large man dressed in full formal uniform Scottish jacket and kilt. A pale thin scar ran down his cheek. He was very quiet, and she noticed, that he had a tear in his eye as well.

"Family or friend?" she whispered.

"A wee bit of both," a Scottish accent answered.

Agnes was holding a three-month old girl dressed in a silk and lace Christening dress trailing a full yard below her tiny body. As her godmothers, Ellie and Agnes presented her to the vicar of the church in Hillford for baptism.

"Charlotte Nova, I baptize thee in the name of the Father, the Son, and the Holy Ghost," pronounced the vicar.

With that, the vicar handed the baby to her parents, Margaret Louise Shelford Drummond and Nigel Crampton Drummond. An emotional glance between Agnes and Maggie was shared by Nigel and the Shelfords. The senior Shelfords knew that Agnes was not just the baby's godmother, but the senior Drummonds were not aware of Charlotte's actual origin. They were just as delighted to have their first granddaughter as were the Shelfords with their first grandchild. Agnes had chosen the names, asking for Nova as the best way to remember the Novak brothers. And Aunt Charlotte felt honored beyond measure.

The Christening was followed by a luncheon held at Oakstone, an emotional reunion of family and friends, now that war was truly over and everyone was home again. Small groups gathered throughout the country manor. There was a mood of optimism, the whole world was changing, beginning with them.

Lady Archer joined the older generation who sat in the sitting room.

"I haven't felt this alive for a long time," Gran told Ladies Jane, Charlotte, and Louisa Shelford, and Carolina De Wever along with Matteus Willems. "During our escape, there was no time to wallow self-pity over the Occupation or my sprained ankle. For a brief time, I was no longer seen as old and fragile. Of course, being with young and active people gave me renewed energy. After Matteus arrived here in May, I made sure he had the chance to recover and find the same new energy."

Matteus grinned. "Last winter didn't kill me off, but Granada's care was nearly as intense as the hunger and cold served up by the Germans and Mother Nature," he said as he took her hand. "I had to marry her, just to calm her down from all the fussing. Well, tomorrow is our day. And what a better way to do that, than with all of you. After our honeymoon, we shall return to Leiden, and we expect many visitors to come our way."

"Be honest, Matteus," Carolina said. "After surviving that winter, you needed fattening up. And Gran's new energy needed an outlet. I speak for all of us when I say we are so happy for both of you," Carolina said. "Coordinating these family events has been perfect for all of us."

"Amen to that," Charlotte agreed, as did her old classmate, Jane Archer. They were in tomorrow's bridal party, with Gran's daughter Carolina as Matron of Honor. "We shall miss you, but we promise that lots of visits shall definitely be in order."

Matteus let the memories of that harsh winter flash up and disappear. The final throes of the occupation were focused on individual survival for both the Dutch and the Germans. No real attention was paid to the disappearance of Ben. Ellie's blindness and Gran's 'broken ankle' were accepted as reasons for their invisibility long enough to be forgotten. Thanks to the work of Pieter and Mr. Brinker, the crown molding throughout the house had been stored with food, and they all made it through what was now called The Hunger Winter. The molding made good firewood as the storage areas were emptied. Pieter's parents came home, with crates of furniture and supplies from Canada. The Brinkers were back at the elder Van Horn's house, helping the remodeling and restoration efforts. Dora stayed with Ellie and Pieter and was helping them remodel their city home. A new nursery was nearly complete.

The rest of the men were in Oakstone's library. Now that the war was over, some of them had returned to their first careers. Clive was back at his pre-war medical practice and helped returning veterans with their problems. Pieter was welcomed back to Leiden University which had reopened. His new interest was in high demand: restoration paints and finishes for art and architecture throughout Europe. Herbert was taking over the management of Oakstone and replacing his father in the House of Lords, who was content to be retiring.

The others were entering new professions. Sam did not stay in England to lead Shells Bakery. He moved to Canada to marry Agnes' nursing friend Vera. He was promised a position with her father's grocery empire. They promised to carry Arrow Teas and Shell's Biscuits in their stores.

Nigel was part of a civil engineering firm transforming old RAF stations into civilian airports throughout England. Passenger and cargo travel were growing fast, and he was a rising star in the air transportation industry. For now, they would live at Oakstone to be near London.

Arie retired from the Queen's company and the Dutch military. He wasn't sure yet what was in his future.

The girls sat in Oakstone's sun room. Just as Arie was leaving his service to Queen Wilhelmina, Ellie was officially entering the Dutch foreign service. She was translating and speaking with foreign diplomats and businessmen in their work with their Dutch colleagues. She was excited to be living in Leiden again. The Brinkers and Pieter had finished repairing their house, just in time to welcome their second child, Margriet, named for her godmother, Maggie, born six weeks ago. She reluctantly left Margriet at home with Dora, but brought several pictures for all to see. Wim made sure everyone saw them, when he wasn't sitting next to Arie. Arie didn't mind. He and Wim were kindred spirits through their war experience. It would be hard to guess Wim's wartime memories. He was as chatty and active as any child his age, but he was very protective of his mother and his new sister.

Maggie was expecting the birth of their first child in May. The adoption of baby Charlotte, the war orphan, was welcomed by everyone, but only a few knew who the actual mother was. Her world was spinning in several directions. A mother, pregnant, and learning how to run Shell's Bakery, now that Sam was moving to Canada. She smiled. None of that should require much driving. She planned to treat herself by hiring a driver, a personal treat.

She still had her personal notes from the war. A collaboration with Mr. Philips, Max, and Ollie on the 'real' story of the war? Someday, perhaps. When she had time.

Lady Jane had only one concern left for this group. Agnes. Clive had been consulted and had agreed that Agnes should return to active work, perhaps some form of nursing duty. She spoke to Agnes in general ways and saw how she perked up when hearing about a position with the International Red Cross. Emergency medical teams went to disaster areas all over the globe. Whether man-made or natural disasters, the need was enormous. Medical teams, directing the building of health facilities, teaching basic public health were in constant demand. In and out, fast action, short term work allowing time to visit home as often as she wished.

And Agnes was willing to give it a go.

Lady Jane Archer knew that the future was good for these three. She was heading back to St. Martin's, eager to discover the next batch of students who could embody the spirit of these girls in the new postwar world.

The Girls' Secret Code

Write the date of your letter on the top of the page. The date tells you where the coded message can be found. So, Jan. 1, 11, 21, or 31 is a '1'. 4, 14, and 24 are all treated as '4'. And so forth. That becomes the key to the code.

1, 2, 3, 4, and 5 mean the first, second, third, fourth, or fifth letter *counting from the left edge of each line* of the message. 6, 7, 8, 9, 0 means you *count from the right edge of the letter*. '0' is the last letter on the line, '9' means the second letter in on the end of each line.

'X' or 'Z' finishes a word, sentence, or thought.

EXAMPLE

May 7, 1936

Dear Maggie

How are you. We just went to the beach, and

I wanted to tell you how hot it was when we

sat in the sun. I wore my blue and yellow

hat along with my new leather sandals. I'm

excited that you want to come to the

beach with us next week. Love and extra

kisses.

Deciphered message: **hello.**

Questions and Topics for Reading Groups

1. What episodes in this book sound familiar to you? Are they similar to ones you have heard from your own family and friends? Or experienced yourself?

2. Which of the themes in the book spoke to you – historical details, growing women's roles, PTSD, wartime censorship, love, loss, friendships?

3. The three girls don't always realize their strengths or talents. What do you consider your strengths, even if you don't think they are special?

4. Who is your strongest friend? Why?

5. Which characters would you like to meet? Who do you identify with?

6. How do creative solutions including pranks play a role in your life, especially when they challenge rules or social norms?

7. Lady Archer stayed in the background, but had enormous influence for the entire book. Do you have people who have helped open doors for you, or connected you to the people you needed?

Interview with the Author

What was your inspiration for this book?

When I first learned the stories of my family's experiences during World War II, I knew that I wanted to record them somehow. Then I began hearing about other people's experiences. Their stories were funny, personal, powerful, unique. My imagination took over, and I wondered what it would have been like if I had lived through the war. That's how Ellie, Agnes, and Maggie were born.

How did you do your research?

General history books first. Then figuring out how to give each girl an important but relatively invisible life. When I did more research, the details came out. I didn't write every day. Sometimes I didn't write for a week or two while the history and my girls came together in one story. I pretended to be that character and walk/talk the scene with them until it 'felt right.' Then in one afternoon, a whole chapter would come out intact. Still, lots of grammar checks and revisions along the way, but the story was set. Checking dates and details often led to yet another story line.

Who is your favorite character?

Who is your favorite child? Whoever you're thinking about at the time, I guess. I also had fun with the minor characters and they are also favorites when I think of them. I wish they were all as real as the people who they represent.

A favorite part of the book?

Like a favorite character – the one I remember at the time. I guess, those parts that I felt were the best blend of fact and fiction. I heard about the beer keg delivery by Spitfires to the Front from a museum docent. Then I heard of my friend's parents who got married at an airbase. Her father was there training up a new group of pilots. Those students buzzed the wedding reception, and wound up in Army jail along with their instructor – the groom – for a week. The bride and her sister enjoyed the honeymoon suite on their own. I knew both stories had to be in the book. Hence Stan and Agnes in northern France.

Why the title?

I have been asked if it is being humble or insecure. Neither really. I wanted to keep the girls from being too extraordinary. They were great students, came from wealthy backgrounds, and had family connections. However, none of that counts if you don't use them wisely. They worked hard and earned their places in the story. They did what they could, to the fullest.

What's next?

I might write a story that brings the children of these girls into their own adventures. The 60s and 70s, when they become adults, is a very full era to work with. Or a 'prequel' of the mothers of this group. That would be World War I and the Suffrage years. Who knows?

Acknowledgements/notes on research

First, last, and always, to my husband, Fons, for his incredible patience, sense of humor, encouragement, and love. To our daughter, Katie, for her editing (4 years as an English teacher should be worthwhile). To our local librarians, especially Sam the Interlibrary Loan guy, and the Lopez Island Book Store also get big thanks. To Ron at Paper, Scissors on the Rock for his technical help. And to all the family and friends who have contributed their stories, wished me well, and encouraged me along the way.

There are libraries full of books and official resources for World War II, it seemed at times almost too many. As important were BBC's Peoples' War series, and Wikipedia, and many websites of varying quality that helped when I had to get details just right.

And then I just had to imagine what could have worked. I gave Agnes an 'experimental' nursing curriculum because I couldn't find much about nurse training in the 30s, or Maggie's experience in the Military Communication Unit. A reminder – writing fiction means I'm allowed to make stuff up, provided that it makes sense.

There are some odd true bits, too. Unknown girls sometimes were presented at Court, prison teaching in the Netherlands happened throughout the war, tea and tobacco are known emergency medicinal aids. Pieter's escape from The Netherlands, is absolutely true – it is the journey my father-in-law made and is as accurate as it was told to us by him and his brother. In honor of him, Pieter used my father-in-law's 'real' alias and false profession.

Thanks to all!